ONE FOR THE MONEY

Also by Carol Clewlow

KEEPING THE FAITH

A WOMAN'S GUIDE TO ADULTERY

LOVE IN THE MODERN SENSE

ONE FOR THE MONEY

Carol Clewlow

MICHAEL JOSEPH

LONDON

MICHAEL JOSEPH LTD
Published by the Penguin Group
27 Wrights Lane, London W8 5TZ
Viking Penguin Inc., 375 Hudson Street, New York, New York 10014, USA
Penguin Books Australia Ltd, Ringwood, Victoria, Australia
Penguin Books Canada Ltd, 10 Alcorn Avenue, Toronto, Ontario, Canada M4V 3B2
Penguin Books (NZ) Ltd, 182–190 Wairau Road, Auckland 10, New Zealand

Penguin Books Ltd, Registered Offices: Harmondsworth, Middlesex, England

First published 1994

Typeset by Datix International Limited, Bungay, Suffolk
Filmset in Goudy Old Style
Printed in England by Clays Ltd, St Ives plc

ISBN 0 7181 3608 X

FOR RICHARD

Well it's one for the money
Two for the show
Three to get ready now go cat go . . .

I

Flight time the night time lights they shine
Rain on the runway on my mind
I wish I'd never read that last letter
Maybe I'll sleep and then I'll feel better
I'll take another drink
I'll watch the ocean shrink
I'll work out what I think is wrong

    Maybe I'll see you
    Vancouver Tuesday
    If my plane lands on the runway
    And if I find you what will you say
    If I see you
    Vancouver Tuesday . . .

Kent came for me last Monday. It feels longer. It feels as though I've been here for weeks, for months. It amazes me that it was only last Monday.

I was working at the café. I don't usually work on Mondays this early in the season. On Mondays we're usually quiet.

It was around eleven when Grace rang. I was stumbling around trying to work out the moves that make up a cup of coffee. I still don't take naturally to mornings if you understand me.

'Can you believe it,' Grace said. 'Coaches. Unbooked. And still only May.'

There was a crash in the background and I heard her turn away to call down curses on Rene's head.

'I'm on my way,' I said.

It was one of those early summer days that still has the tang of spring about it. On a morning like this, even ten years or so on, I can still walk out of the cottage and lift my nose like a dog and take a sniff and get a shot of something that I know is nothing more or less than Life.

The market-place was golden with sunshine when I bounced in across the cobbles in the old Mini. The locals were beginning to go lazily about their business, sticking their signs out, pulling down their awnings. Even so two coaches were parked out front of the café and a crocodile of grockles was threading its way through the door.

Morning coffee and lunch had both come and gone when Rene came into the kitchen.

'There's someone to see you,' she said.

I glanced across at Grace holding her coffee mug suspended in the air. She sighed.

3

'How many times have I told you Rene?' she said. 'When someone asks for Joanie always find out who it is.'

Poor Rene. It wasn't her fault. She's quite new. Probably it hasn't happened since she arrived. It was just at the beginning I guess, when I first went to work at the café. Then it always seemed like the same people, the same four at the table, with the same solarium tans, the same sunglasses, the same shirt-sleeves rolled up and the same silly girl, laughing too much and too early as he asked it.

'Excuse me but aren't you . . .?'

No, not any more.

Hey Joanie, Joanie. Tell 'em who you used to be.

'It's a man,' Rene said. 'On his own.'

Grace grimaced. Let me tell you, for a woman on her own, a mystery man in the same situation and asking for you is seldom good news. More than likely he'll be from the Gas Board come to tell you your gas is getting cut off, or from the DHSS hot on the trail of an extra hour's illegal work. At the beginning I learned a lot about such things. Life is easier now. Even so I grimaced at Grace.

'It'll be the decorator,' I said. 'After the money for the kitchen.'

But it wasn't the decorator. It wasn't even the Gas Board or the Social Security.

He was sitting at a table in the corner as I came out wiping my hands on a tea-towel.

He'd lost weight, I could see that, but still his size escaped over the edges of one of our spindly bentwood chairs. He was frowning and his head was bent as he played with a packet of sugar. As I made a movement he looked up, his eyes hidden behind the dark glasses that are his only weakness in an otherwise blameless existence.

'It's Richard,' he said. 'He wants to see you.'

*

I guess it was the fingers that did it more than anything else, country-boy fingers, thick and stubby and passing the tiny packet of sugar backwards and forwards between them.

The only time those fingers look small are on the frets of a guitar. Then they look tiny. Delicate. Dancing.

Where was it? Amsterdam? Paris? Rome? Yeah, maybe it was Paris. I don't know how many times I played Paris but I know I never bought a postcard beneath the Eiffel Tower or walked up the Champs-Elysées. Hey, poor little rich girl huh? Doesn't your heart bleed?

Still I know how you get to Paris. You get to Paris the same way you get any other place. You get into a car that comes to your door, and then out of it, and on to a plane, or a helicopter, or a tour bus, and some smokes, some toots, some slaps of bubbly later, there you are. Wherever it is.

One night Leon seized the mike adrift somewhere in a world of his own making.

''Allo Munich,' he roared. Which came as a surprise to everyone.

We were in Milan at the time.

No. Wait. It wasn't Paris. Maybe it was somewhere hot, somewhere sweaty and steamy. One of those places with a night sky like black velvet that pressed down on you and on the rainbow of lights overhead. Bangkok maybe. Singapore. Manila. 'Tin trannie' countries. That's what Richard used to call them. Places where the music came out at you in waves like the heat, from every darkened doorway, from every street stall and over-painted jalopy. Where it hit the air like an infection and you figured it was sounding the way it was always supposed to sound, hot and battered and out of tune. Like something from the fifties. Like freedom. Like rock and roll.

Or there again, perhaps it wasn't Asia at all. Perhaps it was Africa, or America or Australia. And what does it matter, because wherever it is, in the end, the hotels were the same and there were the same skyscrapers and the same neon flashing on and off as you came in from the

5

airport, and all about you, as you got out of the car, that same heavy smell of heat and gasoline. And afterwards there was that same walk through a breeze-block tunnel and out into the light where you could swear the same faces were waiting for you.

Afterwards they'd ask you. What's it like to play a place like Shea? Seventy thousand people? What's it like? And you'd have to answer them, that you can't remember, because there's nothing to remember. Because a stadium is just another stadium. And it's not like the early days when you had to hump the gear in and out yourself, which is how you remember exactly how the swing-doors clashed because they caught your fingers, and where the holes were in the stage because the piano leg went down one of them, and the face of the asshole of a barman who refused to give you that last drink.

And now I remember. It wasn't any of those places. It wasn't hot. It was cool. A champagne tang to the air. Like a fresh lick of coke.

It was some sort of festival. There were fireworks over the harbour. As I came out of the hotel, I heard a whizzing sound and when I looked up, there was a catherine wheel pinned and trapped and whirling overhead.

That's me up there, I thought.

It flared up with a fizz like it was teaching me a lesson before cartwheeling off into the night.

Yeah, I thought. That's me up there.

Because I was stoned all the time by then. Staying up there. Never coming down. Passing over to the place where even I knew it was better off not to be.

That afternoon waking up as usual to the dead sound of the silence behind the thick hotel curtains I'd said to Kent, 'Where are we? What day is it?'

He'd come in like the nursemaid he was with the bowl of porridge which was the only thing I could get into my stomach by then, the only thing that could get me, technically speaking at least, up and on to my feet.

6

No, I wasn't eating by then, but then I wasn't doing much of anything, just stumbling my way through the gigs and in and out of the planes and cars and hotel bedrooms.

More often than not I would be on my own when he came in. For some people coke is a sex drug but it never was for me. One lick and I just wanted to be left alone, to crawl into that little private space that only those who know about it inhabit.

This time though there was someone with me. The sax player I think. I remember, he had hair that stood up on his head like the startled crest of a cockatoo and trousers with a thousand zips and pockets. I remember the hair and how the trousers looked lying half inside-out beside the bed. I remember the bulge of his arms above the elbow and the hairless hollow of his chest. I even remember the precise way his fingers pressed down on the sax when he played. But I can't remember his face. I could never remember their faces.

When Kent came in the sheet was a long crumpled line down the centre between us. Normally if there was someone there when he came in he would just order them curtly from the room. This time he just stood there looking.

His look took in the bed and the broken glasses and the upset bottles and the blotches of wine on the hotel carpet. It took in the ashtrays full of dumps, and the Ludes beside the bed and the line of coke, bright and white and forgotten about on the bamboo glass table.

'Where are we?' I said drowsily again and when he didn't answer I began to shout it at him, angrily. 'Where the fuck are we? What day is it for Christ's sake?'

He put the cup down on the table beside me and walked over heavy and unhappy to the window. There he pressed a button and the hotel curtains pulled back with a swish. Framed in the window was the harbour. It was breathtaking, the mountains still snowcapped in the distance, the green of the forests and the glittering blue of the water. I lifted the sheet to shelter my eyes.

At the window he turned to face me, dragging a weary hand through his hair.

'It's Vancouver,' he said, 'so I guess it must be Tuesday.'

Something happens on a tour like that. You're pushing every day. Going deeper, going farther. On your own journey to the centre of your own earth.

Around you the atmosphere grows electric. They feel it, the crew, look at each other as you pass, talk out of the sides of their mouths.

They're waiting and wanting and dreading at the same time. Not wanting to lose their jobs but still hoping to be there, to be in for the kill, to be on the tour that makes another footnote in rock history.

Vancouver. The night I came down from the piano, mumbling and stumbling, haranguing the crowd, playing Janis, Janis who paved the way for all of us to be like the boys and make idiots of ourselves on stage.

'Hey can anyone tell me what day it is?' I said. I'd forgotten by then.

That was the night I distinguished myself by eventually passing out, coming heavily to rest on the keyboard, the last sound in my ears my own E minor carrying me up and up and out and over the rainbow of lights to oblivion.

It came to me as I lay there face down, what I'd been trying to remember all day. I tried to tell Kent as he tried to prise my fingers off the keys. I tried to tell him but for some reason he didn't seem to hear, and anyway it was all white by then and I was fighting whatever it was they were putting on my face.

Then I heard him say, 'What is it Joanie? Tell me what you're trying to say,' and I smiled at the sound of his voice. Told him to come near so I could whisper it in his ear.

I said it over and over again, that thing that Janis said at the end of her own ball and chain. I said, Don't you understand man? Can't you see it?

The last time I said it the dark was closing in.

I said, It's all the same fucking day man.

And now here he was before me, that same Kent, staring down into the coffee cup.

'I thought you'd know,' he said. 'The papers . . .'

'I don't bother much with the papers,' I said.

I smiled at him, surprised at the sheer pleasure I felt in just seeing him. I took a pack of cigarettes out of my apron pocket. He looked up at the flare of the match and I smiled.

'My only bad habit,' I said.

Later, after he took me home, I threw a few things into a bag and locked up the cottage. He was inching the Land-rover back down the hill when he said, 'You took some finding Joanie.'

The sun was gone by then and the mist was rolling in. The smell of woodsmoke that I love so much was coming in through my open window.

'It was what I wanted,' I said. 'At the time.'

We hit the hairpins then and he hunched forward, like the driving was taking up all his attention. But I knew it wasn't. Because apart from anything else he's a farmer's boy and well used to hills and hairpins like these. But besides that I know him, we've been a long way together. Brothers and sisters in rock and roll.

And so I knew that he was letting the words hang there in the air till he was good and ready, when I knew he would catch them down again, turn his head, try to throw them at me squarely in the eye.

9

Ah yes, I know him you see and so I was too quick for him. I leaned my head back, closed my eyes.

'At the time . . .?' he said.

But I pretended not to hear him.

We were on the Hammersmith flyover when I finally asked the question.

'How long?' I said. 'How long has he got?'

He was hunched over the wheel in the way I remembered. A thousand miles. A thousand motorway services. A thousand journeys in a beat-up Bedford van. Because it was always Kent who drove. Always Kent who found the place. Always Kent who took care of the things while we bitched and barracked and bickered in the back.

He shrugged, shaking his head.

'Not long I guess,' he said, this Kent who now a thousand years later was taking me to see Richard.

There's a story my father tells in his book, about a beautiful young man loved by Apollo.

Because Apollo loves him so much he offers him a divine gift. The beautiful young man reaches down and grasps a handful of sand and holds it out.

'I wish to live as many years as the grains of sand in my hand,' he says.

And so he does. He lives a thousand years and more. He just goes on. Living.

But in his greed for life, his greed for living, he finds he's forgotten one thing. He's forgotten, asking for Eternal Life, to ask for Eternal Youth to go with it.

And so he grows old. All his beauty falls away. His back bends, lines come and go and disappear into the folds of flesh.

10

But no matter how he withers and wastes, still he can't die, and as the centuries roll on so he becomes this grotesque shrivelled thing, no longer even recognizable as human.

And then one day, finally, the last tiny scrap of him disappears, so that all that's left is his voice, the voice that once had asked Apollo to be allowed to live and live, now endlessly begging to be allowed to die.

But it's no good. Even for the gods some things are impossible.

Divine gifts, once given you see, can never be recalled.

It's Richard's hair that shocks me most. It shocks me more than the face turning into a skull or the folds of grey skin or the dull opaque eyes I'd rather remember as honey. It shocks me more than the dials and the tubes standing out steely and cold against the warmth of the damask and rosewood and mahogany. It shocks me more than the scene outside the house which shouldn't have shocked me at all.

'Jesus,' I said as they jammed and jostled against the Landrover.

Looking at the notebooks and the microphones and the cameras pressed against the window makes me realize I've been away longer than I thought. It makes me realize I've managed to forget the absolute certainty of them, their absolute sameness, their absolute lack of dignity running like some animals joined at the knee.

'But why complain?' as Robin Phillips said to me once with that knowing smile on his face. You always know when you're falling out of favour, I've found, because it shows on other people's faces.

'It's a symbiotic relationship after all,' he said, 'You're happy enough when we give you a leg up at the beginning. You can't complain if we give you a shove when you're on the way down.'

11

That was the night of the music awards when I threw my drink over him. I wasn't there to get one you understand. Those days were long since gone. I was just a cheap turn brought in to entertain the suits. A left-over. A forgotten performing bear.

Still, to be fair I was forgetting things myself by then. Within an hour of the incident with Robin Phillips I was denying it had ever happened. I was still protesting my innocence the following morning when Francis brought the papers in. But there on the front page was Robin brushing the drink off his dinner jacket. And there was me, *in flagrante*, with the glass in my hand.

'Hold on,' Kent says as we squeeze out of the Landrover. He grabs hold of my hand and we push through the scrum together, the flashbulbs popping in the evening sky.

We're within reach of the gate when I feel a sharp determined clutch on my shoulder. It catches in my hair and drags my head round. I find myself staring into a white face and a jagged and twisted mouth and a pair of eyes straining with pain and the effrontery of *possession*.

'Help me,' she screams. 'I have to see him.

'He's a *friend* of mine,' she says.

On the steps as we wait for someone to open the door, I turn once looking back at the scene. Lot's wife. Turned to salt.

'Jesus,' I say a second time. Because although I've seen it, lived through it, I know I've never seen it like this before, the sheer numbers of them, the towering scaffolding and lights.

It reminds me of something. For a moment I can't think what it is. And then it comes to me. Of course. What else would it be? The Last Great Gig.

'They're waiting for him to die,' I say, turning away in disgust.

Then I remember. They're always waiting for you to die one way or another.

At the door as Kent introduces us, Donald's eyes are

12

cool and curious, neither friendly nor unfriendly, like his conversation, courteous inquiries about our journey as we mount the stairs. It makes me feel that sense of time past again and I wonder what Richard might have said to him about me, and with each tread too I wonder too what I will say to Richard, what I can say after so long. But then while I'm still thinking about it, Donald is opening the bedroom door and there he is lying back before me.

He's propped up on the bank of white pillows staring into an ivory hand mirror. With the fingers of the other hand he smooths the patches and the threadbare stubble that is all that is left of his hair. And so I fail the first test, dropping my eyes. It's just for a second but he doesn't miss it. When I raise them again his own are full of disdain. They say, 'If I can bear it, so can you.' They make me angry those eyes. Mercifully they make me forget about the formalities.

'You should have called me before,' I say belligerently.

He says, 'I wasn't dying before Joanie.'

Yes, it's Richard's hair that shocks me most of all.

As a kid I'd watch chaste old ladies stop his mother in the street. I'd see their hands itching at their sides, fighting for the right to remove a glove and take a farewell trawl through the richness that was Richard's hair.

His hair is the first thing I see of him. I come out one morning and there it is, a mass of watery blackness lying on the garden wall. A weak old British sun came through the clouds as I watched and made a bee-line for it. The hair caught the feeble rays and threw them back again, and danced shot through like silk.

He sat up then and turned and I remember my surprise. How entirely exotic he was. How unlike anything I'd seen before. His brows though were drawn sulkily together.

'Is it always so bloody cold here?' he said.

I remember too how impressed I was with his use of the swear-word. I was seven then. He was eight.

'This is warm,' I said.

He put his hands round his knees then and hunched himself up shivering.

'I'm going to hate it here,' he said.

'No you're not,' I said.

'Really. Why not?' he said. He sounded quite interested.

'Because we're going to be friends,' I said firmly. I'd already decided.

I wrote a song for Richard once.

> *You with your leaking liquid eyes*
> *And the treasure you call skin.*

I guess Richard got his looks from his father which pretty much ruled out the faded sandy-haired Englishman standing next to his mother in the wedding picture we found one day in the chest in the attic.

'Gosh,' I said innocently, we must have been about eleven at the time. 'You don't look much like him.'

He got his looks from his father. That great voice though he got from his mother.

Once, humping the gear into some peeling plush and plaster hippodrome in the early days, I spotted this ancient poster on the corridor wall.

'Hey,' I said to Richard. 'Look at this.'

'Well, well,' he said. 'If it isn't old Carl . . .'

'. . . old Carl with a "C",' I finished for him.

'He changed it darlings you see,' his mother would say

to us, twisting her scarf around her neck. 'He was German, of course. But he thought Carl with a "C" would sound more romantic.'

We must have heard the story a million times. She'd sit at the three-mirrored dressing table as she told it. Behind her back, as I sat upon the bed transfixed by her glamour, Richard would wink and make faces and raise an old man's mocking eyebrow.

'Ah yes,' she would say. 'More romantic. More *Italian*,' and here she would give her scarf a last mournful toss as if the mere mention of the word 'Italian' created in her this vague existential longing.

She'd talk of this man who founded the opera company where she'd spent a decade fondly and intimately as though they'd been friends.

'Dear Carl . . .' she'd say, her eyes misty. At the same time as she said it, she'd pat her hair and look at us sideways, pursing her lips as if gauging our reaction, as if, at the same time, she was concerned to forestall any notion that we might have . . . that she and Carl . . . just because she spoke of him this way . . . oh no . . . oh dear me no . . .

The fact is though that old Carl-with-a-C was eighty years dead by the time Richard's mother joined the company. All her intimate anecdotes ('. . . his wife you know . . . Euphrosyne Parepa-Rosa . . . such a name . . . we called her "Preppy" . . .'), all these were just folk-lore, received showbiz wisdom, the sort of stuff passed down from back row chorus to back row chorus, which is where she was languishing on the wrong side of thirty the night she met the man whom the world called Richard's father.

Edward was an archaeologist already fusty at forty by the time he met Mirabel. He was about to return to Ceylon where he was employed by the Government restoring Buddhist temples. They were married in haste three weeks after the first meeting.

You've read the novel. You've seen the film. Fill in the

gaps for yourself. The failed wedding night, the prudish Englishman, the brown and beautiful punkawallah.

Richard was born three years into the marriage in the mission hospital at Kandy and if his appearance caused a scandal over the chotapegs we'll never know.

'Why don't you ask her?' I said to him years later. 'Don't you want to know who your father was?'

'It's her business,' is all he would say.

It's too late now. Mirabel's over eighty and in a nursing home.

'How is she?' I asked him yesterday as I sat by the bed talking.

'Happy,' he said. 'In her own little world.'

Donald visits her every week, another of the loving tasks he performs for Richard. When she asks where he is, he makes excuses, tells her he's on tour. She clicks her tongue pretending to be vexed but later boasts to the nurses.

'That son of mine. Away again. Of course I know what it's like . . .'

For sometimes, according to the staff, she thinks she's back with the opera company. Suddenly a cracked old voice will break into *Butterfly*. For she has Alzheimer's disease now. She can remember things a long time ago now but not what happened yesterday.

There's an irony here that sticks in the gut, for the disease has taken the same toll on Richard.

'They should put us on the same ward,' he said.

It's one of the few times I hear him speak bitterly.

'At first I thought I'd kill myself,' he said. 'I thought, Why sit around, wait for it to get you? I had everything to do it. I remember thinking at the time how crazy it all was. That they could give you all this stuff to kill yourself but nothing to keep you alive. I sat at the dining table with the tranquillizers all around me. I even got a bottle up from the cellar to wash it down. Then I reached into my pocket for a handkerchief, pulled out the card they'd given me with it. I picked it up. I was going to tear it in two. I thought, Shit ... counselling ... I'd rather *die*. Then I reached behind me, picked up the phone, I still don't know why and it was Donald who answered.'

'You were always into everything,' Richard said, 'what d'you make of that?'

I shrugged. 'Deus ex machina?' I said.

Naturally my father loathed Mirabel.

'You spend entirely too much time in that place.'

That was his favourite saying of the time.

Note the use of the word 'loathe' here. My father did not dislike or disapprove of things as other people did. My father loathed them. He expended time and energy on it, this business of loathing. He took it entirely seriously.

Herewith an off-the-top-of-my-head list of some of the things my father loathed.

television ('no civilized person would wish to look at the thing Joan let alone lay out good money to buy one ...')
magazines ('picture books ... full of women's stuff')
newspapers (other than *The Times*)
housing estates
clerks (pronounced with an 'ur' and a curl of the lip)
comprehensive schools
instant coffee
Arnold Bennett novels
day trippers
package tours
picnickers
paperbacks
caravanners

17

department stores
tinned salmon

Such things were 'execrable' and 'obnoxious' and 'nauseous'.

He had a private lexicon of such words. As he said them the bushy brows would draw in together and the broad slightly hooked nose lift in distaste. He poured into them all his reserves of disgust and contempt. And something else too. Resentment.

For my father was that other cliché of stage and screen, the disappointed man. His disappointment though was less a complaint or a simple displeasure than a disease which infected every last corner of his life.

When I think of him, I think of the sound of heavy journals slapping down in academic high dudgeon, or the angry scratch of his replying pen across the page.

Dear Sir, I really must take issue with Professor Blah Blah on his assertions concerning the influence of Mycenaean culture on the Homeric tradition . . .

My father, you see, believed himself a scholar of great note. He believed his rightful place was up there among the dreaming spires, drinking sherry at high table. Instead he was just a humble classics master in a third-rate country prep school.

In lieu of a decent salary, they gave him the gate-house on the edge of the school grounds at a peppercorn rent. His finances meant that we lived in that genteel, stiff-upper-lip, put-on-another-sweater poverty, another of those things blown away by the sixties.

My father loathed everything about the school and that included its pupils. 'The sons of clodhoppers and Johnny-come-lately car salesmen' was what he called them.

I can't tell you anything about my mother. She died when I was born. There were no pictures of her around the house and he never talked of her. I imagine she irritated him with her death. I imagine he found it inconvenient. Almost certainly he couldn't forgive her for landing him with me.

There's this line. In *Twelfth Night*. Viola says it, masquerading as a boy. I remember how it hit me when I was fifteen and studying it for O-level. 'I'm all the sons of my father's house . . .' Well, that's how it felt as a kid for me. That's how it was with my father.

Because it was a son that he wanted, a son to whom he could be a father, to whom he could pass on all the things in life he loved and cared about, all his passions, just as any father would wish to do. It wasn't his fault his passions happened to be Plutarch and Homer and Ovid.

When my father was thwarted, when the son he had assumed would appear didn't materialize, but turned out to be a daughter instead, he took revenge the only way he knew. By simply ignoring the facts. By bringing me up precisely the way he would have done a son.

I remember some female rock writer asking me once, 'What's it like to be a woman in rock and roll?' I remember how lost in thought I was, how I couldn't answer. Because I'd simply never thought of it before. Never pulled the thing out and examined it. The fact that I was female. I'd had to fight against a few things in my life but not that one as it turned out.

'You can do anything you like in life Joan,' my father used to say. 'All it needs is work.' And there was the rub. For work was my father's creed. He had no other. He dismissed religion. He didn't even bother to include it in his list of loathing. No, it was work that counted for my father.

'Work Joan. Work is what makes life worthwhile.' I must have heard it a million times.

Each night when I came home from the small private school to which he sent me, I faced another three or four hours of study. First my homework had to be done on a table in front of his desk, and after that it was piano practice.

It never ceased to amaze me, seated at the Bechstein, how he could be so immersed in his work and yet not miss my smallest mistake. His pen would not falter or his head raise, as the precise dusty voice cut through the music.

'Since the composer gave us an F sharp Joan perhaps we could play that and not an F natural . . .'

I remember one Saturday morning, squirming in my chair as the sun came flooding in through the French windows and I could see Richard already lying on the wall. Before me my father strode endlessly up and down tapping his glasses on my exercise book, expounding on the flaws in my homework. In the end I could stand it no more.

'Can I go now?' I said, jumping in as he paused for a second, his glasses in the air.

'Go?' he said looking up in surprise.

'Why?' he said. 'Where?'

'To play?' I said. 'It's Saturday. Richard's outside.'

He closed the exercise book with a snap and threw it on my table, striding over to his desk where he sat down.

'Of course,' he said. 'By all means. Go.'

His voice was angry and sarcastic but, when I hear it now in my head, also very sad.

'Yes go,' said Dr Gradgrind.

'Go,' said Pygmalion.

'Go out and *play*,' said my father, sneering over the word.

I guess one of the reasons he got married again was to try to help counteract what he saw as the pernicious influences from next door.

20

I was ten when my father arrived home with Joyce. She wore one of those wide-skirted frocks with a little hat on her head and was surprisingly pretty. She looked up and saw me staring through the bannisters at the top of the stairs and smiled.

My father saw me too. He said, 'Joan. Come here and meet your new mother.'

I must have looked puzzled because Joyce turned to him, an expression of distress on her face.

'Maurice,' she said, 'you don't mean . . .'

As she stared at him, she looked like something was occurring to her which hadn't occurred before. She clutched at his arm and turned away whispering but I heard her anyway.

'Don't tell me,' she said, 'this is the first time you've told the child.'

'Certainly,' said my father.

I never quite figured out why Joyce married my father. I asked her once when I was older. It was not too long before she died.

'I loved him,' she said simply with a sad smile. She didn't say whether she still did.

Joyce was the best thing that happened in our house, and even as a kid, it didn't seem right. There she was, ridiculously kind and bright and pretty as well, and all she got in return was this selfish and angry man.

'He's had his sadnesses my dear,' she would say defending him to me. 'He's had his disappointments.'

When she talked like this, I always knew she was referring to The Book. *The Lives of the Greek Gods* by Dr R. M. J. Harrington.

'A great universal drama Joan.' It was the only time I saw a gleam of life in his eyes.

'Gods and men Joan. Gods and men. None of this Christian nonsense of sin and salvation.'

He spent most of his life working on it like some old Casaubon but then couldn't find anyone to publish it. It

21

didn't help that he had De Vere next door with his 'damned' detective novels.

De Vere was Richard's stepfather, the reason I had discovered him that day lying on my garden wall.

He met Mirabel on the boat home from Ceylon which she was taking after Edward had succumbed to malaria. The second marriage was as speedy as the first only De Vere was a much better catch.

De Vere was our town's first celebrity since Joseph of Arimathea. He wrote detective novels one of which had been made into a film. His hero was a handsome charismatic ex-army man, clearly an alter ego of himself.

My father detested De Vere almost as much as he detested Mirabel. He made more effort though not to show it. For De Vere's mere presence ground in his own lack of success. He made every effort to avoid De Vere but sometimes he would find himself caught.

'How's it going old man?' De Vere would shout across the hedge, swivelling his pipe in his mouth and pausing for a second with the shears. 'Any luck with a publisher yet?'

My father did find a publisher in the end, a minor press in Oxford, only the book never brought him the academic acclaim for which he yearned. No one even bothered to write those searching, nit-picking letters about it which probably hurt him most of all. Universities bought a few copies for their libraries where, I'm sure, they've long since been packed away to the basement.

He sent an inscribed copy to me, a sad, awkward little gesture.

To my daughter Joan, with best wishes from the author.

Things were already on the slide by then. With exquisite timing I'd just taken a large toot when Francis brought it in and I pulled the paper off.

Flipping it open, I began to read the introduction.

What were the gods to the Greeks? *my father wrote.*

22

They had no moral or spiritual superiority, indeed they were gods precisely because they were possessed not just of the same failings and follies as mankind, but with those failings and follies in abundance and on a far grander scale.

They were not even really immortal, those old Greek gods, according to my father. Their only immortality came from their divine food and drink. Their ambrosia. Their nectar.

To feed on ambrosia, as he pointed out, would make any man immortal.

Or there again, I thought, with my head down doing another line, at least damn well make you feel it.

Donald cooks every day. Three courses. He's at it here now in the kitchen, poring over recipe books, boiling and baking. The house revolves around the rhythm of it, which I guess is part of the plan. I figure he tells himself that if he can keep it going, this routine, it will help keep something alive. It will help keep someone from dying.

Donald is a glorious cook, one of those truly gifted cooks who turn food into something more than just eating. I don't mean all that food art stuff. You know, sunbursts of shredded vegetable finished off with a grape. Believe me, I've laid out for a few platefuls of that in my time. And mostly I just ate the grape. No, Donald's food isn't like that. Donald's food is plain and simple, wholesome, almost old-fashioned you might say. But it tastes better than anything you've tasted in your life.

Because, of course, it's Richard that Donald is cooking for. It's all that's left to him now. That and the small tender tasks around the bedroom. It's his last way of saying 'I love you.'

Each night he mashes the food up carefully and

discreetly. He does not cluck or fuss, just lays a tray with the best silverware and a white damask napkin. Then he takes the wine upstairs and they drink a glass in a small ceremony together.

'Oh robust Richard ... very robust ... oh and blackcurranty ...'

He likes to eat with Richard too, holding the fork for him if he is too tired to lift it himself, filling the spaces with gentle inconsequentialities.

'They say this farmed salmon tastes the same but really Richard I'm not sure ...'

At those times, if it's what Richard wants, we eat at a table in the alcove by the window, Donald and I and often Kent too, for he has taken to appearing at dinner time.

At other times though, when Richard has fallen asleep, or if he is irritable or angry, and sends us away, we eat downstairs in the kitchen, around the long pine table, where it is warm and bright and comforting somehow unlike the splendid grand tented dining room.

Maybe it's the billows of material depressing the spirits in there, or the mockery of the ormolu, the mirrors and the candelabras. Or maybe it's the laughter of the chairs holding out their arms and beckoning around the black lacquer table.

'See how you made merry when you bought us,' they all seem to say.

'See how we will make merry when you are gone ...'

Donald likes to cook to Bach. It's playing now. *The Art of Fugue.* My father's favourite.

'Conceived on the very threshold of eternity Joan.' An oddly reverent thought for my father.

It suits the house, the sound. Perfectly ordered on the surface, frantic underneath.

'Contrapuntal mastery Joan. Duality combining to pro-duce a perfect unity.'

But it was his precious *Art of Fugue* I ripped off that day to put on Eddie.

I figure now that was the final straw. Seeing his beloved Bach tossed aside like that on the floor. That and the sacrilege of seeing Eddie on his turntable.

Because if there was one thing he'd come to loathe more than anything else on that list, it was the new and creeping menace that went by the name of 'pop music'.

Pop music.

Even the word won't work in his mouth. It's too small, too pathetic. It rolls around in there, a ball in a bagatelle, before popping out again, the 'P' hard with hate.

'*Pop music.*'

'*Vilia miretur vulgus* Joan,' he would say, his favourite Latin quote, lifting his nose higher than usual in the air.

He liked to scrabble together all his worst words for it ... *execrable* ... *obnoxious* ... *nauseous*. But there were others he used too, dark ones that gave the whole thing a forbidden ring. 'Music of the mob ... idiot sounds ...', and once, when he thought I wasn't listening, 'jigging and yapping negroes ...'

When a new record shop opens up at the bottom of the High Street, he writes to the council and the local paper demanding its closure and is genuinely surprised when nothing happens.

'O *tempora* O *mores* Joan,' he said, his lips drawn tight in disdain as he tossed into the bin the letter back from the council.

From then on he did the only thing open to him which was to take a long and ostentatious detour so as not to pass the shop. Which was just as well since I was in there all the time with Richard.

25

I was just thirteen when I bought 'Three Steps to Heaven' and I used the five shillings my father had given me for my birthday.

'I don't want you wasting it. You'll either save it or buy books with it,' he said, but I wasn't about to do either.

I figured I was safe that day, that my father would be away with Joyce for several hours. I also figure now I had my first orgasm to Eddie.

That's what it felt like anyway, a wonderful and mysterious something exploding like a firework inside me. I don't know. Maybe it's the rush of childhood you try to copy years later with coke.

I don't know either how many times I played that record or how many times I danced around the room to it. I only know my back was turned and I was still dancing when it happened, so that the first thing I knew of my father's unforeseen return was the outraged scrape of stylus on vinyl.

'*How dare you?*' he screamed.

It's only a question on the page, never in real life. In real life it's a statement of impotence and outrage and intent. *How dare you?* is what they've screamed since the beginning.

There was something erotic about his rage. I can still see him standing there, his whole body shaking, the record arm still in his hand. His face, generally so pale, was purply-red with the pressure of it. Veins pumped in his forehead and his body, always calm and cold and upright, bounced as if the pressure of his fury blew him out like a balloon. His words too were no longer dry and dusty but flew at me wet with spit.

'I will not . . . I will not . . . I *will* not . . . have this abomination played in my house.'

For a moment we stared at each other and then he said,

26

'Go to your room,' but it wasn't that easy any more. Because in the first place his voice had the faintest tremor in it and there was something new too in his eyes. It was just a flicker. A flicker behind the fury. But it looked like fear.

Afterwards I told Richard what had happened.

'I don't care,' I said, jumping, skipping, running, throwing my school beret in the air.

'I'm going to buy his next record,' I said boldly, 'and his next and his next after that I'll buy an LP,' but Richard only laughed.

'You can't,' he said.

'What do you mean?' I said, misunderstanding him. 'I'll save my pocket money. I'll wait. Use the money I get for Christmas.'

'It's not that,' Richard said. 'He's dead. Didn't you know? It was even on the television.'

I remember the disappointment, how it lay heavy and cold in my stomach. I remember too how strange it all seemed, that this being so far above us, from another planet, an American yet, who made *records*, had died so near to our home.

'There's a bridge there,' Richard said. 'It's on a bend.'

'I've been past it,' he said proudly.

They say he was homesick, Eddie. They say he had trouble sleeping. They say that was why he decided to fly home for a break, why he was there racing up to London, late at night in that taxi.

He'd been supporting Gene who was already washed up. Getting a grand less. Stealing the show. Eddie, the clean liver. Gene, all pills and paranoia.

Gene was in the taxi too and so was Sharon, Eddie's fiancée. They all survived including the taxi driver. All except Eddie. The world's first writer–producer.

27

And that's the thing about rock and roll deaths. You can't fake them. They're mundane in their own way, all death is, but still they're always stranger than fiction. For instance the first local on the scene of Eddie's crash found the doors open and the boot up and sheet music blowing around in the wind. And while Eddie's last minutes ran out on the verge, his Gretsch lay in the middle of the road uninjured.

Gene lasted another eleven years. Petered out in the end from stomach cancer.

'Hey guess who's died,' Richard he said looking up from the *Evening Standard*. We were in the dressing room at the time waiting to do *Whistle Test*.

'Better to go early than become a boring old fart,' Leon said, waving his bourbon bottle belligerently at Richard.

He'd been on one of his three-day benders, arriving late and rowing with the rest of us who were worried that he wasn't going to show.

'Hope I die before I get old,' he said, putting the bottle lasciviously to his lips.

'Oh you will Leon. I'm sure you will,' said Richard.

'Why you?' Robin Phillips said to me once. It was the first time he tried to sell me the idea of the biography. But there was a fix to his jaw and an envious glint to his eye.

'Why you?' he said. 'Why not any of the rest of us who strummed our racquet heads and listened to Radio Luxembourg under the blankets? That's what the world wants to know.'

'Talent Robin,' I blustered. 'Must be talent.' I was on the slide then and we both knew it.

'Could be, could be,' he said, fixing me with a lazy stare.

'Or there again,' he said, 'maybe you just wanted it more . . .'

*

28

There are those who will say when the time comes that they always knew you were different. There are others who'll say, 'She was nothing when she was here.' There are those who'll say that you've changed, that you've grown vain and obnoxious, and others who say you still drop by for a beer. Some will say you've given the place a bad name, others want a plaque on the wall. And all of these things are what they want one way or another. But then there are the others, the seekers after truth, whose eyes mist over and who mumble and shake their head. 'I just can't see it,' they say.

What they mean is they just can't make the connection between the kid they knew then and what the kid afterwards became. And they're the ones who've got it. Because there is no connection. Because it's the one major thing the business offers you not normally available to ordinary mortals. A clean break. A fork in the road. A step off the straight and narrow that ploughs through the minefield of identity.

It's a chance to play God, to remake yourself, changing your name for instance, like I did. Refashioning yourself. Like Didi does, all the time.

Re-inventing herself. Removing a rib.

Re-creating herself.

Only this time in her own image.

There's a picture of Didi on Charisse's bedroom wall. From the early period. All tattered virgin voile and earrings. Half covered with heroes who came later. Linus is there. But not Angus. The photo is curling at the edges now. Faded in the sun. Gone the way of all flesh. All flesh I guess except Didi's.

Charisse is Grace's daughter. Grace has a penchant for exotic names. I sleep in Charisse's bedroom sometimes now she's away at university, normally when I've been hitting the red wine after a tough day in the café, when I'm too drunk to drive home.

Charisse was just a kid when she put up the picture. She smiles when she looks at it now.

Because now she calls Didi a Post-modern Icon. She says Didi's Post-feminist. Perhaps even Post-structuralist as well.

'She's anti-patriarchal,' she said to me once.

'I'm not a bit surprised,' I said.

My father refused to call her Didi.

'Ridiculous name,' he would say, emphasizing every syllable. He insisted on calling her *Diana*, which was too large for her, and overwhelmed her as she tottered about the house. When he spoke it she would move, instinctively, towards Joyce's skirts, bumping into things to get away from him.

From the start my father was remorselessly unkind to Didi. He breathed heavily when she was around. He spoke her name ironically, with a smothered grimace, in patient weary tones.

'Joyce,' he would shout through his open door. 'Could you *please* come and remove Diana. She's got into my study again.'

He spoke about her as if she was some small annoying animal. As if she didn't belong to him.

I was eleven when Joyce brought her back from the hospital, a purple thing, crying, with a wide open mouth. Like she knew, for all the world, what was coming.

The awful truth about Didi is that she was the only thing that ever united us, my father and me, for from the start I understood his dislike. I could see that he'd married someone quite selfishly to cook and clean for him and then had realized too late what he'd done, that he'd given up the solitude which he'd then found was what he really wanted, and worse than that had been punished for it with Didi.

'Who's that?' someone would say at the Cococabana.

It was the coolest place in town, or so we thought, with formica-topped tables and spindly chairs and an espresso machine that gushed and hissed and steamed up the glass.

'Over there look. At the window.'

Oh yeah. And a juke-box. Which is why we'd sit there, Richard and I and the rest, for hours at a time.

'There's someone. A kid. Waving at you.'

'Where . . . no not for me . . . must be waving at someone else . . .'

And somewhere, if you listened carefully, a long way away, in the distance, behind the gushing and the steaming, between the notes of the music, you could hear a cock crow in the Cococabana.

Later when I got home Joyce would be laying the table.

'We saw you didn't we Didi?' she'd say. 'We waved but you were with your friends and you didn't see us.'

I'd mumble then, about the noise, about the crowds in there, how the machine steamed up the windows.

'Never mind,' she'd say, pausing for a moment with the knives and forks in her hand. For a second she'd look at me, her eyes clear and empty of unkindness.

'Never mind,' she'd say again quietly.

'You were like some sort of golden couple . . .'

I remember the way Didi said it. With her eyes closed and the sun on her face. Like she was making an effort to show me it didn't matter. I remember the exact line of her head as it leaned back on the lounger, like something from an old movie, white swimsuit and hair caught up in a towel. I remember the soft chuckle of the water as the Filipino raked a stray leaf from the pool and I remember,

31

above all, the picture-postcard blue of the intractable Beverly Hills sky.

'Oh come on . . .'

'Yes, really. He was so dark, you were so fair. How I wanted your hair. I used to pray for it. For hair just like yours. Did you know that?'

'Oh for God's sake Didi,' I said, swinging my legs off the lounger in irritation. 'It's all so long ago.'

'What would it have cost though?' she said, remorseless herself now. 'A lousy smile or a wave through that window?'

'For fuck's sake,' I said, exploding, forgetting my mission, 'what is it with you?'

I was staring at her now but her eyes were hidden behind the glasses. She smiled though with a calm smile that said she'd won.

I ran a hand through my hair and shook my head.

'It's not like it was Swallows and Amazons for any of us Didi.'

I wrote a song for Richard once.

> You
> *A survivor of the war*
> *Where your mother and her man*
> *Fought a bitter battle for*
> *Your soul . . .*

Richard despised De Vere from the first, from the moment I guess when De Vere swung him too high in the air and too near the ship's railings and then tried to comfort him with the crassness of his cravat pin.

'What a cry-baby,' said De Vere as Richard wept. And from then on the battle lines were drawn.

'That boy . . .' as De Vere would call him. 'There's something about that boy, Mirabel . . .'

32

From early on Richard could do a faultless impersonation of De Vere.

De Vere was past his prime when he met Mirabel. He'd been married a couple of times before and liked to think of himself as a ladies' man. He had an old-fashioned raffish quality about him that he liked to encourage. He always looked like an actor playing the part of the cad in one of his books, bright-buttoned blazer and club tie or cravat. And none of this sat easy with Richard.

De Vere sent Richard to my father's school.

'Toughen him up Mirabel. The boy's tied to your apron strings . . .'

Richard's response was simply to get his mother to write notes excusing him from all the things he despised like rugby and cross-country running which, naturally, infuriated De Vere. He also joined the school's dramatic society, appearing one year as Faustus, and another, much worse for De Vere, as a disturbingly lovely Viola.

'That boy, Mirabel . . . that boy . . .' De Vere blustered, apopleptic at his own inability to formulate the accusation he needed. 'He's turning into a real namby-pamby, that boy.'

'Nonsense . . .' Mirabel said calmly, tossing her scarf. 'He's going to be an artist De Vere . . . just like his mother . . .'

Richard was lazy too which allowed De Vere to bitch about the fees.

'Might as well throw the money away Mirabel. Throw it down the drain . . .'

His revenge for all of this was to start muttering about the army: 'Make a man of him Mirabel.' At which point Richard decided it was time to come up with an alternative plan.

To keep De Vere quiet, Richard invented a passion to get into Cambridge, something De Vere's brothers had done but which De Vere had never managed. For a couple

33

of years then, with some help from me, he turned into a swot.

I used to coach him, help him with his Latin and Greek. If it was warm, we'd meet in the summerhouse at the bottom of our garden. We were there one evening, around May it must have been, going over a translation.

I was sixteen then, he was seventeen and changing by the day. It was like he was filling out. His legs and arms had lost their boyish stick-like quality and the skin on them seemed to have taken on a new depth of shine. Also it was 1963 and the Beatles and the Stones had arrived, and to De Vere's disgust Richard's hair had begun to creep down steadily over his collar. In short there wasn't a young woman of any taste or discrimination for miles around not half in love with him.

We were sitting on a rug on the floor this night, our heads bent over Richard's exercise book. Outside the grimy fly-spattered windows, the garden was bursting with colour and blossom. The evening rays were warm through the window and I had rolled up the sleeves of my school blouse. Richard had on a T-shirt. It was the simplest moment, a collision of bare arms, but the effect was like a thousand-volt charge.

Afterwards it felt like there should have been a roll of thunder to announce it with some decent-sized forks of lightning, or perhaps the ground should have split asunder in sympathy.

It was one of those quantum leaps in the science of puberty. An earthquake in growing up that would shoot right off the Richter scale. Everything stopped, what I was thinking, what I was saying. Life came to an end with the touch of his arm and for that one amazing eternal nano-second, all I could feel were the things that came from him, his breath on the side of my face, a tiny tickle of his hair and the faint sweet rich exotic scent off his skin that still remains for me the essence of Richard.

'Are you all right Joanie?' he said.

34

I didn't answer him. I couldn't. I just stared straight

ahead. All I knew was, I didn't want to move. I wanted to stay there, frozen, with that bare arm against mine. I wanted to hold on to it, whatever it was, consider where it left me, this feeling that had suddenly appeared out of nowhere for this strange being I had previously thought of as Richard.

And then suddenly the spell was broken. A long piercing squeak broke the silence as the door began to inch slowly open. One tiny foot appeared around the side and then, grasping the door frame, five little pudgy fingers.

When the face finally peered round, the lips were trembling but the eyes wide and brimming with hope.

A hand reached forward from behind her back and held out to me a limp clutch of flowers.

'You screamed at me over and over to get out.'

Her eyes were misty and looking past me as if she were staring at the scene.

'You said I was fat and ugly. You said you hated me.'

'Jesus Didi,' I said wearily. 'It's all so long ago . . .'

'You said you wished I was dead. Or that I'd never been born.'

Her voice came from a long way away as she spoke and there was a small bitter curl to her lip.

'You ripped the flowers out of my hand and threw them in my face.'

'Look,' I said eventually. 'I'm sorry. If it's what you want Didi I'm sorry.'

But she wasn't listening. She put her head back, slowly, elegantly on the back of the lounger. When she spoke eventually it was an icy hiss.

'And you want me,' she said, 'to lend you money?'

*

35

Once before dinner, after Donald had left the room to check on the food, Richard lifted his wine glass to me.

'My only vice,' he said grimacing.

'Funny you should say that,' I said.

'Do you miss it?' he said.

'Every day,' I said. 'Like a lover.'

'Me too,' he said.

'Ah . . .' he said, laying his head back on the pillow, 'the cruising . . . the new face through the steam . . . another night . . . another body.'

He said, 'You know, sex *solved* something for me.'

'I know,' I said. 'It was the same with dope for me,' I said. He gave me a mocking mournful smile.

'Ah,' he said, 'but I was in love every time.'

'Ah, but so was I,' I said.

He'd been at Cambridge just a term when he called me up. It was his first day home and when he spoke his voice was low like he had a hand over the mouth-piece.

'Come on over,' he said. 'I've got something you've got to try.'

My father caught me as I was leaving the house. Joyce was in the hall putting her hat on to go shopping so we had one of the three-cornered rows that he so much enjoyed.

'Tell me, are you going to let her go out like that?'

It was black plastic masquerading as leather and shorter than the length he considered proper.

'Really, I'm sure it's all right Maurice.'

'It's not allright. It's not all right at all.'

'Don't worry my dear. All the youngsters are wearing them. Why only the other day I saw the vicar's daughter out in one.'

'I don't give a damn about the vicar's daughter. It's my daughter I care about . . .' And so it went on.

When he got really angry he liked to hold Joyce as a sort of interpreter between us, imprison her, as it were, in his own hate.

'Has she done her homework?'

'Tell him I've done my homework.'

'Let me see it then. Tell her I want to see it.'

'There's no need. I've done it. There's no time. I'll be late.'

'Late? Late for what? Where is she going?'

'Where are you going darling?'

It pierces me still, the memory of that *darling*.

'Just next door. That's all. For a coffee. With Richard.'

'I will not, *I will not* have her spending so much time in that house . . .'

Behind me, as I slammed the door, I heard the old defrauded howl.

'I blame you for all this. You're supposed to be her mother.'

And the soft answer, a breath on the air.

'She's just young Maurice. There's no harm in it I'm sure . . .'

De Vere was away promoting his latest book and we knew Mirabel would never disturb us. So I lay back on the bed with the joint in my hand as Otis swam out of the stereo. *Ah beeeen . . . lovin' you . . . toooo lauuuuung . . .*

'I hate him,' I said to Richard, taking a sniping awkward little puff. 'God how I hate him.'

On the bedroom floor, lounging against the side of the bed, Richard shrugged the 'so what' shrug he saved for all fathers, mine, De Vere.

'Sure,' he said. His voice was soft and soothing. 'So what?' it said again as the long honey arm held up the joint.

Some time later, so long later I was surprised that we

seemed to be still on the same topic of conversation, Richard said, 'What does it matter? You'll be away from the old bastard soon. You'll be at university.'

But the hash was starting to take effect by then. Something was Starting to Happen. The stuff was hitting the backs of my knees, and somewhere behind my head, and somewhere else too. Somewhere, wherever it was, where my confidence was located. Belief in limitless possibilities seemed all of a sudden to be ballooning up inside me, or mushrooming like a large white puffy nuclear cloud. Suddenly I felt wonderful. More wonderful than I'd ever felt before.

'I'm not going to university,' I said.

Richard looked up from the floor, his lips crinkled in scepticism.

'Oh yeah,' he said.

'No,' I said. 'Really. I mean it.'

My eyes were shining. From the inside. I knew the time had come.

'The thing is . . . I've been dying to tell you . . .

'I've met this guy,' I said.

There's a myth isn't there that great bands are born and not made? Because, I guess, we like our witches on the heath and our blind beggars by the roadside. So once there's a classic album in the bag, the word is that it could never have been any other way. That this band is more than the sum of its parts. Brought together so to speak by the gods. Except that the reality is always rather more mundane than that. One person who plays in a band brings another person who plays in some other band round to a third person's house. And the rest, as they say, is history. Disappointing isn't it? Still, for those who need some demonstration of that old Deus ex Machina, you could say that it was just by chance that I happened to be there that day outside the pub when the riff rang out. And it might have been the pretty one who couldn't play who came out to catch the bus instead of Kent.

I was feeling good that day because I'd just had my last piano lesson. I'd persuaded my father to let me give them up. I'd said I needed more time to work for my exams. We had to go through the grand charade of him considering the matter. In the end he allowed it, looking down his nose at me, like a potentate granting a great favour.

'Very well,' he said, his fingers twitching over his papers. 'Under the circumstances . . .'

My teacher was sorry to see me go. She crumpled her lace handkerchief sadly between her fingers. I was her only Grade Eight and besides that pupils were hard to come by.

As I was leaving, she fumbled around in the window-box beneath the aspidistra and the sleeping cats and pulled out an ancient copy of *Les Adieux* which she pressed into my hand at the door. I'd just celebrated my de-mob by tossing it with the rest of the music into the bin at the bus stop when the riff corkscrewed out above my head.

There's something about the sound of a raggy band coming out through a pub window, something rich and raw and unexpected. In that moment I thought that riff the sweetest sound I'd heard in my life, an opinion, as a matter of fact, I've never seen the need to reconsider. It went into my soul and out the other side without leaving a hole. A bus came up over the hill and I stepped back to let it pass and turned instead towards the front door of the Fat Ox.

I remember how courageous it seemed walking in. My father didn't go to pubs. I thought someone would stop me as I walked up the stairs. I kept turning round expecting a hand on my collar.

It's an old place, the Fat Ox, fourteenth-century with old beams and plasterwork and uneven wood floors. The upstairs room was so small and dark I could hardly make out the figures at the end. The only light came from a shaft of sunlight dancing with dust specks seeping in from a tiny leaded window. It hit on the two guitar players, one a pretty boy, all long blond hair and hollow cheeks. I figured the riff had to belong to him, until it wound out again and I looked at the other one, a shambling fat thing with farmer-boy jeans. I saw him raise his head towards the dancing dust specks and close his eyes and squeeze up his face, the way he still does, as though what he had to play could only be got out this way, with this enormous pain that was also pleasure. And I knew it had to be him.

It seemed too good a chance to miss when the pub door opened and he came out towards the bus stop a few minutes later.

'I heard you,' I said, 'through the window.' I didn't say I'd been up there to watch.

'I sing a bit,' I said, 'play some piano.' I said it casually, like I thought it should be said, but I needn't have worried. He wasn't even looking at me.

His eyes were on the music still sticking out of the rubbish bin. As I stood there, shifting from foot to foot, he put his case down on the ground and reached forward and began lifting it out sheet by sheet.

I was struck dumb watching him. The way he did it. Tenderly. Like the stuff had been violated. As he lifted the sheets out, he laid them on his arm where he stared at them silently. His eyes were full of something. At first I couldn't figure it out, then I saw what it was. A hunger. He looked like he was staring at something hiding between the dots. Something he wasn't even sure of, but whatever it was, he knew that he wanted.

'Take them if you like,' I said carelessly. 'I don't want them.' I was trying to sound off-hand but it wasn't working because a chill hand of embarrassment was beginning to crawl up my back.

'I chucked them away,' I said. 'I just had my last piano lesson.' But still he took no notice of me. His eyes were fixed on the sheets of music which he stroked gently as if trying to comfort them for their distress.

'I hate the stuff. It's not what I want to play,' I said. 'I want to join a band.' I was defensive by now, talking too fast.

Eventually, as if finally registering my presence, his eyes dragged up to mine. There was no censure in them, there never would be, only absolute amazement.

'*You threw them away?*' he said.

And that's why, in the end, it worked so well between us. His admiration for my ability to make sense of the little black dots on the page, mine for his, the natural talent he got from his father, the one that allowed him to hear a tune once and then reproduce it, entirely faithfully, only a thousand times better.

There's a story, maybe you know it, about a well-known drummer who shall be nameless, who came to audition for us after Leon died. Wandering along the corridor he heard a break that broke his heart, something he knew, solid drummer that he was, he couldn't come anywhere near.

He thought he'd take a look, just if you like for posterity, to see who it was who was clearly going to get the job. Pushing open the door a crack and looking inside he saw there behind the drums the man who was supposed to be the band's lead guitar.

'So who else is here?' I said that first time we met to rehearse.

There were keyboards there and a drum set as well as the several guitars. Nearby a sax spilled half out of its case, in a corner.

'No one,' he said. He had that familiar embarrassed look on his face.

'You play *all* of these?' I said astonished.

41

'Oh no,' he said, as if I was crazy, smiling and shaking his head.

'I just mess with the sax.'

We played surrounded by bales of straw and harnesses and rusting farm machinery, and by the occasional hen strutting in through the door, to turn its head and cluck, I liked to think, appreciatively.

Sometimes as we played Kent's kid brother and sister would come in. They'd sit together on a bale of straw watching us very seriously. Sometimes, too, Jenny would join them, Jenny who had been going out with Kent since they were both fifteen and who wore neat cardigans and skirts and worked as a secretary for the local solicitor.

As she sat there beside the kids listening silently like them, she'd put her chin on her hands and her eyes would glaze over. She looked like she wasn't hearing us any more or seeing us either, but instead was staring at something else, some vision, a long way in the future.

And lastly, occasionally, there'd be another shape in the shadows, another silent watcher, Kent's father, stick in hand, scratching the ground, this expression on his face. Not unhappy exactly, more bemused. Uncertain. Apprehensive.

As a child in this village where he was born, Kent placated the gods, once a year with the rest, marching around the village, in clumsy schoolboy shoes.

Earth feet, loam feet . . .

With the vicar at the front of the procession swinging the incense burner, and the farmers like his father appearing as if by accident, hanging over their hedges, prodding the ground with their sticks, praying, as had always been

42

prayed, for a good harvest, for sun and rain in moderation and in the right order, and for an absence of disease.

'Except that now the chemicals have taken over the business of the gods.'

'Yeah . . . well . . . sort of . . .'

Such colourful concepts always sat uneasily with Kent.

When Kent said, 'Come and see the farm,' I tried to make excuses. I said 'I will' vaguely and then 'Some time' but Richard wasn't having any of it. He waved a hand in the air from the pillows, said, 'She'd love to go Kent. Take her away for the day. She needs the air,' like I was some sort of consumptive Victorian heroine. Then he said campily, 'I'm sick of seeing her long face around the place anyway,' and I knew it was no use protesting.

The truth was you see that while I wanted to see the farm it was no use pretending I wanted much to meet up with Miranda. They're still together and I can only be happy about that. It was one of the first things I asked him as a matter of fact as his fingers played with the sugar the day he came for me in the café. 'How's Miranda?' I said with a smile that ten years on was still faintly apologetic.

I guess he knew what I was thinking yesterday about Miranda when I made my excuses beside the bed because he said, 'Miranda's not crazy on the country actually. Prefers the city life,' and his eyes stared into mine unashamed. He said, 'She's stuck in the studio anyway mixing.'

It felt like I had to say something then so I said politely, 'She doesn't use the studio at the farm?' and he said, 'No. She has a place in town she uses. She likes the sound there,' and there was pleasure and pride in his eyes and just for a moment, hiding there in the civility and the politeness, was a wish that there wasn't.

I wondered then if I should say something like 'Doesn't she want you there? In the studio?' But then I knew that if

43

she'd wanted him there, he'd have been there. Because he's Kent after all . . .

So this morning he arrived in the Landrover at the back door to pick me up looking the way he always looks when he comes straight from the farm, desert boots caked in mud and a sack of something balanced on his shoulders.

'Aha, what have we here?' Donald said, peering over his spectacles from the sink with that determined and gentle cheerfulness which is his last loving gift to Richard.

'New potatoes,' said Kent, lowering the sack to the floor.

He drew a hand across his eyebrows where beads of sweat had gathered and sank down on a bench.

'Blight-resistant,' he said with a farmer's air of triumph.

I know all about organic vegetables from Grace. She likes to serve them in the café and scowls when the customers complain at the extra cost. In retaliation she reads me lectures in the kitchen.

'Did you know there are already two diseases which attack barley that are untreatable?'

'No, I didn't know that Grace.'

But she never waits for my answer.

'And why . . .?' she says. 'Because the planet is fighting back.' She gets angry then and clashes things extra loudly in the sink.

'I mean have you ever heard anything like the macho names they give these damn chemicals? Assassin, Avenger, Commando. I mean if that doesn't say it all.' Most things in life equate to a masculine conspiracy for Grace.

She turns, Cassandra, her face a picture of severity.

'Mark my words,' she says. 'We mess about with Mother Nature at our peril.'

And so I asked him this morning as we headed out of

town on the motorway, 'Is it true?' and he shrugged and pulled a face. 'Pretty much,' he said.

The shrunk and crumpled T-shirt from many tours ago strained across the broad, country-brown arms, frilling on the edges of the sleeves. Small waves on a peaceful sea.

'You know what they say,' he said. 'This year's spray contains next year's disease.'

'But . . . what?' I said. 'A plague? Armageddon. Whole crops wiped out.' He shook his head.

'No,' he said, 'probably not. But don't think it's something farmers haven't thought about.'

They laughed at Kent's father the first time he left his fields fallow. Mocked him. Every Thursday. At market.

'They don't laugh at him now,' Kent said.

Because now they come from all over to see how it's done. Who, oh everyone from serious farmers wanting to go the same way to city dwellers on a day out with their BMWs and their Barbours and their bought-for-the-occasion green wellies. Not to mention the VIPs.

'By Royal appointment even,' I said laughing, looking at the picture on the dairy wall.

'So what did you say to him?'

'The same as we say to everyone. That it's a different sort of farming. That to make it work you have to build up a relationship with your land. Get to know it. Feel it. Smell it.'

He spoke with the old embarrassed passion I remembered from years ago when I'd watch him at press conferences or interviews where he was forced to talk about his music. Then he'd shift in his seat and shake his country-boy head as if he feared talking too much about himself, or being praised too much, as if in the shifting and shaking he were freeing himself, like a dog with fleas, from the deceit and the sycophancy of journalists.

In the yard, a stable girl laughed with a white-muslined cheese-maker as the shepherd whistled his dog.

45

'There's nothing new in it. It's just going back to the old ways,' he said, turning back from the window.

'Really it was always my father's sort of farming,' he said.

His father never tried to stop him though when he said he didn't want to become a farmer, that he wanted to go to London instead, try his hand in a band. His father never even said, 'Don't go.' He just permitted himself one great moment of rage, kicking the high hat hard which fell over on to the bass drum with a crash and a tinkle and an empty disconsolate boom. Then he walked out of the barn without speaking, and over the fields, his fields, his father's fields before, his father's father's before that. The fields he had always thought he would pass on to his favourite son.

He couldn't help treating Kent as his favourite. He was the first-born after all. And so he did with Kent all the things a farmer will do with his first-born, let him ride too high on the tractor when he was far too young, took him to market, to early morning milking.

And the older Kent grew, the more he began to look like his father, with the same long face, the same wide eyes and the same head-down, wellington-boot walk.

I'd feel a catch in my throat when I'd see his father years later, at gigs, walking down the centre aisle to the seats at the front, an old farmer with a farmer's walk and a comfortable farmer's wife on his arm. I'd see this look on his face, dignified, defensive.

'I'm out of place here I know,' it said.

'But it's *my* son I've come to see.'

It's not hard to hide on a six-hundred-acre farm and the morning we left for London his father was nowhere to be found. His son was hunched sorrowfully on the bench on the station platform when he heard the juddering scream

46

of a tractor being driven into the station yard at high speed.

I guess his father had fought with it since early morning, had felt it churning around inside him, the anger, the disappointment, the loss. But in the end he knew he had to let Kent go. For what was his son but a part of himself? And what was his sin but inheriting his father's quicksilver fiddler's fingers?

In the yard, the small man dragged his big son's neck down in an awkward hug. Then he pushed a handful of notes into his hand and was gone, clambering up on the tractor and roaring away.

'You're lucky,' I said staring enviously after him. 'You get on with your old man.'

'Yeah,' he said, and then, 'I'm sorry.' But it was too late. I'd turned away.

'By the way, I'm changing my name,' I said.

My father wrote me a letter in London.

> I gave you everything, *it said*. I could have given a son no more. But you've thrown it all away. You'll do nothing . . . be nothing . . .

The last of his great rages wasn't the puce affair of five years earlier. This time there were no veins pumping in his forehead. This time he stood before me pale and perfectly still, only a hand clenching and unclenching betraying the white-hot fury.

'It's disgusting,' he said, 'disgraceful. I believe you did it on purpose.' And in a way he was right. I didn't want to go to university so I didn't trouble working for my A-levels.

'You'll spend the holidays revising,' he said. 'You'll prepare for your re-sits.'

To everything, though, there is a time and a season, not least the absolute authority of parents.

'There's no point,' I said, shrugging. 'I'm not going to university.'

'Of course you're going to university,' he said, but his voice had a hollow ring to it and the mask of cold certainty on his face suddenly looked to me exactly that. A mask, nothing more.

In desperation he summoned up one of the twisted superior smiles that once would have frozen me to my soul.

'You forget,' he said, 'You're only eighteen. I am still your legal guardian.'

But I only smiled, taunting him with my indifference.

'What are you going to do?' I said. 'Send in the troops? Have me taken back to school by force?'

From a chair by the window, Joyce half rose, trying to make peace.

'What do you want to do darling?' she said. 'Tell us what you want to do.' But all she earned for it was an explosion of fury.

'Be so kind as to mind your own business,' he said, rounding on her. 'She's my daughter. I will decide what's best for her.'

To annoy him I spoke to her.

'I want to go London,' I said. 'I want to get a job, that's all.'

'No it isn't,' he said, flapping a hand at me as if trying to attract my attention. 'It isn't *all* at all. Don't think I don't know why you failed all your exams. Don't think I don't know what you've been doing down there at that damned farm.'

But it was all too late like I say. Eighteen summers of suppressed insolence were uncurling on the carpet towards him. And so came the dying gasp, the bushy eyebrows drawn, the nostrils flaring one last time.

'I forbid it,' he said. 'Do you hear me? I absolutely forbid it.'

But he'd been forbidding things tooooo lauuung. He was just an old cracked record playing over and over and now even Joyce knew it too.

'Nonsense my dear,' she said in a firm voice of infinite sadness. 'You can't forbid things any longer. It isn't the way. It can't be done.'

And I guess that was what did it. For suddenly it was all over. In one long stride he had reached his desk and dropped down heavily behind it. As we stared he turned over the pages of a book with a studied dismissive air.

'Very well,' he said. 'Since you appear to have worked it out between you. Since it's a *fait accompli*. Do what you like. I wash my hands of the whole affair.'

When I went into his study to say goodbye a few weeks later, he was standing with his back to the door looking out of the French windows. A closed thumb and forefinger conducted the invisible cello whose doom-laden notes filled the air.

'Contrapuntus fourteen . . .' he said without turning.

I had seen my father angry many times in my life. I had got used to his anger. But I had never seen anything like his face when he turned. It was cold and flat and so full of disgust it took my breath away.

'I gave you this,' he said, his voice a whisper, 'I gave you all of this.'

He walked over to his desk, as he always did, to take refuge in his papers. As he turned them over listlessly, he recited the list like a mantra. *Bach, Beethoven, Ovid, Homer, Shakespeare, Eliot* . . .

'I gave you all of these,' he said, the voice still full of the suppressed rage, 'and instead you chose this . . . dross.'

'It's not dross,' I said.

'It is. Dross is exactly what it is,' he said. 'It's debris. Detritus. The scrapings of what passes for culture today.'

'In your opinion,' I said mutinously.

49

'*No*,' he said and with the word brought his fist down hard upon the desk.

'Not in my opinion. In the opinion of every civilized and educated person like myself who has devoted themselves to the study and enjoyment of the very best that mankind has produced down through the ages. And at the end of it . . . what? I have to watch you choose . . . this . . . instead.'

His voice had dropped, falling lower and lower. At the end it sounded so full of despair that I was sorry for him despite everything. I walked towards the desk, twisting my hands as I bent over him.

'But why can't the sort of music that I want to play be part of the best too?' I said. It was a genuine question, an earnest question, but for him it was the final heresy.

'Get out,' he hissed, staring down at his pages.

'Get out. Get out.'

And I did.

'I guess he just doesn't understand, Joanie,' Kent said. He was sitting opposite me in the compartment which we'd got to ourselves. He strummed softly as Salisbury Plain passed outside the train window.

'Oh, he understands,' I said. 'Believe me, he understands.'

And he did. And I knew it even then. Of course he understood. They all understood. Who were *they*? Oh, the outraged, the disgusted, the appalled, the ones who stood outside with the placards way back at the beginning. The ones who wanted Elvis Presley to stand *still*.

Basically, beneath it all, my father thought rock and roll was dangerous. He thought the blast of it would bring down the walls. He thought if it was given its head it would take over the world, storm through it like some

50

mad power-crazed monarch spreading mediocrity like a disease.

His greatest fear, I see now, was a sort of armageddon of vulgarity, a Second Coming, Rock and Roll as King, trailing its courtiers, blue jeans and Coca-Cola in its wake.

He argued about it till the end, more with himself than anyone else.

'It won't last,' he said to me nervously, pettishly, that last time I saw him.

'It already has,' I said.

You still see Kent's father around the farm. He's almost eighty now and when you see him it's like a rare sighting of some shy but indigenous species, always in the distance, appearing from behind a tree, striding on his farmer's bow legs, head down and prodding the soil with the stick that seems to grow off his hand like a sapling.

When he saw us this afternoon, he raised the stick to us in an old country greeting which said, 'Fare you well and fine by me but no need to come nearer,' and I figured it had to be because of me.

'Your father still doesn't like me,' I said but Kent shook his head vigorously.

'He does that to everyone. He wouldn't even know who it was at that distance.'

We were sitting in the barn by then, the barn where it all started, except that now of course it's not a barn any longer.

'Bricks and mortar. Bricks and mortar,' that was McGarvey's advice when he passed those first fat cheques across the desk to us. Ironical when I think about it. We clinked our glasses and toasted and chuckled in a small ceremony. McGarvey liked small ceremonies. They were his smoke-screen. His camouflage. The thing he practised in lieu of humanity.

Richard bought the Boltons with his money and I bought my beloved Stoneham. But Kent set about converting the barn.

He'd arrive at the studio covered in dust like a labourer because he'd been searching out old timbers or stone or stained glass.

It was an exquisite conversion, the sort you see in *House and Garden*, except that Kent would never have let a journalist within a mile of the place. He probably would now except they'd have to be *Living Earth* or *New Farmer and Grower*.

The heart of the place is the lounge on the first floor which stretches the length of the old barn. Once in a previous incarnation the polished wood floor was scattered with toys. A fire was always smouldering in the canopied fireplace in the centre of the room even in summer, sacred coals on a sacred altar, with Jenny always around somewhere, sewing name-tags on school shirts, or finding lunch boxes or parting a pair of fractious twins. And perhaps it's because I remember it this way that the place has such a melancholy feel to it now, as though a dust of a thousand memories has settled so firmly that it can't be displaced even by the weekly cleaning woman.

For now it's a spartan place with a bachelor feel to it, a small galley kitchen where no one cooks and a couch in the corner with a cover hastily thrown over it that looks too restlessly, too carelessly slept in.

Miranda's not crazy on the farm actually. Prefers the city life . . .

His guitars are there and some coffee cups scattered about the place but not much else. There's a picture though above the couch. The twins. Angus. And Andrew.

It still has the beautiful view, of course, looking out over the fields, sweeping down to the cut and the copse and the cottage.

'Who lives there now?' I said. From the window I could just make out the small wisp of smoke from the chimney, the only way that you'd know the place is there, hidden as it is by the trees and the green fold of the hill.

Green. Green and clean. The reason why Leon loved it.

'The shepherd,' Kent said, spooning coffee into the cafetière. He didn't have to ask what it was I was looking at. As he poured the hot water in, he made the soft sucking noise I remember that tells you he's thinking carefully about what he will say.

'You know . . . it's all a long time ago now Joanie,' he said. And so it is. Twenty years.

'Do they still come?' I said. He sighed. 'Regular as clockwork,' he said. He handed me the mug of coffee and sat down.

'Who are they?' I said.

'Oh . . . taxi drivers . . . tree surgeons . . . traffic wardens . . . take your pick.' With only one thing in common. The desire to worship at the shrine that is Leon.

'You despise them,' Dr Linquist said to me once in the clinic. 'Who?' I said, surprised. 'The fans,' he said. 'Why?' I said. 'Because they feed off you,' he said. 'Because they want you to do the things they don't have the courage to do themselves.' And it's true. But there are other people I despise more. The rock journalists who play the same game, the Robin Phillipses of this world, squalid purveyors of the same creed, worshippers around the throne of the great trinity, sex and drugs and rock and roll, hypocrites, half in love with easeful death. As long as it isn't their own.

'Oh, for fuck's sake,' I exploded once when I saw the headline over Rory's shoulder. 'Mystery. What fucking mystery?' Rory is Charisse's boyfriend. He's doing politics at the same university.

Rory has a T-shirt with Leon's face on it and THE LEGEND underneath. He was wearing it the first time I met him. When Charisse introduced us, he said 'Hi' in a cool and faintly accusing manner. It was like he was blaming me for something and I figured afterwards it could only be for not having the decency to die like Leon.

That was the day Rory told me that Leon was a rebel, that he didn't give a shit about authority.

'Really?' I said. 'That's amazing. I never noticed.'

'He lived for today,' Rory said.

'He had no choice,' I said. 'He couldn't face the future.'

'He was a *real* rock and roller,' he said with a meaningful sniff.

'Oh God Rory,' I said. 'This is all so much shit.'

After that I made myself a promise that I wouldn't argue with Rory. But then I came upon him reading this Sunday supplement piece. You know the sort of thing. Ten years on from the Great One's death, twenty, and now the silver jubilee. Which is why I exploded.

Rory lifted his eyes up wordlessly when I began to rave. When they looked into mine they said, 'Really?' and 'What would you know?' which made me very angry.

Sometimes like the rest of the world I try to imagine what it would have been like if Leon had lived, if he'd just gone on growing old like the rest of us. I do it perversely, off-handedly, trying to catch myself unawares. I have to do it this way to keep up the fantasy, because I know that Leon never could have lived, that Leon alive is not one of the options available, not even among the trillion zillion possibilities in those endless parallel worlds.

And yet what people like Rory want to believe is that his death was somehow unpredictable, that it was random, bad luck, a wrong turn of the wheel. At the same time they want it to be truly tragic. In the real sense of the word. Like Macbeth's for instance. Predestined. Foretold by spirits. Predetermined by that famous tragic flaw.

It's a tough life being a drummer. I mean it's physically tiring. And all rock history would seem to show that it's a better than average breeding ground for tragic flaws.

This business, as we all know, is famous for the neuroses and paranoia and general personality defects of those who

54

take part in it. But there's one thing on which most of us would agree and that is that drummers, as a breed, are more over-burdened with these little difficulties than the rest of us.

Passing the time sometimes on long journeys, on the bus, say, on the plane, we'd tried to figure out the mystery of this.

'They're jealous,' Richard said once. 'They're stuck at the back. The girls can't see them.'

That's part of it, I'm sure of that. Because, as a female who spent the best part of her working life stuck at the back playing piano, I can tell you that anyone who doesn't understand that the rock guitar is a) the greatest phallic symbol invented by mankind and b) the heart of rock and roll is misunderstanding the medium. And apart from anything else it goes a long way to explaining why all the great tales of excess on the road are attached to drummers, why, shall we say, they over-compensate after hours. And why, more importantly, the drum machine is reckoned by most people to be *the* great musical invention of the late twentieth century, something which has added to the paranoia of all but the most intelligent drummer.

For what the drummer knows, essentially, is that he's the unsung hero. Without a good drummer you have no band. The same goes for the bass. You think the bass does nothing until you take it away, and then all you have is this ethereal nothing without the blood and guts that makes it rock and roll. But the bass man at least has the compensation that he gets to stand out front along with the others and collect the kudos. All the drummer gets is those endlessly dreary conversations from earnest young men who want to tail him afterwards and tell him about what a great drummer X is and why exactly Y is so brilliant, conversations guaranteed to bore the ass off any red-blooded women.

Because the truth is that, generally, as a breed, women aren't interested in drummers. Women at a concert will

55

do exactly what the rest of the band does in those boring and obligatory drum solos which all bands have to give their drummers for no other reason than to keep them happy. They go off and get a drink or go to queue for the toilet. And drummers, while they're not known for their sensitivity, can't help but realize this. Not exactly, when you think about it, a tribute to your art. Which as a matter of fact is something quite fine.

For the irony about good drumming is that all the worst clichés are true. When you hear one of those boring young men say, 'It's not what he does, it's what he doesn't do,' he's actually speaking the truth. Even though, half the time, he doesn't really know what he's talking about. For simplicity, not flashy solos, is the name of the game when it comes to great drumming.

'Sounds like he's putting a roof on a shed,' I once heard Leon sniff about the drummer in one of our support bands, which is not only one of the funniest things I've ever heard about a drummer but also one of the best. Because that's what it's all about. The difference between good and bad drumming, the bang bang bang of a hammer or the infinitely delicate driving simplicity that keeps the whole thing together.

'We've got bugger all else to do but drum, that's the problem,' is what Leon said about the business in one of his more lucid moments. And that exactly sums it up. Which is how he could end up stoned out of his brain as was his custom with a bunch of free-loaders he called his band, crooning nonsensical scraps into his Revox. Those same nonsensical scraps which the fast-buck merchants turned into The Basement Tapes after his death.

No one could have been *surprised* at Leon's death. Given Leon's life, it could only have been expected. The how of it was always a foregone conclusion, and the only cards he kept up his sleeve were the *when* and the *where* which he clutched to his chest, a dirty old man in a raincoat, fanning them out like smutty postcards with a 'psst' and a 'wanna see . . .'

And if there's a rock and roll heaven, which on the balance of probability I'm bound to say seems unlikely, then let me tell you that Leon is up there laughing at it all, the book and the film and particularly the tie-in T-shirt.

Leon had to die because he was the lightest of us, the vaguest, the wicker man waiting to be made whole, waiting to be plumped up and filled out and coloured in by those vampires and necromancers whose job it is to twitch straight the tablecloth of history and make sure that the myths are in place. People like Robin Phillips.

The mythology has grown up around Leon like a thicket and it's mainly thanks to Robin. A hard man, a drifter, a North Country lad lost in the big city. A real drummer, you might say. But there were thousands of Leons in London by the time he walked into the pub where we were playing. The place was full of them, a whole mafia moving south once again in search of work.

We played Leon's home town once, a club there, grey and grubby like the place itself.

'Close the window for fuck's sake,' Richard screamed as we pulled off the fly-over, the cloud of smog like dirty cotton wool beneath us. He began coughing in disgust.

'Christ,' he said. 'How do people live here Leon?'

It was like this between them from the first. Richard would camp it up and call Leon 'our working-class hero', while Leon would come back with 'bourgeoisie'. This time though Leon said nothing. Just put the old belligerent bottle to his lips.

It was in the early days and we were dossing down at Leon's parents for the night. It turned out to be a council house, pockmarked pebble-dash in a grey sea of the same, all with threadbare unfenced lawns outside them and the occasional bottle, can or chip paper caught in the grass.

'Oh very gritty,' Richard said. 'Very northern.' It hadn't been a good gig and worse for Leon because it was his

57

home town; heavy metal fans who clearly didn't care for us plus a few adventurous punks.

Inside the house it was all black plastic and plywood and there was a smell of fat over everything. Upstairs we could hear his father coughing.

'Emphysema,' said Leon. 'You don't know what emphysema is do you Richard?'

He was very drunk and very stoned and pretending not to care in the way that he did all the time, especially when he was teetering on the edge of fury.

A few joints later he jumped up and threw open the front door.

'So convenient eh Richard?' he said. 'Straight in from the street. No hall or lobby or vestibule . . .' He said the words slowly and mockingly, a cigarette hanging from his lips.

It was when Richard wouldn't answer, turning away in disgust, that Leon hurled himself out into the street. He threw his arms in the air and began singing raucously and bitterly.

My kind of town . . .

Lights were going on up and down the street and someone was yelling from a window as Kent and I jumped up to try and drag him back in.

'Leave him,' Richard said. 'He's a maniac.'

'Yeah, leave him,' said Hammy. He always sided with Richard. It was one of the things I despised about him.

We caught up with him halfway along what passed for the main street, a road of down-at-heel pubs and shops and shattered bus stops. Glass from shot-out street lights crunched beneath our feet as we finally managed to grab hold of him.

'Come on Leon,' I said. 'Let's go home.'

We were standing in front of what had once been a cinema, a handsome old place, with an art deco frontage behind the boxed bingo posters and marbled mosaic beneath the grime.

He'd actually turned to go when there was a movement at the top of what had once been the elegant curving steps.

'Come on Leon,' said Kent, sensing trouble. But it was too late.

The smell was sudden and sharp and surprisingly strong. It hit our nostrils harder with every drop as it trickled down the mosaic. Before we could stop him, Leon was up the steps and grappling with the hunched figure at the top, screaming and swearing as he tore at its back.

'Dirty fucking filthy bastard . . .'

He caught the guy off balance as he was buttoning himself up and they toppled and fell together, rolling down the steps and in and out of the rivulet of urine. His leather jacket was wet and he stank of it by the time we managed to drag him off and the drunk stumbled away, muttering and frightened, into the night.

'For fuck's sake Leon . . .' I began but stopped as he dropped down on to the steps, his whole body an expression of despair, and buried his head in his hands. When he raised it, I saw that he was crying.

'I hate this filthy stinking town,' he said.

Kent bent over him and lifted him up. His shoulders were shaking.

'Let's go home Leon,' he said gently, but he pulled away from him. His face was fierce now and his eyes wild. He stared upwards towards heaven like he was pleading.

'You know what I want?' he said. 'You know all I want in life?' He lowered his head and looked backwards and forwards, between the pair us.

'I just want to go somewhere where they don't piss on the cinema steps . . .'

We'd almost pulled out of the place the next day when Leon said, 'Take a left.'

He said it so urgently and so sharply that Kent did it

instinctively, without signalling, which was unusual for him. Behind us a lorry braked sharply, its load clanking as the driver swore at us behind his windscreen.

'Oh for fuck's sake . . .' said Richard.

We knew what he meant. Leon's love life on the road affected all of us. We'd grown used to shifting up in the back to make way for some girl that Leon had picked up at the gig who'd sit there next to him, trapped and embarrassed and monosyllabic, unable to deal with the boredom and irritation towards her which soon he was beginning to make no effort to hide in her presence.

Once he brought two of them back to the van, and when he was made to choose, he did it like a man selecting merchandise, which was pretty much how he treated women. Well, at least until he met Lois. He never even troubled to kiss the beaten finalist goodbye, I remember. She walked off, torn tights and a pair of boots, into the night.

'We haven't got *time*,' I said as the van lurched and regained its equilibrium. And I was right. We didn't. We had to make the ferry for what we were laughingly referring to as our Northern Ireland tour.

But Leon ignored us.

'Straight ahead . . . straight ahead . . .' he said, flapping a hand at Kent, as we drove through streets as grimy and grey and pebble-dashed as those we'd just left.

'Oh for fuck's sake,' I said, 'we're back where we started.' But we weren't. It was just that every street was the same where Leon lived.

'Here,' he said to Kent, and when the van stopped he jumped out and ran up the same tarmac path between the same threadbare unfenced lawns, pulling a key out of his pocket with which he let himself in.

He must have been in there all of three minutes. When he came out he had the look of a man who had got away with something. But as he half ran up the path the door half opened and a thin white face looked out with smudged

60

black eyes and a pile of wisping dark hair. And from somewhere deep inside, like an echo, came the sound of a child crying.

Marge. Marge and Linus.

'You never told her did you?' I said, as he clambered past me into the van.

'You never even told her you were playing here.' But he didn't answer, just pulled out his dope and began, immediately, rolling a joint.

'Christ, you really are a bastard aren't you Leon?' I said.

Like I say, there was always a girl with Leon. There was something aggressive about it. Something overt and extreme. Most of the time he treated them like he despised them, and the thing that lodged in the craw looking on was that they seemed to accept it.

Leon's meanness was legendary on the road, not an unknown failing in our business, believe me. His favourite trick was to get them to pay for everything, his drinks, his food.

'Come on darlin',' he would say in his hoarse unaffectionate North Country drawl. 'Get your hand in your pocket.' And they always did.

What he liked best were the occasional private gigs we got, the balls, the birthday parties.

'Rich pickings,' he would say, leering and rubbing his hands in the back of the van. And they usually were.

'They like a bit of rough,' he would say, and they did too, fanning their taffeta tails for him like peacocks, yahyah-ing in his ear, side-stepping, like old professionals, the chinless wonders they came with.

It was Arabella's party this night, which I guess gave her the right to dump Jocelyn or Julian or whatever his name was, just another drunk on the dance-floor as far as we were concerned, distorting his vowels and his body in an approximation of dancing.

The atmosphere wasn't good when we found her in the back of the van. We were at that stage which comes to all bands at one time or another, good or bad, the make or break time when it might go either way, when people are becoming restless and getting on each other's nerves and at the same time looking for someone who might be responsible.

Normally in this frame of mind Leon would bait Richard, which he tried, but to no avail, because Richard wouldn't rise, simply slumping away in his seat in a bored fashion. So all Leon could do was turn on Arabella.

We'd pulled up at these traffic lights when he said, 'Fancy something to eat, something sweet,' and he leered at her. 'There's a grocer's darlin', jump out and get me a Mars bar.'

She looked round at him like he'd just crawled out from under a stone. She was angry by now and getting cold in her taffeta. What was worse she was coming to realize she'd made a fool of herself with a lout. 'Get it yourself,' she said curtly.

When she said it Leon's head went up. His eyes glinted like an old revolutionary. He began to move in on her menacingly. 'Got no money darlin',' he said.

'You've been paid,' she said, sniffing, turning away, but Leon said, 'Boss keeps all the dosh,' with a jerk of his head towards Kent, and made a dive for her bag, but she was too quick for him, wrenching it from him and sitting on it to keep it from his grasp.

'If you *must* play the yob,' she said sneering, 'I suggest you get out and steal something.'

He reared back in surprise when she said it and stared at her with a mixture of hate and reluctant admiration. This way have the likes of Leon looked at Arabellas for generations. Then he shook his head and the next minute was out of the door.

When Kent heard the door go he looked up into the mirror and cursed. We'd been at a set of lights which were changing. Now he had to crawl along the inside lane with traffic hooting and flashing behind us.

Leon caught up with us at the next set of lights. As he hurled himself in, banging the door, a shopkeeper in a brown overall ran out on to the pavement cursing and waving his arms in the air.

'Go. Go. Go for fuck's sake,' said Leon.

As he fell back in his seat chocolate bars began spilling from every pocket. He bent forward as they tumbled into his lap, lifted them up and began dropping them over his head. 'Christ Leon,' I said as he threw one at me.

It struck me then, not for the first time, that he'd done the whole dumb thing more to impress Richard than anything else. But Richard only grabbed a bar and huddled himself up back in his seat so that Leon was left alone again.

In desperation Leon began eating the bars suggestively, pulling down the wrappers, putting his lips over the top. When this provoked nothing from anyone he began advancing on Arabella.

Normally they squeaked like mice when he got up to his horseplay. It was pretty much all that was open to them. But that was below Arabella. Beneath all that taffeta she was as tough as they come. She stared down at him with disgust, a marchioness right down to the last pearl in her choker.

'God you are revolting,' she said.

By this time he was sticking bar after bar in his mouth and the bottom half of his face was smeared with chocolate. As he moved towards her, Richard and I started to protest in the back saying things like 'Oh, for God's sake Leon', but not really defending her or helping her, because that was the way we did it. That was the way things were in the back of the van.

And so in the end all she had to call on was her own resources of which she had plenty. She ignored him, turning her head away as he shoved his chocolatey face towards her. She looked down her nose at him in a gesture of superiority which took in not just him but the rest of us as well. It amazed me. It seemed to come from a long way back. It belonged entirely to what she was and what she perceived us to be, a look perfected, probably on the way to the block.

I tell you that look drove Leon to distraction. If it was revenge she was after then she got it. Because that look burnt like a brand on his working-class soul. In a second he was on top of her, grabbing the bars, tearing them open with his teeth, trying to jam them into his mouth and hers as well. But it took more than this to wipe the centuries of breeding from her face. Her lips remained clamped closed and she stared down at him with loathing, still refusing to scream.

I was trying half-heartedly to drag him off as he pushed the bars between her breasts and up her skirts where the chocolate lay like blood above her suspenders by the time Kent, swearing loudly, threw on the brake and jumped out, hurling open the back door to sort things out. Richard meanwhile was laughing like a maniac while Hammy kept up a running commentary from the front seat . . . 'Jesus Christ . . . I mean for fuck's sake . . . bloody hell . . . we're late already . . .'

'You're an animal,' she said, when order had been restored, resting against a speaker smeared in chocolate, like the victim of some crime. But all he did was laugh, his mirthless croaking laugh.

'And don't you just love it,' he said.

All of his life Leon acted like a man intent on forgetting something.

'Ah, so many different drugs . . .' he would say in a sort of toast, his nose dipping to the coke or dropping a tab on his tongue, 'so little time . . .'

So many. So much. The story of Leon's life.

While the rest of us were still sitting at the feet of our accountants, Leon was already out of the door, renting a Bentley with an option to buy.

There was something almost girlish about the way Leon shopped. Coked up, he and Marge would go on absurd sprees, shopping wherever was most convenient, which was wherever they were at the time, in Bond Street, where the jewellers scraped and bowed, or at the tacky tourist end of Oxford Street among the postcards and the T-shirts and the Union Jack underpants where they would buy mountains of cheap toys for Linus.

Leon shopped like he lived, grabbing, plundering, stuffing it all into the cheap plastic carrier bag that was his life. The floor of the Bentley would be covered in bags by the time he got home. Once there he'd throw them into one of the many unused rooms in the four-storey house that he rented in Notting Hill, which is where they stayed most of them until the day that he died, room upon room of them, unopened carrier bags, the flotsam and jetsam of his life.

He never got round to buying a house, just like he never got around to buying basics like furniture. When he first moved in he called up an interior decorator who scattered a few rugs about the place and some oriental chests. When the bills began coming in, though, he went off the whole idea. There was never anything more than cushions to sit on in his lounge, while the same grubby old curtains he'd inherited stayed hanging at most of the windows.

Looking back, I figure that the only thing that really gave him any pleasure besides the dope was the Bentley.

For a while, when he first got it, it seemed like he lived in it. He drove around in it all day, drinking and doping up. At first he drove himself, very badly, not surprisingly since he'd never learnt to drive. After the first crash though and the first court case, he was persuaded to get a chauffeur.

The Bentley was cream with tinted windows which is what he loved most about it, the whole see-but-not-be-seen thing. But here's the irony. His big joy was to be spotted in it, this thing that showed, in his own mind, the fact that he'd made it. It's why he'd bought it in the first place. So he had to wind his precious windows halfway down, which is what he used to do, lounging on the back seat, pretending unconcern, pretending he needed the air while waiting for the rush of feet at the traffic lights.

He had a special look of surprise that he'd rehearsed in front of the mirror for when the hands and the autograph books and occasionally even the items of underwear appeared through the window.

He liked to pretend when it happened that he was in a rush. That he was off somewhere important, even though all he was doing was driving around all day. So he'd scribble a signature or two and push the books back through the window. Then he'd tell the chauffeur to step on it and as the girls ran beside the car he'd press the button to whizz the window up, trying to catch their fingers.

He managed it once when I was in the car with him. We were at the lights just around the corner from McGarvey's office. At first she laughed as we edged away from the lights, trying to stare in through the window. As we began to speed up though her expression changed first to panic and then to one of absolute terror.

'Press the button. Press the button for fuck's sake,' I yelled at him, lunging towards it. But he covered it with his back, staring at me as he reached slowly and leisurely behind him, pressing the button at last and freeing the hand.

Behind us the girl fell away sprawling on to the pavement, white-faced and weeping.

'Fuck you,' I said coldly. 'You enjoyed that didn't you?' But he wouldn't look at me, just leaned his head back on the seat, his face flat and empty.

'You really do hate them don't you?' I said. I shook my head, appalled.

'What is it with you Leon?' I said.

Leon's exploits on the road were the stuff of which biographies are made. You'll find them in Robin Phillips's book. Some of them happened the way he tells them, some of them didn't. And some of them never happened at all.

It's true though that when we arrived in a new town the art gallery or museum wasn't automatically the first place that Leon searched out. It's also the case that his capacity for stimulants of all states and persuasions were capable of surprising even his most battle-hardened companions.

One night the roadies who he'd been partying with pulled the large mirror off the inside of his wardrobe door and put it in his bed beneath the bottom sheet. He woke up the following afternoon to find the bedclothes covered in blood and his back cut to ribbons from the smashed glass.

'Slept like a baby,' he boasted proudly.

If there was bad company to be had in town then it's also true that Leon would find it, for the hard-man reputation was not entirely unfounded.

One night, tired and trying to get to our beds, we found no one at reception. A roadie was behind the counter trying to find our keys when the desk clerk turned up and began giving him ear-ache for being there. When Leon started swearing at him, the desk clerk turned on him with the sort of middle-class pompous rude-speak you come to dread as a band staying in British hotels. He even had the misfortune to wag his finger at Leon.

'I've met your sort before,' he said.

It was as far as he got. I still don't know how Leon did it but he was over that counter in one. He had the clerk jammed up against the panelling with a fist under his chin.

He didn't even look angry, Leon, in fact he was grinning now benignly at the quaking jobsworth.

'Oh no you 'aven't,' said Leon.

I'll tell you what happened to Leon. I'll tell you why he never made it. Leon saw a picture of himself and thought that it was him. A fatal mistake in our business.

Perhaps it was the picture that Robin Phillips used in the book. Leon with the Three Witches. Thane of Glamis, even of Cawdor. Never to be King.

They curve into him in the photo, one at his feet, the second at his elbow, the third, tall and towering and staring over his shoulder.

They were the most famous groupies around. Always together. Always hunting in a pack.

When we touched down in LA, they'd be waiting for him on the tarmac, secret black and midnight hags, their long hair and dresses lifting in the wind, their eyes drawn out to their ears.

Sometimes they travelled with us on the bus, a coven with Leon in the middle. Back in his hotel room after the gig, they would dance around him, doing his chart, rolling his joints, cooking his smack. Serving him honey slides on a plate.

Eye of newt, and toe of frog . . .

They slept with him too, all three of them together. I walked in on them one night in search of some more coke and there he was, passed out with them on the bed, curled in among them, a smile on his face like a baby.

One died of an overdose not long after he did. Another was last heard of in Mexico.

The third cleaned up and went to college and became a lecturer in feminist semiotics.

She's writing a book on Didi now.

*

68

'What made him want to do it?' I said to Kent. 'Your father? Go organic?' We were still sitting in the window seat looking out at the farm.

'An oak tree,' he said. He pointed the coffee mug, fingers through the handle, out through the window.

'Over there,' he said. 'Between those two fields. Past the studio block.'

'Where?' I said peering.

'It's not there any more,' he said.

It was his father's favourite tree. It had been standing there for three hundred years. Should have gone on for another three hundred. Then one day . . . for no reason . . .

'Pesticides . . .?' I said. He shrugged.

'I don't know,' he said. 'Neither does anyone else. What I do know is that the fields on either side had been sprayed regularly twice a year for fifteen years when suddenly it died.'

I stared out through the window. I was suddenly very cold. What felt like an ancient shiver twitched my shoulders. Once I might have said, 'Someone just walked over my grave.'

'I think we should go home,' I said.

I knew something was wrong as soon as we walked in. No Bach playing in the kitchen. No pans boiling on the stove top. I guess Kent must have felt it too because without speaking we headed towards the stairs together.

We heard Donald's voice about halfway up. It was strained and strangling with pain.

'It's what Richard wants,' he was saying. 'It has to be Richard's decision. And Richard doesn't want to go into hospital.'

We could see the difference in Richard from the door. Nothing startling. Nothing noticeably greyer or more sunken. Just the sense of something further having slipped away, of some new stage having been reached.

By the side of the bed a doctor stowed away a stethoscope. He was a man in his fifties, handsome, grey-haired, a certain briskness disguising the sorrow. I know him. He's been Richard's doctor for many years. Perhaps even his lover. And yet it's more than that, the sadness on his face. It says he's tired himself, that he's played out this scene too often.

'But if there is an emergency . . .' he was saying with a sigh.

From the bed there came a small unexpected clicking of teeth. Richard's eyelids shot up and the eyes rolled up in mockery.

'*An emergency* . . .' he said.

'I used to talk to it at first,' he said. 'Reason with it. Curse it. I'd visualize it as an alien creature invading my body.'

And now, I wanted to say. *And now.*

I was sitting by the bed. Donald was washing Richard's body with sweeping tender strokes. I'd made to leave when he'd begun but Richard had just flapped an irritated hand that said he was past all that now.

'You go through everything at the beginning,' he said. 'Anger. Despair. Disgust. Denial.'

'I can understand the anger,' I said.

'No,' he said. 'It's not what you think. I was just angry that no one would tell me how long I had. I thought they were keeping it from me but of course they weren't. They just didn't know themselves and now I'm glad. Because they might have said a couple of years and in the end . . .'

In the end it was seven years. Seven years since he was diagnosed. Two more hit albums, a couple of world tours, half a dozen more of his outrageously inventive videos.

'He never even slowed up,' Donald said proudly with

one of the long loving strokes. He held Richard in his remorseless smile. 'Even in bed he's been planning songs for a new album haven't you my darling?'

But that was when I saw Richard turn away from him, when I saw for the first time that look of suppressed anger and utter weariness on his face in Donald's presence. It made me see the dark side of Donald's love. How desperate it has become and because of that how pitiless.

'In the end,' Richard said, as if he had not heard him, 'I was just left with amazement.'

'Amazement?' I said, not understanding. 'Because you got it?'

'Good God no.' He let out a deep raucous chuckle of remembrance and for a moment he was lost in some memory. Then he turned a pair of calm eyes to me from the bed.

'No. I was just amazed that having money made no difference. That in the end there was nothing they could do for you no matter how much you were willing to pay.'

What shall it profit a man . . .

I go to church sometimes, right? No big deal. It's just something I do. It's mainly because of Paul. Paul's our vicar. He lives alone in the boxy little rectory behind the church. A property developer who got out before the crash lives in the old rectory now.

Because he's on his own, Paul takes his breakfast every morning in the café. A croissant and a good cup of coffee. A bachelor's breakfast.

He takes a beating for it some mornings trying to hide behind his *Guardian* as Grace rages against the Colonel, more often than not to do with the hunt. Grace organizes the local saboteurs and has felt the crack of the Colonel's crop across her shoulders.

The Colonel runs pretty much everything in our village

71

and that includes the parochial church council. Occasionally Paul will make a sort of statutory effort to defend him.

'The wonder of God's love,' he murmured once, 'is that it includes all . . .'

'No, the *wonder* of God's love,' Grace rejoined sarcastically, 'is that it includes the Master of the Foxhounds.' Grace has no time for the church.

It's part Norman our church, the rest fine perpendicular. A chocolate-box church for a chocolate-box village. It's why they come, why they feel quite at ease walking around it. They like the carved pews and the screens and the ancient effigies and the fact that it has a properly musty smell. It allows them to feel comfortable in the place. Relieves their embarrassment. It means they can treat it the way they feel happiest treating a church which is as just another tourist attraction.

Our church rates a page in Pevsner, so you can understand why the Colonel's daughter, who has long since flown the coop, should none the less wish to get married there.

Her bridegroom – husband now – deals in futures. He's one of those guys who appears on your TV screen dragging a hand through his hair and screaming down the phone like a maniac as the newsreader's telling you it's the end of the financial world as we know it. I don't imagine the happy couple were avid church-goers, which is their business. Still, in the manner of the times, they showed up one Sunday, pale from their hangovers, to hear their banns read. And, all in all, you might think it quite fitting that our man from the money markets just happened to be there the day that Paul preached that number about camels and needles' eyes and the difficulty of getting into heaven if you're loaded.

Poor Paul.

'But it was the reading for the day,' he kept saying, genuinely hurt after the Colonel had caught him in the vestry afterwards and called him a Trotskyite. The Colonel, you have to understand, has never seen fit to update his vocabulary.

Because it wasn't a personal thing at all. It was all a complete misunderstanding. It's because he's short-sighted that Paul leans out from the pulpit and stares like that. And it was pure bad luck that, given the habit, he appeared to be addressing the prospective bridegroom personally when he pronounced the offending words, 'It's not that you *can't* get into the Kingdom of Heaven if you're rich . . . It's just that it's going to be that much harder, that's all.'

For myself, I have to say that watching the Colonel turn that interesting shade of purple was worth every last penny I put in the collection plate. I got quite excited at one point. I thought maybe he was going to spontaneously combust like some character from Dickens.

'Great sermon Paul,' I said afterwards, grinning from ear to ear, and refusing to sympathize. And so it was. And since the futures king had spent the best part of the previous day getting pissed in the Stawell Arms and boasting noisily about the killing he made on Black Wednesday, I figure there were a few other people in the congregation who thought so too.

But you know what breaks me up still about that whole camel and needle's eye thing? The young man. The one who brings about the whole episode. I can see him so clearly. So rich and yet so thoroughly decent. Not the easiest thing to be, believe me, when you've got money.

He must have been smart. Because you've got to be smart to have that much money and to realize, at the same time, it isn't enough. But even being smart didn't help him against the power that is money.

In fact, in the end, his wisdom was the worse for him, which to my mind is the ultimate cruelty of the story. Because, in the end, he had to carry it away with him, his insight, like a pack on his back or a curse from the gods.

He knew it wasn't enough and at the same time he knew that knowing it didn't make a ha'porth of difference. He knew he still wasn't able to part with his money.

Sell whatsoever thou hast and give to the poor . . . Not a chance. I figure it lay there in piles laughing at him, taunting him in his dreams, the way it did with me, the way it did with Silas Marner.

And he went away sorrowful for he had great possessions . . .

I saw it all that day in the church, what money was, what it had become, how it had changed its very nature, leaping across the elements, a base metal at the beginning, dug from the earth, nothing more than a token of exchange, and then a commodity, gold to make more gold, lent out in usury. And now what? Nothing more than figures flickering on screens around the capitals of the world. Numbers growing longer every day. Gaining noughts but never materializing. Never becoming anything. Never taking shape. Nothing but air. Whimsy. Existing only for the players in the game.

People like the bridegroom.

People like McGarvey.

Where would I go to find McGarvey today? To his apartment perhaps in New York, or Paris or Rome? Or then again to the town house in Chelsea, or the chalet in Switzerland? Or maybe he's in Ireland on his estate, or at his place on the beach, in Palm Beach or Malibu. Or he could be away from it all on the small private island they say he's just bought somewhere in the Antilles.

McGarvey. *A man with enough homes in enough countries to pay tax in none of them.* Robin Phillips wrote that. One of the better things he wrote. Except that *home* is not a word which suits McGarvey. Neither does it suit the echoing empty mausoleums around the world where small

74

armies of attendants change linen which no one sleeps in and put out new towels which no one will use, and all in the unlikely event of a visit by the Scarlet Pimpernel the world knows as McGarvey.

Robin Phillips spent the best part of a year tracking McGarvey down and where he found him eventually surprised just about everyone.

The Cordillera has to be one of the planet's most inhospitable spots. It's one of those places you figure must have been behind the door when they were handing out the extras in creation. I mean this place has *nothing*. Twelve thousand feet up in the Andes, it's less the roof of the world than its grey gravel drive. Distinguishing features are hail-stones the size of golf balls that break out of clear skies and a wind that would cut you in two.

They say up there where the condor flies that anything can happen and usually does. Which is guide-book speak for watch out for your wallet and don't do drugs because the boys who do them up there are serious.

For this is the land of the coca plant, the place where it all begins, where the air is dry as a bone and sharp as a needle and you get cold and very hungry, which is why they began chewing the stuff in the first place.

You get a headache all the time that high up and it's hard to sleep, that is unless you're a native with a barrel chest and big lungs and one of those silly bowler hats that was the conquistadores' thank-you present for the silver and the tin and the several million trillion zillion pesetas' worth of purloined GNP.

It was the rainy season when Robin Phillips arrived and the trains weren't running, which didn't matter a toot because the railway line didn't go anywhere near Mc-Garvey and neither for that matter did the buses.

Where McGarvey lived was so far off the beaten track that the only thing Robin Phillips's trusty guide-book could suggest was trying the local lorry drivers. In the market-place where he went in search of one, all went well until he mentioned his destination, when the driver all but made the sign of the cross before slinking off into the night.

Determined not to be defeated, he decided to drive himself. Only no one would hire him a jeep which is how he found himself in the ramshackle tin-roofed office of what passed for the chief of police.

From then on it was like something from a Graham Greene novel. Fan grinding slowly overhead. The air heavy and hot. Half-moons of sweat beneath the police chief's arms. And defeat at the hands of a pitiless implacable courtesy.

The police chief told Robin Phillips he would need a pass to proceed any further and when he asked why, the man merely shook his head, and sighed and stroked his moustache and muttered the mournful word *bandidos*.

When Robin Phillips asked how long it might take to acquire such a pass, all he got was much shifting in the seat and the spread of a pair of deprecatory hands. Finally the man slung his feet off the desk and got up and walked over to a bureau whose roll-top he threw up to reveal some glasses and a bottle of best Chivas Regal.

It wasn't a good sign and Robin Phillips knew it, the equivalent of a month's wages this high up in Cordillera. And he drank the stuff like tequila. He drank it like there was more where that came from. He tossed it back in one, insisting Robin Phillips did the same, pouring out another and another.

The more the man drank, the more he talked. And the more he talked, the more incoherent he became. But it didn't matter. Robin Phillips had already got the message. Summed up, it was the inadvisability of making a journey which might in any way inconvenience the inestimable Don Carlos McGarvey.

'CARLOS.'

'It was worth going', he wrote afterwards, 'just for that.'

He was drunk by then on his own admission, so drunk that he fell about laughing.

'Carlos . . .' he told the puzzled police chief, shaking his head.

'Who'd have thought it . . . of all things . . . I mean *Carlos* McGarvey.'

No one ever knew McGarvey's first name you see. To everyone he was just *McGarvey*.

The cheques though were scrawled with a C. *McGarvey*, so that with nothing better to do and too much of something or other inside us, we'd speculate along with the rest of the world what the 'C' might stand for.

'Charles . . .'

'Cecil . . .'

'Oh God no. He's not a Cecil. Cedric maybe.'

'Nah. One of those girl's names. You know. Like Carol.'

We met McGarvey in the Auchnasomething ballroom where he was the manager on the last night of what by then we were only sarcastically referring to as our Northern Ireland tour. It's not there any longer, the ballroom. It was blown up. The IRA claimed responsibility but there are those who've never ruled out McGarvey.

It was '71 when we got there. Bands with more clout than us were refusing to go. But we were just glad to get the gigs. At least we were until we got there.

There was always something suspect about those gigs. Leon got them from a man he met in a pub who claimed to be a promoter. A few years later though he was done for gun-running for an extreme Protestant para-military organization.

Unpacking and repacking the van is famous as the down-side of the business. Out in cowboy country though, searching for obscure villages, we were doing it several times a day, every time a squaddie didn't like the look of us or was just bored on patrol. And that was most of the time.

As for us, we had no political opinions about the Troubles. Frankly we couldn't see why the Protestants and Catholics were having trouble getting on. To us they seemed like they had everything in common. For whatever they were, wherever they worshipped, they sure as hell hated the band. Each night it was the same. They wanted sharp suits and slick hair and 'Send me the pillow that you dream on', not a verse of which we had between us.

McGarvey's ballroom was on the outskirts of town. It had a daisy chain of lights across the front that flashed the name on and off. The foyer was faded red plush with holes in the seats. There was a large mirrored ball in the centre of the dance-floor which switched itself on to the sound of 'The Last Waltz', another number we didn't play.

The strangest thing about the place though was its entrance, which was an amusement arcade, complete with slot machines so old they still showed you what had once thrilled the butler. There was a Haunted House too and a Tunnel of Love which you went through on a sort of railway. Best of all was a tacky flaking Hall of Mirrors.

What you might term artistic tensions within the band had resulted in a rather higher level of substance abuse than usual. We were running short on reality. As a result we were like kids in the place, pulling faces, cavorting and screaming with laughter.

Even at the time I remember thinking there was something creepy about the mirrors, the way they transformed us into these strange shapes and sizes. Because the weird thing is that, in some way, they turned out to be prophetic. I was thin then for instance, but I remember still how I looked in one mirror, barrel-fat. A bit like I look today. In another Kent, who always had plenty of flesh on him,

78

became thin and drawn, the way he did after Andrew's death. Richard, stretched out, became more elegant than ever. And Leon? Well Leon had stepped before a mirror that waved and dissolved him so that he simply drifted apart like ectoplasm.

We were standing in front of the one that turned us into sticks when this apparition appeared behind us. He looked like one of those shadow puppets, all hook nose and spiky fingers.

Or like Nosferatu.

Nosferatu, the vampire.

A laugh died in my throat as it opened its mouth to speak.

'McGarvey,' was all that it said.

From the first day he moved into the Boltons Richard bought tastefully and carefully and wisely to furnish it. Today if you walked around the house there's nothing to tell you the occupation of the person who owns it. You might imagine, for instance, fingering some of the fine pieces, that the place belonged to a rich businessman, which in some ways is what Richard is, or perhaps an antique dealer or one of those interior decorators who use their homes as a showroom. What I mean is you won't find any gaudy gold discs trailing you up the stairs (why do they always put those damned things up the stairs?), no ugly little statuettes on the mantelpiece.

Any stuff like that is banished to the study at the very top of the house. Push open the door there and you feel like an archaeologist excavating the tomb of some ancient king who draws a blank in the ante-chambers, but goes on hacking his way through, until suddenly there he is, in the inner sanctum, and there it is too, the evidence of all his theories around him on the walls.

Here you'll find the gold discs and the awards, here the newspaper cuttings, the pictures, the lists, the letters, the schedules, in short, the paraphernalia of a quarter of a century, soon to be a lifetime in the business.

And something else too. What the likes of Robin Phillips would give their right arms to possess? A priceless artefact. A piece of rock history.

The only known picture of McGarvey.

It's just another part of the legend. Another piece of the myth. The way McGarvey point-blank refused to be photographed.

In publicity pictures he'd always stand firmly aside from the band. Photographers knew in the end not to try and include him. Because from the first there was always a heavy on hand to rip a camera from an uncooperative neck. From the first there was always this sense of menace about McGarvey.

There were few occasions anyway for an idle picture of McGarvey. His visits to music business back-slappings and jamborees were always brief. A fleeting appearance for appearance's sake, and before you knew it, no more McGarvey.

He set about tracking down all of the pictures of himself early on, gaining a reputation for making offers that no one could refuse. In a few years he was supposed to have tracked down the negatives of every known picture of himself. Except one. The copy of which is there on Richard's wall.

It was taken that first night we met McGarvey, by a pop fan with a yearning to become a professional photographer. He snapped bands appearing at the ballroom and then pestered the local paper to use them.

We didn't want our picture taken that night and it shows. We wanted to load the gear and get away. Things were so bad by then that we were on the verge of splitting up. It seemed like we were going nowhere, and after those weeks on the road together, we'd come to the conclusion that there was nowhere anyway we wanted to go. The end was in sight and you can see it written there on all of our faces.

We're in a line in front of the stage, bored, mutinous, scowling. No one's speaking to anyone else. We're in our own little worlds. Even Kent can't muster a smile.

It's a lousy picture. It's not even in focus. A kid with a box brownie could have done better. Still, there behind our heads is what makes it all worthwhile. Badly cut hair and too tight suit, the blurred but still distinguishable figure of McGarvey.

By the time McGarvey caught up with the photographer a few years later, he'd progressed, but only to a grimy studio at the wrong end of town where he scraped a living doing weddings, and christenings and first communion pictures.

The story goes that McGarvey offered him more than he could make in six months for the negative but for some reason the guy turned him down. Pride. Pig-headedness. Who knows why? Anyway, when his car was found at the bottom of the ravine off the bad bend, with the guy dead inside, no one really thought much about it. He'd had a drink problem, his business was bust and anyway his wife was divorcing him.

With a couple of kids to support she gladly accepted McGarvey's redoubled offer.

To this day, or so I've heard, she won't have a word said against the name of McGarvey.

I used to think afterwards how accidental for us the whole thing was, how, if another half-decent band had come McGarvey's way before we did, then it would have been them instead of us. And for him things would have gone on just the same. And for us? I don't know, probably not judging from the mood in that picture.

It was money that won us over to McGarvey. We'd never had a manager. We got paid cash on the nail each night, so that every night, it being part of the tradition, we always had to haggle.

'Fifty-five . . .'

'Sixty actually . . .'

Sometimes the try-ons were outrageous. Sometimes they were merely petty, and that was worse, knowing that it was all merely sport for them. Sometimes they backed down with a careless laugh. Sometimes they called their gorillas in, so that if you had fingers to protect you backed down, slunk away, knowing you'd been fucked, from the back and against your will, and that all in all it was just one more thing in life that you had to go through for this thing called Money.

And that's how it happened every night. Every night that is until we met McGarvey.

'Nice set,' said McGarvey tersely as we were packing up the gear.

This is the way McGarvey talked. Not staccato. Low and soft in fact. But never using three words where two would do. As if he knew that the only thing that could pin him down to his place on the earth was his Ballywhat-ever voice, which should have been easy to fix, easier for instance than his face which the wilder rumours claim has fallen beneath the knife now as part of the man's fanatical fixation with anonymity.

McGarvey held out the wad of notes.

'Seventy,' said Leon, who'd taken to playing the hard man to get in first with the try-ons.

'No, sixty actually,' said McGarvey coolly, holding his eyes. 'But I've stuck in an extra tenner.'

Leon reached out and snatched the money from his hand. To save face he tried to outstare McGarvey. But

McGarvey fielded the look, held it like it was nothing. In the end it was Leon dropped his eyes.

'So who's managing you then?' said McGarvey.

The Big Whore. That's what Leon liked to call McGarvey. He growled it, whistled it through his teeth.

It was the Big Whore who made us get rid of Hammy.

First of all you have to understand that we didn't exactly sail back across the Irish Sea in a flurry of expectation because of McGarvey's offer to manage us. We'd had managers before and what we'd found in the past was that most of them just wanted the title to pull women. We weren't even particularly excited when McGarvey appeared at one of our gigs a while later, sat down with us afterwards trying to pull his shirt-cuffs out of the beer on the table-top, gave us his card.

His office turned out to be a suite in Soho with pot-plants and a lip-glossed secretary, but we were still cool. We'd been in offices like this before, and let me tell you, if you're making a list of the fun things to do in life, taking demo tapes around to A and R men is one you can strike from the list.

Often we never got past the secretaries. Those amazing secretaries. There must be some place where they order them up along with the desks and the chairs and the photo-copiers. That's what they're like. Photo-copiers, spewing out identical answers . . . 'X X is not in right now . . . X X is in a meeting . . . Is X X expecting you?'

Sometimes we'd sit there all day, refusing to budge, because we figured that was the way you had to do it, the way it happened in the movies. You sat there all day so that just by chance old X X caught you as he flew through.

Impressed by your tenacity, he took you into his office then, and put your tape on his machine . . . and ker boom. Fame and fortune. Except that it never happened to us, and in the end we'd just surrender up the tape in the boring buff envelope and slide off sick at heart, knowing the game was already over and that our boring buff envelope would just go on the pile with the rest.

Orphan tapes you see are next to useless. There's an expression we have. 'Talk it up.' It's what you have to do and it makes you sick to your stomach. Talking it up. Laying your soul on the line. Because a tape's not enough. In the end you have to convince them they need *you*. It's a decision, believe me, they can't make on their own. Which is what you have to understand about the people who make the decisions in the music business. That basically they don't have any taste or vision of their own. They don't know music from shit. The old cliché is true. They might as well be selling soap powder. All they know is *product*, and for them product is whatever made it last week. And when, by some fluke, you'd get in to see someone, they'd put the tape on the machine, stand hot-fingered in front of it, whizz it through, ten seconds a track, while all the time the wodge of sickness and anger and disappointment was rising in your throat, and you'd think to yourself that when the time came, if the time came, someone would pay for this humiliation.

Afterwards they'd sit down at their desk, start fiddling with their pen, tell you it sounded like album stuff, they really couldn't hear a single. They'd tell you that what they really needed was another this or another that, another whatever, but always what someone else had done before.

They're know-nothings, do-nothings, counterfeiters and poachers, these people. I still despise them. I can still get angry. It's despite them not because of them good music makes it. They deserve what they get, what they're getting already, which is video games, three notes playing over and over. Plumbers and hedgehogs, the growth area of the business.

May they rot in this hell of their own making.

I sound like my father.

Now isn't that funny?

'We're not signing anything mind,' Leon said, as we sat before McGarvey trying not to be impressed. There was just the four of us. We hadn't bothered to take Hammy.

McGarvey held him in a gaze like a snake, reared up and unblinking. Leon never even saw the tongue flick out.

'Oh, I wouldn't expect it,' said McGarvey.

Opinions have always differed on just how McGarvey managed to set up so quickly, how, for instance, he got the college circuit sewn up, those dog-day evenings dodging beer cans with audiences too drunk to hear that taught us our trade, just where he got the money from to rent the flash office, start the label, hype the records.

It cracks me up still, all that outrage about hyping. I mean who *cares*? There's nothing more absurd to me than some current affairs reporter who was in Africa last week covering the famine coming over all serious on the television about malpractice in the music business. Because it's not the Olympics we're talking about here and everybody knows it. There's nothing clean-limbed and honourable about the music business. Test the industry for bribery and corruption and any other of those illegal substances and you'll have no runners left in the race.

Sure McGarvey hyped our records at the beginning. So what? So did everyone else. *Creative marketing* they called it. Probably still do. The only interesting question in this case is where McGarvey got the money to do it.

At the beginning people used to mutter about the Northern Ireland connection. Colourful scenarios involving paramilitaries of one persuasion or another. Money-laundering

. . . gun running . . . take your pick. For myself I always thought there was a simpler explanation. I just thought McGarvey was the Devil's representative sent ahead to set up the evil empire on earth.

Not that it would have made any difference if we'd have found out he was. Because if there are bands out there who would decide against handing over their souls in return for a chance to make it, then all I can say is, I've never played with them. And anyway losing track of your soul isn't something treated as too much of a big deal in the music business.

I had the measure of McGarvey from the beginning. I figured out early on he didn't give a toss for our music. I knew, like I said, if it wasn't us it would be somebody else. Just the same, I knew what we all knew, which was that if we were going to make it we needed this man McGarvey.

'Will you do it or will I?' was all he said about Hammy.

'We'll do it,' Kent said. He was the only one to speak.

Leaving McGarvey's we stood staring inwards at each other, backs to the wall of the lift, watching the indicator flash down through the floors.

'For fuck's sake,' Richard said, 'the bastard can't even keep time.'

It made us feel a whole lot better.

'It was my band,' Hammy bleated all those years later to Robin Phillips. And it was true. It was his band. But only in the time-honoured tradition. It was his band because it was his van and mostly his gear and because we rehearsed in the basement beneath his dad's shop. None of which made Hammy a better bass player.

On stage Richard would go crazy, lashing the mike lead, flinging the stand about, trying to drag Hammy along with him.

86

'It's him or me,' he'd say in a loud voice every night in the back of the van. 'And I don't give a fuck if he hears me.'

There's always a slacker loading and unloading the van and of course that slacker had to be Hammy. To be fair he wasn't that strong. He was scrawny and he limped a bit from some disease as a child. That didn't make any difference though to Leon.

'Let *me* do that Hammy,' he'd say sarcastically as Hammy lifted a lead, or 'Whatever you do, don't *strain* yourself Hammy.'

He was sick though, Hammy, the night we fired him, shivering and shaking in the toilet. 'For God's sake Hammy,' Richard said, trying genuinely to be kind. 'You should be home in bed.'

'You wish,' Hammy said bitterly. 'You wish.' You could see he knew by then what was coming.

We left Kent to do the dirty work. I saw him take Hammy aside, after the gig, at the end of the hall. I looked away. Concentrated on coiling the leads.

When I finally got the courage to lift my eyes, Hammy was putting his guitar into his case. He had his head down and Kent was still standing over him. I could tell by the sad bend of his body and the look on his face that he was saying something like, 'Sorry Hammy.'

I caught up with Hammy in the car park at the back of the pub. He was walking, head down, his guitar case in his hand, across it.

He was beside the van, no longer his van, a brand-new van that we'd bought a few days earlier with McGarvey's cash along with a stack of new gear. Something that must have told him what was coming.

'I'm sorry Hammy,' I said. It was a bitterly cold night and frost had formed like a carpet of diamonds on the windscreen of the van.

'Yeah,' he said, a hunched thin figure staring into the distance. 'But not for long eh Joanie?'

He lowered his case to the floor and leaned his forehead against the glass, idling a finger in the frost as if he expected me to speak.

'Hammy . . .' I began, but then I stopped because I had nothing to say, and in the end he turned his head slowly to look at me.

'Yeah . . .' he said. 'Exactly . . .'

He pushed himself up off the windscreen and turned to face me. There was angry resignation in his face.

'You don't care do you?' he said, turning his head. 'You're a hard bunch of bastards.'

He bent down, picked up the case. 'Well . . .' he said, 'I guess that's what it takes. I guess it's what you have to be.'

He'd already turned to go when he stopped and lifted a finger and began writing on the windscreen. He wrote slowly and thoughtfully, jabbing his finger in a last satisfied dot. When he'd finished it, he stared at it for a moment and half shook his head before finally walking away.

'Keep on trucking then Joanie,' he said over his shoulder.

I shouted after him. 'This is crazy Hammy. Don't you want a lift?' but I guess he didn't. I guess the last thing he wanted was that ride home in the van.

I left what he'd written on the windscreen. Somehow it seemed the right thing to do. I saw it one last time, sitting up the front by Kent, in Hammy's old seat, before it was swept away by the wipers.

'And fuck you too Hammy . . .' I said softly.

He was glad of the company when Robin Phillips came to call. He was pleased to have someone to talk to.

'It was my band,' he said, 'and they just threw me out.'

He died in the end in another of those great traditions of the business, old and cold and alone and before his

88

time. His gas had been cut off and his electricity. It was years since he'd had a telephone.

The latest music shop had failed a long time back and his wife had left him. Even his daughter never visited. But despite all of this it turned out to be our fault that he died.

We stood guilty as charged. Not his country, not the authorities. No, us. Whose crime was a simpler one. Two decades before we'd sacked Hammy from the band.

'*They* let him die,' she said, his harridan of a daughter, sitting on her over-stuffed sofa in her six-hundred-thousand-pound house, her neck and her arms full of developer's gold.

It was our fault for letting him die, our fault for forgetting. It was even our fault for not sending a wreath when everyone knew that all it would have done was enshrine our hypocrisy.

'NOT EVEN A WREATH.'

The words of the headline, the words from the daughter who only visited at birthday and Christmas, but who knew all about her father, knew all his most intimate thoughts, just how much we'd hurt him, just how much the heartbreak had preyed all those years on his mind. How our names had been last on his lips, this man they took two weeks to find.

'I could have been there,' Hammy said to Robin Phillips. But it wasn't true. Because if Hammy could have been there, well then Hammy could have been somewhere else, Hammy could have *done* something else, instead of doing what he did do which was to die old and cold with the rent due in his council house. Don't give me the might-have-beens. There's too many in this business.

I could have been there. The words they should have chiselled on his tombstone. For what are tombstones for but lies? *Devoted Husband, Loving Father.* Which is the lie I put on my father's.

I gave my father a small marble mausoleum when the

89

time came, a heavy thing that lay on top of him, trapping him there with its classical splendour. It had to be specially designed and executed and it cost me twelve thousand pounds.

It was that twelve thousand pounds that the perfectly manicured pale pink fingernail of my Inland Revenue investigator pointed to on the bank statement.

'And this amount, what is this amount for?' she said.

I shrugged. Reached into my pocket for my pack of cigarettes, pulled them out. 'I prefer people not to smoke in my office,' she said sharply.

Later she leaned back in her chair, stared at me very hard. 'You sign a cheque for twelve thousand pounds,' she said. 'And now you tell me you cannot even remember what it is for.'

I blew through my teeth noisily, shrugged again. Next to me David, my earnest young accountant, frowned. 'It's a while back,' I said. 'How should I remember?' For it was true. I couldn't.

She got up from the chair then, walked to the window. She didn't look round when she spoke and her voice was very cold.

'Are you aware,' she said, 'that that is as much as some people earn in a year?'

I stared at her back, hating her with every fibre of my body.

'Perhaps so. But is that my fault?' I said.

II

Strange kind of business this
Do I need it
Strange kind of creature this
Kills those who feed it
There's the people who can do it
The walking dead who blew it
Those who just go through it . . .

This is one for the money
Now go man go . . .

I read somewhere that it's an opportunistic disease.

For a start it provides the opportunity to care.

I read somewhere that it's casually transmitted.

By gossip for instance, graffiti, fear-for-sale tabloid stories.

Milton came this morning.

The crush outside the house meant that he had to park his new BMW a good way up the street and I could see from the window that he wasn't pleased. His lips tightened in the way that the wise have learnt to avoid. He lowered his head to push his way through them like they were a pack of dogs, snapping about his heels, dancing in front of him on their hind legs looking for some titbit from his hand. Which is what they want, why they hound us when we come and go. Some small morsel about Richard. Dying.

In the hall, shaking his dark coat which he wears at all times regardless of the weather, he shrugged his shoulders and his back at the same time, as if he were a dog himself now. As if he shook them off like fleas.

Handing the coat to Donald, he made a small sound of disgust, but Donald only smiled and gave one of his world-weary shrugs.

Milton touched his upper lip then in a movement that I remember, as if he smoothed down a moustache which he does not wear. He put a hand to the grey-black hair and lifted the briefcase and began climbing the stairs with his old walk, tough and hunched and a little tired, a walk that says, 'Don't bother me, I've heard it all before.' Which of course he has being a music lawyer.

Milton's head always bends as he walks, like a head happier in its yarmulke. Because of this he didn't see me till he had almost reached the top of the stairs.

'Joanie,' he said in the old neutral voice. 'So Kent found you. I'm glad.'

Coolness. Neutrality. Qualities that in the end I came to admire. A flatness of the face, practised and necessary. Disguising, what? Dislike? Disgust? Contempt?

'So he died on my sofa. So what, is that my fault? Why should I have to give evidence?'

'It's the law Joanie. It's tiresome I know but it's the law.'

Perfectly formed hand-cut phrases murmured softly across the desk. In this way Milton played a game with you, a game you deserved, gave you plenty of rope to hang yourself if that was what you wanted. But at the same time he offered you, like some ancient archangel, a moment of truth, a burning bush, a ram caught by its horns in the thicket.

For you could sit in front of Milton's desk and discuss with him, without embarrassment, all your worst excesses, and just how he was going to get you off the hook for them. And you could trip merrily out of that office, if that was what you wanted, convinced that he thought none the worse of you for them, convinced in fact that, being your lawyer, Milton must live like you, according to that first rule of rock and roll, the one that says that you are what you are and you do what you do, and that includes by rights being the biggest asshole in the business. Which in fact was an attitude of mind of all things most abhorred by Milton.

For Milton is not like other rock lawyers. Most rock lawyers are exactly what you would expect them to be. Lawyers who want to be rock stars. And so they dress like them and talk like them, and drink like them and do drugs like them, and when the coke goes round, well, take it from one who knows, it can be pretty nigh impossible to tell the difference.

He's Jewish, yes, but not like the others, the ones with their stage Yiddish and their flamboyant donations to Zionist good causes, whose functions they attend like tacky potentates, with their remodelled shiksa girlfriends on their arms.

For Milton's religion regulates his life, and this application to the faith is part of the reason they fear him, these other lesser players in the game.

He unnerves them, Milton, because they know he can't be bought, because they know they have nothing to offer him. And it's why those on the other side, the ones who make the music, have always queued up for Milton, why he has one of the richest practices this side of the Atlantic. Why anyone who's anyone wants to be with Milton.

It's not unknown for some poor sucker due in court the following morning against their record company (and remember most people go to court against their record company at one time or another) to see their lawyer coming out of a restaurant and being caught in a warm mafioso hug of farewell by a vice-president from that very same record company. What I mean is, if all the vice-presidents who started off as bona fide lawyers and got bought off with shares were laid end to end, well, that might be the best thing. And perhaps only Milton would be left standing.

Milton, keeper of so many secrets. Keeper of mine.

'I thought under the circumstances you would not mind if I gave Kent your address.' I shook my head wordlessly, surprised at the lump in my throat.

'Good to see you Milton,' I said. 'How's Lois? The kids?'

*

95

The last time I saw Lois I was in the charity shop with Grace.

I remember the first time we went charity shopping together. We hadn't been friends for long. She was wearing this Jaeger jacket with her jeans.

'Nice,' I said.

'A fiver,' she said. 'My latest bargain.'

'Where?' I said, and she took me.

'Labels,' she said, professional that she is hurling the hangers along the rail. 'Look for labels . . .'

I found a Cacharel cardigan. Put it on over my T-shirt.

'Look at this,' I said. 'What fool would throw this out?' And we looked at each other and laughed.

I've come to like them now, charity shops. I spend a lot of time in them. I like the way they cut you down to size. My old albums for instance, stuck in a box, fifty pence each, sometimes twenty-five. But then above them, on the bookshelf, as if by way of consolation, there's Dickens, George Eliot, Hemingway, Fitzgerald . . . And all half the price of my albums.

That day I saw Lois's picture, I'd picked up a copy of *Silas Marner*. I was handing over the ten pence at the till when I saw Lois, there on the wall.

'Who's that?' I said to the woman behind the counter, unable to believe my eyes.

'Where?' she said.

'There,' I said, 'standing next to Princess Anne.'

'Oh, her. That's our new President,' she said proudly.

The picture was taken at some charity film premiere. At first I thought the feeling I had was that old thing, déjà vu. Then I saw it was something more complicated, more like looking down through some weird extra-dimensional telescope poking back through the fog of the years, showing Lois here and now but at the same time the way she looked twenty years ago.

For what goes around comes around, most of all fashion. And so there she was in a tight dress with long

96

sleeves and a jewel-encrusted neck, with her hair swept up on her head, the sort of dress she wore when she married Leon. And I don't know whether Lois is face-lifted or collagened or lipo-suctioned. Perhaps she exercises each day, is waxed and polished and pampered. But whatever it is it works. Because Lois looks as beautiful as she always looked. And only her smile was different.

For Lois's smile was famous in the old days. It beguiled more than the long legs and the perfect body and the luscious brown hair. It was a warm smile, sometimes a wan smile but a smile born of its time. It started somewhere in the middle with those two slightly larger front teeth, drawing back slowly to come to rest in the delicate cheekbones between the long straight curtains of hair.

And I could see, looking at the photograph, that despite everything Lois has kept her smile. It's still warm, but its wanness had gone. There's something else in its place, something tough and cool and aloof. It's a smile now that beneath the welcome is on perpetual guard. It says, 'I am here by virtue of what I am.' It says, 'I have earned my place.'

It says to Royalty exactly what it says to the rest.

'Don't fuck with me,' it says. 'I'm a survivor.'

Because when I look at Lois now, I know I'm looking at a particularly fine specimen of that rare species of being, the rock wife. And I know that if a visitor from Mars had just flown in knowing nothing about rock and roll, but had explained to it just why someone like Lois was good for the job, well, alien as it was, it would just begin to nod its little green head in agreement.

See, you have to understand that the thing that hurt them most, those people who hated the whole thing, was what the rock and rollers did with their money.

It was OK at the beginning. Because at the beginning

this band of parvenus knew their place. They bought pink Cadillacs and white suits with their cash or fake leopard-skin sofas. But before you knew it they grew up, developed a sense of their own worth, particularly what that worth might buy. They began hoovering up all the fine things of life, antiques, paintings, old houses. And what drove people like my father to despair was the realization that all these things they had thought so special to them, that they thought were theirs by some divine right of taste and education and good breeding, these they saw were in the end just like everything else. Freely available for money.

Soon rock and roll was boasting it could buy all that was best. And that included the best women as well.

The classic rock wife has a CV that goes back to the cradle. She's a goddess herself and a fitting consort for the new rock and roll deity. In the first place, she knows her way around money, because she's born rich and beautiful too and elegant, things that come naturally to those born beneath this most blessed of trinities. She knows good wine and fine furniture and how to hire a nanny. Most important of all though, with generations of good breeding behind her, she knows that boys will be boys, especially on the road, and the trick is to turn a blind eye. In short she brings the class which is the one thing her Johnny-come-lately can't buy and which he thinks he'll inherit like a dowry. And that's just what Leon thought. But of course he was wrong.

There are two reasons, I think now, why Leon wanted Lois. The first was that he actually fell in love with her, or rather fell in love with what she was, that package of beauty and class and sophistication which Marge never had. The second was that he believed she belonged to Richard.

Let me tell you about the way Leon wanted. He tired himself out with it. He wore himself down. He wanted the world. He wanted everything he'd never had. But most of all he wanted to *be* Richard.

For in Richard, Leon saw someone playing the game of life like he wanted to play it. He wanted Richard's carelessness, his ease. He even tried to copy him, but of course he couldn't do it.

When Leon set about winning Lois, Richard just stood by with a wicked smile on his face. Leon was on his own by this time. The shopping sprees with Marge had given way to shouting matches. On several occasions the police had been called, adding lustre to the already fashionably louche reputation. Eventually Marge and Linus had moved out to an apartment and all that was left was for the lawyers to argue over the palimony, for Leon and Marge had never married.

Richard wasn't jealous when Leon moved in with all the tact and sophistication of a ten-ton truck. How could he be? For Lois was no more than a friend, no more than an escort, a camouflage. And at first, I think, Lois was amused too by Leon's rough but enthusiastic wooing, but when it did not stop, when the barrages of flowers kept arriving and the presents and the telegrams, when she had got used to finding the Bentley with this growling, unshaven but imploring creature in it parked outside her flat, or outside the studio where she was modelling, or anywhere else that she went, well then I guess that finally something caught at her heart.

And I don't know why Lois fell in love with Leon for I guess she did. Only Lois knows that and she isn't telling. Perhaps it was the bad-boy image. Perhaps she wanted to save him.

For Leon, I believe, Lois was a dying flash, a last hope of salvation. And somewhere along the line I'm sure he saw it, that with all that Lois was, she might come to represent the best of him, if only he could pull it off. If only he could stick with it. And this is why, I'm sure, he determined to marry Lois.

*

The wedding was one of those fey affairs of its time like a thousand others that look so absurd in the photographs twenty years later, all in white the pair of them, the high-necked dress, Grecian curls and white lips, his flares and long collars.

There were no relatives from either side. Probably it never occurred to Leon to invite his parents and Lois's father couldn't be stirred from his castle in Westmorland. Rumour had it though that Lois's mother was jetting in from Paraguay where she'd settled with her latest lover, an international jet-setter and polo player. So when the heavily veiled figure in the Chanel suit burst in halfway through the reception, most people figured it had to be her.

She clutched the bride first to her gold-buttoned bosom, then putting her aside held her arms wide with a thrilling, throaty 'Leon'.

She kissed him then full on the lips through her veiling. Afterwards she insisted on dancing with him, her new son-in-law, holding him close.

Most people had got the scam by then and they drew a crowd. Those who'd taken more coke than they should like me were laughing. All except Lois.

She stood at the side of the dance-floor biting her lip and trying to smile.

'Hey Lois . . .' I said laughing, but when she turned her face was like thunder.

'Go to hell,' she hissed fiercely, and went to push past me.

'It's just a joke for Christ's sake Lois,' I said and she stopped sharply in mid-step.

She turned her head slowly till it was inches from my own.

'It's nothing,' I said. 'Boys will be boys. You know what Richard's like. It's just band antics.'

'Fuck you,' she said. I'd never heard her swear before.

'Fuck you and fuck your whole fucking band.'

*

100

Naturally things started to go wrong for Leon and Lois early on. Not that they were ever really right. From the start Lois's family treated Leon as an interim, an amusement, an aberration on her part. Someone who couldn't last. Which of course he couldn't.

It was the same story with her friends. But because of what Leon was, because of the times, they camouflaged their contempt with fawning. They toadied about him, leeched and lick-spittled. Sniffed his coke and drank his champagne while laughing at him behind his back. And because of what they were, the background from which they sprang, they didn't even bother to make their ingratiation anything less than transparent.

'I hate those fuckers,' he said to me one day at the retreating back of some scion of an ancient seat who had just bummed a line off him. And he did too. This man who at the same time was heart-sick for them, and in the end wanted them more than his soul would allow.

'Forget them Leon,' I said. But he couldn't and so in the end he found himself doing what he'd always done in his own defence, playing the yob, which when he'd picked it up again, like some ancient cudgel, he couldn't put down.

For a while you see, when they were first married, he'd cut back on the dope. Because Lois had made him promise to do it. And because he genuinely wanted the thing to work. For a while he really tried to be a changed man. At least a part of him did. But there was another part of Leon, like a stream, running along underground, dark, destructive, eating away into the rock, seeping up and out and on to the surface, poisoning everything and everybody it touches.

And dealers, being dealers, knew all about dark underground streams and how they always surfaced in the end. So that when Leon looked like a changed man for a while, they didn't go away. They just crawled off into the undergrowth and sat there, hiding, sticking their heads out occasionally, lifting their noses and sniffing the wind,

101

waiting for it to change. And of course it did. And when it did they came out of hiding along with the two-bit starlets and the models and all the other camp followers whose business it was to be seen with the likes of Leon.

And so, like an old story already told, the scenes in the restaurants and clubs started again, the pictures in the papers in bad company. And while the world had lost the taste for breaking butterflies on wheels, still the police couldn't ignore the Bentley in the middle of a round-about with the packet of white spilling out on to the front seat.

For a while Lois did what she was supposed to do, which was to paper over the cracks and pretend it was still business as usual. One day though she came back unexpectedly from a modelling assignment to find him in bed, their bed, with a couple of bare-assed wannabees. And that was when she decamped for good.

There were those afterwards who said Lois was a fool, the sort of people who wanted her to take something with her, preferably Leon, and straight to the cleaners. For myself, I don't think so. Lois walked out of the marriage with nothing and wanting nothing, except to be free of Leon. And why not? She had her own income and her own career, and a lorry-load of decency, and she declined even to bother with her own lawyer and it was left to Milton to sort out the divorce for both of them.

They were together just over two years. On the day she left, I was in bed when the phone rang. When I lifted the receiver the voice was so slurred with awe and reverence I scarcely recognized it.

'You don't know Joanie . . .' it said. 'You don't know.'

'Leon?' I said.

At the end of the line there was a long low exhalation of breath which carried the words with them.

'It's like a galleon Joanie,' he said, 'sailing you home on soft sweet seas . . .'

102

Lois was gone and Leon felt bad. And someone had given him some smack.

In the dragon lady's dream
No one ever asks why
No one ever says no . . .

I was living at Stoneham by then and developing a few bad habits of my own.

I bought the place, a mere ten miles away from my father, more to irritate him than anything else. I liked to tear over in the Aston, swinging into his drive, making the gravel fly.

'What have you come for Joan?' he would say, refusing to look up from his papers.

'To annoy you,' I would say with my coke grin. 'What else?'

Over the years we became like those figures in a wet and dry barometer. When things were going well for me, he would scarcely acknowledge my presence as I walked into his study. Later though when I was on the slide he began to enjoy my visits.

'I see from the papers Joan you're having problems,' he said once. A small difficulty. A county court judgment out against me on account of a few bounced cheques.

'I thought you didn't read the papers,' I said.

Kent was with me, that first time, when I went to look at Stoneham. I carried with me a copy of the entry from Pevsner that the estate agents had sent . . .

Built by Sir Thomas Sydenham in 1434 for his daughter upon her marriage to John Alford. An enchanting facade includes unusual decorative timber framing on the West Wing. Aesthetically the most interesting feature is the great hall with its majestic double

103

hammer-beam roof featuring fine carving in three sets of arched braces and tracery in the spandrels and eight light windows. The hall gallery is a later addition, probably late C17, with twisted balusters and hung with a fine Flemish hunting tapestry . . .

Ah the tapestry. How I remember the tapestry. For wasn't it behind the arras, just like Polonius, that I received the fatal wound?

'I mean Jesus . . . sleeping with your *dealer* for Christ's sake . . .'

The last Sir Thomas met us at the door. He was in a wheelchair and not troubling to hide his distaste. He didn't want to sell to this harpy chewing gum in a leather jacket. He didn't want to take the rock and roll shilling. He figured five hundred years of history had to be worth more than this. But needs must, and he knew that in the end he had to choose between this she-devil and the deep blue sea of cream teas and postcards and kids with sticky lollies. And in the end he chose me.

His nephew showed us round, thirty-something, buggered by public school in the fullest sense of the word. Overweight. Sweating. Awkward with women.

'Don't I know you?' he said, breaking out into a blush.

'I doubt it,' I said unkindly.

Upstairs the place was pretty much closed up, damp and sweating, like the nephew. Only two of the bedrooms were in use. Both had four-posters with musty old damask drapes. One room smelt of chest-rubs and medication. I thought this had to be the old man's. The other smelt of nothing which somehow seemed right for the nephew.

We strolled along the corridor, Kent and I, getting the evil eye from the ancestors. We'd stopped before a chisel-nosed cavalier with a hook nose and a weak mouth when a piece of plaster hanging from the ceiling slipped its moorings finally and crashed down on to the floor. I hooted with triumphant laughter while ahead of us the nephew bent his head a little lower and sweated his way on down the stairs.

Later we stood on the over-grown lawns, staring at the front of the house and then the other way, down to the slime-covered lake. I picked in delight at one of the statues eaten away by the weather, covered in lichen, a strange thing, a woman in what appeared to be sweeping robes, her hand laid calmly, in full command, on the head of her pet dragon.

Kent meanwhile was trying to be sensible.

'It's a beautiful place Joanie, I'm not saying it isn't. But you know it's going to cost a small fortune to put right.'

I put an arm around my dragon lady with a smile.

'But I've got a small fortune,' I said. 'We've all got small fortunes now Kent.'

After he'd left, I drove round the lake, parked the Aston in between some trees, took some grass from the glove compartment and rolled a joint. I smoked it leaning out of the window, looking up at the house.

'I want you,' I said.

As I said it, the reeds at the edge of the water clicked their heads in consternation.

'I'll have you,' I said.

And a moorhen rose up in alarm.

In succession
Houses rise and fall, crumble, are extended,
Are removed, destroyed, restored . . .

I had the roof redone, the walls replastered, the floors relaid. I had the timbers replaced and the statues restored, the lake dredged and cleaned and restocked with fish, and the gardens relaid to include a swimming pool. And Kent was right. It did take a small fortune.

I bought the place with some of the fixtures and fittings,

the scowling ancestors who now became my own, the four-posters with the mildewed damask hangings and, of course, that original hanging tapestry.

Among the furniture was a handsome old roll-top desk that stood in the old man's study. Inside I found a copy of an account from the parish records of the building of Stoneham.

That everything might be done in order and without confusion, a piece of work was assigned to each labourer. Some dug the clay, some fetched it in wheel-barrows, some heaved it up on the walls. The rustic girls, a great many of whom also attended the occasion, fetched the water, with which the clay was softened, from some neighbouring ditch or pond. When the walls were raised to their proper height, the company had plenty to eat and drink; after which the lads and lasses, with face incrusted with clay and dirt, took a dance upon the new floor . . .

It was my greatest delight in the years that I lived there, often when I was stoned, always when I was alone, to lay my ear against the bulging misshapen walls, to feel the coolness of the plaster against my cheek, to breathe them in and all their occasions, and then to strain for it, to fancy I heard it, somewhere a long way in the distance, the sound of music, that old sound of dancing.

> . . . Feet rising and falling,
> Eating and drinking. Dung and death.

Which, sometimes, afterwards, in my worst moments, I thought pretty much summed up some of the worst goings-on at Stoneham.

I took on Francis playing the lady.

It seems extraordinary to me now, looking back, how accidentally Francis came into my life, just something else wrong with the world, it seems to me, that such a wealth of old-fashioned decency and loyalty and duty could have been waiting there to be hired by the hour.

He came from the agency I'd rung, the first and the last that they sent. His father had been a butler, spending thirty years in the house of a banker. He hoped his only son might follow in the family tradition but instead Francis broke out and studied accountancy. Something of the old family firm had worn off on him though for he stood before me in the great hall as if to the manner born, hands folded before him in a dark suit as faintly out of date as his decency. It was the same suit, I truly believe, he was wearing a decade later the day that he left.

'I need someone to take over the day-to-day running of everything . . . a sort of steward . . .' I told him grandly at his interview, reaching for the word. It was a strange term, awkward, old-fashioned like him, but as it turned out exactly right, for a steward was what I got, a steward with the impossible task of overseeing my spending.

It was Francis who found me Caroline. I played the grand game again with her.

'I just want food on the table,' I said. 'I don't want to ask how . . .' If I'd cared to see it, which I did not, I'd have spotted that first faint flash of contempt from the rounded North Country unaffectedness that was Caroline.

I figure now, looking back, there must be a grapevine which buzzes suddenly into life like one of those old-fashioned ticker-tape machines when there's a new fool in town with too much money.

For soon they began to appear, as on some pilgrimage, or like nomads, plodding in on their camels, to the souks and bazaars, from the desert.

Beware Greeks bearing gifts they say, which is what they were, hiding in their wooden horses and all saying pretty much the same thing Eduardo my art dealer said.

'Oh course it's an investment Joanie . . . if you ever need to sell Joanie . . . just give me a call Joanie . . .'

They came with floorings and furnishings and wallpaper at fabulous prices. They came with rugs and original stair-rods and a ridiculously expensive Heriz silk carpet. They came with chests and china and lamps and screens. They came with things I'd never heard of like canterburies and cadenzas, and things I had, Chippendale chairs and Welsh dressers and chaise-longues. They came with Regency and Sheraton and Chinese rococo. They came with their boule work and their bow fronts and their crossbanding and brass beading. They came, this glorious gaudy caravanserai, laying their goods out on my lawn.

Oh yeah. And one of them came with some coke.

Black night and blue light
Make nervous rainbow
Coke spoon and stage fright
Might make the pain go . . .

And now a small digression. Now I figure it's time to introduce you to my good friend cocaine. You're meeting everyone else after all and it's a character along with the rest. Ah yes, Sex, Food, Work, Love, Life . . . What is there that will not fall beneath the wheels of my friend cocaine?

Lest you should think it though and so be disappointed, this is not one of those cheap, vote-pulling Government health warnings. I don't have any revised manifesto when it comes to drugs despite all that happened. As far as I'm concerned, I think what I always thought, which is that they're here on the planet and some people will do them. And it being the way of these things they'll be punished by their peers who prefer to get blitzed on gin and tonic.

Because I guess what I still hate most is that nasty, Protestant proverb pursed-up way of talking about dope. Like *Coke is God's way of telling you you've got too much money.* Don't ever make the mistake of thinking that's a joke. Let me tell you, that goes to the heart of everything we are. It's like that other tight-assed no-good little panacea *Money can't buy happiness.* And what I hate about them, these little homilies, is the way they ruffle no feathers. Because coke's a movable feast just like money, and it's down there in the moonscapes too where the money is tight and jobs are just a memory. Only there they call it crack and it's Vim-thinned and cut-price, which makes me wonder what's the message from on high for this end of the market?

The best cocaine is sparkling and white and fluffy. Metaphorically though it's black and thick and sticky, the oil that keeps the music business running.

There are tours where 10 per cent of the budget goes on coke and has to be hidden by creative accounting. I've seen crews paid off with it, journalists, DJs. I've seen people you wouldn't believe with their noses down, sniffing coke.

They called it the champagne of drugs at the beginning. The designer drug. Made for the job. The *now* drug. No waiting. Clean and green and free of hangovers. Suitable for work. Non-addictive. Works on all surfaces. Can you believe we fell for that shit?

Not that anything would have changed if we'd known. Or that a warning on the packet would have made any difference. If there's a coke-head out there willing to debate before he toots the philosophical implications of there being no such thing as a free lunch, I never met him, that's all.

I first got into dope as a serious habit on the road, the way everyone gets into it, in the old Bedford grinding up a motorway, with Kent at the wheel and Leon doing every substance known to mankind in the back. And later in the hell-holes they called dressing rooms, which were often just toilets, stinking of urine and occasionally encrusted with crap. Or sometimes between sets in the bar at some pig-sty of a student union with beer swilling on the floor and bottles rolling and cans flying on to the stage. I got into it the way you do, out of boredom, to pass the time, to try and sleep. And I told myself it would go away, this boredom, when the venues got bigger and the dressing rooms better, when there was a proper tour bus to travel on or a plane. But somehow it didn't. Instead it got worse. Because the journeys were longer and you were that much farther away from home.

I remember some journalist asking me once, 'Do you enjoy touring?'

'*Enjoy touring?*' I said, looking at her like she was crazy, not knowing where to begin, how to tell her what it was like spending each night in a different bed in this nether-world where time and place disappears and the base-line of your life along with it, so that sometimes it seems like there's nothing left to hold on to.

And yet I understand the question. I understand the difficulty, where the confusion occurs. Because when they ask, *Do you enjoy touring?* what they mean is, *Do you enjoy playing live?*, and of course you enjoy playing live. Why the hell else would you be in the business? Except, there again, that *enjoy* seems somehow the wrong term, too weak, too inexpressive, and also, on occasions, entirely wrong. Because playing before a room full of people who like your stuff whether it's the Pig and Whistle or Shea can be the best thing in your life, or later on when it all starts to go wrong, the worst.

When it's working there's nothing like it. There can't be. I figure no one's invented a word for it yet, that emotion you feel up there on the stage when everything's going right all around you, and the band is playing like one man, into their own thing and everyone else's as well, anticipating, surprising sometimes, pulling it out of the bag in a way they've never done before and out front is an audience that knows it, that's rising to the occasion just like you, so that the answering emotion from them is welling up over their heads and rolling back on to the stage in huge hot blasts.

And that's how it was for us just like everyone else at the beginning with that first hit album behind us. I'd look across at Leon on the drums and see the arms going like a windmill and the wild grin and the brightness in his eyes busting through the dope, and I'd feel so good I'd even smile at Steve who'd replaced Hammy and who I never really got on with. And I'd take it on the piano then like a message from those that I loved and as I did it Richard would turn from the front, T-shirt soaked in the sweat, and he'd raise the mike in the air in a private gesture of triumph and amazement between us that said we still couldn't believe we were HERE.

And lastly I'd look over at Kent, see his head thrown back, his eyes closed, and I'd *feel* his sound more than hear it. And as it ran through my fingers like my own blood and out over the notes with the sweat, he'd turn and open his eyes and for a second there as we looked at each other, I'd know that nothing, no love affair in the world could come anywhere near this.

Grace asked me once, the only time we ever talked about it, 'Was it ever good?' and somehow I never managed to explain. I just said what everyone says.

'Yeah,' I said. 'It was good at the beginning.'

Faces in the dark . . .
They pay for their intrusion
Into someone's blue confusion
Till the dogs of disillusion
Bark . . .
*

Because all too soon, it seems, the faces out there in the dark don't seem friendly any more. All too soon you can't feel those great rolls any more coming up from the auditorium. All too soon it seems that magic you had together has disintegrated, blown away like the smoke from the dry ice. It's separate limos to the gigs now and bitching and whingeing up there on the stage instead of all that fine fellow feeling.

How long do you get when it's good? So little. So pitifully little. Three albums is the norm. Just what we had. The average life of a band.

Nothing's going right by now. It's not working up there on the stage and it's not working for you either where it really counts, in front of the piano.

Because by now, too, you're not writing any more. You sit in front of the thing idling your fingers on the keys and trying to figure out how it is, what wicked sport of the gods it could be that allowed you to write so fast and so well in those old hard-up days, in those crap-hole dressing rooms and in the back of the old Bedford van. You remember bitterly how the songs fell out of your pockets then, and you wonder how it could all have deserted you here, in this new world of money and comfort, where you don't even need to perform if your promoter has forgotten to supply the fifty different French cheeses for a snack before the gig that you stipulated.

Back home later you sit at the piano idling the same snatches over and over and tooting between them to ward off the paranoia, till one day you wake up to find yourself, a rat on a treadmill, on this wheel going round and round, not sure any longer if you're taking another hit because the songs won't come, or if the songs won't come because you've taken another hit.

Leon used to say about coke, 'It makes you feel like the main man,' and I never heard it put better. It takes away the fear, coke. It makes you feel good. It whispers in your ear, tells you what you most want to hear which is that simplest thing of all. That everything is really OK.

And yet that first time I tried the stuff way back in the beginning nothing happened. I was used to acid and speed. I was used to the earth waving. I was a tryer though. I wasn't about to give in. It took me three or four goes before I got my first rush, that old slam bam of hellzapoppin' happiness, but when I got it, I knew I'd come home.

It's a mealy-mouthed mother-fucking drug as far as I'm concerned, coke. It creeps up on you. And while you know it's all happening, that you're doing more and more for the obvious reason that it's offering less and less, still you think, so what? It's only money after all.

The first time McGarvey pushed that cheque across the desk towards me, I saw a string of noughts I truly believed would go on for ever. And later, when I got into the coke in a big way, I just thought, Well, if it only takes money to stay up here, to feel this good, then so what? I can do this as much as I want, I can stay up here for ever, in this heaven I already know and have inhabited, where no one can touch me, away from all the fears and all the insecurities that lie outside waiting, like guerrillas in the jungle, to ambush me.

I can be *happy* here, is what I thought.

And that's how it is, how it works, until one morning you wake up feeling bad, but you've been drinking the night before so at first you figure it's nothing worse than a hangover. You take a handful of paracetamol to take care of the headache, crawl back to bed. But then a pain starts in your stomach and you feel nauseous and you change your mind, you tell yourself it must have been something you ate.

It's not too long after that you begin to shiver, which makes you think it's flu, and at first you're relieved. You scrape around in your brain for all the tales that other people have told you, things going around, strains from exotic corners of the world. Because you're not about to face the facts, so you dose yourself some more, with Beecham's now, like a child. All you want is for it to go away. Only it doesn't, and as the day wears on, it comes to you that you're feeling worse than you ever felt in your life.

And so you lie there, shivering, with the chills running up and down your body, shaking and hurting all over, in every inch, in every last bone, the worst flu you ever had in your life, and combined with the worst hangover, not even just physical any more but mental too, boring into your bones like a screwdriver, into your very being. And you contemplate dying, but dying is harder than you think. You're not sure how to do it and anyway it takes effort. And so after everything, eventually, you call the doctor.

And if you're lucky then, if your guardian angel, despite everything, is still on duty and sitting on your shoulder, if your doctor is one of the decent ones and not employed by you merely to massage your ego, then he'll tell you the truth. That junkie is the word that suits you best.

But if you're unlucky? Well, if you're unlucky, as you reach for the phone to call the doctor, it rings and it's your dealer, and when he hears how lousy you feel, he tells you he's on his way over.

And when he arrives, he has his own bag of tricks. He fixes you a little something, something you've never had before, something a little . . . heavier.

And in less time than it takes to say *aaaaaaah*, stick out your tongue or take your temperature, you're up on your feet again, out of bed, bouncing and snapping and ready to go clubbing.

Coke can make you irritable, anxious, paranoiac, hallucinatory and possible psychotic. Not, of course, that this is any reason to stop using it. One of the reasons you get like this is because, on top of everything else, you don't sleep well. You're so up with the coke you have to throw down shitloads of other stuff just to get down. And when you do you pass out, you don't fall asleep. And when you pass out like this you don't dream, so you don't get any

114

of the deep, sweet REM sleep that we all need, it now seems, to stay sane.

So you could say coke destroys your dreams.

It's a nice touch, a poetic touch. It's the only reason I mention it.

It was Eduardo my art dealer I have to thank for bringing me my first coke. He gave it to me as a sort of free gift when he brought my madonna.

I showed her off proudly to Kent.

'It's lovely Joanie . . . no, I mean it's beautiful . . . it's exquisite . . . but what I mean is . . . well . . . it's just that it's an awful lot of money.'

'Yeah, I know. But it's fifteenth-century. And it's a pseudo Pier Francesco Fiorentino or something . . .

'And anyway . . .' I said, 'I had to have her.'

I put her in my study over my desk where the light fell on her halo and on the rich ivory of her skin, and on the absurd pucker on the face of her pudgy corn-haired little Christ child. I'd look at her, overwhelmed with the knowledge *I* had her and no one else, that she was mine, overwhelmed with that blissful feeling of *possession*.

She was the thing I was most determined not to part with when the time came. I can still remember the outrage I felt at Didi's shrug, at her cold smile of pleasure.

'Suit yourself,' she said. 'It's up to you. But you'll have to sell her in the end.'

Rory and Charisse disagree about Didi. It's the thing they argue about most.

'It's all bullshit,' Rory says. 'She doesn't subvert patriarchal and capitalist constructs at all. All she does is collude with them.'

Once when Didi came on the television he sniffed.

'She has no political agenda,' he said.

I laughed in the kitchen with Grace.

'Still, look on the bright side,' I said. 'She does have forty million dollars.'

Leon's life fell apart almost immediately after Lois left. She was just what he'd thought she was, his dying flash, his last hope of an anchor.

He had a new anchor of course, that certain something that nails you to your core, the punishing schedule of scoring and fixing and mixing, of finding the perfect combination of pharmaceuticals for every occasion, coke, heroin, speed, uppers, downers . . .

Not that he had to look far for supplies. There was always someone hanging around willing to do a deal with Leon. We'd find them skulking in the corridor, outside the studio, hiding behind the swing-doors waiting for him to come out. Give-away works littered the toilet basins, slipped out from his pockets on to the studio floor.

For it was the smack that Leon had fallen in love with now, a bitter-sweet affair, for every time he shot up it left him with such a feeling of ecstasy and contentment that he was convinced it was the last time. It made him feel washed through with it, pure again and free.

'No more Joanie,' he'd say, turning his eyes to me with calm purpose.

No one knew how many grams a day Leon was doing by then. Only his dealer knew that and maybe his bank manager. He looked as bad as the shit he was shooting though. His face was waxy and his lips cracked. He sniffed all the time from the blocked nose and breathed through his mouth. The green eyes had gone yellow at the centre but worst of all he sweated, all the time, with a sweat that smelt of the chemicals, and that seemed to ooze out of every pore and into every last corner of the studio.

We were attempting to put down the third album by then. Behind us now we had four hit singles and two

116

albums gone gold. But things were already disintegrating, foundering like they always do on the rock they call the Third Album Syndrome.

It's a well-known complaint in the business. There are different reasons for it. The most obvious is that those first two albums are like pots into which you pour all your best stuff, all your hopes and dreams, all those first youthful enthusiasms. You've worked through the stuff too on the road before you've taken it into the studio, or at least you did then back in those long-gone days of the mid-seventies.

By number three as well you've woken up to the fact that you have commitments, some more dubious than others. One way or another anyway you've established the sort of life-style that whispers in your ear at first that it doesn't want to lose you and after that drops the nice-guy stuff and puts its hands around your neck to begin pressing tight.

All in all before you even notice it the feel-good factor of those first years has disappeared, turned in on itself, and the next thing you know it's coming out at you baring its teeth and snapping like a dog. And that's pretty much the way it was when we went into the studio to put down that third album.

It's a goldfish bowl, a studio, a place where everything is magnified, all your petty prides and privileges, your absurdities and insecurities. You swim around in there, bumping your nose against the glass, swishing your tail trying to be top fish, while all the time your mouth is opening and closing in a silent, floundering scream of paranoia. Which is just the reason why the dealers line up, wall to wall, around a studio.

Sitting with our feet up on the desk, smoking and drinking and playing back the tracks, we indulged ourselves in the fantasies that are all part of the experience and the bonhomie and camaraderie born of these occasions, but in our hearts we could hear that on the evidence so far, Album Number Three didn't sound like it was about to give us a hat-trick of gold. It was already taking too long for one thing, for another, thanks to my own little habit, the songs weren't coming like they should. And on top of this there was the problem of Leon.

Because by now Leon's into speedballs, just the right amount of coke to get him up, mixed with just the right amount of smack to float him down again, a great social asset, a speedball, as sought after as a firm hand on a martini. And speedballs just happen to be the speciality of Leon's weasel-faced dealer.

Now some people can still hold it together no matter what state they get into. By some miracle, some reflex action, some people can still play. Only Leon doesn't happen to be one of them. By now his playing is sloppy and getting sloppier by the minute. He's always late and usually stumbling, not just stoned either but drunk too, which makes him aggressive.

One day, arguing with Richard in the studio which he does all the time now, Leon leans out towards him from the drums, the sticks in his hands, his face white and tight, his eyes staring.

'*Nigger*,' he screams and the place stops still like it's been frozen in a bad fairytale.

'Jesus . . . Leon . . .' I begin truly shocked but Richard cuts me short.

'Forget it,' he says curtly. 'He wouldn't even know where he is,' and he doesn't even look at Leon.

Sometimes Leon would turn up buzzing. Sometimes he'd be vague and disconnected. Sometimes, going for the rush that broke his heart a bit more every time, he'd overshoot and we'd find him an hour later passed out in the toilet. And sometimes, when his schedule had gone awry, when his memory had deserted him altogether, he didn't show up at all.

One night, after we'd waited for several hours, Richard finally exploded.

118

'This is fucking useless,' he said. 'That's it. It's got to be done. We all know he can't do the tour and we might as well face it.'

By this time, you see, Leon had been busted again, a bust we knew could be disastrous for all of us. For plans were already being made for the tour and some of the countries on the list had begun to be sticky about letting in people with drug records. The lawyers were worried and we all knew it, something else that was adding to Leon's paranoia.

'Well, if you want to know what I think . . .' Steve began.

'We don't,' I snapped.

It was always this way between Steve and me. Because he'd replaced Hammy I liked to treat him as a newcomer which was crazy since he'd been there at the beginning as far as our success was concerned. Richard had brought him in. They'd met in the same office in London where Richard had worked for a while selling insurance, and for me there always remained something of the insurance salesman about Steve, some well-brushed hush-puppy thing which grated. He was always too *respectable* for me. We both knew that he despised my life-style and I despised his, whatever it was that he did with his life that could warrant the word *style*. I knew when he criticized Leon for his bad habits he was including, although he wasn't saying so, my own.

'It would help,' I said coldly, 'if you'd lay off Leon,' but Steve just ignored me.

'We can't mess around any more,' he said. 'Richard's right. We all know it.

'It's bite-the-bullet time . . .' he said. Which is when the crazy cackle broke out from the shadows and looking up we saw Leon with the gun.

It's not as bad as you think, I guess. I mean we knew he had a habit of carrying the thing. He'd bought it in the States during our first tour. It was a thirty-eight, a Colt,

119

nickel-plated with an ivory handle, a woman's gun, the 'Saturday Night Special', so called because of the number of times it turned up in domestic murder cases when wives shot their husbands.

At the time when he bought it we'd had to stop him trying to carry it back through British customs, bold as brass, in his hand luggage. He'd got a roadie to smuggle it in in the end.

'What else are roadies for?' he said with a grin. Now he was pointing the thing straight at Steve.

I guess it seems strange now that no one took much notice at first. But you have to understand that it wasn't the first time that Leon had pulled this sort of stunt in public. He liked to show the thing off. He'd whip it out of his pocket, brandish it in the air, playing the bad boy. Which is why Kent just turned away in disgust.

'Oh for fuck's sake Leon . . .' Kent said, his voice heavy with irritation. He got up abruptly from his chair, lifted his guitar, turning to fiddle with an amp.

'Now that you're here,' he said.

Richard too was unconcerned. He was at the cona machine now pouring a coffee. So I was the only one, apart from Steve himself of course, who realized the new and menacing way that Leon was advancing with the gun.

'Bite the bullet . . .?' he was saying. 'Bite the bullet eh Steve?'

Leon was almost on him when he raised the gun slowly and placed it in the air on his other hand like a marksman, aiming it at Steve's head. I wanted to yell out, but I felt like I was in one of those dreams that you wake up from in a start, with a strangled grunt in your mouth because you can't scream or use your limbs. Through the window I could see Rory the engineer up on his feet now in alarm.

It was when Leon cocked the thing that everything changed. The double click of the hammer going back made both Richard and Kent look up sharply. Kent began to lift the guitar slowly off his neck.

'Come on Leon. Stop messing about,' he said softly.

But Leon was taunting Steve by now. There was a wide grin on his face as he repeated the words.

'Bite the bullet eh you cunt . . . bite the bullet . . .'

Steve was white to the gills. He sat there like he was carved in marble on the seat. His eyes were locked into Leon's.

'Come on Leon,' Kent said, beginning to move slowly towards him.

'Who's biting the bullet now Steve?' Leon said in his mocking growl, the wide crazy grin spread now all over his face. And in a slow-motion movement he squeezed on the trigger.

It wasn't loaded. Still, the empty snap of the hammer seemed to echo around our heads like the shot that might have been. Steve collapsed on the chair like a puppet freed of his strings, Richard and Kent started shouting at Leon.

In the end Leon lurched angrily out of the studio. The next day, of course, he couldn't remember a thing about it. But I guess, more than anything else, it was what made him realize it was time for the clinic.

'They'll clean him up,' I said to Richard. 'Give him a whole new lot of blood so that the stuff is out of his system. He'll even get the visas for the tour OK.' But Richard only looked at me pityingly.

'You think that'll do it?' he said. He shook his head scornfully.

'It's a new brain Leon needs,' he said, 'not a new load of blood.'

We'd waited, wasted another five hours hanging around for Leon. I couldn't help but know the end was in sight. Still, I touched a hand on Richard's arm as he bent over putting music, note-book, throat spray into his case.

'Please Richard,' I said. 'We have to help him. We can't just get rid of him.'

I touched his back nervously. It was taut like a bow.

'With everything, you owe him that,' I said boldly.

It was Kent who suggested that Leon move into the cottage when he got back from the clinic.

'Good idea,' I said sanctimoniously. 'Get him away from the dealers.' I did not look at Kent as I said it.

He took a little persuading when we met him at the airport. He'd been away for a month in the place in Switzerland.

'What for?' he said. 'I'm clean. Everything's fine. I feel great.' He looked great too. There was a freshness in his cheeks where the waxiness used to be and a light in his eye. He looked newly made.

He changed his mind though when Kent showed him the cottage. For years it had been used as a sheep pen. The slates were gone and the doors and the windows. It was just a shell when the builders moved in. They'd kept its country bulk though, the beauty of its chunky stone walls.

It had a fairytale feel to it, cut off as it was. For there was no road to it, not even a track. It could be reached only by walking, or in the Landrover in which Kent would drive over, delivering Leon's mail and his food. For suddenly being there, away from it all, beyond contact with the outside world, seemed to be what Leon wanted.

'Smell it Joanie,' he would say, leaning out into the night over the stable door of the cottage.

'So clean . . .' he would say. 'So fresh . . .'

And if we'd hoped that the de-tox would get Leon back into the studio, then we were disappointed. Our master-plan turned round on us and it became impossible to shift him from the cottage. In London Richard and Steve were already shopping for a new drummer, and I figure now, without being told, Leon knew it.

Kent tried to get him to work. He'd come to the cottage, bring him back to his studio which in those days was upstairs from the lounge. Occasionally Leon would pretend to work. Lay down a few desultory tracks. But he had no interest in it. It seemed that even the barn and the farm were too much in the way of civilization for him and he could not wait to be back in his cottage.

To encourage him I began driving over from Stoneham and more often than not we would go back afterwards to the cottage. Soon I began to visit him there, even when we weren't working, so that we fell, in those last days, into a sort of easy compatibility.

Soon the things that we would do with our day turned into small rites, climbing to the top of the nearby knoll, for instance, at sunset, to catch the last rays slanting through the tree-tops, or sitting on the huge stones at the top of the waterfall watching the water run down the gulley, coming home to build a fire in the open grate to ward off the evening chill.

Often as we walked back to the cottage, Leon would reach down and pull up clumps of weeds and wild flowers. He did it awkwardly, like a city boy. When we got back he'd stick them clumsily into jam-jars which he'd scattered around the place, reciting as he did so the names which Kent's father had taught him in his mocking throaty growl.

'Vetch . . . Ragwort . . . Bittersweet . . .'

For a strange friendship had sprung up between Leon and Kent's father. Leon took to accompanying him on his business about the farm, striding along beside him with a stick like his own which he had cut and which he grasped in the very same way. Sometimes too Kent's father would stop by at the cottage using as an excuse some supply that Leon wanted. Once there he would stop for a cup of tea with a grunt of thanks, or more often than not a glass of his favourite whisky which Leon kept for him and which he would not drink without him, like some monk delighting in new-made vows.

I can't tell you what they talked about, or why they grew to like each other. Something tells me though that on Leon's side, Kent's father blew through him like a breeze of fresh air after all the leeching and the lick-spittle and the false friendship that he'd become used to.

'Whoa George,' he said once, hallooing to him through the open door as he went by at a distance, pleasure and pride in his voice.

But George, seeing me, just raised his stick in the familiar greeting, and passed on by.

More often than not when I visited, I would stay over, and when I did we slept in the same old brass bedstead, side by side, without embarrassment, warm and comforted, like children.

Away from temptation, Leon had stayed off the coke and the smack. He smoked the hash or the grass which I came with and drank the claret which he began to enjoy and which I brought from Stoneham's cellar.

He still took the downers prescribed by the clinic to get himself to sleep, though, so that when we both fell into bed we were usually gently stoned and drunk.

Still, sometimes as we fell, we would fall upon each other too, instinctively, as people will. For a few minutes we would make small frantic unabashed attempts at sex. But it would never come to anything. Soon the effort would begin to peter out. Soon one of us would slide off and away into sleep and the next day, when we woke, the interlude would seem like a dream.

I can't remember when exactly things began to change.

Afterwards, looking back, I thought perhaps it had something to do with the seasons, with the freshness of

124

May slipping away into June and July, and then into a hot, used-up August. One day, looking out of the cottage window, I noticed for the first time that the greenery had grown dull, that it looked too heavy and over-blown as if tired of the summer.

That night I woke up in the small hours to see Leon curled up like a leprechaun in the window smoking quietly. The window was open, and as I raised myself a shaft of early autumn air hit my shoulders, making me shiver.

'Why doesn't he come?' he said.

'Who?' I said, although I knew he meant Richard.

The next time I pulled up outside the cottage in Kent's wagon, I heard a discordant jangle heaving out through the window. I knew immediately what it was. The basement tapes, those scraps of melody, banalities masquerading as lyrics.

We began to fight almost as soon as I got in. He stood in front of the tape player, tapping his cigarette on the ashtray, getting up, sitting down. He kept asking me what I thought of them and in the end I told him for by then we were arguing anyway.

'It's just acid-head stuff Leon . . . stoned crap.'

He called me then, I remember, 'a hypocritical bitch' and of course he was right, for my own coke habit had continued unabated when I wasn't with Leon. I'd even done a line in a lay-by on the way over to the farm and being an old hand he knew it.

Suddenly he was tearing my bag up from the sofa, rummaging through it, throwing the contents over his shoulder.

'Where is it?' he said.

'You've got some,' he said, throwing the bag away, coming towards me. 'You've got some and I want it.'

I lied to him then, backing away.

'I had some but it's gone. I did the last. On the way over.'

125

'You're lying,' he said, and he lunged at me, grabbing my arms and pushing me backwards.

'Calm down Leon,' I said, trying to pacify him, but he just gave me another hard shove, pinning me back against the wall.

'I want it Joanie,' he said.

I gave him a shove then which caught him off guard so that he stumbled and I slipped from his grasp. He was turning to come after me when he saw the corner of the packet sticking out of the sunglasses case.

'Ah . . .' he said, with a delighted smile.

Before I could reach it he had snatched it up and was laughing and holding it over my head like a child.

'Don't Leon,' I said.

Before me his eyes had turned vacant and cold.

'We'll share it,' he said and I saw the old crazed grin was back.

'It'll be just like old times Joanie,' he said.

I was picking up the stuff that he had thrown out of my bag when he came up behind me. I felt his hands around my waist, his face at the side of my head.

'Go away,' I said.

By then though it was too late and the coke-confident hand, no longer that of a friend, was up between my legs.

'Come on baby,' he said.

Something in the voice and the hand made me shiver. Because they were both his but not his. It was like being in some sci-fi film where the victim discovers the man she thinks she knows is not a man at all but a machine made in the same mould.

'Get off,' I said crossly. But by this time his hands were round my neck.

We did it half on the sofa in the end, half on the floor, because that's how you do it when the coke is calling you.

126

We did it back to front, frantically, like dogs, which I was glad about at the time because it meant I couldn't see his eyes. We did it with a lot of howling and grunting and screaming, and lots of 'Baby, baby' which both of us knew meant nothing. And when we'd finished, and crawled apart, he got up abruptly and began pacing up and down, and I dragged my clothes back on and finished throwing the things back in my bag and walked out.

He was drinking the whisky that he kept for Kent's father when I left and scrabbling on the floor for some downers he believed that he'd lost. I didn't say goodbye and he didn't notice me going.

The last thing I saw as I pulled away was a jam-jar of flowers in the window. All the water was gone and they were brown and brittle and dried out. Useless. Like a memory.

Vetch. Ragwort. And bittersweet.

I've been crying today
Over someone I barely knew
Our lives were bound together none the less . . .

Nobody had to tell me Leon was dead. Nobody had to say the words. When the phone went by the bed early one morning waking me from a deep sleep it was Kent, and I was already halfway there.

'Joanie . . .' he said. 'It's Leon . . .' and I put the phone down without hearing the rest. It was all I needed to know. I didn't want the details. I didn't want to see what it was on Leon's postcards.

Leon killed himself a day after the album was released, for which case of impeccable timing McGarvey got down

127

on bended knee in grateful thanks to whatever perverted patron saint it was that had the responsibility for looking after the fortunes of B Whores like himself.

Meanwhile the rest of us stood by amazed watching as the conspiracy theorists began to crank up the industry which would become Leon, and an album no better than it should be turned into that capricious thing Rock Gold.

Never let the facts interfere with a good story. That's the way they work, these guys. And it didn't matter that Leon scarcely played on the album, suddenly the thing was full of all the moments and all the touches that went to show Leon at his best, the unfulfilled Leon, the Leon who might have been, the Leon who was going to do so much.

Leon never showed up again in the studio after I drove away from the cottage that day. The following morning Kent went over as he normally did to see if Leon needed anything, but the place was all locked up and the key left where it always was beneath a stone in the outhouse.

It took another three weeks or so for Leon to surface and when he did, it was clear he wasn't going on tour with us. In fact it was clear that he wasn't going anywhere with us.

He was back in the serious smack-head stage, stumbling and incoherent and stinking of the old chemicals. He was ranting too, buttonholing any hack who would listen and there were plenty of them, claiming we'd thrown him out, keen to tell them about his new band. And in the end it was left to McGarvey to bring it all to a close with the usual bullshit about 'musical differences'.

Since Leon was found with his works still hanging out of his arm, it wasn't too much of a problem figuring out how he died. One of the bitches of coming off the stuff is that when you back-slide and pump in your old dose, your body can't take it and you OD and that's what happened to Leon.

Besides the coke and heroin, the post-mortem also found a liver blown up to twice its normal size from the alcohol, and a distended and exhausted heart. A routine case of death by rock and roll you might think. For the ghouls and the necromancers, though, a heart distended and exhausted wasn't enough. For them it also had to be broken.

The hate mail and the death threats and the rest of the shit began pretty much from the moment the body was discovered in that back-street in Hamburg. It fell to Lois to organize the funeral since she was still legally married to Leon and his parents were old and overshadowed with grief. She went with Milton to bring back the body and between them at some point they decided on the cremation. I guess they figured that what the world didn't need right now was another graffiti-ed rock grave.

I drove up with Kent to the funeral. Steve came with Richard who had Mikhael in tow. McGarvey sent his excuses.

As we turned off the slip-road it was raining, a steady relentless determined rain that turned the cotton wool that hung over the town heavy and sodden. The main street where we'd chased him that night was as grey and as shoddy-looking as ever. The old cinema looked even worse. One of its art deco doors had lost its glass and was boarded up. The steps were encrusted with dog shit and on the top of them a wino's bottle rolled backwards and forwards in the wind like it had been placed there for the occasion. As we pulled into the crematorium a trickle of smoke inched out from the chimney into the filthy grey sky. And I guess that was what finally decided me.

'We can't . . . we just can't leave him here,' I said.

Lois looked extraordinarily beautiful at the funeral, dignified too in her black. Milton held her arm at the elbow as she edged her way through the crowd.

The fans were out in force. I heard a faint hiss as we walked up the path. The police were there too keeping them back. They saluted, as they do on such occasions, as

129

the coffin was carried past. A nice touch, I thought. Leon would have liked that.

Inside, the crematorium was packed, mainly with kids from the town laying the local hero to rest. There was a greyness about them that they'd caught off the town, a pinched quality, as if they'd been too long without sun. Scattered in among them the visitors glittered like diamonds, strangers from another planet, an A and R man McGarvey had sent, the Basement Tape cronies, a handful of wannabees, one eye open for the press.

Marge had moved to California by then, but never one to miss an opportunity to show off her connections had come back for the funeral. She was sitting in the front row, a happy smile on her face, like me as coked up as the place where Leon was going.

Marge though in her vanity had made the mistake of sitting herself too near Lois, who made her look mucky and sluttish in a black dress, expensive but too tight and wrong for the occasion. Beside her Linus in a little boy's suit looked about him with wide eyes that were already too old for his outfit.

We all went back to Leon's parents' place afterwards because they'd said it was what they wanted. They lived in a little bungalow by then which Leon had bought them. The black plastic was still there though and the same smell of fat. I was drinking my tea and chewing on my fairy cake when I noticed the picture on the sideboard, short grey pants, skimpy jacket badly buttoned and the same cheeky schoolboy face that was printed on Linus.

Lois's eyes behind the stiff smile were cool when I kissed her. Still she listened, nodding her head, to my suggestion.

'He was happiest there,' I said, as we stared at each other, no love lost between us.

'If he was happy anywhere, he was happy there.'

And I think in the end she was grateful for the idea, his

130

parents too, because ashes are tricky things you never quite know what to do with.

That night, laying out a line back at Stoneham, I unscrewed the lid of the fancy urn that they'd given us and sprinkled a little in.

'For old times' sake Leon,' I said.

Everyone knows what happened at our private 'funeral' thanks to Mikhael. It's all there in the film, that first great *rockumentary*. They should bury the damned thing in a canister below some new building, an abattoir perhaps, or maybe a slab of new motorway.

When Richard said he wanted to film the tour I said, 'You're mad.

'You're mad,' I said. 'Tell him Kent. Tell him he's crazy. On top of everything else. All our other problems. Leon gone. The way everyone's feeling . . .' But Richard was adamant.

'It'll be good for us Joanie. It's what we need,' and in the end, as usual, Richard won.

I was furious when he turned up with Mikhael outside the cottage where we'd arranged to meet.

'It's supposed to be private Richard,' I said, 'just the band,' but Richard just laughed in a way quite unlike him and I realized that he was stoned. An unusual occurrence for Richard.

'I'll wait at the top,' Mikhael said with the polite insincerity which was the thing I always most disliked about him.

'Do that,' I said coldly.

It had been wet for a few weeks and the gulley was very muddy. We slipped and slid down the sides, the four of us, grabbing hold of the trees.

It looks so foolish now, the whole thing, and so it was, even then past its time. And all I can say now in my defence, for it was my idea, is that I wanted Leon to have

131

something, something dignified, although I know that's not the way it turned out, but something more than the Twenty-third Psalm and the turgid hymns they'd picked for him at the funeral. I wanted something more too than a filthy trickle of smoke inching up into a gun-metal sky.

So I gave him the Keats, read it from one of the large stones by the waterfall where we used to sit, he and I, during that short sane intermission.

'. . . I have been half in love with easeful Death,
Called him sweet names . . .'

The only sound as I read was the water rushing over the stones. It gurgled and rattled like it was laughing. Apart from that the place was silent. No birds, nothing. It was as if they'd all been warned off the thing by Mother Nature herself, instructed not to participate. At one point a small shaft of sun came out from between the storm clouds and slanted between the trees as if snatching a look. I guess it didn't care for what it saw because it went in again just as quickly.

I'd taken the lid off the urn and I was all ready to sprinkle the ashes and I'd just got to that bit, 'Thou wast not born for death, immortal Bird!' when Richard let out the guffaw. The next minute he was capering like some pathetic old folk rock wizard, catching at the silver birch trees with fey mocking hands and swinging himself round, parroting the lines as he went.

'Thou wast not born for death, immortal Bird!'

I'd jacked myself too far up in preparation for the occasion and now was dropping down fast. The whole thing was falling apart around me and I was beginning to feel fractious and a little weepy. I brushed a muddy hand across my eyes and began yelling at Richard.

'You're a bastard Richard, you know that? You're such a bastard . . .'

And then before I knew it, I was shouting other things

132

too, things I knew I shouldn't shout, things that weren't even necessarily true, but things I wanted to shout anyway. I heard them spinning and echoing around the trees.

'It's your fault you know that don't you? You know what you did. It's you that made him unhappy . . .'

When I shouted them he was half behind a birch tree. He stopped mid-caper and his head shot up. When he turned all the fey foolishness had fallen away and his face was as black as thunder. But it was too late. I was leaning forward, the urn still open in my hand, the words already spewing out.

'It's your fault he killed himself . . .'

'Shut up Joanie. This is crap. That's enough.' It was Kent but it was too late. Richard was already springing forward, wrestling the urn from my hand. Now it was his turn to scream.

'Come on then. Let's do it.' His face was contorted in fury. 'Let's *sprinkle* Leon, that's why we're here . . .'

And that's when I heard it. Between the shouting and the scrabbling as we fell together to the ground, the faint evil whirr of Mikhael filming.

It made Mikhael's reputation that piece of film. I'm sure that you've seen it.

There we are, four figures from hell in a dripping Cocteau forest, in dark glasses and regulation rock and roll black. Richard and I wrestle on the ground, covered in the mud and the leaves and bits of broken branches, while the urn which has slipped from both our grasps lies upended with what was Leon spilled out and ground beneath us in the mud.

Beside us in this black comedy Kent lumbers forward, a hand stretched out to try and stop the mayhem. His face is a Kent face, full of anger and pain. Yet it's Steve in the end who says it all.

133

He's staring upwards, face fixed and white, peering at something high up above us.

For a long time I couldn't put a name to it, what it was on his face. It was only much later that I saw it. I saw then too what had thrown me, which was that the expression was so out of keeping.

Out of place for us. Out of time. Not part of what we were.

A fine Old Testament terror.

In the dragon lady's dream
She scans the starlight for signs . . .

'So what have you got for me Joanie?' Richard said. He was lying back on the pillows, his eyes closed, very tired. He is like this a lot now and sleeps much of the time. Still there's that old touch of mockery on his lips.

'Trouble is,' he said, 'everyone expects you to have some sort of conversion on your death-bed. They're disappointed if you can't offer them some sort of spiritual awakening.

'So what have you got for me Joanie?' he said. 'You were always into everything.'

It's true. We ticked them off together on our fingers.

'Zen Buddhism . . .'

'And that other thing . . .'

'Krishnamurti. Sufism . . .'

'God and you looked so dreadful in orange . . .'

'Primal Scream . . . Gestalt . . .'

'Never did understand that stuff . . .'

'Neither did I. Anthroposophy . . .'

'Anthro-what . . .?'

'Forget it. Just flirted with it. Tai-chi . . .'

134

'Transcendental Meditation . . .'

'Oh yeah. The white handkerchief . . .'

'Oh and your *mantra*. What was your mantra again?'

'I still can't tell you. Channelling . . .'

'Oh God channelling. I'd forgotten channelling. What were you again?'

'I don't know. Can't remember. A vestal virgin probably. The court of King Rameses . . .'

'Seems unlikely . . . Astrology . . .'

'Well of course . . . Numerology . . . the I Ching . . .'

'The Devil's work', Egan called it. When he burst in we were throwing the sticks on the hotel bedroom floor.

'Save her. Save her. Save her dear Lord from this wickedness.'

He was on his knees, tearing at the sticks, snapping them, ripping up the charts.

'What the fuck . . .'

'Pour your mighty spirit on her Jesus.'

I remember how he sweated in the southern heat, how he held the Bible up, brandishing it before him like a cross or a torch warding off evil, how I screamed, first of all in fury. 'Get him out . . . get him out . . .', how I turned on Steve jabbing him hard in the chest so that he fell backwards, how the I Ching freak in her long floating dress cowered against the wall covering her heart with her hand, how I yelled for Kent, the tour manager, the roadies, anyone.

'Get in here . . . for Christ's sake . . . get this crazy out of my room.'

By the time Kent came in Steve was on his knees too, holding up his hands awkwardly, sneaking looks out of the corner of his eye at Egan to see how to do it. And all the time Egan's voice.

'Save her Jesus. Save this life. Save this soul in distress. Bring her to yourself . . .'

'You stupid fucking asshole . . .'

Me threatening Steve now, pushing him, kicking him, Kent holding on to me.

'Take it easy Joanie . . .'

'You tell me to take it easy. Fuckhead here busts into my room with this maniac and you tell me to take it easy . . .'

And Steve, eyes wide and earnest, trying to explain.

'Can't you see what's happening to us Joanie . . . we can't go on this way Joanie . . . you don't want to end up the same way as Leon Joanie . . .'

All this and suddenly the evil eye whirring again from the bedroom door.

'Turn that fucking thing off. Tell him to turn that fucking thing off.'

A hand, my hand, pushing into the camera.

'Turn that bleep bleep bleep bleep bleeping thing off Mikhael . . .'

It was Kent's father that Steve had seen staring down at us from high up on the ravine, the face that Mikhael missed, a face like some ancient god's or prophet's, flat and carved in stone, reflecting all the folly it saw beneath it.

He never got over the sight, Steve, and I guess with all that had happened, Leon pointing the gun at him and everything, it really wasn't surprising. He tried to explain it as we sat watching Egan on the river bank.

'All I mean is it's crazy . . . the way we live . . . like no one ever tells us we can't do anything any more . . . no one ever says no . . . and in the end . . . well you just end up wishing someone would . . . wishing for someone . . . something . . . bigger . . . higher . . . than yourself . . .'

We were a couple of months into the American leg of the tour by then and the album was locked in securely at number one on both sides of the Atlantic. It should have been a good feeling. Instead it hung like an albatross around our necks.

From Mikhael's point of view, though, things couldn't have been better. The death threats were continuing unabated. Because of them security was tight. Minders with names like Bud or Buck and sinister bulges beneath their tour jackets added colour on the bus for Mikhael but didn't do much for the rest of us. Our new drummer took the next plane home after he got back to his hotel and found a fan in a Leon mask waiting for him with a gun. It turned out to be fake but with a wife and children he didn't wait to find out. We scrabbled around drafting in session men but the tour was falling apart and we knew it.

I was in bad shape by this time. You might think that what had happened to Leon would have slowed me down too, but as anyone with a habit from smoking upwards can tell you, other people's experiences never register on your own Richter scale. For wherever we looked, Leon was there like Banquo's ghost. I'm surprised he didn't show up on Mikhael's film like one of those blurs in a picture trying to prove the para-normal. Interviews and press conferences became a nightmare. He was all anyone wanted to talk about. After a couple of bad scenes where we'd stormed out, we laid down a rule that we wouldn't talk about him any more. But that only made things worse. First we'd killed him. Now we wouldn't even mention his name.

Mikhael had become a serious bone of contention between Richard and me.

'We want different things, that's the trouble Richard,' I raged at him one day.

'Well maybe that's something we should discuss when we get home Joanie,' he said coolly.

So altogether to say we were all jittery is an understatement. There was a feeling of hysteria lying just beneath the surface ready to break out at any time which communicated itself to the humblest roadie. It's that feeling of hysteria, so they say, that makes the film the classic it is.

And all I can say to that is that while it might look fine from your cinema seat, it wasn't that much fun being in the middle of it.

I can't remember now the name of the place where Egan entered our lives. It was some small place in Texas I believe, a one-horse town that trebles in size for the festival.

It was July when we got there, with a sun so strong it seemed to grill you when you walked out in it. We came off after the first set limp like rag dolls to find the air con off in the trailer and the beers boiling in the fridge.

'Oh for Christ's sake,' I said, 'I know where I'm going.

'And don't think you're coming,' I snapped at Mikhael.

The creek that snaked around the festival site was lying like a streak of welcoming silver and I just grunted when Steve asked if he could come too. Things were pretty touchy already between us by then but it was too hot to argue so we grabbed towels together and strolled down the hill towards it.

When we got there it was full of old gold hippies bare-breasted and beautiful, washing their pots and pans and their baggy-nappied babies.

At first I scarcely noticed Egan a little way downstream, waist-high in the water and haranguing the crowd that watched from the bank with his tales of sin and salvation. I only started to take a lazy interest when a line began forming from the river bank and the Jesus freak began leading the lambs out towards him.

'Welcome to the Bible belt,' I said to Steve, who had his eyes screwed up in the sun and was staring out over the glittering water towards them.

He did good business in baptisms that day, Egan, and I figure it had to have something to do with the heat, or maybe it was the high level of chemicals or perhaps that simple old disillusionment with life. Or maybe it was a combination of all three. I said as much to Steve. But he still had Leon on his mind and that face between the trees which is when he started in trying to explain.

'There has to be . . . something else,' he finished.

'Of course there's something else,' I said sharply. 'But it's sure as hell not what he's offering.'

There was silence then as I lay back and let the sounds of the festival, the music and voices and the heat of the sun drift over me with the water. When Steve's voice came it was from a long way away.

'Do you ever feel,' he said, 'we've gone too far?'

I let it rest for a minute then I said coldly, relentlessly, 'Too far?'

'You know,' he said.

'No,' I said. 'I don't know. Tell me.'

'Well . . . Leon and everything,' he said.

I made a sharp movement then, pulling myself up and out of the water. I knew what he'd been waiting to say and I didn't want to hear it. I reached for my clothes angrily.

'Leon has nothing to do with it,' I said, dragging on my shirt. 'Leon has nothing to do with anything.'

'But don't you think . . .?' he began but I cut him short.

'Leon was Leon,' I said. I was dragging on my jeans furiously.

'Leon did what he did. He's dead. We're alive. End of story.'

I was shouting at him by now and a couple of people nearby had looked up.

'I'm going,' I said, snatching up the towel. I didn't ask if he was coming with me but it didn't matter because he wasn't, and I figure it was already beginning to happen in his head. He just went on sitting there, his arms round his knees, shaking his head dumbly and staring at Egan across the water.

You know the rest. It's all there on the film, Steve beaded and bangled, bare chest to the sky, arms stretched out like the crucifixion before Egan pushes him under the water.

I figure now that Egan couldn't believe his luck when he found out just who it was he'd baptized. Mikhael had come back with the news so that we were waiting for Steve back in the caravan, the air con blissfully re-established, when he walked in glazed and euphoric with Egan.

'Oh God,' I said in disgust, taking a large swig from my beer can. I held it up towards Mikhael, threatening him with it.

'Turn it off,' I said, but Steve was already in there.

'No,' he said. 'It's OK. Keep filming.' He cleared his throat like he was making a speech.

'I want the world to know,' he said. 'In fact I want to tell the audience, tonight, on stage.'

You know what happens next. You can see it on the film. The hands across the eyes, the shaking of heads. No one knows whether to laugh or cry. In the end I toss the can angrily into a bin.

'Like fuck you will,' I say.

'No way!' I say, jumping up and throwing the beer can into a bin. 'Tell him Kent.'

But Kent is as stunned as the rest of us and even he can't think of anything to say. So it's left to Richard, to my mind the one great moment in the movie.

'Oh why not?' he said, pursing his lips, acting up for the camera.

'We've tried everything else after all.'

He did too of course. It's all there, walking out front between a couple of numbers in the middle of the set a few gigs later. He gave them the whole red-hot-seen-the-light-found-Jesus-changed-my-life bit and some laugh and some boo but most of them just look bemused. Still, the press loved it, and the day after Born Again Steve was on the front page of all the papers.

By this time Egan had become an uneasy addition to the

tour. I was outraged when Steve wanted him to travel with us on the bus.

'Christ,' I said, 'if we don't have enough problems with fucking Cecil B. De Mille on our backs . . .'

'But Joanie,' Steve said, trying to be reasonable in a way I was beginning to find annoying, 'we've had half a dozen of your gurus on the bus.'

It was true. And it didn't help.

'That's different,' I said grandly. 'Nobody objected.'

'Nobody was asked,' he said.

In the end though he hired a car and the two of them travelled separately, with Steve driving and Egan giving him Bible study on the way.

Things came to a head a few weeks later when Steve and I found ourselves together doing a plug for the concert for a local television station. I don't have an entirely clear recollection of what happened for obvious reasons, but it seems the two of us ended up shouting at each other, or rather I was shouting while Steve was still using his new more-in-sorrow-than-anger voice of sweet reason.

It's true I had to be bleeped out a few times but the reports afterwards about me having to be dragged from his neck and after that from the studio were really vastly exaggerated. However the fact is that I managed to insult not only Steve during our twenty minutes or so on the air, but more importantly every last member of the religious right who was listening. Words like 'Weak-minded mutton-heads like you who need this sort of crap . . .' are the ones so I understand that did the damage.

To Mikhael's delight when we turned up to the gig that night they were waiting for us with banners already unfurled.

'Hey, quite like the old days,' I say gaily into the camera as a banner hits the side of the Lincoln. Richard and Kent though don't look happy.

'This is not good Joanie,' Kent said privately to me later.

141

Banners outside the gigs then got so frequent that Mikhael even got bored with filming them. To his delight though they soon began unfurling inside the hall. One day when 'Turn on to Jesus' opened up suddenly in front of the stage, I reached down ostentatiously and took a joint from a fan.

'Hey . . . whatever . . .' I said.

'Leave it Joanie,' Richard hissed.

But I didn't. I did it other nights too, and early one morning after I'd retired to bed with one of the drafted-in drummers there was a fierce pounding on my hotel room door.

The guy got to the door eventually and turned the key. As he did, it flew open and Kent was there, striding to the bed, dragging me up from beneath the covers and shaking me.

'Where is it?' he was saying.

'Where's what?' I said blearily.

'You know for fuck's sake,' he said. 'The stash. They're on their way up.'

And they were too, storm-troopers, with dogs. But by then Kent had ripped open my bag and flushed several thousand dollars' worth of best coke and grass out into the city sewers. And let me tell you, if you think you may have missed something in life by not being busted in the boondocks, forget it. On the list of most fun things to do it's down there around one thousand and eight.

I sat on the bed, my legs stretched out, smoking a cigarette and trying to look insolent, as they turned over everything in the room from my dirty knickers upwards.

At the door as they left one of them turned and tipped his hat with a mastery of the art that must have gone back several generations.

'Sorry to have disturbed you . . . ma'am,' he said with his mocking Southern-boy grin.

It's all there, captured beautifully on camera.

*

Naturally the raid, unsuccessful as it was, made the papers. All of which helped when Steve came to paint his grim and seedy picture of life on the road for an evangelical newspaper, an account which, while it named no names, managed to leave the world with the impression that at least one female prima donna piano player in the band had some worrying anti-social habits.

'That's it. That's it,' I said, waving the paper in McGarvey's face. Things were so serious by this time that McGarvey had had to get out from behind his desk and fly over to sort things out, something which always deeply annoyed him.

'I'm not going on stage with that bastard, McGarvey.'

McGarvey's voice though had those slivers of ice in it.

'You've got no choice Joanie,' he said. 'Half a dozen more gigs then it's over.'

'OK but then he's finished, right?' I said. But McGarvey never answered.

It didn't matter anyway. There was no way that Steve was going to want to stay with the band. In Seattle with just a couple of gigs to go, he gathered his own press around him to announce that he was leaving the band at the end of the tour to work full-time with Egan's New Life in Christ Foundation.

A reporter caught me just as I was going on stage, asked me how I felt.

'I'm heartbroken,' I said. 'God knows how I'll get over it.'

And so we limped on to the end of the tour, and I wish for you, for Mikhael even, for all of us, I could write in one last great gig in LA, a gig where it all came together, where some of the old magic shone through despite everything reminding us of what we were, what we had been, what, perhaps, with a larger pinch of salt than the gods were prepared to sprinkle, we might still have become.

But this was not to be. We got through that LA gig by

the skin of our contractual obligations, something painfully apparent on the screen.

Still, despite everything, because of everything, it went gold that album, it went platinum. It stayed and stayed. They called it a 'classic', they still do. It turns up with frightening regularity in those tedious New Year page-fillers where people of no consequence and with nothing better to do choose their favourite albums of all time. And I've come to the conclusion now that it must be what people want, this pretence. The truth of the fairy tale must be that in the end no one *wanted* to see the emperor naked. Maybe it's just like the poet said, we're really not that crazy on reality.

It was our third album and without doubt our poorest. Still, it sold in the end better than the others put together and all because it's supposed to be Leon's last album.

'Listen . . . *listen* . . .' Rory said to me once, face aglow. 'I mean that is the *definitive* Leon.'

'It would be,' I said, 'if it was Leon playing.'

We left Leon's name on those tracks. Of course we left Leon's name on those tracks. What else would we do? But it's still Kent you're hearing on drums most of the time on that album.

And in case you're curious, the answer is no. No, I don't know any more about the facts surrounding Leon's death than you do. I don't know who, if anyone, he'd gone to see in Hamburg with his Basement Tapes under his arm. I don't know who was with him that night in the hotel. I don't know who it was gave him the bumper dose and why they left him to die when they saw what had happened.

As for how many dumps there were in the ashtray or what colour the lipstick was on the glasses, or how many people the desk clerk claims he saw go up to Leon's room, I don't know about any of these things. And the only difference between you and me is that I don't care.

I don't care because it doesn't matter. Only one thing

matters and that's Leon is dead. But if you want a dirty postcard, I'll show you a dirty postcard, Leon's dirty postcard,
the one he kept up his sleeve, the one entitled *Leon's Last
Goodnight*; the man himself collapsed head back on the
bed on the floor, a contented smile on his face, a hand
clutched round his bottle of bourbon, his works still
hanging out of his arm.

It's like I said, Leon was always going to die and for that
I'm sorry. I'm sorry he lost it. I'm sorry he gave it all
away. I'm sorry that he's gone and I'm glad that I'm alive.
And for me that's all there is to it.

There's only one thing worse than touring and that's not
touring any more. Arriving back home afterwards.

For despite everything you're restless when you come
off tour. Because the strange thing is that however much
you know that you hated it, when you get home, at least
for those first few weeks, it's worse. For bad as life is on
the road, at least it means your day is taken care of. You
don't have to think about anything, what to do with your
time for instance. What to do with your life.

It's why, for some people, gigging becomes a serious
addiction. Harder to give up than the dope. Because
while it's happening, for better or worse, touring becomes a way of life, until suddenly, bang, there you are
home again with twenty-four hours stretching out emptily in front of you every day and no one to tell you
what to do with them. In fact, all of a sudden, there's
no one there at all. You're alone for the first time in
months. And although you remember yearning every
night in yet another breeze-block hotel bursting with
loud-mouthed roadies for the peace and quiet of your
own home, still, when you get back there, the place
seems empty and lonely and all you can think of is how
to fill it.

And that's basically how the party season got started at Stoneham.

In a business whose by-word is excess her parties became legendary . . .

Legendary. Now there's a word abused by the media.

Legend has it, for instance, that following the crucifixion, Joseph of Arimathea set sail from the Holy Land carrying the Holy Grail, and arriving for no good reason in the town where I was born, hid the thing down a well. Legend also says that a jealous witch, chasing an ungrateful and eloping daughter, hurled a thunderbolt after her to halt her flight which missed but as it landed split apart the hills, thus forming the nearby gorge, into which the wicked witch tumbled.

Now that's *legendary . . .*

And *cool.* There's another over-worked word, disapproving too and parsimonious, especially when hitched as it always is to amounts of money the envious consider unearned or even better misspent.

As in: *One party alone is reputed to have cost a cool quarter of a million pounds . . .*

Well, he should know, Robin Phillips. Because he was there and hoovering up my coke along with the rest.

Once, standing in the gallery and looking down into the great hall with too much of everything inside me, I saw them all turn into animals. Perhaps it was the sun setting through the huge leaded window, but I saw the walls turn the baked red brown of the Serengeti where I went that time with the Dentist, and I watched as they swished their tails, fat contented hippos at my watering-hole, drinking my drink and munching my food, tooting and snorting and nudging their frail gazelles.

It was common for guests to receive airline or rail tickets in the post and to have hotel rooms waiting for them when they arrived . . .

146

'Book the Lamb and Flag Francis,' I would say.

One day as I said it, I saw a look of pain cross his face.

'I was thinking Joanie . . . really I'm not sure . . . their rates have gone up and everything . . . and I was just wondering . . . I mean is it really necessary . . .?'

Oh Francis my Francis. My one honest man.

'Francis,' I said, laughing, 'I do believe you're trying to save me money.'

There was a gentle dignity in the way he drew himself up, inclined his head.

'It's the reason you employed me Joanie,' he said.

Once I had a Russian party with a balalaika band and real Russian caviare and an ice rink laid out on the lawn. Once it was the Arabian Nights with belly-dancers and waiters dressed up as genies and gold minarets on top of the marquee. There were lasers in the sky for the Star Wars party and palm trees, specially planted, for South Pacific. I remember a Fifties party too with juke-boxes and skiffle groups, a Forties one with fireworks exploding like the blitz. And, of course, what else? A Twenties party, the Jazz Age, complete with the Valentine's Day massacre laid on by actors in the hall.

Afterwards we did the Charleston, beneath the fairy lights on a dance-floor laid out by the lake. And while I was not Gatsby standing behind the French windows, watching and smoking quietly as the curtains lifted in the breeze, still like Gatsby I have seen my drive fill up with cars, with the automobiles that bore them there when they might just as easily have been somewhere else, and I have seen them leave, just as he did, in the great tradition of Gatsby parties, not even knowing whose party it was at which they had been.

For I have done time with the vulgar. I have measured out my life with the sluts and the tramps of all persuasions, the arch and the camp and the odd minor deity from hell. And once – a medieval party it was – staring down at the Vanity Fair below, the guests, two-thirds of them out of

147

their brains, and mingling with the jugglers, the fire-eaters, the clowns and the conjurors, I saw how impossible it was to tell the difference. And I thought I saw an ancestor smirk and another one lift a mocking eyebrow. And it came to me then that what they were saying was that Stoneham had come of age now, had come full circle, with paste and pinchbeck ruling supreme, and good old-fashioned mummery and mask.

And I thought, as I looked, that one, a superior cavalier, gave me a pitying smile which said that he had seen it all before and this was nothing new to him, this world of charlatans and quacks. And he told me to remember this, if I remembered nothing else. That a fop and a fool was a fop and a fool, no matter what age they came from.

The party that hit the headlines though was the one with the avant-garde production of *The Tempest*.

I'd become something of a patron of the arts by then.

'This new project I'm involved in Joanie . . . this new exhibition Joanie . . . new play . . . new book . . . new film . . .'

The play was performed on the lake shore. I don't pretend to understand the finer points of the production, but Prospero was gay and whirled his cloak about a lot while Miranda and Caliban spent most of the time in the nude. There was a lot of shaking of thunder sheets, coloured smoke and some enthusiastic incantation of spells. For added dramatic effect, it was performed at midnight beneath a full moon, which all goes to explain how a bunch of locals stumbling home the worse for drink after a night's poaching managed to assume they'd walked in on a black magic orgy.

Being simple country folk, they did the only thing they could think of to do, which was to go to the Sunday papers. And the papers, it being their way, turned up a

Barbie doll who claimed to have been at the party in question and pumped full of drugs, and all but sacrificed to the Devil on a black magic altar.

'Sue them Milton,' I said, slapping the paper down on his desk. But Milton only sighed.

'Look I don't even know this girl. I've never seen her before in my life. I don't suppose she was even there at that party.'

'Ah but can you be sure?' Milton said quietly.

'Of course I can't be sure. You know how many people come to my parties. But so what if she was there? There was no black magic Milton. It's all garbage. Lies.'

Milton made a gesture then with his hand. It said, 'Yes . . . so what?' He got up, went to the window, jiggled with the cord of the blind, a ruse I knew he used when he was biding his time.

'Of course,' he murmured comfortingly. 'But still . . .'

'Still what?' I said.

He turned then to face me, his arms across his chest.

'What normally goes on at your parties Joanie?' he said.

'I don't know what you mean.'

'Yes you do.' His eyes stared at me coolly, taking no prisoners.

'A lot of drink Joanie. Some drugs. Brought in by your guests.' His eyes were polite and calm, refusing to accuse.

'A small orgy perhaps. In the summerhouse say. In a bedroom. It's a big house Joanie. You wouldn't even know what was going on.'

'OK Milton,' I said. 'I'm not pretending they're always vicarage tea-parties. A little sex yes, some drugs. That's rock and roll. But not black magic Milton. Not sacrificing virgins. I think we should sue.'

I liked to use the 'we'. It gave me a feeling of solidarity. But he just stood there, arms biting deeper into his chest, an expression he managed to make regretful on his face.

'What we have to face up to Joanie is that there are questions which a clever counsel would put to you in the witness box which you might find, shall we say, awkward

149

to answer.' He paused gravely, allowing the discreet truth of what he said to sink in.

'What I'm saying is that we cannot presume that the average juror would be sympathetic to a life-style such as yours, a life-style, I can assure you, that any defence counsel is going to paint in glorious technicolour.'

I couldn't look at him.

'So . . .?' I said mutinously.

'My advice is that while the thing is doubtless annoying, we let the matter drop Joanie.'

'So . . .' I said later at the door. 'We're like the Royal Family are we Milton? We never sue.'

'Something like that,' he said smoothly. There was the ghost of a smile on his lips.

'But normally for different reasons.'

The parties were so frequent at Stoneham that in the end it wasn't worth taking down the fairy lights. They stayed up strung out around the lawn.

Sometimes, when I was there on my own, I would have Francis put them on, sit down on the steps, take a toot, stare at them wonderingly.

Once, strung out myself, I thought I saw a figure in the half-light standing beneath them.

'Leon?' I said, rising in alarm, but then it was gone.

The lights were still there the day I left, swinging in the wind, dangling and dripping.

The last thing I heard as I got into the van was the sound of them tinkling and clinking.

'Play something Joanie,' Richard said this afternoon.

When he said it the back of my neck went cold and I began to stammer.

'I don't know Richard . . . ummm . . . I'm a bit out of practice . . . I haven't played much lately . . .'

I looked over sharply and nervously at Donald for help but he was beyond it, his face naked and sorrowful.

We've suspected, you see, for the last few days that it was happening. From certain things that Richard said, things that slid off the side, didn't quite add up, so that at last we saw it was here, this moment that Donald has been so much dreading, Richard's mind gently uncoupling itself, drawing itself apart, separating itself off into two tracks, one which will go about its daily business, with Milton for instance, putting the final touches to the will, discussing without fear or prevarication the inevitable; the other, this track where time stands still, where it stretches back into the past and more importantly forwards too, unhindered, into the future.

Because the truth is I haven't even touched a piano for ten years, not since I moved down to the cottage, and Richard knows that.

There's no evidence of my previous incarnation in the cottage. The Bechstein went along with everything else in the Great Stoneham Bankruptcy sale, sold at the time to a mystery buyer whose identity I guess I always suspected somewhere at the back of my head.

The only musical instrument I carried with me into exile was the Martin that Kent had bought me a decade before in those heady happy days of the first American tour. Even that's gone now. It went a year after I moved down when Linus came to stay.

For the first few years of my new life in the cottage I avoided pianos like the plague, rather as lapsed Catholics will avoid churches, deliberately, angrily. For a while, the thing was obsessional. I didn't want to see one or hear one, let alone play one again. I wouldn't go into the Stawell Arms, for instance, if the sound of the old pub piano was coming out through the windows. Once, not long after Grace and I had become friends, I stormed out, slamming my drink down on the table, when she joined the rest of them trying to cajole me into playing. She caught up with me as I was striding across the market-place.

'For heaven's sake. What have we done?'

'You don't know?'

'No.'

'What do you want me to play? "Daisy Daisy"?'

'No. I mean . . . I thought . . .'

'You thought what? I might want to play some of my old stuff? Some of my old *hits* . . .'

I was standing by the car by this time, twisting the car keys between my fingers, trembling with rage.

'No . . . look . . . I mean I didn't think . . . I'm sorry.'

But I was in no mood for apologies. It was an opportunity I couldn't miss. A chance to vent my spleen, to get rid of all the suppressed fury.

'Rule one. For future reference. Never ask a musician to play. For *fun*. At parties.'

'Like I said. I'm sorry. I didn't know.'

'You know now.'

'What can I say? I'm sorry.'

'It's OK. I have to go now.'

'Don't go.'

'I have to. I want to.' But the key wouldn't fit into the lock. I fumbled with it, unable to see it for the mist of tears. In the end I thundered a fist down hard on the roof of the Mini.

'Don't you understand,' I said, turning to her, 'what it meant to give it up?'

Later, calmer, sitting before her fire, I tried to explain.

'I had to,' I said. 'I needed to cut myself off from it completely.'

'But why?'

'Because I couldn't take the chance. It was too risky.'

'How do you mean?'

'I didn't want to want it all over again . . .'

It was true. It was for the same reason that I'd switch off the television at the first glimpse of any music programme, determined to cut myself off from my old life entirely.

Even so when I was not quick enough I would occasionally catch sight of Richard. Once too I saw Kent beside him and a strong dark dart hit my heart as I snatched at the zapper. Still, a few days later when Milton mentioned during one of his phone calls that Kent had requested once again my address I just grunted my refusal as usual.

For that is how it has been you see for the last ten years. During that time I did not see or speak to either Richard or Kent which perhaps will make you understand how it felt to see Kent sitting there that day in the corner of the café. And with Richard the break has been even longer. Fifteen years when I add it up. The ten years since I moved down to the cottage and before that the five years after the band finally disintegrated and he and I went our separate ways. In those years I avoided him assiduously and more often than not ostentatiously at music business jamborees and the other places where we would occasionally find ourselves on opposite sides of the room. Our only communication then, if such you wish to call it, was my well-publicized one-sided slanging match in the music press.

'Sure. I mean his stuff is great. If muzak is your thing . . .' It became one of those music business feuds, none the less famous for being so one-sided. Perhaps you remember it.

I've tried saying sorry to Richard about the things that I said then but he refuses my apologies, just waves that old airy hand on the pillow.

'Water under the bridge darling,' he says, which it is, especially I guess for him now that it's the dark and unfathomable Styx which flows under the bridge on which he is standing.

He bears no resentment for anything I did or said

153

during those years, something which humbles me. But then I remember he always had this careless equanimity about him. I think back to the beginning when we were kids and I would rage about my father and he would just shrug the wordless shrug that included all such fathers, mine, De Vere.

'Fathers. So what?' it said.

It was with that same easiness that he never bothered retaliating to all those snide little comments I'd make to any music journalist willing to buy me a drink. But then the truth is that he didn't need to answer them for he knew what I knew. That I was going down as fast and as surely as he was going up and the things that I said were only born out of wicked old-fashioned jealousy.

We've talked a lot about these things since I arrived, Richard and I, and only got near to arguing once. I'd been telling him about the cottage, Grace, the café, when suddenly he grew angry.

'It's ridiculous. Burying yourself down there in the back of beyond.'

'I like it.'

'Well, it makes me angry.'

'I'm happy. I have a life there.'

'A *life*. What? Waiting on tables?'

'It's what I want.'

'You make me sick Joanie, you know that. And you know why? Because what *I* want is to go on making records. But I can't have what I want. Because I'm dying. I have no more time. But you, you have all the time in the world but won't do anything with it. I think it's disgusting refusing to even play the piano.'

I understood his anger. How could I not? His life curtailed like this when he has so much left he still wants to do, so much Life left inside him being drained away, day by day now, by the disease. And it was because of this I shivered this afternoon when he said, 'Play something Joanie. One of those old classical pieces you used to play,'

154

knowing as he said it that another stage had been reached in this draining away, that the dark water beneath the bridge had risen that bit higher.

I wondered then, looking uncertainly and unhappily into his eyes which had grown misty, what was in his mind as he asked it, just where he was at that moment in the history which we share together and which stretches out now behind us, whether for instance he even realized that the piano he was asking me to play was my old Bechstein. For it was he who was the mystery buyer that day at the Stoneham sale.

I was moving from the doorway towards the bed that day I arrived when it caught my eye in the bay window. I stopped, just for a second, caught by the thing, surprised and unamazed at the same time.

When I turned my eyes back to his they were staring at me steadily from the bed.

'I kept it for you Joanie,' he said.

'You won't refuse it this time will you Joanie?'

'Play something for me Joanie,' he said. And so in the end this afternoon I got up and walked over to the piano with nervous sweating steps, feeling Donald's fear behind me, wanting to make it work for Richard, wanting to keep any charade that was necessary, wanting to pretend, wherever he was at that moment, that I was with him there too.

I sat down at it slowly, lifted the lid and laid my fingers on the keys with a feeling of doom. As they touched them though, I felt a strange tingle of recognition, the sort you might get at a handshake or an embrace from an old long-lost friend. I looked down at them for a moment stretched out on the keys, which is when it happened, a small miracle, a memory from long ago taking over so that I watched, disconnected in amazement, as my fingers, like

Sparky's from that old kids' record, began to wander over the keys.

Where it came from I still don't know. A gift from the gods I guess, Chopin, a nocturne, the E Flat Major, the piece I played for my last piano exam, well practised in the old days and lodged somewhere in the deepest recesses of my brain which is why I guess it was the one which came back to me.

As I stumbled my way through it, wincing over the mistakes, I felt more nervous, more tested than I did in front of that examiner thirty years before. When I'd finished, I laid my hands in my lap just like then, not daring to look at Donald, waiting fearfully to be found out by Richard.

But he only yawned on the pillow.

'Lovely,' he said.

His eyes were already drooping and satisfied and he swallowed on the edge of sleep.

'But you're right. You have got a bit rusty Joanie.'

The E Flat Major. The great nocturne to my mind. It was just about the only classical piece, mutinous as I was, that I enjoyed playing. It was the only one I put back into my satchel that day when I tossed the rest of them into the rubbish bin.

I liked it because it seemed so modern, because it came the nearest to the music that I wanted to play. It always seemed like a song waiting for words. It still does.

One day as I was playing it not long before the exam, I caught a movement out of the corner of my eye.

It was Didi. She'd crept in through the French windows and now she had her arms raised above her head, a six-year-old, hair stuck out in stiff bunches, plump and un-gainly and standing on her toes. On her face though was an expression of absolute happiness. Her podgy feet turned with surprising grace in time to the music. As she lifted a leg, the pleats on her cheap little skirt fell away and for a moment she balanced, caught in her own concentration. Then she sank down. A small swan. Dying.

And what did I do? Did I play on for her? No. I went to the door and called out in the voice that I had learnt from my father, 'Joyce. Could you *please* remove Didi from the study. She's interfering with my practice.'

It was a few days later when I heard them arguing, Joyce and my father. I was passing their bedroom door on the way to the bathroom and I heard every word. I heard her pearls drop on to the little tray on her dressing table which along with its glass pots and silver brushes was pretty much all she brought with her to her marriage by way of a dowry.

'Please . . .' she was saying. 'Please. Didi wants so much to learn.'

My father made the harsh thin tching sound through his teeth that he made when he was annoyed.

'And where do you propose,' he said, 'I find the money for ballet lessons?'

I heard the wardrobe door go now, and I guessed she was hanging her dress up and must be standing there in her underwear. The thought made me shiver. Still does. Her voice was gentle. It attempted to be persuasive. It said it knew the difficulty of the task in hand, but despite this was determined to appeal to his better nature.

'But Joanie has her piano lessons . . .' she began, but my father broke in harshly.

'Don't call her that,' he said. 'How many times do I have to tell you? Her name is Joan.'

I heard her pick up her hairbrush, heard the sound of it on her scalp. She seemed to be waiting, as if this was what she had learnt over the years, to let his anger settle like this.

'Please Maurice,' she said eventually, softly. 'It's important to me.'

'You want Diana to have ballet lessons,' he said, 'you pay for them.'

And now the wardrobe door went on his side. I imagined him turning to face her.

'She's your child after all,' he said.

I never noticed Joyce dying. But then I never noticed Joyce living. She just seemed to fade more and more into the background.

'Where's Joyce?' I would say, swinging in on one of my sparring trips over to see my father, but he would just shrug.

Often I never saw Didi either but I'd feel her, a presence in the house. I'd know that she was upstairs listening to us, my father and me, laughing. For it became something of a challenge to me in my later years to try to drag from him one of the harsh little barks that had so little to do with laughter. Later, as I drove away, I'd see her face staring out from an upstairs window, fixed and flat and full of longing, but full too of a proud refusal to raise a hand in farewell.

Didi was sixteen when Joyce died. She stood rigid as a tent-pole by the grave-side in her school uniform, staring fixedly ahead and refusing to cry.

Joyce had been popular and the funeral was crowded with people from the town. Afterwards my father stood at the lych-gate receiving condolences with a weary pompous showmanship.

'You old humbug,' I said, leaning into him, murmuring in his ear. For over the years, as I had grown older, become an adult myself, so this rough half-bantering honesty had grown up between us, the nearest we got to affection.

There was no funeral tea afterwards for the mourners at the house. Instead it was just my father and I who retired, a couple of cool retarded human beings, taking sherry together in his study.

Something, though, some mood to do with the strange honesty that had come to surround us, had affected me during the day. It lay there in the darkening study.

'Did you ever really love her?' I said, staring into my sherry glass. He sat at his desk determined to prove it was just another day.

'Love,' he said. 'A meaningless word. A word for pop songs.' The old 'p' popped in contempt.

'Or my mother?' I said. 'Did you love her?'

'I really can't remember,' he said. The voice was dry, dusty and uninterested. Which is when it came to me, and to this day I'm not sure I quite know why or how.

'You're gay aren't you?' I said.

It amazes me now that I said it so calmly. I wasn't straight of course. I'd always found that a hit before seeing my father helped the relationship. And I don't know what I expected by way of a reply. Outrage I guess. I thought his eyes might blaze, that he might leap up shouting from the desk. His lips merely curled in disgust, though, pedant to the last, at the perversion of the word.

'Gay . . .' he said, with his bitter little bark.

'When was I ever *gay*?' he said.

And that was it. The great moment of truth past and gone. For that was what it was, I'm sure. He never chose to deny it.

Later I said, not unkindly, seeking to let him off the hook, 'You must have been horrified to get a daughter.' He was pouring me out a second glass of sherry without asking, another of the little ceremonies which passed for intimacy between us.

'It was not the fulfilment of my wildest dreams,' he said with his thin sardonic smile.

'And not once,' I said. 'But twice . . .'

He took a long sip from his own sherry, walked back steadily to his desk. I see now, old ham that he was, that he was measuring the moment. He even sat down, flipping his jacket up at the back, taking his time, arranging himself carefully lest anyone should think he was in a hurry with what he had to say.

'That child is not my daughter,' he said.

'I agreed,' he said. He said it grandly, as though he should be judged magnanimous. 'It was what she wanted.' He kept his voice purposefully dull and uninterested, continued the old trick of shuffling his papers.

'She used her own money, arranged it herself. I had nothing to do with it. She went off one day on the train. Some place in London. Great Portland Place I believe.' His old man's face creased up with a child's look of pride at his own cleverness, at the preservation of the futile little detail. I turned away, ashamed of my own cheap complicity in his mockery.

It came back to me then, the memory, like a snapshot, myself as a child, crossing the hall, eleven I must have been, hearing the raised voices behind his study door.

'. . . or I shall leave you Maurice I promise you that.'

I remember how her voice stopped me in my tracks, because I had never heard her speak that way before. It was hard and angry and cold, quite as hard and angry and cold as anything I had heard from my father.

'And you will miss me Maurice,' it continued. 'Do not forget that.' It took a tone as mocking as his own.

'You will miss me cooking and cleaning for you Maurice.'

'So . . . who . . .?' I said, still heavy with my own shame, to my father. But he just went on rustling his papers.

'I really haven't the least idea,' he said, affecting the especially bored voice he brought out to show that a subject was at an end. 'Neither had Joyce I understand. Probably an out-of-work actor or an impoverished *clergy-*

man.' He looked up now, pleased at the thought. His voice rolled with disgust over the word.

'I gather those were the sort of *people* who did it.'

And that was when I heard what sounded like a movement outside the door. I got up and walked over and opened it but there was no one there. I called out Didi's name but it just echoed emptily around the hall. Upstairs though I heard the click of a door.

Walking up the stairs slowly, taking each tread respectfully at a time, memories jumping out at me like the ghosts and screaming skulls in an amusement park haunted house. Outside Didi's bedroom door I tapped, for the first time in my life, deferentially.

There was an imperious ring to the 'Come in.' When I entered, she was sitting dry-eyed on the bed, cross-legged and posed as if ready to receive visitors. She was still in her school uniform, cheap blouse and skirt that made her look lumpy. Her hair was still wild and wiry, but her eyes were cool and superior and empty, challenging me to ask if she had heard.

'Uh ... Didi ...' I began uncertainly, not sure what to say. But it didn't matter because she didn't let me finish.

'I want to leave here,' she said. Her face was absolutely flat as she said it, the way she would be, I would find, when it was necessary to do something she despised but which she knew had to be done.

'Talk to him,' she said. 'Tell him you're taking me with you.'

She looked at me with such imperious scorn when I said, 'Perhaps he won't let you come with me.' Her eyes said I must be a fool or else a thousand years younger than her.

'Of course he'll let me come,' she said. 'He despises me.' There was not even any malice in her voice, just a harsh flat acceptance.

161

My father, though, put up a fight.

'Absolutely not,' he said.

'I don't believe this,' I said. 'You don't even like her. You've told me that. You say she isn't even your daughter.'

'I need someone here,' he said, head bent over his desk. 'To look after me.' I shook my head in wonder at his selfishness.

'I'll get you a housekeeper,' I said, 'someone to come in every day.' He didn't bother looking up.

'Very well,' he said.

There was just a small case on Didi's bed when I went upstairs to fetch her.

'Is that all?' I said. 'What about all your clothes?'

'I have no clothes,' she said. It was true too. I went to the wardrobe and opened it up but all that was there was a couple of crumpled old dresses.

'But I sent you money,' I said, 'you and Joyce. Every month.'

She smiled her chill little smile.

'I saved it,' she said. 'Apart from what I spent on my dancing lessons.'

I sent Didi, at her own request, to a school which she chose herself several hundred miles away.

'I want somewhere I can board,' she said.

Towards the end of her first year they sent me an invitation to Speech Day.

'I'll come up Didi,' I told her on the phone.

'There's no need,' she answered politely.

For her seventeenth birthday I gave her a car, a Mini, the one I still have today. I also gave her a party.

I was surprised when McGarvey turned up. McGarvey never came to my parties.

'Actually I came to see Didi,' he said.

162

Later, fighting down my displeasure, I tried to throw an affectionate arm around Didi's shoulders.

'McGarvey tells me you've been writing songs,' I said. 'He tells me you've sent him a tape.'

Her hair was no longer dark now and wiry. Now it was bleached and short and there were pins and things in her ears. Her dress, a strange thing that she'd chosen herself, was all rips and zips and fell off the shoulder.

'That's right,' she said coolly.

Later, when most people had gone and there was just the hard core of liggers left in the library, I said, 'Let's hear your tape Didi.'

She blushed crimson, hissed at me, 'Not now.' But I wouldn't have it.

'No, no,' I said. 'Come on. I'm sure we'd all love to hear.'

And so I put her tape on, one of the worst things you can do, one human being to another. I made them all stop talking, sit there dutifully and listen while Didi sat on the sofa smoking and chewing her fingernails. Several times she jumped up, tried to press the stop button, but each time I forestalled her.

'No, no we want to hear it *all* Didi,' I said.

When finally we were alone and the last of them had left she forced herself to ask the question.

'What did you think?' she said.

If the cock crowed in the Cococabana, it fell off its perch weeping now.

'It's *fun* Didi,' I said.

It wasn't true. It was rough, what else could it be, put together on a tape recorder with a few friends from school? But it was a hell of a lot better than *fun*.

If it hadn't been, I wouldn't have done what I did, which was to try to take her hand, go into my patronizing routine.

'It's a tough business Didi . . . you have to realize you need something special . . . it wouldn't do to get too excited . . .'

163

The eyes that had looked up at me for that moment naked with hope were dull now and disappointed.

'Perhaps the best thing would be to concentrate on your exams for now Didi,' I said.

'McGarvey thinks it's good,' she said, staring straight ahead. 'He says he's really interested.'

'Oh, McGarvey,' I said dismissively.

'What do you mean?'

'Well darling McGarvey would say that wouldn't he?'

It pierces me still, the memory of that *darling*.

'I mean you are my sister after all.'

'No.' The word shocked me it was said so forcibly. Her eyes when I turned dared me to make the next move. For a moment we stared at each other.

'No?'

She'd regained herself by now. She was back in control. Her smile was as thin and cold as her eyes.

'Half-sister surely?' she said mockingly.

Sound check and run through
Same old routine
One two and one two
Where the hell have you been . . .

There's a point in Mikhael's movie, perhaps you remember it, a sound check where everything's going wrong.

I arrive late and Richard's fuming.

'Well thanks for coming Joanie. I mean we've only waited two hours . . .'

'Leave it Richard. She's here now.' Kent trying to make peace.

Because I'm out of my brain. It's all he could do to dig me out of my pit. To prove it I trip over on the way to the piano. And that's when I see Mikhael and start swearing.

In the end I turn on Richard. 'We're living our fucking lives out on this thing. Can't you see it?'

I figure now that just about sums up the difference between Didi and me. I always hated cameras, they never liked me, whereas the opposite is true of Didi.

They say Didi doesn't want to live off camera. They say that's the essence of what she is. And I don't pretend to know why she prefers it, this celluloid between her and the world. Except perhaps in some way it's easier for her. Perhaps in the end, pretending to show all she is, she shows nothing so that we're the ones in the end who are fooled. Perhaps the core of her is there on the outside like one of those crazy bullet lifts in extravagant shopping malls. Didi's ego, shooting up and down like that on the outside, mocking us all as we stare in.

Didi brought in Mikhael to do her tour movie. I saw some of it on TV a while back.

In Didi's movie there's a sound check too, only heads snap back, fingers twitch as Didi arrives.

She does her stuff, goes through her paces, but then things start to go wrong. She can't hear herself, there's something wrong with the monitor mix. She storms up to the front, eyes flashing. 'What's happening?' she says.

You can feel the tension from the other side of the TV screen, the tremor of ancient heads rolling.

She's looking about her now, side of stage, out into the darkness. Nothing moves. No one wants to be the one in the wrong. And so she stands there, hands on hips, foot tapping.

'I am *waiting*,' she says finally, icily, into the silence.

What Didi does is less a concert than an extravaganza. A stage twice the size of an aircraft hangar. It takes a convoy of trucks to carry it there, a crew of three hundred to put it up.

For the finale Didi descends the flight of stairs decked out in silver, trailing her troupe of dancers behind her.

165

Astarte. Queen of Heaven. Something coming full circle.

I'm proud of her if you want to know.

———

III

Delay below us we must wait
Memo to me I must get straight
I find it hard to walk a straight line
As we cross another date line
I'm drunk on altitude
Brandy and airline food
They say my attitude is wrong . . .

As I lay in the middle of the great hall at Stoneham, on that last day, neither sad nor happy but in that limbo of feeling, lying on the sofa which was pretty much all that was left, with the handful of packing cases scattered around and the rain spattering against the windows and the tapestry mocking me from the gallery, telling me it had been there for three hundred years and asking me if I thought *I* of all people should be the one to disturb it. As I lay there surrounded by all the lost loveliness, it seemed to me that I had been there before, that somehow I knew the scene. But when I struggled with the idea, tried to pin it down, it slipped away somewhere around the sides, sticking its grinning head out, like a kid playing behind a wall, ducking back the moment I turned. So that in the end the van driver came in, coughing politely at the door, saying, 'Stuff in here now is it miss . . .?' and I nodded and swung my feet off, and lost for anything else to do, wandered aimlessly around the place, grimacing one last time with the ancestors, touching the tapestry, taking one last look at the view from my bedroom window, the lawns down to the lake with the fairy lights still tinkling, drew a hand along the marble surround of the bathroom, looked in the mirror one last time with the long flat dull look of one who knows they no longer have to check for a smut of coke. And then I said, 'Well . . .' to my reflection, which was the only thing it seemed like I had to say, and I came back down the stairs and walked out of the front door and clambered into the Mini and watched as one of the removal men pulled the door closed for the last time, and I turned the keys in the ignition and revved up the engine and started down the drive, not even looking back, for all the world like it was just another day, like I

169

was going out for a while. For all the world like I wasn't leaving Stoneham for ever.

And I forgot about the feeling I'd had, that image of myself lying there in the middle of the great hall, and never thought about it again, not for ten years, till now. Till scribbling here in the window, with Richard sleeping and the voice soaring softly beside the bed, which is when it came to me, the covered portraits, the packing cases, Violetta, dying, centre stage, on the bed.

Of course. *Traviata*.

We had a visitor today.

When her car drew up the press jerked to attention on the railings where they had been lounging like collapsed puppets. They swarmed about her car as they do now about every car that pulls up outside the house. Only this time they fell back instinctively, deferentially, when they saw who it was inside.

Her chauffeur was young and tall and haughty, the sort of young man who once would have delighted Richard's heart. His uniform was dark, perfectly fitting with tight jodhpurs and a jacket with many buttons and epaulettes and a peaked cap pulled down low over his face.

He opened the door as if the reporters milling about him did not exist. As one tiny foot felt its way out of the darkness on to the pavement, he extended a crooked arm in a formal movement that seemed to belong to another century. A gloved hand appeared with a bracelet falling over it with many diamonds and then an arm. It laid itself flat upon the chauffeur's arm with a calm assurance, and then the grand lacquered head appeared, swathed in its veiling, and the grand echo-chamber of the bosom. As she steadied herself on the pavement, drew herself up to her full tiny height, so the peaked cap dipped and the heels met in the smallest suggestion of a click.

170

In the hall, muffled by the fur despite the warmth, she raised the netting across her face majestically. Beneath it the skin was strange and flat and ageless, painted like an Old Master in rich colours, grand and dignified but still soft.

As I watched from above, she laid a motherly hand on Donald's cheek. She pulled his face to hers, murmuring softly in Italian. When he drew back, eventually, there were tears upon his cheeks which she stroked away with her gloved thumb.

'*Coraggio* . . .' she said sternly.

And so, together, they mounted the stairs, slowly, she leaning upon Donald's arm, placing her tiny feet carefully upon each step. As Donald pushed open the door to Richard's bedroom, her own voice from the stereo swirled out into the hall.

'*Cara*,' I heard in a merry voice summoned with who can know what effort from the bed.

'You see how I was waiting for you.'

They play her records all the time. It is the only music that Richard will allow in his room.

I have seen them remain, an hour at a time, listening as it plays, holding hands in silence, Richard against the pillows, Donald beside him by the bed.

Sometimes at the end of *Traviata* or *Bohème* or *Butterfly*, there are tears on Donald's cheeks but never on Richard's. Sometimes, though, the tight angry look which lurks all the time behind the archness and the camp theatricality and the mockery which he summons up for himself or for us, I'm not sure which, sometimes this look disappears. Once I even saw him lift Donald's hand as they listened, and carry it slowly to his lips in a gesture that laughed at himself and was wry but also tender. And I saw then how fitting it all was, how death needed this flamboyance and grandeur.

'Catharsis Joan,' as my father used to say. 'From the Greek Joan.'

Katharsis. The core of tragedy. Passion. And pity. And fear. And I see why only the divas will do for Richard now.

'And this is where I thought we'd bring in the opera singer . . .' I remember the studied casualness with which Richard said it, not looking at Kent or me.

'*We . . . opera singer . . .*' I shook my head in disbelief.

'Oh yeah,' he said. 'And I've had a great idea for the video . . .'

What will you remember him as? The Emperor Napoleon? The mad Sun King? The Phantom of the Opera? Will you see him as Dracula or Frankenstein or the Man in the Iron Mask? Will he always be a gangster to you or a naked Greek god? Or a housewife? Or a hooker? Or Hamlet with a skull in his hand?

Richard took from everywhere for his videos. From everyone. From Warhol, Wells, Fritz Lang. From Cocteau of course and Busby Berkeley. From Eisenstein, Dali, Diaghilev.

Trains ran for Richard, armies marched. Whole towns grew up in aircraft hangars. And in the middle, Richard, like Prospero conducting the storm.

I hated making the videos from the first. They were Richard's thing not mine. They were his outlet for the flamboyance and the theatricality which were always too extravagant for pure rock and roll. But I wasn't Didi and I wasn't Richard. The camera never loved me.

'Listen Joanie,' Richard used to say when I complained. 'The video's as important as the song now . . .' And that was just another reason I hated them.

172

When he made me do some damn fool thing I didn't want to do I'd scream at him, 'I'm a songwriter Richard, not a fucking actress.'

Making the videos shot my coke consumption up considerably. I'd sit in the caravan provided doing line after line, Leon with me in the early days for he hated it too. We'd stare out bitching and belligerent at the phantasmagorical set that Richard had dreamed up, watching the dozens of people we didn't know and didn't like doing things we didn't understand, wheeling lights about and cameras, walking around with clipboards in their hands.

It was worse after Leon was dead because then there was just me in the caravan. Sitting there one day while the extras milled outside for the video for the fourth album, I stared miserably down into my hands.

'I'm not saying you're not clever Richard,' I said, 'you may even be a genius, but . . . well . . . it's not what I want, that's all.'

It was a weird way to hold a conversation, I remember. We were in costume and waiting to go on. I was a man, painted-on moustache and evening suit. He was a woman, perfectly made up and truly stunning in fish-tailed evening dress, his glossy hair pinned up on his head.

He licked his lips, looking at himself in the mirror, tucked away a stray curl.

'You're sticking so much of that stuff up your nose you don't know what you do want Joanie,' he said.

But even the small army of extras couldn't do it for that ill-fated fourth album. Following that old Rock Gold was always going to be an impossible task, especially with Steve gone as well as Leon. We should have thrown in our hands then, quit when we were ahead. It was Richard who insisted we could keep going.

'We'll draft in session men,' he said. 'It's all we need.' He looked at me sternly.

'I've told you before,' he said, 'it's the video anyway that's important now.'

And so things got worse. We were going in different directions, and if I hadn't already known it there were plenty of people around more than willing to tell me.

'I mean for God's sake . . . you'd think it was his band. He's turning into a real prima donna Joanie.'

Ah yes. Your special friends, the ones who drink your drink and snort your coke and take you by the hand to lead you up that high mountain to show you the future laid out before you. Tell you all the things you want to hear.

'And his stuff Joanie . . . I mean for God's sake it's crap. It's just not a patch on yours.'

And once you've seen that vision, believe me, it won't go away. It's fixed for ever in your sights. You can slink back down the mountain if you like but it won't matter, it won't make any difference, because it's too late, you've opened Pandora's box, taken a bite of the apple, and it'll always be there now, staring out at you in glorious technicolour, from the back of your head.

'And it's not as if he's the only one in the band with a decent voice Joanie . . .'

For all you can see now, whichever way you look, is that vista imprinted on your brain, the view from the mountain carved on your heart. A beautiful panorama. Empty. Nothing but YOU as far as the eye can see.

'Frankly I've thought for a long time you should do a solo album Joanie.'

The end came in the end like the big things of life always do, the ones you wait for and find are there, suddenly, taking you by surprise, so that it's all over before you realize it.

We were in Kent's studio, upstairs among the ancient beams, Kent and Richard and I, pretending to put down a

174

few ideas for the fourth album which I guess we pretty much knew, all three of us, wasn't going to make it.

Jenny was away this night and the au pair had called up asking Kent to come down to settle one of the twins who'd woken up after a nightmare, so Richard and I were alone. Around me as I sat on the floor waiting the walls glowed a deep misty melancholy yellow.

'It's not working Richard,' I said sadly, but as much to myself as to him.

He came over then, got down on his haunches in front of me, put his hands either side of my head and swept back my hair. It was a gesture of great tenderness but his voice was hard.

'What do you *want* Joanie?' he said.

And so, suddenly, out of nowhere that last great row was upon us.

'I don't know. But not what you want. Not all this pomp rock stuff . . . opera singers . . . videos . . . it's not my thing Richard.'

He got up abruptly, clicked his teeth, reached for the cigarette he smoked only occasionally and then badly. It was an argument we were having all the time now.

'We're going in different directions Richard and we both know it.'

He took a sharp puff of the long thin cigarette.

'There's only one direction you're going in Joanie,' he said, not looking at me.

It was true. I was having trouble holding it together by then. Not much had been done that day thanks to me. Still, Richard's sharpness fuelled the fire already burning inside.

'What I do is none of your business. Anyway it's under control . . .'

'Oh *sure* . . .'

It was his tone that did it, superior, dismissive, like in some way he'd written me off.

'OK, so I'm doing more than I should. You want to

175

know why? I'll tell you why. Because I can't face playing your fucking muzak any more.'

He was bending over his bag by this time which was on a chair against the wall. As I said what I said, he straightened up slowly. He didn't turn, just stood there, the back tense beneath the shirt, a back that knew the moment had come.

'I won't even call them *songs*,' I said.

When he spoke it was to the wall.

'No one's ever suggested my stuff's as good as yours Joanie. But we wouldn't be using it if you'd come up with something.' But I'd scrambled to my feet now and was spoiling for the fight.

'But you see it's not that easy for me Richard. I'm not like you. I don't just cart a bag of riffs into the studio, let everyone fill in the spaces. I don't compose by numbers. I take my time Richard. I work on my stuff to get it right.'

And that was when he turned. He spoke slowly, softly, everything about him full of scorn.

'Oh yeah? And what are you *working* on now Joanie?'

He leaned back against the wall, his movements still slow, crossed his arms across his chest.

'I'll tell you what Joanie, why not try it my way for a change? Why not bring a little bag of riffs into the studio, see if there's anything there we can work on.'

'How fucking dare you.'

He shoved himself off the wall with a snort of derision.

'A bag of riffs? The state you're in? You should be so lucky?'

It was the last straw. I felt like he'd stripped me bare. I hated him so much in that moment I wanted to kill him.

'I write *songs* Richard. You don't even know what songs are. I don't write sound-tracks behind videos Richard, I write *songs*.'

But he'd hitched the straps of his bag over his shoulder and lifted his jacket. On the way past me he paused for a second.

Richard, my oldest friend, my brother, had eyes half an inch from mine.

'Did Joanie,' he said contemptuously.

'Correction. You *did* write songs Joanie.' And he was out of the door.

And after that it was all over bar the shouting but there was plenty of that, on my side at least, sucked up and savoured and spat out on all sides by the music press.

'Well, looks like I made the right decision,' I said, slapping *Melody Maker* down on the table. We were in a coffee shop around the corner from McGarvey's. Kent didn't look up from his cup.

'Read that shit,' I said. 'Seems like Richard wanted out too.'

Kent lifted it, cast his eye over it. It was a mild enough piece. Just Richard talking about his plans for the future.

Kent laid the paper down on the table-top again. He didn't look at me as he spoke.

'What would you know?' he said, his voice edged with bitterness. 'What would you know about what Richard wants? When did you ever take the time to find out what it was other people wanted?'

'That's not fair,' I said angrily. 'You knew it was all over, same as me. But it had to be me who did the dirty work and broke it all up because you wanted to go on playing Big Daddy and Father of the Band who holds it all together.' It was a nasty thing to say but still true and he acknowledged it, shaking his head ruefully.

'Yeah,' he said, sighing heavily, 'you're probably right.'

He raised his head then and looked at me. 'So what are you going to do now Joanie?'

'A solo album,' I said. 'Will you play on it?'

'Of course,' he said.

'He says there,' I said, shoving the paper, 'you're playing for him.' But he just looked at me steadily.

'For him too,' he said. And he did too, through the years that followed till everything fell apart for me, playing for both of us, giving us both, man that he was, equal measure.

Later as I got up to go he said, 'So when do we start?'

'Not for a while,' I said. I raised my head triumphantly.

'First,' I said, 'I'm off on tour. With The Man.'

I opened the door once at Grace's to be greeted by the familiar quavery whine.

'Still whingeing on about the War huh,' I said, leaning over the back of the sofa. I know how much Rory hates this. 'Still if it works . . . hey . . . why fix it?'

Before me The Man sat on a chair at the front of the stage, bending over his guitar sharing all his pain, just the way I remembered him. As I watched he lowered his head purposefully to his harmonica. A soft adoring cheer came up from the fans as the notes began to wheeze slowly out.

'Really Rory,' I said, 'I think you have to ask serious questions about a man who can play a musical instrument for thirty years and still not get any better.'

The boys in the pool hall
say lonely's a crime
They say you can fool all
the people some time
If you can't understand it
then don't criticize
I'm in love with the lady
with the diamonds in her eyes

178

Yes I'm in luuuuuuv with the lady
With the diamonds in her eyes

'You know I wrote that for you Joanie,' he said one night about halfway through the tour. And then he began to sing it to me. *His own song. In bed.*

'I know,' I said shakily. 'Let's not tell anyone. Let's just keep it as our secret.'

Every story needs a fool, that's for sure. Shakespeare knew that. And when I try to figure out what part The Man plays in this tale then I guess it has to be that one. And when I think of him now that's how I see him, cap and bell and patchwork trousers. Which come to think of it is pretty much how The Man still dresses.

I figure that in everyone's career as a human being there has to be one person you're deeply embarrassed at having gone to bed with. I'd say you're ahead of the game if you can narrow it down to one. No prizes for guessing who it is in my life.

It pains me to admit it now but The Man was once a hero of mine, from the early days. Once, not long after Kent and I had met, when we were scouting around for gigs, we called in at the local folk club. There was a list on the door as we went in. 'Hey,' I said. 'What a swine. Look who we missed last week.' But Kent only grunted. Kent was never a fan of The Man.

But as for me. Well. I had Kerouac in my pocket and when The Man sang about the road, and The Man always sang about the road, just like he always sang about getting high, well then I *understood*. I sat with him and Jack on the old broken-down river pier and I saw the long, long skies rolling over New Jersey and I wanted it, all that raw rolling land. I wanted the immensity of it, coming from this piss-small four-square island that I did. I wanted their space just like I wanted their rock and roll.

179

So it was just about the biggest thrill of my life when way back in the early days we did a couple of gigs supporting The Man. The Man's been up and he's been down more times than a yoyo, but he was up then and it was just cream on the cake when we ended up in bed together.

The Man's call asking me to play piano in his band was perfectly timed. While I was publicly sounding off about all the thrills and spills of going out on my own and how much I was looking forward to it, the truth was I was more than a little nervous so The Man's offer seemed like a neat interim measure. It also seemed like the sort of move I should be making. Being part of a good old-fashioned band again. And the good news is that the band was great. The bad news was The Man.

On the road with him I saw why he toured. All the time. I saw that he couldn't live without it, the adulation, there every night live in front of him, a shot in the arm along with his smack.

By a month into the tour I'd actually begun to hate his audiences, something that had never happened to me before. It wasn't just the adoration that you could feel heavy in the air like the scent of some left-over sixties joss stick. It wasn't the way they crowded at the front and shook their heads from side to side, their long hair just like his, it wasn't that they cheered every time a song mentioned getting high, and if you know The Man's stuff then you'll know too that most of his songs mention getting high. No, the worst part about it was that virtually all of the audience were men. Ninety per cent I reckon at least. And all there for Him. All desperately bonding if you understand me.

Because this audience *adored*, like no other, his every breath, his every weak joke, his every incoherent ramble which kept us waiting, sometimes up to ten minutes between numbers.

I'd stand there, hands folded behind the piano as he

180

postured as the Eternal Rebel, hating the way the hall fell into respectful silence for him as he banged on about Ireland or Red Indians or fluoride in the water, or, more often than not, about the deeply spiritual qualities of life as experienced on what he liked to describe as 'his spread' in Montana.

'This here's for a friend of mine,' he'd say in his fake Southern-boy voice. I mean hell's teeth, he's from Winnipeg after all. Then he'd turn round and look meaningfully at me and slug into those first dreary chords of 'Diamonds'.

> Go up to Montana
> For two days or three

Because by this time, you see, The Man had decided in a sort of Messiah-ish way that I was to be his Mary, the woman chosen to bear his child.

'Oh I don't *know*,' I said, overcome.

'Can I really be that worthy?'

Kent came to see us like the trouper he was at the London gig.

'Well,' I said glumly. 'One thing you have to say. It's a good band.'

'Oh it's a good band all right,' he said, and it was. Because by the time Kent came to see us, we'd been on the road several months and we were *tight*, I mean *tight*. And we were tight first of all because we were having a ball playing together. I was even cleaning up for it, getting my act back together. We were tight mainly though because we had to be. We had to get tight and stay tight just to keep ourselves awake as we dragged along to The Man's dreadful dirges.

Now I have to hold up my hands here and admit like

181

I've told you that I'd been a fan of The Man from the early days. And over the years, one way or another, I'd never really re-examined the myth. But it only took a couple of months on the road with him to show me in glorious technicolour the mistake I'd been making. In short an hour or so of playing his stuff every night taught me that while The Man had a way with melody, lyrically he was as mediocre as they come.

Let me tell you something about The Man. You know where he goes down best? Those tin trannie places, those rock and roll countries where the climate is hot but not so the spoken English, at least after they've dispensed with the formalities like 'You want young girl . . .?'

I noticed that once we hit Europe, particularly the sophisticated bilingual countries where English as a second language was pretty much as fluent as the native tongue, in short the nearer we got to the mother country, the smaller the audiences became. Now let me ask you. What does that tell you about The Man's lyrics?

Luckily for us The Man's main defining feature was his vanity which meant that he was too blind to see that the tighter the band got, the more the music exposed the banality of his lyrics. I figured he got his revenge every night though when he put us through that famous saga of 'William Smith and Pauline Jones'.

> *He said can I see you again*
> *She said yes and he said when*
> *They played the games young lovers do*
> *But this was different and they knew*
> *They could feel it in their bones*
> *William Smith and Pauline Jones*

*

182

Look, everyone has A Song. He can't be blamed for that. What I mean is everyone has a song that they have to sing, that they loathe doing, because it's a lousy second-rate thing that they didn't like when they wrote it and was only included on the album for lack of something else, but which afterwards went on to be a massive hit. This is something we accept, along with the fact that we're duty bound to sing it as part of the deal that we've signed with the Devil. And so we do sing it, dutifully, like a penance, prevailed upon and protesting. Which is the way The Man should have sung 'William Smith and Pauline Jones', embarrassed about it, losing it between a couple of other numbers, a token couple of verses to keep the fans happy. But he didn't. He didn't sing it like that at all. He sang it out loud and clear, all fourteen verses of it, every damn night.

What I'm trying to tell you is, he sang it because he *liked* it.

It did well for him, the song, of course. Bought a fine head of steers I'm sure for the spread in Montana. Is it steers they have in Montana? I don't know. I never did find out. It was a hit twice over, this tale of the two lovers torn apart by the Vietnam War, first when the war was on and then again on the soundtrack of all the Hollywood re-creations.

'For Christ's sake, I mean I'm a half-decent piano player. I'm not the best and I'm not the worst either, but I challenge anybody to do something interesting for fourteen fucking verses.' It was like this every night. Every night we'd get The Man out of the way, get a roadie to baby-sit him, feed him his smack and a groupie. Then we'd sit around on someone's bedroom floor bitching on about Smith and Jones.

Lennie, the bass man who'd lied shamelessly to The Man about loving his stuff to get the job, was the one who was easiest about it.

'Forget it,' he said, 'or look on it as the price we pay.'

'For what?' I said.

'For the pleasure of playing together,' he said, raising

his bottle in a toast. He was only twenty-three and on his first major tour.

Lennie had taken to chalking up the verses in the air behind The Man's back as we ploughed our way through the thing. One night he got himself off the hook by turning down his volume knob and mouthing and gesticulating wildly for a roadie, pretending his sound had gone. That was the night I bet him a thousand bucks he couldn't do the same for all of us by somehow persuading The Man to do the thing solo.

It was the next night, when he managed it, that I saw clearly for the first time the nature of The Man's vanity, how it was like a shield, hard, shellac, between him and the world. Because I couldn't believe when Lennie started in on what a brilliant song it was that The Man couldn't smell the scam.

'I mean that song man . . . I can't tell you . . . that song is our *history* man . . .'

For back at the hotel that night Lennie had worked his way through the scrum to The Man's side, while the rest of us were jammed in, lost in admiration, behind the sofa.

'For me man . . . I gotta tell you this man . . . that song is the *moment* do you know what I mean man . . . I mean that song is the *essence* . . . what I mean is for *me* personally . . . that song is where it all happens in the set man . . .'

I'm surprised now, telling the story, how bad I feel about it, even for The Man. I want to shrug the thing off but it's not easy. There's something sad beyond measure in the way his head kept nodding like the toucan in the old Guinness advert, over the top of the sofa, his voice slurred with the smack.

'You think so man . . . maybe you're right man . . .'

Lennie hit The Man where it hurt most, in his weakest spot, the vision he had of himself. A lesson for all of us.

'I watch their faces man . . . I see what you don't see . . . they don't want us man . . . it's you they want man . . . it's you they've come to hear . . . just The Man . . . The Man and his guitar and his harmonica . . .'

184

And it worked because the next night The Man took us aside, told us he was going to do the thing on his own and we all had to try to look disappointed. Behind his back as he shambled away Dis the drummer punched the air and mouthed a long screaming 'Yeeeeeeeeessss.'

Later that night I tried to hand over the thousand bucks to Lennie.

He pushed my hand away, put an arm around my waist.

'I got a better idea,' he said.

The last gig was New York, Lennie's home town. Relations hadn't been good between Didi and me so as a sort of peace gesture I flew her out for the party. She grimaced and raised a satirical eyebrow when I introduced her as 'my little sister'.

It was a night of some excess. I couldn't even if I wanted to fill in the details. End-of-tour parties are always like this, especially if something good has been going on in the band. I was feeling better than I'd felt for years. I was even writing again and we'd talked about getting together again for my album.

It must have been around five in the morning that I went looking for Lennie, which given the time probably means I wasn't intent on discussing things musical.

The door of Didi's bedroom leading off her suite was open a crack and I heard the sound of her tape coming out. I pushed it open a bit farther with a toe. The first thing I saw as I did it were Didi's eyes. They were wide open as if she'd been waiting. As I watched her, she arched her back and pouted her lips like she was doing it for a camera. Above her Lennie gave a last gasp and came.

We went on like that, just staring at each other, me arms crossed in the doorway, until at last Lennie rolled off and after some more gasping and blowing opened his eyes and saw me.

185

'Hey Joanie,' he said, with a grin that said he'd been caught and knew it. 'I was looking for you.'

'Yeah and I'll bet you looked really hard,' I said.

As I turned to go, there was a hard thump on my back which I recognized as a Winnipeg hello.

'Ah an orgy . . .' said The Man, amiably out of his brain and leering.

'C'mon Joanie,' he said grabbing my hand. 'Let's join.'

I slammed the door shut hard, almost catching his foot.

'Joanie . . .' he said, hopping with pain in the hotel corridor.

But it was all too much for me. I threw a wobbler, a wild one, then and there in the corridor. I told him all the things you might expect me to tell him, that his songs stank along with his playing and I made several inventive suggestions about what he might like to do with his harmonica.

I did it all on the run and at the top of my voice. As I stormed down the corridor, kicking the room service trays, he shambled alongside of me, smacked off his head but still amiable.

'C'mon Joanie . . . C'mon Joanie . . .' he kept saying blearily.

The place was full of businessmen on some sort of convention. We had to share a floor with them, not a wise thing for a rock band. Soon doors were opening and heads peering out, all of which enraged me even more.

'And what the fuck are you lot looking at?' I yelled.

I was fumbling for my key when The Man caught up with me. He tried to grab me but he was staggering and the shove I gave him knocked him off balance.

'But I wanna marry you Joanie,' he said, smiling vaguely, his voice slurred as he slid down the wall opposite. 'I want you to come to Montana.'

The heads poking out had recognized us by now and were beginning to look pretty interested. I turned the key in the lock and kicked the door open savagely before turning.

'I wouldn't go to Manchester with you let alone fucking Montana,' I said.

'Now ... did everybody get that?' I said, looking one last time down the corridor.

The last sound I heard as I slammed the door was a smack-filled sigh as he appealed to his fellow guests.

'And I wrote "Diamonds in Her Eyes" for her,' he said.

'You're only eighteen years old. You're far too young. You can't possibly expect me to say "Yes",' I said grandly to Didi the next day.

'Say what you like,' she said shrugging, 'but I'm staying anyway.'

When I went into her room answering that old imperious 'Come in', Lennie was gone but she was packed and ready to leave, her hands folded before her.

'You don't even know him,' I said. 'For heaven's sake. He's a musician. He has girls all the time.'

'That didn't seem to bother you,' she said.

I sat down on the bed, lit a cigarette with a shaking hand.

'I'd be worried about you,' I said. 'Here on your own.' She raised a contemptuous eyebrow.

'Worried about what?' she said. 'That I might get into trouble? That I might get into *drugs*?' It hit hard and I guess she knew it.

'So what do you want Didi?' I said, trying to stay calm. 'To enrol in a few trendy New York dance classes, hang out with a few alternative film makers? OK then. If that's what you want. We'll call it your finishing school shall we? Because you'll want me to pay won't you Didi?'

But she could play the game as well as me. She too was calm.

'Yes,' she said, her eyes staring into mine clear and unashamed. 'Yes I'll want you to pay. Till I get on my feet. Till I can pay you back. Which I will eventually. I'm getting a deal with McGarvey.'

It was a shock but I tried not to show it. I gave her one of my special grown-up if-that's-what-you-think-but-I-know-better-than-you-Didi smiles.

'Sure,' I said.

Like the Judas I'd learnt to be I walked over to her and put my arms around her. She strained to get away from me but I would not let her go.

'OK,' I said, hugging her, kissing her on the cheek. 'Do what you want. Enjoy yourself. But don't be disappointed if it doesn't work out.'

'Oh it'll work out,' she said.

The last time I saw The Man was at the festival the day my father died. He hung over me, pinning me against the side of the stage, the fringes of his suede jacket swinging.

'Poor old Joanie,' he said. 'Done all her best shit first. Now she got nowhere else to go.'

It was true. I was pretty much flat busted by then and everyone knew it. Still I shoved myself forward, jabbing at him, pushing him aside.

'As opposed to what?' I said coldly. 'Churning out the same old crap as you?'

In the trailer, before he went on, he held the syringe up in the air like a crucifix. Outside the crowd was already chanting his name.

'We who are about to die . . .' he said, saluting me.

I looked away not wanting to see but the mirror on the wall caught the reflection, the needle poking into the soft brown of the bruising, the blood curling back into the barrel like a feather.

Later, much later, when I went to get my stuff from the

trailer he was in there with a couple of girls, lying blank-eyed like them on a couch.

He was shaking and sweating so much by this time that he couldn't get a grip on his works. So his man was there to help him. The man to The Man.

He was shushing him tenderly, rolling up his sleeve.

Fixing it for him. His good and faithful servant.

'Well done,' I said.

One afternoon, in the height of the season, as Rene and I hurled from table to table and the coach trips stacked up at the door, a familiar voice squeaked my name.

'*Joanie* . . .?' it said.

I could hear the delight in the voice, the sweet satisfaction. I turned round to meet a pair of eyes bulging with revenge.

'Hello Molly,' I said, sighing.

Molly. Molly By Appointment. Queen Ligger Molly. Molly fucker of the famous, free-loader to the stars. I threw Molly out of one of my parties once.

'Thith ith Ruthell,' she said, in her little-girl lisp. 'Ruthell's in a band.'

'Thath nith,' I nearly said. 'The special by the way is fish pie.'

'I expect you're wondering what we're doing here,' Molly said, jerking her head at the pimpled pony tail next to her.

'Not really,' I said. 'Oh yeah, and the soup of the day is artichoke.' Molly though had already started to ramble.

'London was so hot . . . so dirty . . . so full of bloody tourists . . . you know how it gets . . . we thought we'd get away for the weekend.'

'Great,' I said. 'You want chips or salad with your pie?'

Later as I cleared away the plates she leaned conspiratorially across the table. 'We're staying here tonight,' she said, 'at the hotel. Up the road. Why don't you join us there Joanie?' When she looked up her eyes were wicked and shining.

'We've got a little something I'm sure would interest you Joanie.'

I slapped a hand on my forehead.

'Gee Molly,' I said. 'What a swine. The one night. But it's my car maintenance class.'

Her lips tried to smile but rippled instead like Charlie Brown.

'Oh well,' she said. 'Just an idea.'

At the door as she was leaving, she dropped a handful of pound coins ostentatiously into the saucer. She said, 'Well ... see you then Joanie,' and I said, 'Yeah, see you Molly,' and she turned and reached for the latch. As she lifted it she stopped like something had occurred to her. When she turned it was complete with brand-new smile.

'By the way Joanie,' she said, 'did you know that the Dentist was dead?'

Your world narrows when you get seriously into dope, that's the bitch of it. That's the cheat. The first time you drop a tab of acid and the world around you sings and comes out in colours, you think you've discovered the Tree of Knowledge. You quote Huxley and you think it's all about your reality expanding. And when you move on to coke and the world begins to zap and zing, you feel so good that you think you know why the whole thing is forbidden. And if later it begins to take a little more of that old stardust every time to get you back up there, well, you think, so what? These things happen in Eden. And it's a while before you begin noticing that the universe that seemed so spectacularly to have broadened out has shot into reverse all of a sudden, so that one day there you are, a heroine in some old horror film, strapped to the mill wheel, lost for a hero and watching the walls and the ceiling move in on you.

By then you're not going out any more. By then everything is just too much effort. By then your idea of a good time is a video you won't even remember and some mush from a jar you call food. Plates in restaurants become something to push your salad around on, places to stub out your fag. Because staring in the mirror at the You you always wanted to be, you divine one of the sweet mysteries of life, that meals are for other people, for lesser mortals, not for the likes of yourself who need only another cigarette, another glass of wine, another line of something to keep yourself alive.

And down there what you know although you don't say it is that given the necessity, you'd sell your grandmother to raise another toot. Still you go on mouthing the thing you're most proud of, your code, the commandments you cling to, the sum total of your rat-thin little moral universe, words of wisdom engraved on your heart.

'I never take dope from strangers,' you say.
'And never, ever, sleep with my dealer.'

News travels fast
When you're sleeping with your dealer
Word gets around when you make it with your man . . .

It does too. Around you the mob raises its own coke-eaten nose with the pleasure of it and sniffs the wind and turns its eyes up with the pleasure to the sky to look for Icarus on her way down.

'I mean I ask you . . . how low can you get?' Molly said.
'I mean fucking your *dealer* for Christ's sake.'

*

191

'Weird,' she said now, standing in the door of the café, holding up the flow and preventing a family of six from getting in.

'I mean is that weird or what? In the end he dies jumping off a bridge.'

I shook my head. Only a fool would think the Dentist would go the same way as his clients and Molly is of all things a fool.

The Dentist started his career with the Australian army. He stole his first drugs while still in training, taking advantage of the key to the dental hospital medicine cabinet.

He was from Melbourne but of old Irish stock, tall and wiry with red hair and a pale skin scattered with freckles. He lived in an apartment stretching over several floors on the top floor of a converted warehouse on the edge of the Thames, Jacob's Island Dickens called it once, Fagan's hang-out, 'filthiest and strangest of many localities in London'. Not any more though thanks to dockland redevelopment. Although sometimes staring out at night at the river from the Dentist's windows I'd think there was still something dark and Dickensian about the place.

It was a splendid conversion. The old windows were still there, vast things from ceiling to floor looking out on three sides to the river. The floors were polished wood, and brass-railed staircases curved up from level to level, so that altogether it had the look of an old ocean liner about it. In the corner, in the lounge area, set between two of the huge windows, there were a couple of original Lloyd Loom chairs beneath a bright yellow parasol, a souvenir of the Raj which Eduardo brought back for the Dentist from India. *House and Garden* were effusive about the place. They did a piece on it. They described the Dentist as a 'commodity dealer'.

It was Eduardo who took me along to the Dentist's Christmas party.

*

The Dentist's Christmas party was famous among those on his client list which was probably the most distinguished in London. I figured afterwards it was his idea of a joke.

He decorated the place with holly and mistletoe and candles so that it looked like the set for one of those squeaky-clean Christmas TV specials. You expected a bunch of toothpaste-smile chorus girls done up in skimpy Santa outfits to come high-kicking down the stairs, or better yet, Bing Crosby to appear singing 'White Christmas'. Now what a nice touch that would have been.

The parasol got pushed out for the tree at Christmas. It winked with lights and brightly coloured decorations and the tiny packages, wrapped and innocently bowed. The branches were touched with spray snow. I saw an MP once who briefly made the Cabinet blitzed and trying to snort the stuff off.

After dinner the Dentist would disappear, to reappear a short time later done up as Santa when he'd distribute the 'presents' from the tree.

'Your free gift,' he'd say, bowing in front of his guests. 'Having bought goods to the value of . . .'

Like I say, he liked a good joke, the Dentist.

Harold answered the door the first time I called round after the party to negotiate a serious purchase of my own. Harold was the Dentist's heavy, the runner who brought the coke to your door. The Dentist never dealt from home. He kept the coke in a series of deposit boxes in various banks, along with the bundles of pre-laundered cash. Another neat touch when I think about it.

Harold wore black leather and a lot of chains. He was a keep-fit fanatic with a fondness for sado-masochism. His most common accessory when he answered the door was a leash with the Dentist's two Dobermanns straining on the end of it. No one, to my certain knowledge, ever considered calling him 'Harry'.

The Dentist was in his gym when I arrived. His eyes

were closed and he was on a bench straining with a weight. Previously I'd thought him thin, almost scrawny. Stripped down to his vest and shorts, though, I saw that his body was like alabaster, honed and hard. I watched him from the doorway in the mirrored wall. The sweat ran down his chest and arms. It looked out of place, like it could never have come from him, the way it would look on a statue.

'I didn't know you worked out,' I said, laughing uncertainly when he opened his eyes and caught me looking. He got up lazily from the bench and reached for a towel.

'Well . . .' he said, draping it around his neck, 'I imagine there's a million things you don't know about me Joanie.'

Later he insisted on taking me around the place, showing me how to use the machines.

'You should have a gym installed in Stoneham,' he said.

I was sitting on a bench straining to drag down a bar to my chest. He sat down behind me on the bench pushing me forward with his hands on my waist. Reaching up either side he pulled down the bar with me but, as it rode back up, let go of it so that my arms were left, locked in the air. He stroked a hand thoughtfully and without insolence down my side.

'You have a good body,' he said, staring over my shoulder at me in the mirror. 'You should look after it.'

'Why?' I said.

'So you can do things,' he said.

'What things?' I said.

'Things,' he said remarkably softly, moving the hand to my neck.

We'd been together for several months when he said, 'I'm going away for a while.' I smiled the ironical smile that I kept for such occasions.

'Business?' I said.

194

'Business . . . and pleasure,' he said. 'Why don't you come?'

We flew first to Algiers where we stayed for a few days before clambering into an ancient Dakota which carried us across the mountains to an ancient oasis town in the middle of the desert.

I lay by the pool in the flashy tourist hotel or sipped cold drinks amongst the marble and the fountains. Outside in the palm-tree-lined street, camels and cars jostled for space among the markets and the cafés and the crowds of Arab tribesmen in their long robes and towering turbans.

I was staring at a camel train one day when I said, 'They look so supercilious.'

'It's because they know the hundredth name of Allah,' he said unsmiling. 'Man knows only ninety-nine.'

'You're a mine of information,' I said and he was.

Somewhere among the crowds and the cafés, the Dentist went about his business. What that business was I took care not to know. One morning though he woke me very early.

'You have to see the sun rise over the desert Joanie,' he said.

The air was so cold when I stepped out of the hotel it took my breath away. The first thing it hit was my nose. I'd taken a toot in the bathroom against the Dentist's advice before I came out. Now the inside began to burn like it was stuffed with dry ice.

Outside the hotel, the jeep was waiting for us. A driver, turbaned and in fatigues, clambered out.

'This is Mustafa,' said the Dentist. I got in the back shivering petulantly in my ski-jacket.

We must have driven for an hour or so. Around us the world was a moonscape of sand, smooth and flat and shifting. Occasionally the jeep would swerve as Mustafa missed a stone or a pothole. Sometimes we hit one and he swore lightly as the impact shuddered our bones.

We were parked on a rocky outcrop with the desert

spread out below us when they appeared with the first rays of the sun, a great train of them, supercilious to the last, stretching away and over the horizon.

'God,' I said. 'How many are there?' But the Dentist didn't answer, and when I turned round he was standing up in the jeep, the binoculars clamped to his eyes.

I thought the desert was plain yellow, or the day-glo orange of tinned peaches that I'd seen from the sky when we flew over it, until the sun rose like a fireball and the sand began to explode into a thousand shades of pink and purple and violet. The air too had become electric as the warmth from the sun fought it out with the bitter cold of the night. My body tingled as I got out of the jeep and walked to the edge of the cliff to watch them as they stepped out between two rocky bluffs, a thousand feet below us.

They were so stately, so full of dignity, their haunches swaying, the heavy packs slung across their humps lurching from side to side.

'I wonder what they're carrying?' I said, but he didn't answer, which is when it came to me, suddenly.

'You were expecting them,' I said, turning, amazed. But the Dentist wasn't listening.

He was still standing up in the jeep but the binoculars were on his chest now. Instead his hands were stretched wide on the top of the windscreen. The sun was shining on his dark glasses making stars of light. He lifted his face towards it.

'Ah, *Africa*,' he said.

We were clambering back into the jeep when there was a movement from the rocks behind us. A donkey appeared and then several more and after that a young girl behind driving them.

Her head was covered with a brightly coloured veil that

wound about her face and her neck and her wrists clinked with beads. She could only have been about ten or eleven and yet she showed no sign of surprise or fear at the sight of us. Instead she stopped before Mustafa, hands folded gravely, and began speaking. He replied and together they conversed in a strange repetitious sing-song.

'What are they saying?' I asked the Dentist.

'Hello,' he said.

'Seems to take a long time in the desert,' I said.

Afterwards Mustafa translated it for me, this strange formal greeting.

Is it peace?

It is peace.

What have you heard?

Peace.

What have you seen?

Peace.

Peace. Peace.

Kallaha. Kallaha. Kallaha.

> *If you lie down with shit*
> *It's a shame isn't it*
> *What is this?*
> *Who can get an equal measure*
> *When you're mixing pleasure with business . . .*

And yet the truth is it wasn't hard at all mixing the two with the Dentist. There was a coldness about him that suited me well, a neutral non-judgmental quality. 'Do what you do,' it said. 'It's nobody business but yours.'

Testing his wares, he'd dip the tip of a finger in, place it on his tongue, lick it and frown like a connoisseur. But he didn't use the stuff himself. His trip lay elsewhere, heart-stopping chemical highs, hang-gliding, free-fall parachuting, the crazy bungee-jumping that killed him. And all this

197

paid for by the couch-potatoes he despised, people like me who preferred the easier earth-bound routes.

Once in one of those moods of self-pity and self-recrimination so familiar to the coke-head, I made the mistake of trying to accuse him of hypocrisy, of complicity in my crime of self-destruction. His face clouded with disgust.

'You want it,' he said coldly, 'you have it. You're an adult. It's your responsibility. Don't try laying that one at my door.'

He was right of course. During the time we were together he never even gave me a discount.

Basically he was just what he told *House and Garden* he was.

Basically he was a commodity dealer.

The only time I saw love on the Dentist's face was when he looked at the Zambesi. The only time I saw respect was when he clasped hands with Elias.

Elias was from Brooklyn. He cut his teeth on the rapids between Franklyn and Myrtle on the A train that runs through Bed–Stuy. By the time he got there the Zambesi was an old friend to Elias.

It was a roundabout route from Brooklyn to Zimbabwe and it included Vietnam, which is where in some bar in Saigon he bumped into the Dentist.

I liked Elias from the start, especially when he started laying into The Man.

'Like it ain't enough man we're stuck in some stinking hot jungle with a gook behind every tree waitin' to stick a bayonet up our asses, fightin' a war we don't give a fuck about 'cause we know win or lose it ain't gonna mean shit to us. All this ain't enough but we gotta hear that honky white-boy peace stuff from back home.'

Elias rowed the inflatable that took the tourists down

the rapids. He talked like a rapper before rapping had been invented.

'This here is your life jacket. Learn to love it, learn to fix it, one, two, three. This baby could save your life.'

The river was in full flood from the July rains when we got there. It rushed and sucked like it was after blood. Up front in the inflatable Elias gripped the oars and grinned at the tourists.

'Let's rock and roll,' he said.

One set of rapids they called Stairway to Heaven. We heard it rumbling a long way in the distance. It was just low at first but the nearer we got the more it began to roll like thunder. We'd already lost a couple of compadres by then. They'd gone over the side like rag-dolls beaching up on the rocks where they lay winded and gasping and waving feebly in the direction of the helicopter.

'Stairway to Heaven, gateway to Hell,' moaned Elias, closing his eyes as the halo of spray rose up behind him.

'Ooh, it's blaaaack down there,' he taunted. 'Two seconds gonna feel like your life.'

It was all tourist talk of course but it did it for me. There was no way I was going anywhere with a chance of my life passing before my eyes. I grabbed on to the side-ropes and held on for grim death as the prow of the boat hit the sky.

The dinghy wheeled and bucked then like it was in league with the river. Once it turned over and I was underneath. I survived though to fly back up again in what seemed like an arc. All the time the only thing in my ears was this deafening thunder of water.

The dinghy shuddered one last time like it was coming to a climax and then it was all over. When I dragged myself up I found just Elias and the Dentist and myself left in the boat. We were gliding in a gorge so spectacular it didn't seem real. The sides were sheer and so high that they cut out the sun. Everything was dark, in shadow, silent too. Way back I could still hear the rapids rushing, but here the water was like glass, pitch-black and so entirely still.

Elias rested on the oars, and the Dentist leaned back looking up at the sky. There was a flash of white from the end of the boat.

'Welcome to the cluuuub . . .' crooned Elias.

But there were other sets of rapids too that Elias didn't take the tourists on and these were the ones that the Dentist had come for.

'Is it dangerous?' I said

'It's a *ditch* . . .' Elias said, grinning.

'No, seriously?' But he just shrugged.

'You can get dragged under by a stopper . . .'

'A stopper . . .?'

'Standing wave. Drags a man under, holds him down.'

'Jesus . . .'

'Your boat can fold up on you so you can't kick free.'

He put a black finger out, wiped it slowly across my top lip.

'Everything's dangerous,' he said.

He held the finger up in the air, grinning, the black top of it tipped with white.

'Now this stuff's *really* dangerous,' he said.

The water was bubbling and foaming like it was getting ready for the fight as they set off in the canoes. I watched from the helicopter as they bounced off the rocks, twisted and turned like dancers. Most of the time you never even saw the canoes, just the froth of the foam around them. In the end you got used to seeing them smash against a rock, turn over and bob back up like some kid's toy in the bath-tub.

They were on the last set of rapids when the stopper caught the Dentist. It was all just like Elias described it. They'd gone over so many times between them but bobbed back up that I'd grown blasé looking down from the air. It took a while for me to realize that the Dentist wasn't turning back over again.

'Christ,' I said, noticing that the pilot was quietly, carefully beginning to drop the helicopter lower.

Elias was in front of the Dentist when he looked back and saw what had happened. He began turning the prow of the canoe, trying to inch back towards him. Muscles bulged in his face and his arms from the effort of the paddling but the flow was too strong for him.

I had the binoculars clamped to my eyes. The sweat ran down my face around them. My palms were sweating too and the small of my back and I was soaked with the stuff beneath my armpits.

'For fuck's sake what can we do?' I said wildly to the pilot.

It was a weird sensation, watching the thing in the glasses, seeing it all happen in front of you up close but being helpless to do anything about it.

Suddenly, though, everything was OK again. The Dentist was rolling back up. I stared at him resentfully through the binoculars for, soaked as he was and pale, still you could see that his eyes glowed and his face was shining.

He and Elias were slapping palm to palm below me as I took another hit in the helicopter.

'Good trip?' I said later, lying on the bed in the hotel room as he came in.

I said it sarcastically for the eyes and the face were still shining with satisfaction. He didn't rise, though, just threw himself down on the bed and put his head back with a sigh.

'The ultimate,' he said calmly.

In my experience, it's not a good idea when you're scrabbling around on your knees in the wreckage to try to

201

figure out how much it cost to get you there. Frankly I still don't know what I spent on dope during those years. I never managed to work it out, and my only consolation, if consolation it is, is that the people whose job it was to do it for me, the accountants, the Inland Revenue, never managed it either. What I do know is that eventually the coke bill at Stoneham dwarfed all the other bills put together, and those included the tally for food and drink and accommodation run up almost every weekend.

For the party season at Stoneham had continued unabated. And why not? By this time I needed all the fawning I could get. Because by this time I'd pretty much stopped working altogether. The solo album had sunk without trace and to make things worse I had to watch Richard's solo career going from strength to strength.

I was living on credit by now, not just financial credit either, which is bad enough, but that other sort of credit, creative credit, the sort fed and watered on past glories and by the lick-spittle and boot-licking that had brought down Leon.

The excuse for the party the night I threw Molly out was that it was the Dentist's birthday.

Stoneham's full of nooks and crannies, priest holes, little tunnels, that sort of thing. Behind the tapestry in the great hall there's a door with a small flight of steps that leads up to the next floor. The room it came out into then was the one I used as my bedroom.

When I lived there I kept it secret and locked. It gave me a useful quick exit when I needed a small private toot in a hurry. And that's just what I'd been doing when I opened the door to let myself back in and caught Molly's wicked little giggle.

'I mean when you're fucking your dealer you *know* it's the end . . .'

Pushing aside the tapestry and stepping out, I found

Molly with Annabelle, a scrubby female DJ who like herself was a regular at Stoneham. Their coke-bright lips drooped as I appeared and their eyes clouded over with fear.

'Molly . . .' I said, 'and Annabelle . . .' putting an arm around each of their shoulders.

'My friends . . .' I said.

It gave me a rich sense of pleasure to see the way their lips began to quiver back upwards with relief as they convinced themselves I had not heard. I kissed them both on their cheeks to prolong the agony and then I drew back.

'Drinking my champagne,' I said, grinning, flicking a fingernail at Molly's glass, 'snorting my coke,' and I waved a mocking admonitory finger in their faces. As I did it the small tight little smiles began to waver as their eyes remained fixed on my face.

My fingers clutching their shoulders were digging into the flesh now and I saw them wince with the pain. I gave them a smile of ground glass, looking from one to the other.

'The thing is, girls,' I said, drawing them into me, speaking softly, 'you have three minutes to get your nasty sycophantic little fannies out of here before I get Harold to set the dogs on you.'

They did too. I watched as their dope-thin legs and tight little skirts scurried out through the door and down the drive to their car, the Dobermanns snapping at their ankles.

Behind me as I watched, the Dentist threw a lazy arm about my shoulders.

'You know Joanie,' he said, 'I've been thinking for some time. You need someone to protect you from these people.'

*

He suggested we get married in the States.

'I have to go next week,' he said. 'We could mix business with pleasure.'

I proposed some crazy cowboy town. 'You know, where the sheriff still wears six guns.' I was entering into the spirit of the thing by then. I guess the idea was salvaging my pride for what had happened behind the tapestry.

I'd just had a fresh hit when I got so enthusiastic I announced it like a breathless teenager from the gallery.

'Listen everyone . . .' I said. Thirty seconds later, it couldn't have been any more, I felt a grip on my arm like steel.

'I have to talk to you Joanie,' said Kent.

He hadn't wanted to come to the party. He didn't care for my parties. He made excuses. Jenny was going to be away. He hated leaving the boys on their own, even with the au pair.

'But they're fourteen now,' I protested.

'You've got to leave them sometime.'

In the end he said he'd come for an hour. Now his head was down like some old bull charging.

I was laughing like the maniac I was as he propelled me through the crowd towards the study door. He kicked it open with an angry foot. Free-loading bodies draped over the sofa and on the floor.

'Get out,' he said and they did.

He grabbed my arms then, pinned them to my sides.

'Are you so far gone?' he said.

I wrestled free from him, lifted a cigarette from a box, my hand shaking.

'It's not what you think,' I said. 'It's not what people say. He has business interests actually.' But he cut me short with a contemptuous expletive.

'Don't treat me like a fool Joanie,' he said.

He sat down then on the sofa. I could see he was trying to stay calm. He did what he always did when he felt this way which was to pick at his fingers and chew them. He said, 'Sometimes I think I don't know you any more Joanie.'

'Perhaps you never did,' I said grandly.

He pushed the old hand through his hair. 'We go back a long way Joanie,' he said. It tore at my heart to see him. I began to bluster, unable to look him in the face. 'It's nothing . . . It's OK . . . It's under control . . .' but it was useless, he was up on his feet now and shouting it at me across the room.

'He's your *dealer* for Christ's sake Joanie.'

Which is when the door opened and he looked around sharply, his lips turned down in disgust.

'Well well . . . right on cue,' he said.

'Everything all right in here Joanie?' said the Dentist.

I don't know how long we stayed that way, carved in stone, or like characters caught in a spell. It was only seconds, a couple of lost heartbeats of life, no more. But it seemed like hours to me.

Before me Kent had his head up staring over at the Dentist. The look of disgust had turned to one of pure hatred. In return, the Dentist leaned lazily against the door, a careless air of triumph about him.

We might have stayed there all night if the phone hadn't chirruped suddenly on the table. I reached to pick it up, but the Dentist was there before me, striding across the room and snatching it up to his ear.

It was obvious that he'd been expecting the call. He turned his back with a curt acknowledgement to the person the other end.

'Business call is it Joanie?' Kent said sarcastically.

I took a step towards him because stoned as I was I knew I wanted to do something, lay my hand on his arm perhaps, show him I knew that everything he'd ever tried to do for me, he'd done out of affection. But I never got that far because in a sudden sharp movement,

205

surprising for his size, he was past me and had torn the phone from the Dentist. It flew in an arc through the air, flex curling like a snake, crashing against the skirting board with an empty plastic clatter.

They fell together then, rolling down the sofa like a couple locked in a violent embrace. A glass table crashed away beneath as they slipped to the floor, seething and punching and struggling.

Not surprisingly, the Dentist was getting the better of it. The hard lean body was uncoiling like a spring and blood was already running from Kent's mouth. I flung myself on them inexpertly, rapping my knuckles on their backs as they turned and twisted together.

As I was tearing at them, screaming at them to stop, a glancing blow from the Dentist hit the side of my face and all the bones beneath my right eye went on fire. The world began whirling with the shock and the pain but my fingers held on like they had a mind of their own to something that turned out to be Kent's shirt.

I could feel it tearing beneath my fingers, hear the sound of it, when suddenly I felt hands on my own back dragging me up roughly. For a moment my face was crushed against something dark and rough and unfamiliar before I felt myself pushed away like a puppet, reeling away towards the corner of the room.

As I crashed down, I saw something dark and round rolling towards me. I reached out for it, grasping it instinctively as the world went black around me.

Squeezing an eye open what seemed like days later, I was astonished to find myself holding on to a policeman's helmet.

Naturally I thought it was a raid. I remember the surprise when I looked up and saw that they were ignoring me and talking instead to Kent. One of them had laid a hand on his arm. He was saying something to him slowly, clearly, as if it was important, as if he needed to make himself understood. Kent meanwhile was shaking his head from side to side like a man who'd woken up to a world no longer familiar to him.

I remember now other things too, like the look on Francis's face as he stood behind the second policeman staring at Kent. It wasn't just fear, something worse, something terrible and *final*.

I remember too how they parted in the hall for Kent walking with a policeman on either side, how they moved back as if keen not to touch him, as if they thought they might become tainted in some way by the tragedy.

Still not fully comprehending, I ran after him, down the hall, through the trail of silence left like a wash in his wake.

'Kent,' I said, grabbing his arm on the doorstep, and he turned back to me.

His lip was bleeding and he was wiping it absent-mindedly on the cuff of his shirt which flapped in a torn triangle across his chest. He looked at me as though not sure who I was, his eyes empty. He shook his head as if in confusion and then was gone.

I stood on the steps watching the tail-lights of the police car as it made its way down the drive.

Then I dropped down shivering where I stood and started weeping.

There comes a time . . . when the past weighs so heavily that the only answer is to tear it up and start again . . .

The quotation seemed so much of the moment, so much to the purpose when I read it framed on the wall over Angus's mixing desk that I shook my head in wonder.

I was worried about seeing Angus again. No point in

pretending I wasn't. I hadn't seen him for twelve years after all. Not since Andrew's funeral.

I wouldn't have been there, at his studio, if it hadn't been for Richard. He'd been chivvying me again about holing myself up down in the country.

'Really, it's too stupid Joanie.'

Because I'm used to it now I didn't mind. I figure he uses it sometimes to get rid of the remaining anger and I can't mind that. So I just smiled and shrugged like I usually do, gave him all my non-committal replies.

It wasn't enough for him this time. He began to go on again about the waste. He was in the middle of it when suddenly he stopped dead, clicked his fingers.

'Of course. Should have thought of it before. Great idea. We'll re-form. A sort of anniversary album.'

It was the twin-track thing again, of course. Real time and imaginary time. Although which is which I'm not sure. Because for Donald, Richard's plans for the future are the real time, the time that counts.

'Hope . . . belief . . . you can't put a price on it. It doesn't come in a pill.'

He'll quote chapter and verse then, refusing to catch my eye.

'Given up for dead,' he will say, the loving zeal on his face.

'Still alive, five years later.'

So it's a rule of the house that we play along when Richard makes his plans for the future. Still, when he said that out of the blue about making an album I faltered.

'Well, I'm not sure Richard . . . I mean . . . after all these years . . . People would think we're crazy . . .'

'Phff . . .' He waved a hand. Blew through his teeth.

'Darling everybody's doing it. It's the only growth industry.'

He was up off the pillow now, shot through with the idea.

'Say you'll do it.'

'Um . . . well, I guess we could maybe . . . uh . . . try out a few things in the studio.'

At that moment the door opened and Donald and Kent came in. Their mouths fell open when they saw Richard up and leaning forward, directing operations from the bed.

'Donald fetch some champagne . . . we're celebrating . . . we're going to make an album again . . . Joanie's agreed . . . Kent we need to think about this . . . we want one of those new young buck producers . . .'

Even Donald was still frozen in surprise in the doorway as Richard snapped his fingers.

'Of course,' Richard said. 'Why didn't I think of it before? I mean it's obvious. He's hot at the moment. Just the sort of name that we want.

'We'll get Angus to produce the album.'

Richard wouldn't rest until we'd agreed to go and see Angus. 'No time to waste,' he said. 'We all know that.'

That's when we saw the peculiar nature of the thing, saw that he wasn't riding along on one track or the other, but instead was somewhere between the two, straddling both the real and imaginary time.

'I know what you're thinking,' he said, staring at us, forcing us to drop our eyes. 'You think I can't do it. You're humouring me.'

Donald was the first to recover himself.

'Of course we think you can do it Richard,' he said briskly. 'We *know* you can do it.' Perhaps he even believed it himself for he turned on us fiercely.

'You'll go and see Angus now won't you,' he said, 'the pair of you,' and we said 'Sure' and 'Absolutely' and backed out of the room uncertainly, unhappily, like children.

Going down the stairs Kent said, 'We have to go.

Angus would like to see you anyway,' and I said 'Sure' a little doubtfully.

We were threading our way in the Landrover around Hyde Park Corner a short while later when I got round to saying what I'd been wanting to say for a long time. Since the beginning in fact. Since he'd come for me at the café.

'Kent...' I said. 'What happened ... at Andrew's funeral...?

His smile tried hard to be kind. He even waved a dismissive hand. I was surprised though at the weariness in his voice.

There was silence for a while and I thought his attention was taken up with the traffic. But then he spoke again, and when he did his voice was fierce and so was his face as if something dark and impenetrable that had settled a long time ago on his soul had surfaced again suddenly.

'Did it all wrong Joanie,' he said.

I was shocked. Cut to the quick. That after what he had said I should find myself, despite everything, unforgiven.

'I'm sorry...' I began again, but he cut me short, rounding on me savagely.

'No, not you ... me.'

And so, as we edged through the traffic, he spoke haltingly, his voice hoarse with self-recrimination. He stared fixedly out through the windscreen, his knuckles white on the wheel.

'It was selfish I know that now ... losing myself like that in my own grief ... taking all those sessions and things ... when he was in so much pain himself and needing me ...'

I touched his arm. The sense of loss in his voice drove an arrow into my heart.

'They don't do night school in being a parent,' I said. It's what Grace says, all the time, when she does things wrong. He turned briefly, gave a sad grimacing smile.

'He blamed me of course ... for everything ... I understand that ... for Andrew's death ... naturally ...

210

and then for Jenny and I splitting up . . . He couldn't forgive me . . . for any of it.'

Angus stood next to Jenny at Andrew's funeral in his heavy spectacles and grown-up suit, his head held high by the graveside, staring straight ahead, determined not to cry. The way Didi did for Joyce. The way the experienced do cast out so suddenly from innocence.

It seems to me, looking back, that there was something grave and solemn and fearful about Andrew's death. Something awe-ful, in that proper sense of the word. Something almost Biblical. It reminds me of that story in the Old Testament. Abraham being told by God to sacrifice his son Isaac. Except for Kent there was no last-minute reprieve. No lamb caught by its horns in the thicket. Instead 240 volts shot up through a new Les Paul into Andrew's fourteen-year-old arm.

My son, God will provide a lamb . . .

Kent had given him the guitar for his birthday several weeks before, not because he was a spoilt rich kid but because his playing deserved it. That's how good, how much like his father Andrew had already become.

There was regret I'm sure in his mother's eyes when Andrew pulled the wrapping paper off at the table and some time later, probably that night as they were about to get into bed, for at this time such things happen between couples, they will have begun to argue.

'He spends far too much time in the studio. You shouldn't encourage him. He's falling behind in his schoolwork.'

It was all true. Angus was the studious one and Andrew the rebel. All Andrew cared about was music.

'He does what he wants to do.'

At the same time as he said it, being the man he is, he will have been ashamed of himself, knowing that he ought to take the criticism better, that he ought to agree with her, back her up. But how could he do that? How could a man who had sat side by side with his fourteen-year-old, heard him rip off a riff already that even he would be proud of, do that?

'I asked him where he got it,' he'd told me just that night, laughing to cover his pride at the party.

'"From you" he said.'

There in their bedroom together I can hear their argument growing more angry, she telling him he should talk to his son, tell him to work harder at school, otherwise he won't get into university, he biting the bullet, telling her the truth.

'But he doesn't want to go to university.'

And so Jenny will have said then all the things a parent should say. 'He doesn't know what he wants . . . how can he know . . . he has to be told what's best for him,' and when I hear her voice in my head something snaps closed. A fastener. A lock. And something else comes full circle.

And so, with the argument out in the open now, they will have turned to face each other, his old country-boy determination rising to the surface.

'But maybe university won't be best for him. Maybe he won't need it.'

'Don't do this to me Kent.'

'What?' But he knows of course.

'I don't want another one in the family.'

Understand me. I don't dislike Jenny. I look at all she is, all she said, and I don't even disagree with it. And I think she knew of all of us, sitting on that bale of hay, what was coming. Because she'd hated it all. Right from the beginning. She wanted Kent to stay a farmer. But she loved him and she married him. And while poorer might have turned to richer in some people's eyes, to her own mind better became worse.

'I hate it. I hate it all,' I heard her shout, a little drunk, unusual for her, when she'd been dragooned into one of my parties.

They were sitting in a corner, the pair of them, on spindly chairs. Later I overheard them still talking.

'I know it's difficult Jenny . . . when I'm away on tour

and everything . . . and I know things have been left to you . . . but you can come with me . . . I've always wanted that . . . I'd like you to come with me and later on the boys too when they're old enough . . .'

'*Are you mad?*' I remember the way her voice lashed out cold and full of fury.

'Honestly Kent,' she said, 'sometimes I wonder about you. I wonder what you see.'

I heard the angry scrape of her chair as she got up.

'Do you seriously think,' she said, 'I'd let any son of mine go on the road with *her* . . .?'

From Stoneham where I sat on the steps watching the lights of the police car disappear down the drive, they took him straight to the hospital. But because Andrew had been pronounced dead on arrival the body had already been transferred to the mortuary. He was standing there beside the steel trolley, holding Andrew's lifeless hand, stroking it and weeping, when Jenny walked in.

She wasn't crying though. In fact her face was entirely without expression. She clicked across the tiles to him on her high heels like the secretary she used to be. She looked businesslike. She might have had a file beneath her arm. She didn't even look down at the body. Just reached up and struck Kent hard across the mouth.

Everything was in the gesture and who could blame her? He hung his head and howled.

Jenny had been in London with Angus, staying overnight at the flat so that he could see some exhibition in the Science Museum. Kent was working on some stuff of mine, some scraps for the second solo album. Which, when you think about it, seems to make it worse.

Because Jenny was away, Kent was able to indulge himself, guiltily, like a man with a secret vice, allowing Andrew with him all day in the studio.

No one knows why Andrew went back into the studio that night after Kent had left for the party. Maybe it was to practise, maybe it was to lay down on tape the simple little four–four blues riff that he'd produced like an old hand for his father that afternoon.

The au pair found him on the studio floor when the lights fused and she went to investigate. She called the ambulance and Kent's father who ran all the way from the bungalow they'd had built across the yard, using what breath remained, fruitlessly, to try to breathe life into his grandson.

The verdict was 'accidental death' which it was, a simple accident, a small studio, too many wires, an effects unit running over a frayed cable. A simple accident, that most impossible of things to accept in a world where God is dead and science is supposed to guard against such eventualities.

He couldn't forgive himself, Kent. Who would? Who could?

At the church gate afterwards, with the grave-diggers already moving forward as the mourners filed away, he stood white and haggard with his outstretched hand.

'Thank you for coming,' he kept repeating. 'Thank you for coming.'

I have never felt pain in my life like I felt watching him. I was waiting at the end of the queue not wanting to talk to Richard who was up ahead of me. Seeing Kent's haggard face, I thought something inside of me would burst. I thought anything would have been easier, anything that could have happened to me in life rather than have to watch him as those people filed past him.

'Thank you for coming . . . thank you for coming . . .'

I wasn't used to pain. I disliked it. It was something, in the world in which I lived, with the things which were available to me, I considered unnecessary. Which is why in the end I turned around from the end of the queue and walked back up the church path and into the porch, murky now with shadows from the late afternoon sun, and took a quick toot.

I was sitting on the stone seat, breathing in deeply, laying my head back against the yellow crumbling wall, when suddenly he was there.

'Joanie?' he said, peering in.

I got up in the darkness, eyes sparkling and out of place, and went towards him.

I know now he must have needed what happened next and I don't begrudge him one second of it. I never will. As I approached him and the light fell on my face, his own went dark with anger.

'Oh *God*,' he said.

His face screwed up, became ugly, unrecognizable, the voice too. It was so full of disgust it raked down me, across my face, my chest, my heart.

'You couldn't do it could you?' he said. 'You couldn't do this one thing straight, not even for me? Not even for Andrew?'

And that was when the fury burst out of him. He pushed me hard on the chest, once, twice and then over and over again, yelling it at me as he pushed me, '. . . not even for me . . . not even for Andrew.' I staggered back with each push, the thumps on my chest almost winding me, till I could go no farther and I felt the studded oak door of the church at my back.

I was hysterical by then and crying. I turned, fumbling for the handle to get away from him, but it was locked for the vicar had long since departed, and so I was spread-eagled against it trying to get away from his wrath. By now though he was pummelling my back with his fists, tearing at me, my hair, my clothes, pulling my head back by my hair, shaking it and all the time howling out like a child.

'Couldn't you do it? Couldn't you do this one thing for me?'

I remember no tears like that, his tears, running down through my soul. I shook from them, my face pressed

215

against the door. They hurt so much I scarcely noticed the battering. The huge iron nails pressed into my forehead and hands as I was pushed against them. And all I could think of was that it was OK, that I wanted them, these tears. I wanted all his fury. I wanted to be crucified like this on the church door.

Then, all of a sudden, he was still. He was turning me round, his hands in my hair at the back, stroking it, his forehead against mine, murmuring faint and sorrowful apologies.

As he drew back, he traced the long third finger of his right hand hopelessly across my forehead, that third finger that bent all the beautiful blue notes on his guitar, that drew out all the pain and love and longing from it and which drew out mine now, touching the stigmata from the nail on my forehead.

His eyes were blank and lost and empty.

'No, of course you couldn't,' he said. His voice was dull. He shook his head and pulled me to him, burying his face in my shoulder. For a moment we stood there in the helpless embrace then he raised his head.

'No, of course you couldn't,' he said again, his voice full of the hopeless sorrow.

And I knew that I preferred his anger.

Relations pretty much broke down altogether between Kent and Angus after Andrew's death. For it was like Kent said. Angus blamed him for everything.

I guess that Angus must have felt like part of him had been lopped away when Andrew died, so close had the twin brothers been. And I think now, all these years on, that what must have frightened Angus most was that what had been lost might in some way be the better part of him, the Andrew part, the part most loved by his father. For he was always the quieter one was Angus, always the student. 'The Professor' we used to call him sometimes as a kid. And while I guess he was able to accept without rancour or jealousy while Andrew was alive the added dimension his brother's musical talent brought to his relationship with their father whom both of them adored, it must have been so much harder to accept after Andrew was gone.

I know this is what Kent thinks too.

'I've asked myself . . . a million times . . . I still do . . . was it true . . . was it right . . . what he shouted at me?'

We were edging through the Soho back-streets by then, searching for somewhere to park near Angus's flat. He frowned heavily at the memory.

'Even though I *know* I loved them both the same . . . treated them the same way . . . I swear to God . . . even though I know it's not possible . . . still I ask myself . . . did I even half think it . . . against my will . . . in my worst moment . . . somehow give him the idea . . .'

I never knew about the terrible scene in the studio until he told me this afternoon. Twelve years on the pain was still etched so much on his face that I turned away as we walked along the pavement together from the empty meter we had found.

It happened the day Jenny told Angus that she and Kent were separating, that the pair of them, she and Angus, would be leaving the farm and moving up to the London flat.

Kent was away the day she told him, away as he was so much of the time, snatching at any sessions offered him to try to get away from his sorrow.

As Kent told me the story, I could see it all in my head, Angus, this proud sorrowing fourteen-year-old, turning on his heel after his mother had told him the news, going up to his room, watching her through the window as she got into her car to go shopping, picking up the black refuse bag then with an angry shake hurling in all his records and

217

tapes. They found it later stuffed into the dustbin, a telling testament to what he felt about his father.

What he did next was a massacre, no more and no less. He was still smashing the things systematically as they stood resting innocent and undefended on their stands or against the walls when Kent, returning home unexpectedly and hearing the noise, ran into the studio.

Even as Kent ran in, Angus did not stop, just went on kicking the things, jumping on them, picking them up and hurling them by their necks against the walls. His father had to drag him off in the end, pin his arms behind his back, eyes blank, body twisting. And that was when Angus screamed it into his face.

'You'd rather I'd died wouldn't you? You'd rather I'd died than him.'

And so Kent did everything he could, said, 'No, no' over and over again, tried to hold Angus, hug him, but he only squirmed angrily away so that in the end it was his father who broke down, collapsing on the floor, head in his hands, crying.

Some of the world's finest guitars lay in pieces around him, collector's items, a Gibson dot-neck, a blond one, a Firebird Seven and the Gretsch White Falcon with the rhinestones in the head that he brought home, nestling it like a child on his knee, from that first happy tour of America. Only one concerned him, though, the Les Paul that he had given to Andrew for his birthday. It had become like an icon to him. I can see him now clutching what remained of its neck like a torn limb, wires splayed out and waving, nestling it, weeping as Angus stood staring down at him.

'Why?' he said, not even able to look up. 'Why?'

'Because I hate it,' Angus answered coldly.

He was absolutely quiet now. He stood staring down at Kent impassively, arms folded above him. It was as if a chill had settled upon him following the storm, entering his very soul and freezing it up.

'What?' said his father, the child now, his face wet from his tears. 'What exactly?'

Angus lifted his foot and kicked a piece of wreckage.

'This,' he said. It was the fingerboard of the old red Hofner, his father's first guitar.

'This,' said Angus, 'all this.'

There comes a time . . . when the past weighs so heavily the only answer is to tear it up and start again . . .

You can hear the sound of tearing on AOI tracks. You're supposed to . . . It's what it's all about. Scratch and mix. Beats and breaks. AOI, the hottest hardest dance beat on the street. AOI, for those who are serious about facing the music. AOI. The Arrival of Irony.

If you don't know AOI your kids will. You won't find any pictures though of Angus on anyone's bedroom wall. Anonymity is the essence. All your kids will know is the band. Except, there again, *band* could not be a more inappropriate term for this brainchild of Angus.

AOI, the name behind the biggest pop singles of the year. And last year. And the year before that. Purveyors of 'post-modern pop', or 'the new punk', or 'the anti-song', take your pick among the music writer's pretensions. For myself I prefer 'product, pure product' which is Angus's definition, the one he gives with the cool smile of the pop technocrat, the young man who has made it.

Product. The word that separates the two sides of the business, that falls like a dead hand on the heart of those it hurts, freezes them, reveals the truth. That in the end, to those whose job it is to sell them, the deepest stirrings of your heart are no different from soap powder.

'Product,' as McGarvey said to me not long before the end.

'It's product we need Joanie not words.'

219

But product holds no fears for Angus. Because Angus has beaten the business at its own game. For AOI is product and proud of it, one hundred and twenty beats a minute of it, which if you hate it, is the sound from hell and not a bad way either to describe it, this Dante's Inferno of the ear. It's the sound you hear pounding out of the XR3 driven by the young man you hope and pray your daughter will not marry, that speaks of drugs and dives and discos uncovering your deepest fears, the most serious of which is that you're getting old. Because when you hear it you want to say that thing your parents said, which you swore on your first single you'd never say, which is *You can't call that music*, which is right again, because it's isn't *music*. It's good and it's clever but it's something else, something bordering on music and so it needs another word. But then finding new words for things is something we've been good at since the caves.

AOI tracks have weird and witty titles. 'Ions in the Fire'. 'Penny Arcane'. 'Kitsch in Sync'. They're maelstroms of sound, stutterings and screamings, crazy laughter, choirs of new-age angels, whispering half-phrases you can never quite hear, and over it all the voice of the rapper throwing out the phrases which though nonsensical still jar with their unsettling juxtapositions.

> *When is life?*
> *Where is good?*
> *How is God?*

Oh yes. And something else. AOI's signature, its hallmark. Fragments of news broadcasts. Homelessness, joblessness, wars, famines and plagues. Hymn of a new generation.

The nightmare of today I read in a review framed on Angus's studio wall *contrasted with the wet-dream of yesteryear* . . .

220

'If I still call it a studio?' I said, shaking my head at Angus and at the VDUs and computers and the bank of gear I no longer even recognized.

He did his best to talk me through it. Loops and patches, TVFs, megabytes. He talked in that way the very bright do talk to those less mentally agile than themselves, looking for simpler words and limping through it, like a crack athlete tied to a round-the-block jogger in a three-legged race.

'Really,' he said, 'there's nothing complicated about it. All you're doing is reducing sound to basic visible units and then editing it on a screen just like you would words or graphics.'

'Is that all?' I said.

He gave the sampler a satisfied tap.

'Mozart would have one of these if he was alive today,' he said.

He looked up with an innocent smile.

'He'd want the same as me,' he said, 'music without musical instruments.'

It was a smile for his father with a barb in the back of it but learning to become affectionate.

'Music,' he said wickedly, 'without the irritating necessity of musicians.'

Music without musicians, made quickly and cheaply without concern for quality. The opposite, in short, of everything his father stood for. Some call it post-modern, others reparation. For, of course, it was our stuff, in particular his father's riffs, which Angus most enjoyed feeding into his mincing machine.

> *You've got power*
> *But your hour may be past. . . .*

221

Remember that one? It gave Angus one of his biggest hits, echoing out with a hollow ring from the middle of the inferno. He called the track 'Memphisaema' which I guess says it all.

Angus did not rebel against Kent. He did not even refuse to see him. He merely treated him for the next decade with a remoteness, with a dutiful politeness that forced further apart the rends and fissures of his father's already breaking heart. During that time, too, he did not trouble to hide from him the utter contempt in which he held his occupation.

For from the time that Angus dumped his tapes and albums into the dustbin, he would have nothing further to do with rock music. He would not listen to it. If it came on the radio or television, he would turn sharply and switch it off as if it offended his ears. The music he turned to was classical, Schoenberg and the like, or chill esoteric jazz.

It's the same stuff you'll find still in the apartment upstairs from the studio which he shares with Anna Lise. He was at university doing computer science when he met her. She was a post-grad, an exchange student, beautiful and as cool as him and with the same lofty intellect. Back home in Germany she'd worked part-time in a studio. One day, on a trip home to meet her parents, she took him into the place, showed him a sampler. And the rest, as they say, is history.

'Of course it's no fun any more now we have to pay for it. That's why we've wound the whole thing up. That's why I've started producing.'

The wicked cool smile was still there for his father.

At first, you see, the likes of Angus got away with it. The industry for once was slow. There were reasons. Sampling was hard to spot. The mixing machine can turn a bass into a castrato. But besides that my guess is that the business was trapped by its own vanity, by the vision it had of itself. For it was a while before those being ripped

222

off got round to realizing that what was happening wasn't homage.

He's done well from the business, Angus. Not a fortune. Not mega-millions. Not the GNP of some dirt-poor South American country. No, this other thing. Smaller. *Cooler.* More manageable. Quietly, carefully, sensibly invested. The studio. The apartment upstairs.

The place belonged to a wholesale drapery firm when he and Anna Lise bought it, a family outfit that had been there for years. They had the architect keep many of the thirties features, the original Venetian blinds, the parquet floor and the white globe lighting. It's all open-plan now, loft style. Spare with many spaces. A place to cook, a place to eat, a place to sleep. A place for everything, calm, clean, uncluttered.

It admonishes me somehow, that apartment. For while it is clever and comfortable with those witty touches which bright young people like them will bring to such a place, still it has a measured quality about it. It spurns luxury and excess in favour of a feeling of money well spent, of reason and moderation and self-restraint, those things which I wish I had had in my life, which I'm not even sure I have now.

'Don't do anything by halves eh Joanie? Always one thing or the other.' Kent's voice echoing in my head from that last day at Stoneham.

Sitting there on my own in the apartment among all this moderation, I found myself yearning suddenly, for the first time in many years, for what had been lost, I, Silas Marner, who had sung the praises of redemption, of the nobility of gold curls instead of cash on the mat, this same Silas Marner who found herself looking round at the orderliness, at the evidence of money respected and well husbanded, found myself yearning, with a new freshness, for what was gone.

'You OK Joanie?'

Kent suddenly beside me all these years later. My friend. Knowing my thoughts, touching my arm.

223

'Sure. Fine.'

He is not so cool now, Angus, when I look at him. He is warming by the day. Towards the world. Towards his father. Perhaps it's Anna Lise. Perhaps these two raging icebergs have consumed themselves. Or perhaps it is something else.

She's pouring the Earl Grey from their post-modern steel teapot when Angus lays his hand on her back, clears his throat like a boy.

'We're glad you came today Dad,' he says. 'We've got something to tell you.'

And I see the truth of it now. The haphazard nature of the thing. How it was started without due care and attention, without due thought for the future. Like one of those horror movies. A mad scientist in the lab. A mutant species out of control. Or perhaps we're more like vampires. Yes, that's it. The undead. The refuse to die. Nosferatus who need a stake through the heart.

'We're in uncharted waters, that's the problem.'

'Sure. But so what? If Eddie Cochran was alive today he'd still be gigging.'

We'd left the proud parents-to-be. We were walking back to the Landrover when I said, 'Hey, how about a quick celebration drink?'

In the pub I raised my glass to him.

'Well, here's to you . . . Grandad,' I said, laughing. He still had the expression of glazed surprise on his face. 'Hey . . . doesn't time fly when you're enjoying yourself?'

He crossed his legs in the old way, cupped his chin on his hands. All of these ways of his I remember.

'Yeah, but I mean, what are you supposed to do? You still want to play. You figure there's no reason you can't go on getting better but you have to put up with some young gun from the music press chipping away at you just because you're getting old. And after all no one expects classical musicians to give up at sixty.'

It's true. It's all true. Growing old has become the crime for which we're most unforgiven, a weird thing to be accused of when you think about it. It's like getting booked for doing forty in a thirty-mile zone. You know it's right and you know that you're guilty. But you know as well that everyone's doing it and you're the only one being pulled over. And let me ask you, why should we do the decent thing just because someone's handed us the gun and pointed us in the direction of the library?

'It's because of what we're supposed to be,' I told him.

'Which is?'

'Oh, you know. Heirs to some pact with the Devil. With a trap-door in the stage through which we're supposed to exit before thirty.'

'Hitting the wall on the Harley. OD-ing in the bath.'

'Retiring,' I said grimacing. 'With *dignity*.'

'Like you did,' he said.

We stared at each other.

'Below the belt,' I said. I got up. 'One more before we go?' But he wasn't giving in. He just looked at me steadily.

'Hasn't it gone on long enough Joanie?' he said.

'It's not what you think,' I said, stung. 'You make it sound like some sort of penance. Some twisted retribution.'

'Isn't it?' he said.

'I'll get the drinks,' I said, turning, but he grabbed my hand across the table.

'Do it,' he said. 'Do it Joanie.'

'Give it another go,' he said.

By the time we walked out of the place, the sun had slipped down behind the buildings and the streets were in shadow. It was still warm though and the pubs had their

225

doors open, disgorging drinkers out on to the streets, for now the offices had emptied and the place was so full of people they blocked the roads as well as the pavements.

Pushing our way through, I found myself shivering. For there was something oppressive about it all, something dark and dangerous, something *Dickensian*. Screams of Sloaney laughter mixed with that other street-cry of the new egalitarian London.

'Got any change mate . . . got any change . . .?'

In the doorways, among the revellers, the prudent had already picked a doorway and were bedding down for the night. In the hubbub, a familiar sound, hot and heavy, hit us through an open pub window.

> *You've got power*
> *But your hour may be past*
> *You're owin'*
> *And your time is goin' fast . . .*

And something deep inside me yearned for a raggy band.

You might think that what had happened at Andrew's funeral would have changed everything. You might think that it would have been a good moment for me to throw in my hand with my little habit, clean up my act or at least turn to help my old friend Kent who was blundering around like a beast with a fatal wound.

I tried as it happens, or at least I told myself I did, that night, after the funeral. In fact I was on fire with the possibility, as you are at such a time. I raised the last of the coke like a sacrament before me in one of Eduardo's splendid ormolu mirrors in the great hall at Stoneham.

'This is it,' I said. 'This is the last. Work for you,' and I felt serious and sure and wonderfully full of self-denial.

226

Because this is how it works, surprising those who've never been down this path, never tried to give up anything, food, cigarettes, alcohol, cocaine. The folly of it. That you can go through the motions like this, indulging yourself, your brain laughing at you, playing tricks with you, being so sure, even as you light up, or grab a glass or lower your head to a line, that this is the last time. This time it's truly final.

But it isn't. Of course it isn't. And the next day, in my case, it was easier to call up Harold and request a delivery than spend a day without a toot.

'But after this one,' I said by way of excuse.

The memory of Kent's dull and shaming eyes in the church porch, though, stayed with me and I guess it was because of them in the end that I never did marry the Dentist.

He'd gone on to the States as planned, never to return as it turned out. A few weeks after the funeral, a gang broke into the bank where he kept his largest stash of coke and money. They were in the middle of breaking open the deposit boxes when they were disturbed and had to depart in a hurry. The Dentist was just one of the depositees who decided against responding to the polite request from the police to return to the bank to find out if their boxes were among those robbed or the others left cracked open with their valuables spilling out.

He phoned a few times, always from obscure locations around the globe without the benefit of extradition arrangements. But the moment was past by then.

As for those dull and shaming eyes, well, in the end I preferred not to meet them. As he lumbered around in pain to my shame I found myself more and more preferring to avoid him. In the end I did not even take his calls. I would tremble when his voice came on the answer-machine, never quite knowing why. Once he left only a 'Joanie', choking with pain. But still I never rang him back.

I was frightened, you see, it's as simple as that. I knew somewhere in the back of my head that life was rearranging itself and offering me something. But I didn't want it. And I didn't want it for one reason and one reason alone. That I wanted the dope more. I wanted the dope more than anything else in life. More than health, more than wealth. And certainly more than mere ephemerals like happiness.

I didn't need love, you see. Dope was always my grand passion. It was my obsession, my great affair. And there was no room for any other.

At which the gods, tiring of the sport, cast around and in the end their gaze fell on Miranda.

When I think of Miranda, I always picture her the way I first saw her, sitting on the sofa in McGarvey's office, below the framed gold discs, her eyes cast down modestly.

I knew what she was the minute I walked in, not who she was but what, and it was all because of the modesty. I knew modesty and I knew what it hid. I knew it hid talent because I had it once. The talent as well as the modesty.

I wasn't feeling good that day walking into McGarvey's and she was the last person I wanted to see. It was a long time by then since I'd done anything good. It was a long time since I'd done anything at all. And I figured this was something McGarvey was about to get round to telling me.

As I walked in McGarvey got up a shade too quickly like a guilty husband and the pain was a lover's pain straight through to my heart.

She held out a hand but I ignored it, preferring instead to raise my own in a cool hello, as I waited for her to say what I knew, without a doubt, she would say, this thing they call a compliment but is actually a betrayal, a kiss from Judas, a knife in a black velvet glove.

228

'Wow . . .' she said, her face breaking out in childish delight. 'This is such a pleasure . . . I mean . . . oh God I hope you don't think this is pathetic . . . but I've always been a fan of yours.'

Of course you've been a fan of mine, I thought. Only soon you won't be any longer. Because although you don't know because you don't hear it, the starting pistol has already gone off for the pair of us. And already you're up on the inside and heading out front, and soon you'll be there in the winner's enclosure with a seat on the sofa where I used to sit in front of McGarvey.

When she was gone, McGarvey was casual in the way the carefully unfaithful are always casual. He said what I knew he would say, but the knowing didn't help. He took the knife that she'd taken and plunged in my heart and gave it one last quivering turn.

'You know in a lot of ways she reminds me of you Joanie,' he said.

When I produced that first batch of third-rate songs, you see, McGarvey didn't say over one of our long lunches where I drank too much and he drank nothing, 'These songs are third-rate Joanie . . .' He didn't say, 'Hey Joanie . . . go back Joanie . . . try again Joanie.' No, McGarvey said, 'Great songs Joanie,' because McGarvey was my manager and as my manager McGarvey was paid to lie. But lies cost money and the way it works is that the two of them normally run out together.

And when that first solo album did badly and then the next one, McGarvey didn't say, 'What did you expect Joanie?' No, McGarvey shrugged, which is what he was paid to do, and moved the cruet around the middle of the table, muttering commiserations . . . the music press . . . the economic times, so that, mollified, I called the head waiter over, and indulged myself in the sycophantic badinage that is the last refuge of those spiralling gently and inexorably downwards, ordering myself another bottle of champagne.

And when I stopped working altogether, which of course I had by now, McGarvey didn't say, 'What are you doing Joanie . . . you've stopped working Joanie . . .' No, McGarvey went on doing what he was paid to do which was to twitch the nets gently into place, to camouflage the truth from the world and even from me. Although never, of course, from McGarvey.

And when I arrived at the office they still played the game with me, they still parked my car, they still rushed towards me with the coffee, said those words of sweet comfort.

'He's there. He's waiting. Go straight in Joanie . . .'

Until this time, that first time, when I walked into the foyer and they said, 'Could you hang on a minute Joanie? He's got someone with him Joanie,' and at the same time forgot to take my car keys or offer me coffee, so that angry, and knowing things had changed, I just barged on in anyway to find Miranda there on the sofa. And in that moment I wanted to shout it, just what a lover shouts.

'Don't stop wanting me McGarvey.'

You can tell the lie of the land, like I say, by the look in someone else's eye. And in McGarvey's eyes that day there was a wariness, an alertness, a certain distance a man will have when his gaze is fixed over your head and looking at something else, at some*one* else, in the future.

'I've got to tell you . . . Joanie,' she said, this child, with her hand disappointed at her side. 'You're one of my heroes.'

She said my name breathlessly, hesitantly, as if she were afraid of the presumption. It irritated me. This further demonstration of her modesty.

'Since when?' I asked her. Because I was angry now and in the mood for it. And because I wanted it, when it came, full in the face.

'Since I was at school,' she said, and I threw my head back and laughed. With the pleasure of the pain.

She looked hurt.

'No kidding,' I said.

She wouldn't have known then what perhaps she knows now. That we're links in the chain and the curse of the worshipped is they're always caught up by the worshipper.

I knew who she was. Of course I knew who she was. The only thing I didn't know was that she was with McGarvey.

'There's a lot of things you don't know these days Joanie,' said McGarvey. She was gone by then and he was signing a letter. When he looked up his eyes were not friendly.

'You should get off that stuff,' he said. It was the first time he'd mentioned it.

'Well . . .' I said.

I'd seen her, you see, on one of those nameless late night shows full of bad music and young over-loud pre-senters. I wouldn't have caught her but for the fact that the video I'd been watching clicked off at the end of the tape and there she was. I was watching a lot of videos by now.

Because I was very stoned at the time, I wasn't sure if she was as good as I thought she was. So to comfort myself, in the hopes that she wasn't, I went out the next day to buy her album.

I lay on my back in the library listening as the tracks clocked up. I'd done one side and was a few tracks into the second and I was beginning to relax. She was good, yes, but not so good I was jealous. Then it came like a thump in the stomach. The one I should have written, a melody that you'd give a few years of your life for and some lines straight from the Great Rhyme Master in the sky.

> *I live like a stranger and feel like an enemy*
> *Praying for peace in this down-town Gethsemane . . .*

'She's good,' I said grudgingly to McGarvey.

McGarvey, though, would not meet my eye.

'Like I say,' he said, 'she reminds me of you.' His eyes were merciless then.

'When you were younger of course Joanie.'

A short while later he leaned back in his chair, pushed it away from the large walnut desk. He put a perfect pale finger to his lips and looked at me hard.

'So what's happening then Joanie?' he said.

Once it was just a way of speaking. Once it would have been an idle inquiry. Now though it was serious and we both knew. Which is how the tables turn and I end up lying to McGarvey.

'Well you know . . . I've got some stuff coming.'

'Enough for an album?'

'Yeah . . . no . . . well maybe . . . not yet.' All lies McGarvey. Take your pick.

And he did, rejecting them all, with a wave.

Which is when I lost my nerve, moved a hand myself with fake carelessness on the chair. Tried to make a joke of it.

'I know. What about a compilation McGarvey?'

But he didn't think it was funny. He didn't even try to laugh. Instead he narrowed his eyes through the haze of my cigarette smoke, pushed the ashtray with an unfriendly air towards me.

'But what is there to compile Joanie?' he said.

It was soon after that I got to my feet and walked to the window where I shoved a skittish finger through the blinds. Below the Soho traffic was squishing through the rain and the sodden cardboard and the squashed and rotting vegetables.

'I'm in trouble McGarvey,' I said.

'I know Joanie,' he said. There was no help in his voice. Nothing to make it easier.

'I need money McGarvey,' I said.

'You need songs Joanie,' he said, reaching out for a letter.

I snorted with laughter then, brushing my sleeve across the window like a child.

'She's got songs,' I said turning. 'I'll bet she's got *lots* of songs. We all have lots of songs at the beginning.'

It was supposed to be another joke. I'd taken a toot in his bathroom. I was laughing.

'I'll do some of her songs. She'll like that. I'm her hero.' But he just shook his head.

'She doesn't need you Joanie,' said McGarvey.

One afternoon, a while later, the phone rang. I was fiddling about on the piano pretending I was working. It was wet and windy outside and the squalls were throwing handfuls of rain against the windows.

'Right,' said McGarvey. 'Got some dates for you.' His voice was firm like he was expecting trouble. It would have sounded warning bells if I wasn't so far gone.

When he read off the dates I was jubilant. I'd been hounding him to get me a tour. But without new material, without an album, he'd been dragging his feet. On top of that, after the last tour the world at large wasn't too crazy to book me. I'd limped on for a few more weeks after Vancouver but then the same thing happened again, by which time the promoters were panicky, not knowing whether I was going to make it or not. After the second collapse, though, I got on the next plane home clutching a doctor's note and pleading that old stand-by 'exhaustion'. That meant the last couple of dates had to be cancelled which left the lawyers to fight over the penalty clauses in the contracts, something which, naturally enough, did not please McGarvey.

Now, though, I'd convinced myself, with the help of a few extra toots and a closer than usual scrutiny of my bank statements, that I was ready to go on the road again.

'Good one, good one,' I kept saying as McGarvey read out the dates. 'See, I told you. They're out there. Never mind new material, they want to hear me McGarvey.'

I was running on, throwing out ideas for a new band, when he interrupted me. He said, 'We're talking solo here Joanie.'

'Are you crazy?' I said. 'In these size venues?'

I remember how the thought of it ran like ice-cold water down my back.

'Enjoy yourself Joanie,' were Richard's parting words to me when he phoned that last time trying to patch things up between us. 'You'll find it's not all fun being out front.' And I'd found out it was true. Having everything riding on you wasn't the same as being up there at the back of the stage to the left. That was the reason for the over-indulgence and the subsequent débâcle in Vancouver. The idea of being up there without even a band was so crazy I even laughed at McGarvey.

'Apart from anything else I'd be blown off the stage by the support,' I said. 'Who is the support by the way?'

'You are Joanie,' said McGarvey.

I refused of course. I screamed down the line at him. I said, 'You must be joking. How fucking dare you McGarvey?'

He said, 'It's a good chance Joanie.'

'For who?' I said grandly. 'For *her*?' Because of course it was Miranda's tour. Which is when he said it a second time only now he didn't mess around with the emphasis.

He said, '*She* doesn't need *you* Joanie.'

I slammed the phone down in the end. I told him, 'Forget it. Get me something else McGarvey.' A week or so later he called again. This time his voice was flat and non-committal. He said, 'I've got some more dates for you Joanie.'

'See, McGarvey,' I said, determined to be pleasant. 'I knew you'd manage it. I knew it would work.'

I'd just taken a toot so my arrogance quota was up.

'Tell you what McGarvey,' I said, 'I'm busy here at the moment. Shove the stuff in the post. I'll look at it later.'

And so he did. But by the time it arrived and Francis left it on my desk, I was on one of my three-day benders. So it was a while before I got around to looking at it. When I did, though, I went up like a geyser.

'Fuck. Shit. Christ. I don't believe it. Piddling little theatres. Colleges. *Arts centres.*'

There was a letter with the list of dates. It was from McGarvey. It said, give or take some fine phrases, that I should think myself lucky to get these gigs and if I wasn't prepared to do them, I should consider our professional relationship at an end. Mine and my manager McGarvey.

It was a set-up of course. I was never going to do those gigs and McGarvey knew it. Still, I picked up the phone anyway.

I fumed as his number rang out, muttering the names like a curse.

'Solihull. Ilford. *Worthing.*'

In those days McGarvey had a telephonist who chirped like a mechanical sparrow. She also lied really badly. It annoyed me, the fact that she couldn't be better at what she did. Lying after all was her job just like it was McGarvey's.

She pulled her usual trick of asking who was calling before telling me he was out. It was happening all the time to me now. By this stage in my career I wasn't having too much luck getting through to McGarvey.

'Can I get Mr McGarvey to phone you?' she said.

'I don't know,' I said sarcastically. 'Do you think that you *can*?'

He never called of course. Like he said in his letter, the matter wasn't open for discussion, so in the end I decided to try and get in to see him.

It wasn't a good idea.

No one offered to park the car but then no one offered me coffee and it didn't matter because all I wanted was to see McGarvey. As I barged past the sparrow towards his door, though, two security men materialized out of the ether. They had a look in their eyes that told me they'd been waiting.

I was squirming and swearing as they frog-marched me down the corridor. As we reached the lift the bell tinged and the door rumbled back.

'Oh, perfect timing,' I said. 'Perfect timing.' And I started to laugh.

'Robin,' I said. 'And *Miranda*. I'd introduce you to my friends but as you can see we're in a bit of a rush.'

He'd been doing an interview with her I guess. They stood there, their mouths dropping open, as the security men bundled me into the lift.

'So sorry I couldn't make the tour Miranda,' I said. 'Couldn't agree on the billing.'

To Miranda's credit the look of shock on her face had changed to one of distress. I was out of my brain, though, so I only laughed more.

'By the way Robin,' I said, as the lift door began to close, 'Miranda's a big fan of mine. I'm sure she told you.'

The door was shut and we were already jerking downwards so I had to shout the last words up the lift shaft.

'I'm one of her heroes,' I yelled.

I figured a way to get my own back on McGarvey. And I knew just the man to help me.

Harold was slapping into a punch-bag when I walked

into the gym, not the Dentist's gym, not the pristine palace of mirrors and stainless steel but a back-street East End gym, a boxer's gym, grubby and cold.

'Got a job for you Harold,' I said.

Harold was down on his uppers by then. He'd been devoted to the Dentist. Now he'd been abandoned and it showed in his face. When I think about it, there was always something of the Dobermann in Harold.

When the Dentist went to the States Harold was left, like he always was, looking after the apartment, which he did to perfection, all but putting lighted lamps in the window each night to welcome the Dentist home. Except of course that the Dentist never did come back, and the first Harold knew about the fact that he was out of a job and out of a place to live as well was when the estate agents turned up with a buyer.

'Chill winds of the recession Harold,' I said as we drank milky metallic coffee from finger-marked cups in a greasy spoon around the corner from the gym. I reached into my pocket, took out some twenties, opened his hand and laid them in. He fanned them out thoughtfully, selected three like cards, passed the rest of them back over the table towards me.

'So when do we do it Joanie?' he said.

We went on Harold's Harley. His pride and joy. I figured I had to be ahead of the game chasing McGarvey on the Harley.

It was just another of those things about McGarvey you see. That no one knew where he lived. Every night he'd come out of the office, clamber into the chauffeur-driven car. From there he'd drive somewhere weird, Crickle-wood, say, Tooting Bec, where he'd get out of the car, dismiss the driver. He'd walk a bit then, pick up a taxi and for another hour or so that was how it would work, a taxi, a little walk, hacking backwards and forwards across London, leaping from cab to cab like a man pursued, which was what he was. A man pursued by his own fanatical desire for privacy.

Over the years it became a challenge among the more spaced out of his clients to try to follow him, to try to uncover the crypt that McGarvey called home. No one ever managed it, though, and the longer the game went on, so the stakes became higher.

One night a band whose name would surprise you clasped hands across the flame in an orgy of male bonding after the singer put up as first prize a night with his new and lovely wife. The drummer was the first to drop out. Well, he would be. He was the drummer after all. He lost McGarvey's car half a mile from the office. Lead guitar fell away next, too slow off the lights in Ladbroke Road. Keyboards saw the first of the change-overs between car and taxi, but got left behind in the docklands. Bass was still there, though, at least till the taxi began weaving around the back of Waterloo station which meant it was all down to the singer. He upheld the band's honour, his wife's as well, sticking to McGarvey like a limpet, but finally losing him, himself as well, deep in the heart of Deptford.

I figure that over the years McGarvey had developed a second sense that told him when someone was on his tail because it took us the best part of three hours to follow him that night. Six times he went back and forwards across the river. Several times, between taxis, I saw him stop and stare and look around him. Once we watched hidden in the shadows of an alleyway as he craned his neck forward and peered into the darkness.

I'd dropped a tab of acid the better to enjoy the trip. Behind the visor the lights of the cars drew out around me in multi-coloured streaks like a long-exposure photograph, the inky blackness of the river rising up like the Styx. The helmets had earphones in them and the music merged with the roar of the Harley, the car horns sounding like trumpets, a symphony of the city.

I thought it was just another change-over when Mc-Garvey paid off the taxi in the side-street in Acton. No one was more surprised than me when he took the key from his pocket. We were in front of an old thirties council block, run-down, graffiti-ed, cheap gaudy curtains at the windows.

Inside the place was the same, grimy walls, a lift smelling of urine.

Harold did the talking, slipped the porter the tenner to tell him the number where McGarvey lived.

Like I say I'm sure in some way McGarvey knew what was coming. He stepped back wordlessly to let me pass as I pulled off my helmet.

The corridor inside was narrow, chipped and peeling, a low-watt bulb hung from a ceiling. But even that didn't prepare me for what lay beyond.

'Jesus McGarvey,' I said.

It might have been a lounge if someone else, a human being, say, had been living there. There was the same unshaded light bulb. The floor was old lino, squiggly stuff from the fifties, with grubby yellow wallpaper, scribbled on and torn, that must have gone up at the same time. The only furniture was an old red plastic sofa covered in papers and a tacky formica table.

I said it again. 'Jesus,' I said. 'I don't believe this McGarvey.'

That was when I saw the other door off the lounge. It was only open a crack, but it was enough to show a weird light, ghostly green, like something from the underworld. Through the crack came an inhuman incessant chatter. Walking over, I pushed it open and stared in.

The only sign that it was a bedroom was a divan in a corner, a cheap duvet thrown over it. The floor was brown carpet tiles, the sort used in an office. There was no natural light. Whatever windows there had been were

239

boarded up and papered over. The light came from the desk lamp and the spots. And from the wallful of glowing computer screens.

I shook my head in wonder.

'Of course,' I said. 'I should have known. The Ark of the Covenant eh McGarvey?'

I sat down on the bed, lit a cigarette, looked up at him.

'Tell me McGarvey,' I said. 'Just for posterity. Did you fall to earth or are you made up by Dickens?' But he didn't answer. Instead he dropped down on to the desk chair, stared into the screen.

'What have you come for Joanie?' he said.

And now let me tell you, I know the things they've written about McGarvey over the years. I know the lengths they've gone to trying to search out the scandals, the rent boys, the bizarre sex games. But all this stuff is just the world blinded by its own *modus operandi*, by its own *raisons d'être* which have nothing at all to do with McGarvey.

For there are no skeletons in McGarvey's closet. No dark secrets. At least only this one. That McGarvey's weakness is money, not one he has to worry about in the eyes of this world. And so it is and so it will be. Till the day he dies. Or till the day he returns to whatever strange place he came from.

It winded me somehow looking at the great bank of computer screens, the keyboards, the chattering faxes. I sat on his bed smoking quietly.

'Why have you come Joanie?' he said again but I just shook my head dully.

'I don't know. To tell you the truth McGarvey I don't know,' I said.

I pulled a wry smile behind his back.

'What about a drink?' I said. 'A cup of coffee?' It was a joke.

'Well ... perhaps not,' I said. I knew McGarvey wouldn't even possess a kettle.

I got up from the bed then, I don't know why, walked over to him, put my hands on his shoulders, slid them round the front of him to his chest. Beneath the silk of his shirt, silk, for the office, his skin was cold like ice.

'It was me there at the beginning,' I said softly. 'My songs, my money. Now you're dumping me McGarvey.'

He didn't answer, just went on tapping something into the computer.

I lifted my hands then from his chest, laid them on the side of his face. Beneath my fingers I could feel the bones of his skull, the skin, eyebrows and lips. I stroked my thumbs down his cheeks carefully.

'I fucking made you McGarvey,' I said sadly.

He raised his left hand then from the keyboard, placed it on my own, brought it down, palm forward, to his mouth. He laid the kiss in the middle, a Judas kiss, calm and cool and final.

'No, I fucking made you Joanie,' he said.

I went back a few weeks later just to check but of course McGarvey was gone. An unshaven guy opened the door in a dirty shirt, the sound of too many children behind him. When I mentioned McGarvey's name a small vein of greed appeared in his eye.

'Come in,' he said.

Inside there was no sign of McGarvey. The place had been redecorated, bright cheap paper on the walls and light came in through the bedroom window.

'So who was he then?' said the guy. 'Some sort of weirdo?' A baked-bean-encrusted child pulled at his leg.

'You could say that,' I said.

He insisted I stay for a coffee. Behind the kitchen door there was the murmur of voices. When they came back out, he said, 'This is Marlene.'

'Hello Marlene,' I said.

241

'Me and Marlene,' he said, offering me a cigarette, 'we're fans of yours.' He leaned back on a plastic sofa much the same but not McGarvey's.

'We've even got one of your albums. Fetch the album Marlene,' he said.

When it arrived it was old, our first. I signed it across the drink rings in the corner.

'Marlene,' he said, 'nip out to the offy for us. Get a couple of cans.'

'Not for me,' I said, laying the mug down amidst the grease on the coffee table.

The vein winked then and began to glow in his eye. He rested his head on the back of the sofa, staring at me.

'This McGarvey . . .' he said, 'friend of yours was he?'

'Not exactly,' I said.

'Something *naughty* was it?' he said, his eyes trying for a conspiratorial twinkle. 'Drugs was it . . . black magic . . . Something like that?'

'I have to go,' I said, getting up.

'Oh look, don't get me wrong,' he said, leaning forward. 'I mean, me and Marlene like a smoke, don't we Marlene?'

He was on his feet himself now. His legs were bandy, his chest concave. He bent to tap the cigarette in the ashtray, coughing.

'Look,' he said, 'let's be fair. We could go to the papers.'

'About what?' I said.

'About you,' he said, 'coming here. The boards over the windows . . . everything.'

I shrugged. 'Do it . . .' I said.

'Nah . . .' he said. 'Listen . . . Marlene and I . . . we like you. We went to a concert you know . . .'

'How was it?' I said.

He got mad then. 'They'd pay us you know. We could get a couple of grand off someone like the *Screws*.'

'Go for it,' I said.

But he was losing his courage and something else too. The tiny holy grail was slipping away.

'Look,' he said, 'tell you what. A couple of hundred. How about it?'

'Don't sell yourself short,' I said.

He snatched in the air in the end. Pulled the figure down.

'Fifty quid. What would it mean to you?'

'I don't carry that sort of money,' I said, my hand on the door-knob. Behind me he exploded.

'Well you wouldn't would you?' he said. 'You don't need to. Your sort never do.'

'What is my sort?' I said.

'Your sort,' he said. 'People with money,' and I started laughing.

I reached a hand into my jacket pocket. There were some coins in the bottom. His greedy eyes followed my every movement.

'Here,' I said, and I pulled out my hand and tossed the coins at him. Dues. At the Temple. At McGarvey's Ark of the Covenant. He swore as they spun in the air, fell like rain about his shoulders. One slid slowly down his shirt like a tear.

As I thumped the lift button he screamed along the landing behind me.

'Don't think I don't know. I read it in the papers. You're in trouble you know that?'

My laughter echoed along the landing, bounced off the strip-lighting.

'Thanks for the warning,' I said.

Where would I find McGarvey today? I know one place. Number 121 in the *Sunday Times* list of the country's richest people.

One of the more secretive of our super-rich . . . the *Sunday*

Times calls him with the sort of understatement we British do so well.

No known photograph is known to exist of McGarvey.

McGarvey sold the record label several years after I left. He's thought to have made £50 million. Since then estimating his fortune has been a matter of taking the original amount and adding to it in the light of his money-making reputation. At the moment it stands at £92 million.

Robin Phillips never did get to the compound high up in the Cordillera. He'd been waiting almost a month for the mythical permit the night the hoary old Indian eased himself down into the chair next to him on the hotel verandah and told him all he needed to know about the man they called Don Carlos McGarvey.

There, rocking gently in the brightly blanketed chair, with the sun slanting in beneath the verandah roof and the owner of the place resting on his arms at the window, grunting, in agreement or not it was hard to tell, the old Indian described with minimal English but with eloquent dancing hands the high barbed-wire fence, the small private army, the helicopter trips to the capital and the Lear jet that waited there at the airport in an area set aside and strictly guarded, reserved exclusively on the orders of the Government for the new conquistadores like McGarvey.

All of which finally made Robin Phillips see the hopelessness of the task which he had set himself, the sheer folly of thinking he was ever going to get to see McGarvey.

For what he saw then was that he had arrived in El Dorado, and that El Dorado was used to men like McGarvey. He saw that El Dorado was used to *arrangements*.

It came as no surprise to Robin Phillips to learn that McGarvey's method of ensuring his continuing anonymity was the one common to all in his position, a suitcase of notes in lieu of tax, delivered personally every year, at a dinner held in the capital, attended by many lovely ladies including some technically yet to become so, plus certain members of the Cabinet, and even, upon occasion, the country's best-known rich recluse. The Father of the Nation, the *Generalissimo, El Presidente* himself.

Technically McGarvey is still a British citizen by virtue of the house in Chelsea that he doesn't see from one year's end to the other. In reality he's done what he always wanted to do, which is to erase himself from the records. For he appears on no electoral roll, has no tax codes or national insurance numbers to worry about. And if McGarvey's name is written anywhere in the Book of Life it can only be on a ledger lying open on some bare hunk of rock sticking up in the sea where the only thing that grows is money.

And so McGarvey cruises the world in his Lear jet which is also his office, with his satellite phones and his faxes and the rest of his hi-tech paraphernalia, acknowledging no one, caring for nothing but his money mountain that grows higher and higher and more chaste and untouched with each passing year.

What shall it profit a man if he gain the whole world but lose his soul?

I wouldn't know. Ask McGarvey.

IV

After last year's jubilee
I watched the sky turn grey
Come on clouds I'd pray
Pull a cover over me
The city with its sweet excesses
Dulls the edge of loneliness's blade
And midnight proves the stupid moves I made . . .

Today we found a photographer dressed as a delivery boy halfway up the stairs.

Gavin threw him out, lifting him up by the scruff of the neck, hurling him down the front steps, throwing his camera out after him. He worked on building sites before becoming a nurse and beneath the white of the tunic his arms are like steel.

The photographer rolled into a rose bush.

'I'll sue,' he said.

'Good,' said Gavin, banging the door.

It disgusts me. Of course it disgusts me. That the world should want a picture of Richard dying. But it astonishes me more how primeval this whole thing is. How they can know out there in the street. Because they do know. The puppets are no longer collapsed on the railings. You can feel it in the air. The sense of growing excitement that wasn't there a few days ago that would tell you, even if you didn't know, that it will not be long now before the end is upon us.

It's been three weeks since that day when Kent came for me at the café. Richard sleeps most of the time now. That twin track of lives is all gone, that grand burst of energy over the album that sent Kent and me scurrying to Angus, all that is just a memory. Still, I like to remember it as I stare at him asleep now on the pillow, his face greyer than I had thought grey skin could be, the breathing heavy and laboured. I see again the miracle of it, Richard sitting upright and alive on the pillows planning another album together.

A last memory for all of us. Apart from Donald who dare not allow himself a word such as *last*. He dare not contemplate it, less a word than a wound opening up before him.

So for Donald, despite the evidence which he can see in the grey shadow breathing heavily before him, the battle is still not over. Hustling about the bed, for instance, he still keeps up the relentless one-sided conversations which are only for himself now, no longer for Richard.

'You're looking better today Richard . . . Not so tired my darling . . . perhaps you could eat a little something . . . I could do something special . . .'

This afternoon, though, when he sat by the bed I saw Richard's eyes fall on him and focus, and when Donald took his hand upon the cover, he made a sudden petulant movement drawing it away and throwing his head aside on the pillow sharply. For a fraction of a second as he turned towards me his eyes were light and bright and alive again. For that second they were like kaleidoscopes glittering with all kinds of emotion. There was sorrow in there and anger and something else. A bitter disappointment.

I understand, I understand. I see what Donald will not see. For downstairs the inflexible battle against any sort of acquiescence goes on.

'His colour really is better today don't you think?' He raises his head at the sink but only stares at the wall. Gavin and I are sitting behind him at the table but he will not look at us. Instead he strides around the kitchen as he talks, lifting pots and pans and slapping them down on the stove-top very hard as if warning against any argument or attempts at mediation. His speech comes very quickly.

'I've called a priest you know . . . actually called a priest . . . last rites and everything . . .'

He turns, his eyes fierce, challenging, daring us to disagree. And he smiles that dreadful smile, his voice cracked like some of Richard's old opera recordings.

'Still alive today . . . five years later . . .'

*

Sometimes, though, when the lonely one-sided conversations grow so strained that even he cannot handle it, Donald brings a book to the bed, reads out loud to Richard. Today as I came in he was idling through the Sonnets.

'Oh *yes* . . . remember this one Richard . . .

'"*When in disgrace with Fortune and men's eyes . . .*"'

And I stood at the door, miserably wishing Richard was not grey and still on the pillow, wishing he would look up, see me at the door, raise an eyebrow, fix me with that old mocking smile. Wishing Richard would say, 'Welcome Joanie . . . perfect timing . . .'

Word gets around when you're sleeping with your dealer. But no faster than it does when you've been dropped by your record company and no one will give you a new deal.

Which is why Robin Phillips comes down to see me at Stoneham.

'Tea in the library I think Caroline.'

Spoken grandly. To keep up appearances. And in return from Caroline, who I know has grown to despise me, a dutiful smile which hides her disdain, a disdain she also disguises with the discreetly closed door. Another discreetly closed door, another salary slipping away down the hill of money which unlike McGarvey's has long since stopped growing and instead diminishes every day.

'You have to understand I don't see this as just another rock biography. I see it more as a study in the phenomenon which *is* rock and roll.' Robin Phillips was always heavily into italics.

It's an excuse coming to see me about this airy project and we both know it. What he's really come for is to see if the rumours are true, the *raison d'être* for all such as Robin Phillips. Still, I entertain him, mainly because I

251

have nothing better to do. I'm not working any more. I'm not writing. I'm not touring. I'm not doing anything much but stuffing a lot of white powder up my nose. And whereas I dislike Robin Phillips, at least he's a diversion. He's a change from the films and the kids' programmes which I watch all afternoon on the television.

'For me that last album, with Leon, that's the classic.'

With the band note. With long-dead Leon. And no mention of my solo albums.

'It's timeless. People will always want to buy that album.'

Words strain and crack and sometimes break, did you know that? Words like *classic* and *timeless*.

Words like *awful*.

'That's awful,' I said to my father. 'That's awful.'

It was the last time I saw him. The last time anyway I saw him alive. The next time would be in the hospital mortuary, his face white and cold, but surprisingly undifferent from life.

It was a day for *lasts*. My last gig. The last time too I saw The Man.

When I told my father that I was playing at the festival, he turned his nose up at his desk.

'Oh *God* . . .' he said. 'Not that thing. Sandals and joss-sticks. *Nuclear disarmament* . . .'

'Oh come on,' I said, with a joviality born of the last toot. 'Even an old fascist like you can't want the world to end in a nuclear holocaust.' This is the way I was able to speak to him by the end.

'Not the world, no,' he said, showing no sign of offence, feigning disinterest instead and turning a page over with a papery hand.

'Still . . .' he said. 'It might be a solution.'

'You can't believe that,' I said, with a sudden wave of weariness which was more than the coke draining away.

'Really my dear,' he said in his cold polite voice, 'you can't have the faintest idea what I believe.'

He took off his spectacles then, laid them on the desk. He pushed a hand over his eyes in a phoney gesture, for they were not tired at all but wide awake with the possibility of one of the chill and emotionless arguments which were his only pleasure in life.

'When I look around me,' he said, the cold voice enjoying the words, 'I'm forced to agree with Nietzsche that really the great majority of mankind have no right to exist at all.'

He got up from his chair then, walked over to the tiny table by the armchair, poured out the two sherries in that small ceremony which had come to pass for affection between us. As I took the first sip he sat down, laying his own carefully on the table beside him and placing the tips of his fingers together in preparation.

'I'll tell you what Evelyn once said . . .' he began. It was his favourite introduction.

Over the years he'd been asked occasionally to record dry little pieces about the Greeks for the Third Programme. You know the sort of stuff. Interval-fillers for live concerts while listeners go off to make the tea. For him, though, his broadcasts were his finest hour. He was immensely proud of them, boasting about them to anyone prepared to listen. He used them, the only weapon in his armoury, against the headmaster who patronized him and belittled him, treating him as little more than a hired hand.

'I'm so sorry headmaster but I'm going to have to reschedule my Tuesday classes. They want me to do another of my talks. It's irritating of course but still . . .'

The only time I saw him vaguely happy was when he loaded himself into the old Rover with his battered brief-case and set out for Broadcasting House. He was almost

253

humming. When he came back he'd drop the names of the great and the good who he'd gossiped about with his producer. The highspot of his broadcasting career had come years before when he'd been introduced to Evelyn Waugh in a corridor. Ever after that he referred to him as a friend. Now, sitting opposite me, his face had that old pompous look of a man on intimate terms with the famous.

'What Evelyn said was that he could see nothing objectionable in the destruction of the planet and really I find myself forced to agree with him.'

'That's awful,' I said, shocked in spite of myself. 'That's truly awful.'

'A case in point my dear,' he said dryly. 'You see how far we have come. We live in a world where we've lost even our sense of language.'

He'd risen to his feet now, had begun tapping the air with his glasses.

'Oh no,' I said, but it was too late. A lecture was already on the way.

'A proper definition of "awful" my dear Joan is inspiring reverence or dread. It's only in this philistine century that we have come to treat it in this trite and nauseous fashion.'

'This is bullshit,' I said, irritated against my will and enjoying using the word before him.

'You just say these things,' I said.

'*How dare you.*'

The old rich rage from years ago had returned, an old echo from the past. The face was white, the old frame trembling.

'I never just *say* things. I have opinions, opinions that I have gained by reading and study. Opinions I've worked on and thought about over the years, something unheard of in your generation.' The lips curled up into a sneer.

'*Peace,*' he said. '*Love.*'

'You're behind the times,' I said, trying to stop him.

'They're all Thatcher's children now.' But he wasn't listening.

'What do you know? What does your generation know about anything? You don't read. You don't think. You don't listen. You have the attention span of a sparrow.'

His own attention meanwhile was entirely taken up with his rage. He pounded backwards and forwards with it across the rug.

'You're magpies,' he said. 'Picking up things . . . images . . . fragments . . . pulling apart . . . cheapening . . . art . . . literature . . . philosophy . . . And for what? To sell a pop record.'

The old 'p' spat out as he said it. I looked at him in amazement.

'Good God,' I said. 'You've watched.' I started to laugh.

'You old fraud,' I said. 'You've watched pop videos . . . you've seen *Top of the Pops*.' And then it dawned on me and all the laughter fell away.

'You've watched me,' I said.

'Yes,' he said, 'I've watched you.' He was holding my eyes, making me shiver, making me a child again with his disgust.

'And . . .' I said, staring back at him, determined not to care.

'And . . .' I said, grinning.

Something happened then. He pulled back from the brink, I don't know why. Instead of the cold disgusted fury I was expecting he waved a dismissive hand. He even gave a weak grin himself, an awkward thing that tried to be self-mocking.

'*Vilia miretur vulgus* my dear,' he said.

That was the day I gave him the Plutarch. I pulled it out from behind me as I got up to leave.

'Here,' I said. 'You've probably forgotten. It's your birthday.' He hated birthdays.

255

Pieter my antique dealer found the Plutarch for me.

'I want something special,' I told him. 'It's for my father. A book I think. Something to do with the Greeks.'

It was a cruel idea I had for my father's birthday present. I wanted it to be something, quite explicitly, he'd give his right arm to possess. I wanted something he could never afford to buy, not because I loved him, not because I cared, but because I wanted to rub it in, just what the cheap and the shallow was worth. I wanted to pay him back if you like with that old rock and roll shilling.

'It's perfect,' Pieter said when he heard the thing was coming up. 'Plutarch. The North translation. First edition.'

When he came with it, though, fresh from the auction, I freaked out at the price. I knew that I couldn't afford it.

'Blind-stamped calf Joanie,' he said defensively. 'Bound at the time of publication. But I don't deal in books like I told you. I only did it as a favour.'

'Still . . . I mean . . . fucking hell Pieter . . . four grand,' I said.

'I took only the smallest commission,' he said huffily. 'Frankly it never even covered my time.'

'OK, OK,' I said. 'I'm sorry.

'Here,' I said. 'I'll write you a cheque.'

'I suppose,' he said carefully, 'you wouldn't have cash would you Joanie?'

I stood over my father, staring down at him, as he pulled the paper off with an old man's frightened fingers. I guess he had some idea of what was coming.

The paper fell to the floor from his knee as he stared at the spine saying nothing. Then he turned it on its side on his knee, wiping a greedy lover's hand across it.

For a while he sat lost in a world of his own then his long delicate fingers began turning the pages as if they

256

were glass, as if the paper might break at his touch. I dropped my eyes in the end, unable to bear the sight any longer, the look of love and greed on his face for this thing which I couldn't understand and for which he would bear even this humiliation.

He said, 'It's wonderful,' all he ever was, all he had failed to be contained in the words. His voice was thick, perhaps even with tears. For the book, that is, not for me.

In the end he did not look up.

'Thank you,' he said.

'Go now,' he said.

And I did.

I had bought the thing for revenge, but the revenge fell to pieces in my hands.

I knew, at base, he hated my success, you see. And it wasn't simply that it was made by the thing he most hated. He was jealous of anything the world called 'success' and why not? He had worked all his life for a pittance, for the few hundred pounds they gave him for his book, for the privilege of seeing it disappear without trace, lost in the dusty basements of libraries.

And I capped all his anger, all his jealousy with that Plutarch. In one moment I took all the beauties and all the delicacies, all the antiques and paintings and ancient houses which he and those like him thought should belong to them by rights but which the world would not reward them with enough grubby money to buy. I took them, all of these things, bought and paid for them with the rock and roll shilling, and I nailed them, without mercy, to his heart.

They gave me the Plutarch back with his briefcase after the accident. It seems the passenger door burst open when the car hit the bridge and the briefcase fell out. It was still buckled up when they found it with the Plutarch some way away, lying separately half-hidden in the grass.

That's how I know he must have had it out, sitting there on the top of the briefcase, on the passenger seat as he drove along. Perhaps he was looking at it, occasionally removing a hand from the wheel to stroke it. Perhaps he was doing it unwisely on the bend which is why the car went out of control. Perhaps at the same time he was planning what he would say over a cup of stewed canteen tea to his producer.

'Yes, a remarkably fine example . . . first edition, yes . . . my daughter bought it for me actually . . .'

They didn't find the stuff till the next day when they came to tow the Rover away. It had been raining during the night so everything was sodden.

'I don't know if you want this,' the country copper said doubtfully, holding out four grand's worth of collector's item.

They tried to find me as soon as it happened, but it's hard to find someone at a festival among one hundred and fifty thousand people, particularly if the person you're trying to find is nose down in a caravan out of reach of the tannoy, having just scored a gram of good coke.

I was driving away when they got me and I went straight to the hospital. It was too late though. So I sat by the trolley for a moment and held his hand. A dead man's hand, limp and useless. Like our relationship.

He could have gone by train to London. It would have been simpler and easier. But he never went anywhere by train.

'So full of *people*,' is what he would moan.

'Well . . . drive carefully,' I said that day when he told me where he was going. I figured at the time it was what daughters said to their fathers.

The crash was something of a mystery. No other vehicle was involved. There seemed no reason for the Rover to go out of control.

The accident received a larger amount of publicity than you might have thought deserved by the death of an obscure unrewarded Greek scholar. And it wasn't just that he happened to be my father.

It was that it was the same bridge, the same corner.

Exactly the same spot that had killed Eddie.

Didi didn't come to the funeral.

'Really,' she said coolly when I rang her, 'I can't see the point.'

So there was just the vicar scraping around for something to say.

And the man who cut his lawn.

And the woman who cooked his meals.

And a scattering of press.

And me.

And the coke.

For company.

Mr Pitiful.

That came to me a few days later when the house had been cleared and the Bechstein brought over, as I sat down at it idling, my head down on my arms.

For the first time in many months I came up with something. A fragment.

> *Something that should have been so beautiful*
> *Is gone aground and wrecked*
> *When is Mr Pitiful*
> *Gonna give me some respect . . .*

But it was just a fragment.

It didn't turn into anything.

*

'I was sorry to hear about your father,' Robin Phillips said pompously that day he came to see me.

'Really?' I said, trying to force the hypocrisy from his eyes.

I got a lot of shit from Robin Phillips that day. A lot of waffle and pretentiousness. A lot of hammering too, one hand down hard in the palm of the other. A lot of rock as cultural iconography, rock as the new religion, rock some sort of repository of a faith that was lost.

'This is all so much shit Robin.'

I was argumentative by then and why not? He was here to amuse me after all and failing miserably. Besides which it had always been one of my joys to annoy Robin Phillips.

'It's just about a lot of people having a good time while a lot of other people make a pile of money. And the only thing people want to know about rock and roll is the details of the sex and the drugs that go with it.'

And speaking of sex and drugs, and the joys that they bring, Robin Phillips was moving in for the kill.

'So what made you leave McGarvey Joanie?'

A sudden memory of my father and his Eliot voices. Shrieking.

'Oh you know. Time for a change. Pastures new and all that.'

Scolding. Mocking.

'You haven't signed with anyone else yet?'

Or merely chattering.

'No. I've had offers obviously but I'm taking my time. I'm in no hurry. Help yourself to more tea Robin. I'll be right back.'

Because, as they say, I had to go to the bathroom. And Robin Phillips knew it. And here's what he wrote about his trip to Stoneham.

That day when I visited her, the end was already in sight. She already showed all the signs of that tragic slide which is so much a part of the ethos of rock and roll. The evidence of the severe cocaine addiction was available for all who wished to see it as well as the disarray into which her finances had fallen . . .

I don't know how it happened that Robin Phillips always managed to be there at the wrong time in my life like some UN international observer. With determined conviviality I was walking with him to his car when the stranger appeared at my elbow.

'Leslie Harrington,' he said.

He had a flat cap, Barbour and wellingtons. By my side Robin Phillips's ears began to flap.

'Really . . .' I said vaguely, 'I don't think we've met.'

'Coach and Horses,' he said. 'My wife suggested I come.'

It's another of those scenes imprinted in my memory. All the tiny touches. The brown envelope that he held out, the misty rain about us, Robin Phillips's happy little eyes. For Leslie Harrington had run on before I could stop him.

'Yes, it's my wife rather than me. She said after all the business you've given us it would be best to come and see you personally. Because obviously we don't want to go to court. She said it must be a mistake . . . some sort of oversight . . . she said that could be the only explanation.'

'Yes . . . well . . . thanks for coming Robin,' I said firmly, turning with determination. Inside the house I strode with theatrical anger across the hall, Leslie Harrington trailing after me. I pushed open the door to Francis's office, held the bill out imperiously towards him.

'Perhaps you can explain this Francis,' I said. 'Perhaps you can tell me what exactly is going on.'

I even carried on with the charade after Leslie Harrington had gone, not the least bit pleased with the cheque he had good reason to suspect wasn't worth the paper it was written on.

'I don't understand, Francis,' I said, sighing in the voice of one forced to say these things more in sorrow than anger. 'Why have you been keeping these things from me? Why didn't you tell me things had got so out of hand?'

'Oh Joanie, Joanie,' he said, poor Francis, slumping back in his seat, his head in his hands.

'God knows I've been trying long enough Joanie,' he said.

'Nonsense,' I said, petulantly.

'Why,' I said, shamelessly, not able to look at him, 'this is the first I've heard about it.'

I got up. Lit a cigarette slowly. Went over to the window and stared out, like I was thinking.

'Perhaps there's another reason you've been keeping all this from me Francis,' I said.

I heard the sound of the drawer opening then, the scrape of the chair as he got up. He was behind me then, speaking my name. When I turned he was holding out the books, humbly, quietly, an offering before him.

'The accounts are here,' he said. 'By all means have them investigated if you wish. But you will find nothing amiss I assure you. I have kept everything in order.' There was the smallest pause. Not even an accusation. 'In as much as I was able to do so Joanie.'

I had no answer to that and I knew it. But I didn't need one anyway. For there was a mild explosion from the door and Caroline was standing there. I whirled round on her.

'How dare you come in without knocking,' I said.

'You silly cow,' she said. 'You silly selfish doped-up cow.'

Francis came towards her then, a sad protesting hand in the air. 'It's all right Caroline,' he said, but she swept him aside.

'After all he's tried to do for you. After all his loyalty. And for what? When he isn't even bloody well getting paid for it.'

'How dare you,' I said again. The old well-used number. The last refuge of the self-importantly guilty.

'What does she mean Francis?' I said, turning away from her huffily, trying to drag together the rubble of my dignity around me.

'Oh for God's sake,' she said in disgust. 'How much longer do we have to continue with this farce?'

'You're fired,' I screamed, turning again.

'Oh . . . never . . .' she said. All of scathing Tyneside in her voice.

'You can't fire me,' she said, spitting the words. 'You haven't paid me for the last three months.'

She spoke to Francis then as if I was no longer in the room. There was bruised affection in her eyes as she looked at him.

'I'm going Francis,' she said. 'You may be happy to go on working here for nothing but I've told you before I'm not.'

'Get out. Get out. Get her out of here,' I yelled, throwing my arms about, trying to push myself between them. But still she stayed perfectly calm. Spoke only to him.

'I'm off,' she said. 'You must do what you like.'

I ran after her shouting as she walked along the corridor to her apartment.

'Get your stuff together. Be out of here in an hour. Or I'll have Austin throw you out.'

His name hit her like a stone on the back of her head. It shot forward as it struck her. She turned slowly, wonderingly, stared at me.

'Christ,' she said. 'You really are far gone aren't you?'

Austin was a handyman I employed from the village. He mowed the lawns, looked after the cars, turfed out the occasional over-enthusiastic fan. Not that there'd been a lot of call for that lately.

The contempt was still there in her eyes as she stared, and something else too, something that would have worried me more if I'd been in any state to take note of it. The faintest flicker of pity.

'Don't you see *anything?*' she said softly. 'Not even the state of the gardens?

'You got rid of Austin over a year ago,' said Caroline.

I did begin to notice things then. How the lawn was waist-high for instance. How the lichen that Austin had once cleared off the statues had grown back over again. How the dragon lady had slipped from her pedestal and was rolling now in the grass. But still only one thing really worried me. How low my stash was getting. I managed to scrape around in the bottom of some packets though, enough to bring me gaily down the stairs to Francis.

'There's nothing for it Francis,' I said. 'We'll have to sell the lease on the London flat.'

'We did that two years ago,' Francis said dully.

'Well . . .' I said, refusing to be down-hearted. 'There must be something else.' I waved a vague hand. 'Don't people remortgage or something?' He didn't look at me. Just coughed politely into his hand.

'I think you'll find that's already been done Joanie.'

'Oh has it?' I said, deflected. 'Isn't that interesting. Nobody told me.'

'It was when the second album . . .' he began. He was going to say 'failed' but stopped himself in time.

'About the time of the second album . . .' he said.

'What we need is a bottle of champagne,' I said briskly. 'Let's have some champagne Francis.'

He had his back to me. He was sitting at the desk staring into the little drawers and pigeon-holes, a redundant pen in his hand. I saw his head shoot back the same way as Caroline, only with him the movement was smaller, infinitely sadder and more subtle.

'Perhaps . . .' he began, not turning, 'this is not the time . . .'

264

'Oh yes, come on.' I was full of forced gaiety. 'Don't be such a puritan Francis. This is *exactly* the time. When things are bad. When there's some serious thinking to do. Everyone knows that's when you need champagne.'

I was brisker then, back to ordering.

'Go on Francis. Nip down to the cellar. Get the champagne.'

He sighed, laid down his pen, turned to face me.

'There's no champagne in the cellar,' he said flatly. 'There hasn't been anything in the cellar for a long time Joanie.'

I was querulous then. Illogically angry. Forgetting everything that had happened.

'Well, where's it gone . . . who's been drinking it . . .? I'll bet it's that bitch Caroline's been at it.'

'Don't say that Joanie.' For the first time he was fierce.

'Don't ever say that,' he said, getting up.

I knew I'd gone too far. I wouldn't look at him. Just strode up and down in front of him, crossing and uncrossing my arms on my chest.

'Well, just get some Francis. Phone someone up. Tell them to deliver it.'

'We can't do that,' he said. He sat down again heavily at the desk. He turned round and picked up the pen so as not to look at me. 'You know why we can't do that Joanie.'

He spoke as if to a child and in the end that's how I collapsed, a child beside him on the floor, laying my head against his knee.

'What's happening Francis?' I said. 'What's happening to everything?'

I was whimpering now. It wasn't much of a toot I'd managed to scrape together from the ends of the packets and now I was coming down fast.

'I know things are bad Francis. And I know it's all my fault. I know I've been a fool. I'm sorry for everything. I'm sorry for the way things have turned out.' I turned my

265

face up to him, whispering. 'But it's hard when you've had it Francis.'

'I know Joanie,' he said.

'All I want is a bottle of champagne Francis,' I whispered.

He pootered off in his old Renault in the end. I watched him as he went down the drive. To the off-licence. Where he bought it. With his own money. I was lying sulking on the sofa when he came in, bringing it in on a tray with a glass.

'Get another glass Francis,' I said grandly.

He didn't want to. He didn't care for alcohol. Seldom drank himself. But I made him drink a glass anyway. It went straight to his head. He stood, a little tipsily, looking out of the window.

'I used to stand there,' he said, 'down there by the lake. I'd look up at the house. All the lights blazing. The cars in the drive. The *people*.' All the despair at what he had seen was in his voice.

'Don't Francis,' I said miserably. Every word was a stab to my heart. But he went on anyway.

'Those people,' he said. 'Free-loaders. Taking everything. Giving nothing.'

'That's not fair,' I said. 'They're my friends.'

'Friends,' he said bitterly. 'They weren't your *friends* Joanie.'

'Don't say that Francis,' I said.

'If they were your friends,' he said, turning to look at me, 'where are they now Joanie?'

'That's it,' I said, jumping up from the sofa, eyes shining. 'Get a pen and some paper.' I was brisk now, business-like. This also can be the way of these things.

'You'll see Francis,' I said.

266

I chattered as we walked around making the list.

'You'll see Francis,' I said. 'Eduardo's always telling me, "If ever you want to sell Joanie". He'll take the stuff back. So will Pieter. They're friends of mine. They'll do it as a favour to me.

'I'll show you Francis,' I said.

But in the end, when he came back from London the next day, I had to prise the story out of him, bit by bit. He told it in distress. Like a man under torture.

He went to Eduardo first, who must have seen him coming in, looking down on him from his glassed-in office like an eyrie high up in the gallery. And knowing why he was there, the word being out on the street, he told his assistant to tell Francis he was out.

'It's OK. I'll wait,' he said. Francis, my Francis.

And so he sat down on one of Eduardo's Italian leather chairs, put his briefcase on the floor beside him, sat staring straight ahead, his hands folded in his lap, would not even allow himself to pass the time with the art magazines scattered before him on the coffee table, so that at last Eduardo was shamed into seeing him.

'Francis,' he said, coming down the steps, holding his arms wide. 'I'm so *sorry*. They didn't tell me it was you.'

He had his elegant spindly assistant buy time then by bringing them coffee.

'Now what can I do for you Francis?' he said.

When Francis handed over the list, he put his pompous half-moon spectacles on, read it pursing his lips. Then he got up without speaking, began to pace up and down, a man *racked*, tapped his spectacles on the paper.

'Ah, if only it were that simple Francis,' he said sorrowfully.

He sat down then, began to talk to Francis, man to man, resting back in his chair.

'It's my biggest problem,' he said. 'Trying to make people realize how easily the market can change.'

267

He positively moaned then, spreading his hands wide, demanding sympathy from Francis.

'Who would have believed it . . . not me . . . after that first exhibition . . . why, everyone wanted him . . . and now . . .' and here he gave one of his one eloquent shrugs, 'going for nothing Francis *nothing* . . .'

He sighed heavily, a sigh that said he was content that such sacrifices must be made for the sake of humanity.

'It's been a disaster for me too I don't mind telling you Francis.'

He lifted his cup of cold coffee then, stared into it, as a man might, contemplating the very heart of his philosophy.

'That's why I tell people,' he said, 'never buy as an investment . . . buy because you like a picture not because you hope it will make you money.'

He looked up now, staring shamelessly at Francis.

'That's what art should be about after all Francis . . .'

At the door Eduardo put his arm around Francis's shoulders.

'I'm so sorry. What's happened with Joanie. I can't pretend I haven't heard.' He looked Francis full in the eye.

'One of my *dearest* friends,' he said.

'Not to mention one of your best customers,' Francis answered with unaccustomed asperity.

'Oh . . . absolutely,' said Eduardo.

He dropped his arm then, reached back a lapel so that the other hand dug deep into his inside breast-pocket. He pulled out a wallet, poked around in it with his plump, perfectly manicured fingers.

'Perhaps . . . all things considered Francis . . . it would be better if . . .' and he pulled out a small wad of notes, held them out to Francis.

'I should so hate to offend Joanie. Perhaps better not to mention you saw me. Say they told you I was away. You'll think of something.'

Refusing to be defeated as Francis just stared, Eduardo collapsed the money, rolled it, reaching forward to stuff it into his top pocket. But Francis, awaking to the feel of it, jumped back as if touched by fire so that it fluttered down on to the floor around them.

'I don't need your money,' Francis said stiffly.

'Very well,' Eduardo said, unabashed, stooping to retrieve it. As he scrabbled on the floor his voice changed, became harsher, rasped.

'I like you Francis. You're a good chap. Take my advice. Get out while the going's good. Everyone knows what's happening to Joanie.

'It's a tough world,' he said, rising. 'It's good to remember that. Take care of yourself Francis.'

I make it up of course. But who could not, knowing what I know now? And how it was the same too when Francis went on to see Pieter, how he had to listen to the same self-serving moaning.

'Oh my dear . . . I am so sorry . . . oh, poor *Joanie*.'

Pieter slumped down on the red upholstery of his walnut wing-chair, his head dropped forward on to a hand balanced delicately on the extended leaf of his George I bureau.

'Oh if only one *could*,' he said.

He began to talk then, a low agonized voice.

'A secretaire Francis . . . such a piece . . . seventeenth-century . . . such exquisite patination . . . worth seven thousand . . . couldn't get four for it . . .'

He gave a great sigh, opened his arms and his hands wide at his desk. 'What can I *do*?' they said.

He kept up the commentary in the end right out on to the street.

'The truth is I'm over-stretched myself . . . it's between ourselves of course but opening that office in New York . . .

269

well, I'll be frank ... I wonder honestly if we were really ready for it ...'

He clasped Francis's hand in farewell.

'You will tell Joanie won't you ... how sorry I was. So many pleasant times I've had down there at Stoneham.'

His last vision of Pieter was a hand raised in front of the shop, his voice ringing out down the pavement.

'They say there's not a recession but really I don't know Francis ...' Unfortunately the effect was a little spoiled by the broad smile that broke out for a customer just arriving.

'Ah Charles, my dear Charles, that Sheraton knife box you were after. Well, I think I just might have something that fits the bill.'

'There is something,' Francis said.

'Tell me,' I said, still staring out of the window.

Francis was almost out through the door when Eduardo had put the cool hand on his arm.

'I notice the madonna's not on the list,' he said.

'No,' said Francis.

Eduardo shook his head in a puritanical fashion.

'You'll have to tell her Francis,' he said. 'These days ... well, I've told you how things are ...' He raised a magnanimous chin in the air. 'Between ourselves, though, I could probably do something with the madonna.'

'She doesn't want to sell the madonna,' Francis said, but Eduardo only sniffed.

'Well,' he said, 'it's her business of course.

'But needs must the way I hear it Francis.'

'Bastard,' I said when Francis told me. But it was said

without rancour, as if some lethargy at it all was taking over now, beginning to press out even the bitterness.

Later I stood before the madonna with a glass in my hand. I traced a finger over her bemused smile, pushed back a lock of her hair.

'Needs must my darling,' I said, raising my glass to her. 'But perhaps not yet.'

Which is when I decided it was time to go and see Didi.

Read my mind and you will find
the secrets lying here behind
the mask that never slips
don't ask, don't read my lips
Read my mind . . . Read my mind

'So . . .' she said, taking her time, not raising her head from the lounger, 'you come to me last Joanie.'

I'd called her up, made some excuse. 'I have to be in New York Didi . . .'

'What a pity,' she said, playing with me, 'and I have to be in LA.' I knew when I was beaten.

'Well then I have to be in LA Didi,' I said.

Do what you want Didi. Enrol in a few trendy New York dance classes, hang out with a few alternative film makers . . . Remember that little speech? I'd said it mockingly, patronizingly, but of course she did all of that and more.

It didn't help as my own albums mouldered and disappeared without trace that when I phoned McGarvey the mechanical sparrow would chirrup, 'I'm sorry . . . Mr McGarvey's in New York.' And I'd know he was there because of Didi.

And who could blame her? This much I managed to

figure out as I sat down on a lounger beside her. Who could blame her if now she enjoyed her revenge?

She knew why I was there. Still, I tried to keep up the charade, pretending there were other reasons why I'd come.

'I brought you something,' I said, holding out my father's gold watch-chain and a small Meissen group, one of the few good pieces he possessed. 'I thought you might like something . . .' Even I didn't have the nerve to say 'to remember him by'.

It got her head off the lounger anyway. She even took off her sunglasses. She looked at me like I was a fool.

'Why on earth should you think that?' she said.

Her eyes held my own with all the pleasure which was their due.

'Now,' she said. 'Why don't you tell me why you're really here Joanie?'

I said, 'I'll pay you back of course Didi.'

'No you won't,' she said, not troubling to hide her amusement. She drawled it as if wanting to stretch out the moment but her face was as severe as some schoolmarm's.

'You're too far gone. You're finished Joanie.'

It should have hit me like some slap across the face but I hardly felt a thing. Because that's the way things were now, the way things would go on being. Not feeling things any longer, all these things which were happening to me, the world going on by, and me in the middle somewhere, grinning half-heartedly at it all, trying to pretend it was all still a joke. Which is what I was doing now to Didi.

'Oh for God's sake,' she said, seeing the grin, slinging her head back on the lounger in disgust.

I said, 'You seem to know a lot Didi.'

She shrugged. She said, 'Everyone knows about you Joanie.'

272

Later she said, 'What's the point in giving you money anyway Joanie? You'll only spend it on drugs.'

'Oh, I won't, I promise I won't.' I was serious too, taking it all now, this lecture. From my little sister.

It was more to let myself off the hook than anything that I said, 'It's hot Didi. I think I'll go for a swim.'

She said, 'Sure,' in her new transatlantic accent, fresh-made like the rest of her.

'There's some costumes,' she said, 'over there in the cabana.'

I crawled back on to the lounger, winded, coughing, after a length. 'My God you look terrible,' Didi said.

She shook her head as she looked at me critically through her glasses.

'You're in bad shape,' she said lazily, stretching back in all her perfection.

'Not like you Didi,' I said.

It was evening when I was passing her bedroom and heard her call my name through the open crack of the door. The heat from outside was still lying heavily, seeping in through the long gauzy curtains at the wall of sliding windows, the last of the light glittering the pool, turning the lawn a dark deep green beyond.

Pushing the door open, I found her sitting at her dressing table, a marble slab of a thing with mirrors on three sides stretching up to the ceiling with branched candelabras coming out of it, the surface of the marble covered with pots and potions and bottles winking and glowing in pastel shades. There was something *gorgeous* about the scene, her in front of the dressing table. Even my father could only have approved of the word. The stool on which she sat was tiger-skin with a golden sphinx head at either end like something from ancient Egypt.

Astarte. Queen of Heaven.

'Come in Joanie,' she said.

I'd been hard at work at my own marble slab. Old connections in LA had helped me score fresh off the plane.

I'd been nose down in the guest bathroom since coming in from the pool and had also managed to fit in some grass.

'Tell me what you think?' she said.

She was craning forward from the stool towards the mirror, her buttocks two perfect circles, her hands cupped underneath her breasts. She sucked in her cheeks as she looked at herself, turning to the mirrors on three sides. She was like a child again. A child with new toys. There was an expression of happy satisfaction on her face.

'They say you can tell,' she said. 'That they go hard, lumpy, but it's not true.'

'They're perfect Didi,' I said, and it was true. Two perfect globes, the white of the marble, echoing the perfect circles below.

I believe now she had played the scene before because her lips were open a little, red and beautifully painted, and her eyes were lined in and drawn the same way. Her face too had that expression about it, the one I'd seen over Lennie's shoulder, that behind my back, beyond me, there might just be a camera. Still, looking at her, I could see how far she had come, this beautiful creature fashioned out of the ugly duckling with the stuck-out hair and the plump legs which once had been Didi.

'No, feel *them*,' she said.

Her eyes bored into mine in the mirror as I stood behind her. All the child was gone now. Her hands had dropped to the sphinxes' heads at her side.

I stretched forward from behind her, put my hands on her shoulders, first felt the smoothness of them, stroked her neck, the perfection of her back, the rise of her shoulders between the hollow, the childish hollow still there, staring all the time at the alabaster breasts she held out before me in the mirror.

'What are you afraid of?' she said. Her voice was a wicked whisper now.

'Do you think it will be *incest?*' she said.

'You know,' I said.

'Of course I *know*,' she said scornfully. 'I've always *known*.' A smile, mocking, coquettish, tilted her lips at the corners.

'You're the one who's always been blind Joanie,' she said.

I lifted my hands then from the sphinxes' heads, slid them around her, cupped them and spread them on her breasts. The feel of them, their smoothness, the sheen of the marble went straight to my belly. I threw my head back so I should not look at her, stood there, feeling them, waiting for her to make the next move which she did, taking my right hand, lowering it till it lay between her legs.

I cried in her hair as I lay on top of her, lost in her, my head in her neck, one hand across her breasts, the other bringing her off. She did not yelp or cry out as she came, as women usually do. She made no sound at all and in the end it was only the sound of my own voice I heard as I came myself, rubbing and thrusting like a man on her ass.

And I must tell you that over the years I had had, upon occasions, those doped-up intertwinings of all race and gender, those rites of passage, nothing more, solipsistic in the end. But I had never felt anything in my belly like I felt that day lying on that cool tiled floor with Didi.

Afterwards she got up briskly and dusted herself down. She walked over to the dressing table, pushed her toes into film-star sandals, tip-tapped on the tiles to the closet. She even hummed a little as if I were not there. Trying to recover some composure, I pulled my jeans towards me on the floor, fished into the pocket, lit up a cigarette. I tried to be nonchalant.

'So are you going to give me the money Didi?' I said.

She was standing in front of the doors of the great mirrored closet that stretched along one wall. She had thrown hangers along the rails as she hummed, pulled something out, a silver thing, fish-tailed, and pulled it on. She posed now, lost in thought as she stared at herself from all angles. A mermaid made up of chain-mail.

275

'You can pick up the cheque in the morning. I won't be here. Just see my secretary.'

I began mumbling then.

'Thanks Didi . . . I appreciate it Didi . . . as soon as I'm on my feet again I'll pay you back of course Didi . . .' But she broke in on me.

'You misunderstand,' she said coolly. 'It's not a loan.'

I shook my head in confusion.

'I'm buying the madonna from you,' she said. 'It's the only thing you've got that I want that's of value.'

I pushed myself up off the floor against the wall, covering my own breasts with my hands as I smoked the cigarette. I caught sight of myself in the mirror. Thin, grey-looking, circles under my eyes. Naked too and trembling.

'I'm not selling the madonna,' I said.

She clicked her teeth in irritation.

'Don't be ridiculous,' she said.

She tip-tapped back across the room, began drawing out brushes from a thin silver vase, dusting her cheeks, her eyes. Her breasts.

'You still don't get it do you?' she said. She reached behind her to a folder lying on a spindly gold chair, 'Here,' she said, throwing it so that it hit the floor with a slip and turned circles, eventually landing at my feet.

She was clipping on earrings now, taking them from a jewelled box, first one pair, then another. Her voice was matter-of-fact, not even unfriendly. Conversational.

'For what it's worth,' she said, 'my accountant's advice is that you go bankrupt. You're too far gone now according to him. You can't pull back. Not in your condition. Not with that claim from the Revenue hanging over you.'

But I hardly heard her. I had opened the folder now and I was staring at the figures inside, my life and times all laid out on the page. All my folly.

'Where the fuck did you get this?' I said. 'This is . . . private.'

She gave the small explosion of irritation again, the

276

click of her teeth, jabbed the brush with which she was dusting a shoulder now back in the vase.

'Oh, for Christ's sake,' she said. 'Nothing's private these days. Particularly when you're in the sort of shit that you're in.'

She was taking a last lick of mascara to her eyes with an old-fashioned block and brush. She stared into the mirror as she finished with that old smile of pleasure.

'It's a good price,' she said. 'More than you'll get on the open market.'

She stood up now, reached for a fur wrap on the chair, slung it over her arm with one last look in the mirror. As she passed me, at the door, her voice was severe.

'Take it Joanie. Do yourself a favour. Do something *sensible* for once.'

In the mirror now I saw a tossed-aside gigolo on the wall. Suddenly a man could not have been angrier.

She was crossing the hall when I shouted it, leaning over the bannister.

'You can keep your fucking money Didi.'

The Filipino maid who had the front door open looked up with a start. So did the peaked-cap standing waiting by the limo. But I didn't care that they saw me. I didn't even care that I was naked.

The shrug of her shoulders also lifted the perfect breasts. She stared up at me for a moment unembarrassed. Then she turned as if dismissing the matter entirely from her mind.

'Do what you want,' she said calmly on her way out through the door. 'But you'll have to sell it in the end Joanie . . .'

'You have to mourn it,' Dr Lindquist said, 'like a person.'

'That's terrible,' I said and I meant it. But afterwards I saw that he was right. So deep it is, this thing that we feel. This love affair we have with money.

277

'What are you thinking about?' he would say, his pipe puffing behind my head as I lay silently on the couch.

'I'm thinking of the dream,' I would say.

For a while it was the only thing I dreamed, turning up every night on the back of my eyelids, regular as clockwork, like a movie booked in for a long run.

In the dream I'd be sitting in this grey vault with this great iron door in front of me, barred and padlocked, with my money, stacked up in gold piles, all around me. I'd hear the footsteps approaching along the corridor and as I heard them I'd lean forward and put my arms around the money in preparation, pull it to me, rock it like a baby, croon over it and kiss it. Then I'd hear the key turn in the lock and the iron door push open. I never looked up. I never saw their faces. But it didn't matter. I knew why they were there. I knew that they'd come for my money.

I learned a lot about money after I went bankrupt, the old-fashioned paper stuff which I'd forgotten the feel of, the stuff I'd forgotten that people still hand over in exchange for things when they're forbidden the convenience of plastic.

'They'll want your credit cards, your cheque books, that sort of thing,' David told me the day before I was due to go to the bankruptcy court. David, my accountant. Bright and going far but young too and embarrassed.

'And something else Joanie . . .'

'Yes . . .?'

'Don't wear anything expensive, a Rolex, anything like that.'

'Jesus Christ,' I said, shocked. 'You mean . . . they'd take *things* off me . . .?'

Didi was right of course. I had to sell the madonna. I had to sell everything in the end. Stoneham and all that was in it.

It didn't take long after I got back from LA for the great snowball to start rolling. And once it started, it picked up speed surprisingly quickly, growing larger with every turn, carrying me with it as it rolled on down the hill.

The thing that surprises me now is how little I remember. It was as if I was cut from the whole thing. It wasn't just the dope, although there was still plenty of that. By some miracle I always found money to cover life's little necessities. No, it was something else that cut me off, some sort of barrier that had dropped down between me and the world, a sheet of glass that I could press myself against, watching all that went on the other side, but unable to touch it or feel it or join in the experience.

I think of that period now, that last period before I moved down to the cottage, in snatches, in a series of scenes or tableaux, me for instance, sitting at the end of the long leather-topped table in Milton's office, looking down at the line of suits on either side, wondering idly who was paying for them and then remembering it was me.

They were all there and interspersed with their underlings who made notes for them and passed them their files; the bank manager, greeting me without the warmth I remembered, the insolvency adviser who was a lot more friendly for after all I was good business, the VAT man rubbing knees with the ice maiden from the Inland Revenue who declined now even to look in my direction.

Francis was there too. My good and faithful servant with the pile of books and bills and cheque-stubs in front of him.

'I have done what I could,' I heard him say in a quiet dignified undertone to Milton.

'No one would think otherwise Francis,' Milton murmured, laying a comforting hand on his arm.

Most of the time they acted like I wasn't there. I embarrassed them, I could see that. I offended their sensibilities, this blatant example of financial mismanagement, cluttering up the end of their well-ordered table.

'I expect you're wondering why I called you all here,' I said as I came in, trying out a feeble joke, but all I got was a round of chill polite little smiles so after that I remained silent.

I saw that they preferred it this way. That my presence should become no more than a formality. I'd done my bit after all. My part was already played out. That was why I was here, beginning to know my place, at the end of their table.

The only time that they took any notice of me was when they needed my signature. When that happened the papers would be passed down the table so that one of them would have to look at me and when they did I'd catch this slightly bemused expression, as if they were trying to figure out who I was or why I was still there.

Most of the time this is how it was, sitting there like some Jarndyce uninvited, the fog of the jargon around me like a foreign language or distant music, muted and muffled.

Occasionally, as if to free myself from it, to shake it off, I'd get up, walk to the cona machine, pour myself another bitter stewed coffee. Once, as a protest, I sighed loudly when I came back, threw a leg ostentatiously one over the other and Milton threw me a warning smile.

Sometimes, though, a word would break through the jargon, a sharp word, harsh and jarring, peaking up like an iceberg in the fog. A word like *creditor* for instance. Or *debtor*. But sometimes too I'd find myself smiling vaguely, so unreal did the whole thing seem, so impossible was it to take seriously, when they mentioned another debt of grand or unusual standing, the jeweller's bill, for instance, for the round of Rolexes I'd given away one Christmas.

It was my attempt to reinforce the disintegrating Yuletide spirit. I made them stand before me like retainers to open them up, Francis and Caroline and Austin, and even

Austin's father-in-law Bill who sometimes helped him out in the garden.

They opened the presents unhappily, Caroline trying to cover her scorn, Bill scratching his head and looking at it.

'Thass very nice missie . . .' he said in the end. 'But see I got a watch.'

'Ungrateful yokel,' I said, telling the story with a laugh later to Eduardo.

That was the year I gave him the Italian chairs for his gallery, the same ones that Francis sat in when he went for the money. The same ones possibly that Eduardo still has.

Yes, the truth is that even I was surprised at the sheer size and variety of the debts laid out before me, the number of credit cards, the accounts with shops, stores, specialists and suppliers of every variety. The list read like a Yellow Pages of delight, no stone of hedonism left unturned, wine merchants, delicatessens, dress designers, caterers, hirers of marquees and novelty acts, organizers of exotic parties. And it escaped no one's attention, I imagine, aware as they were of the rumours, that at least one major outgoing was missing from the list.

There were the other bills too, large but more mundane. The Gas Board, the Electricity Board, the Water Board, plus of course the Inland Revenue whose total read more like a phone number. The VAT bill too was substantial, as was the one from the Department of Social Security.

'Oh do I pay them?' I said, interested.

'Apparently not,' Milton said drily.

Afterwards, when the rest of them had filed out, and there was just Milton left and David and Francis, Milton said, 'I'm sorry Joanie. We did what we could. But the Revenue won't accept a voluntary arrangement.'

'Oh well . . .' I said vaguely.

'I'm afraid you will have to go bankrupt.'

'But can't I just go on working?' I said, wondering why no one had thought of it. 'Just pay everyone off.'

'But when did you last work Joanie?' Milton said sadly.

They did their best to make me understand what was in store. They tried at the same time to be encouraging.

'You'll be able to keep some basic items to get started again,' David said.

'Oh good,' I said. But then he said, 'Yes. Some clothing, bedding, say, some furniture.'

It wasn't quite what I had in mind. It took me a while to get the hang of it.

'Are you saying they won't let me keep the Aston David?' I said.

He did his best, David.

'You can keep things which are necessary to your business,' he said.

'The Bechstein,' I said joyfully.

'Ah . . .' he said. 'Well . . . Perhaps not the Bechstein Joanie.'

And yet I was not unhappy. For while these great schemes rose and fell around me, I still had my own business to think about. My life was still busy, wheeling and dealing and trying to figure out where my next score was coming from, not to mention how in the hell I was going to pay for it.

I was lying on the sofa one afternoon waiting for a call when Francis came in. He had his coat on and he was coughing sadly and politely.

'I'm off then Joanie.'

'Off . . .?' I said, shaking my head. 'But where are you going Francis?'

'Oh Joanie, Joanie . . .' he said.

He took my hands then, sitting beside me on the sofa.

'Take care of yourself Joanie,' he said.

'I'm sorry Francis,' I said, a shaft of sanity striking

through the madness. 'Of course I remember now. I'm sorry. I'm sorry about everything.'

'Here,' I said, reaching to the table behind me, 'Take this. I want you to have it.'

It was a Baccarat paperweight. One of those empty without-affection business presents that people give. For one of my birthdays, this one. From McGarvey.

He wouldn't take it though. He shook his head. 'I can't Joanie,' he said.

I tried pushing it into his hand.

'Why not? It's not personal. It's not that sort of present. I want you to sell it. To make up for some of the money I owe you.' But Frances only looked distressed.

'The thing is . . . we're not supposed to take anything from the house,' he said.

I exploded, jumping up, stamping my feet in fury.

'For Christ's sake what do you think it *matters* Francis? What do you think any of it matters now? Who do you think *cares* about this lousy little paperweight?'

He just hung his head as if the fault were his.

'I know but still . . . I can't . . . there it is.'

I held it up in front of the fireplace.

'Very well,' I said. 'I'm going to smash it now Francis. Unless you take it, I'm going to smash it here into a thousand pieces.'

'Oh Joanie,' he said, up on his feet now, pulling me to him in a hug as I shoved it into his pocket.

'Don't worry,' I said, drawing back from him, laughing shakily.

'They'll just think I flogged it for dope Francis.'

That night I walked round Stoneham, alone in the place for the first time.

'So,' I said, 'just you and me now,' and I laid my head against the walls. But nowhere could I hear the sound of dancing.

*

Donald's smile is like a clown's smile now. That awful smile painted on the grey face. A face sometimes almost as grey as Richard's. For Donald too is exhausted.

Donald's bed is a couch in Richard's room where he lies down at night but does not sleep, his ears alert for the smallest alteration in the rhythm of departing life which is Richard's breathing.

Occasionally he will get up to stretch his legs and pace the corridor outside. If I awake in the night it is always to the snick of pressed floorboard and the soft tread of his feet.

Once when I could not sleep and got up to make some tea I met him walking up the stairs. He'd been to the kitchen to replenish the oil in the lamp that was once Richard's favourite, that he liked for its old-fashioned glow.

He held the lamp aloft defiantly in one hand, some keys jangling at his belt.

Mrs Danvers watching over Rebecca.

So because days are nights now and nights days, we find ourselves talking at strange times in strange places, at three o'clock in the morning for instance, like this morning, Donald and I speaking in low voices at the window, to the sound of the soft rhythmic breathing.

He was telling me about Dickens. He was an English teacher when he gave it up to look after Richard. I figure some part of him still misses the teaching.

Donald says that Dickens never did get over the Marshalsea. Fourteen weeks was all his father stayed there in the debtors' prison, but it turned into a life sentence for twelve-year-old Charles. He couldn't shift it, the memory, visiting his father in that prison. It became an incubus sitting slimily on his shoulder. It nudged and gnawed at him, distorting his view of money, destroying his belief in it, so that in the end he could come back from a tour of America with twenty thousand dollars in his pocket (and I can show you plenty of bands a hundred years later who've come out with less), an unheard-of amount of profit, but it didn't make any difference, it didn't help. No matter how much he made he still couldn't get over the feeling that one false move and he might be back in the Marshalsea.

It makes me wonder. Is there a Marshalsea that none of us see sitting on McGarvey's shoulder?

No Marshalsea for me though. Just Carey Street. Walking up it, at the back of the High Court, surprised that it exists, understanding where it came from, the old saying. *In Carey Street*. Which means bankrupt. Which is where I am now.

In Carey Street.

Walking up it with Milton, past the old queerly shaped buildings, walking the way they've all walked for so long and for the same reason before me, I feel this tremor in my soul and I wonder if a clerk might not scurry out suddenly in a pince-nez from an alley. I wonder if it's too late to try for a loan from Ralph Nickleby.

Outside the court there's a small knot of reporters. They buzz about me angrily like bees.

What did you spend it on Joanie?

Is it true about the parties Joanie?

How did you get through so much money Joanie?

It wasn't that difficult, I say.

Inside my footsteps echo on the stone floor as they would in a church, and I figure that's right because it looks like a church inside, soaring roof, high windows, and I figure this is the way it should be, a bankruptcy court like a church in this world where money is the new religion.

Milton said to me, 'Be straight Joanie,' not taking any prisoners, and I said, 'Of course Milton,' but I was past caring by then, not too much worried about lying. And anyway there's a fake marble ledge around the basins in the empty toilets where we're waiting which is too good an opportunity to miss.

I've just dusted my nose off when she comes in, still I have the feeling that she knows what I've been doing but she just gives a faint shrug that says, Don't worry about me. It's a whatever-gets-you-through-the-night sort of shrug and it's why I like her. Not judging me in this place which is all about judgment.

As she washes her hands afterwards we begin talking for no better reason than we both happen to be here. But just being here, in this place, means you can by-pass the preliminaries.

'I'd given it up,' she says a little regretfully, savouring the smoke, letting it out slowly. We're grabbing a cigarette, like children, behind a pillar.

I'm raising the cigarette to my own lips when she notices the Rolex which I'd forgotten.

'Take it off,' she says. 'Put it in your pocket. You never know when you might need it.'

Her eyes are dark and flat and empty, drained with the effort of managing without tears.

She's unmarried. She ran the family printing firm along with her brother whom I suspect of small-time profligacy for no better reason except the obvious one, that she's the one who's here and not him. She only shrugs though.

'Women survive it better,' she says, 'a business collapsing. You see it all the time here.'

She goes before me, wishing me good luck. We grasp hands quickly before she's gone like we're on the way to the guillotine.

'You've made it once,' she says, 'you can make it again.'

'Yeah,' I say. 'Why not?' But only because I don't want to disappoint her.

286

Watching her back disappear I wish I'd said something like 'Let's keep in touch,' but it's too late now because the tumbril's bouncing back over the cobbles and Madame Defarge is waiting for me.

I offered myself up for bankruptcy so it's a private hearing, the thing that's irritating the reporters. It's over quickly. Some getting up, some sitting down, a lot of passing paper backwards and forwards. Milton is appointed my trustee.

Later I hand over the cash cards, the credit cards, the cheque-books. They write my name in a ledger the size of a desk.

The clerk bows her head as she writes it. She writes it so slowly, so painstakingly, she might be using a quill pen.

And this also seems to me like something from Dickens.

How different is this night from all other nights . . .

Sitting in the lounge, pretending to flip through a magazine, I heard the raised voices in the kitchen.

'How could you Milton?' I heard Lois say. 'Tonight of all nights.'

'It's because it is tonight Lois,' Milton said.

The angry bees had buzzed around us again as we left the court.

'I don't think you should go back to Stoneham tonight Joanie,' Milton said as we pulled away in the car.

'I think the best thing would be if you came home. Spent the night with Lois and me.'

I wasn't that crazy on the idea of spending the night with Lois but there were questions I still hadn't quite answered. Like just what I was supposed to do without cheque-books and cash cards. I wanted to ask Milton as they took them away but it didn't seem in the spirit of the thing somehow to mention it.

Lois was bending over the platters of food that seemed to cover every available surface in the kitchen as I coughed politely from the doorway.

'Look,' I said as they both looked up, 'it's OK. I understand. There's no reason why you should want me here Lois. Call me a taxi Milton. I'll go to a hotel or something.' I thought it was quite a smart idea. I thought it might precipitate a discussion about money.

It was Lois though who spoke.

'Milton's right,' she said. 'There's no reason to go.' She did not look up as she said it.

Only after she had laid a final lettuce leaf, pushed the plate aside, did she finally lift her eyes.

'It's our Seder night Joanie,' she said coolly. 'You are therefore welcome to join us.'

Everyone who is hungry, let him come in and eat; everyone who is in need, let him come and celebrate the Passover . . .

Lois converted when she married Milton. A determined thing for a non-Jew to do. Shabbas candles and kettles and challah and barucha and all without a mother to teach her.

'I'd never been brought up in any sort of faith. I liked the one Milton offered. I liked the orderliness, the completeness . . .'

We sat on the sofa after the meal. She talked naturally but without any false attempt at friendship.

'Also I wanted the children to be brought up properly in it. I thought they could decide then for themselves whether or not it was what they wanted.'

At the dinner the children sat smartly dressed, merry-eyed but still with that strange old-fashioned sense of *duty* that pervades the house. A girl with a mass of dark hair, only seven or so but on the way to being a great beauty. Boys five and four, bowing their heads in their yarmulkes,

288

peering through their fingers, as Milton dipped the bitter herbs in the salt water, broke the matzah, offered thanks.

Blessed art Thou O Lord our God, King of the Universe. Creator of the fruit of the earth . . . I might have wriggled in my seat like the boys, but I found a few bits and pieces in the bottom of my bag, some Valium, a little grass, some scrapings of coke.

When the time came, the boys ran out, tumbling over each other, to open the front door for Elijah. Their eyes grew wide as Milton touched the table with his knee, making the spare glass of wine tremble. Later they hunted for the matzah, sang rhymes with their father.

'I'll see you in the morning Joanie,' Lois said at the foot of the stairs.

'Yeah, goodnight Lois and thanks,' I said, because in my head I was already out of there. I'd worked out a plan.

The cab cost me the last of the few quid I had in my pocket, but I wasn't worried. I'd figured there'd be someone in the place I could bum a line off and a drink. And whatever came after that I was past caring about.

The entrance was up an alleyway full of bins and fire-escapes. There was a queue at the door being entertained by a couple of buskers. The younger of the two, a skinny thing, played a concertina. The other one, thin too but older and taller, did a Fagin dance, holding wide an old tweed greatcoat, menacing the queue with his hat.

'Thank you ladies and gentleman thank you so much . . . a little something . . . for the *poor* . . . how can you refuse . . .?'

As I strode past him and past the rest of the queue, he followed me, imitating my walk, a busker's trick, making the crowd laugh.

'Fuck off,' I said over my shoulder.

I'd been a regular at the place once with my own special table. It's also true I'd passed a couple of bad cheques.

Still, when the bouncer put his hand across the door I just laughed at him.

'Oh, come onnnn,' I said.

He had that glazed and opaque look only possible from someone acting on instructions.

'Private party,' he said firmly.

'Oh yeah? Whose?' I said, jamming my face up close to his.

When he said the name, I laughed again, shoving against him, feeling the iron chest, at the same time smelling his carnation.

'Great,' I said, 'tell him I'm here.' But the bouncer didn't move. Instead he reached out and caught the hand with which I pushed him, held it by the wrist, and lowered his head. His lips were near my own now and lascivious. Savouring what they had to say next.

'What name shall I say?' he said.

I was on a short fuse and I was about to go up. At my back Fagin danced, played the fool, or maybe the Devil.

'Go screw,' I said but I was getting the worst of it and I knew.

The queue was beginning to laugh behind its hands now. I could hear my name whispering along the line.

'You know who the fuck I am,' I yelled at the bouncer but he just crossed his hands across his chest. It was all it needed. I began punching him and kicking him, yelling it all the time, over and over.

'You know who the fuck I am,' I said.

It wasn't a big shove that he gave me in the end but it caught me off balance. I staggered backwards, felt myself begin to fall. I thought I was there. I'd already seen myself crashing on the ground before me but something caught me the second before I fell.

It felt like wings, that old great-coat, as it folded about me.

'Tell 'em who you used to be Joanie,' he said.

*

In the dragon lady's dream
Things are done more or less
Just the ghost of a chance
That the Devil may dance
Hear him answering yes . . .

'Who are you?' I said once to Fagin, who turned out to be called Max.

'Who do you want me to be?' he said with that strange wolfish grin.

'Journeymen . . .' he said as I stormed away, the last of the laughs from the queue following me down the alley-way. He flourished his hat in a deep mocking bow, dancing along beside me.

'Gentlemen of the road. At your service ma'am,' he said.

'Max,' he said. 'And my good friend Mark. A fan of yours no less.'

'I need to score,' I said, ignoring Mark who was staring wide-eyed with a look of adoration.

'Yes,' said Max. 'I rather thought you did.'

He was like some bizarre old-fashioned showman, or some mountebank, skilled in deception and selling phoney medicines from the back of a covered wagon. He sold my Rolex for me in the pub he took me to, a weird thing like a stage set, standing ghostly and alone in the middle of a redevelopment site, the sort of place that made you think it might not be there if you came back looking for it the next day.

Inside, it was an underworld of thievery and small-time crime, with a Mother Courage of a landlady and camp followers, mostly ladies of the night.

'Four hundred,' Max said, putting the notes on the table.

'It's worth two thousand,' I said, outraged. 'For Christ's sake. It's a Rolex.'

His look wasn't friendly. It said there was a new world out there and I might as well get used to it.

'Things are worth what you can get for them,' he said. 'And here it's worth four hundred.'

I watched him as he played the huckster, selling the watch and afterwards scoring the coke. He moved easily around the huddles of men. I saw the leaning back, the shrugs, the animation and the carelessness, and I saw that what he was most of all was an actor, which was one of the things he claimed to have been along with a priest and a petty criminal. His convictions were mainly for threatening behaviour, incidents while he was begging and busking when he'd bad-mouth the bystanders who refused to subscribe.

Looking back, I think Mark was the only person in the world he cared about. And he did care about Mark, I'm sure of that. It was as if, in some way, he'd taken him on.

Fagin. With Oliver Twist.

I phoned Milton from Stoneham the next day.

'We were worried about you Joanie,' he said reproachfully. 'And how did you get home without money?'

'Friends Milton, friends,' I said.

A few hits of coke and some cheap whisky and all the bad things, the bankruptcy, the Stoneham sale, all this had begun to fade away. Instead, I began to feel a weird sort of satisfaction at the way things had turned out. I had a feeling of clearing out, of new beginning. I liked meeting the hucksters and the down-and-outs that Max introduced me to. I liked this feeling of becoming part of a new and disadvantaged in-crowd. I looked forward to despising

292

everything that had been before in my life, and I particularly liked the idea that I had slipped down a level, that my fall from grace had brought me to this place of belonging.

'Max,' I said, 'Mark,' putting a hand round both their shoulders.

'Friends,' I said, squeezing them to me, 'friends in adversity.'

Max stole a car to get us to Stoneham. I watched him as he jammed the wrench in the door, jump inside in one smooth easy movement.

'Oh God not an *Escort* . . .'

'Just get in,' he said.

It was the first stolen car I'd ridden in, and I liked the sweet feel of excitement. It was the same one I'd felt as a kid, fourteen or so, on the back of a motor-bike, doing a ton which was what you had to do at the time on the long straight stretch of road over the reservoir. It was already too late when I realized the only car ahead was a Rover. Roaring past my father, my head turned away, I'd felt the heart-stopping rush that comes with the feared and forbidden, the thing, I figure now, you try to recover with the coke when there's nothing left to say no to.

It was five in the morning when we dumped the Escort in a backstreet a few miles from Stoneham.

'So what do we do now?' I said.

'Walk,' said Max.

'*Walk.*'

'Don't knock it till you've tried it,' he said.

And it was true. The fields were heavy with dew like diamonds and there were silver spiderwebs on the hedges. A cuckoo sounded as we crested the hill. Below us five hundred years fell away as Stoneham poked through the mist.

'You live *there?*' said Mark

Later in the day they decided to go busking, to try to catch the tourists.

'I'll come with you,' I said.

I wore the ten-gallon hat with the rhinestones I'd brought back from one of the US tours, wrapped on the dark glasses.

Crammed into the back of the Aston with his concertina and my guitar, Mark chattered over my shoulder.

'Pick anything you like Joanie. I can play them all.

'I've got everything you ever did,' he said.

We set up our pitch in the market-place opposite the record shop that my father had continued to make detours around till the day of his death. If he was looking down from his Greek heaven, well all I can say is, he got his revenge.

'Christ,' I said in disgust, looking at the handful of coins after an hour's work. 'What a bunch of tight bastards.'

'Makes you wonder doesn't it?' Max said smirking.

'Not at all,' I snapped.

Luckily there was a better way of raising money to fill the fridge and replenish my stash.

'I was an antique dealer for a while,' Max said and I believed that too, watching him cast a knowing eye over the wares in the house.

'I'll take care of it,' he said. And he did, for Max was taking care of everything now.

He took to his new role of master of the house as if to the manner born. I was lying on the sofa one day when he came in looking every inch the successful businessman dressed in a suit the Dentist had left behind, a charcoal-grey number with a black silk shirt.

'Have a good day at the office darling,' I said mockingly as he swept the Aston keys up from a table and put the pair of French bronzes beneath his arm. He looked back at me from the door in the same mode.

'I'll bring back a little something for you shall I darling?' he said.

It was Max who had the idea for the party. We were sitting in the library in front of the fire. I was drunk and maudlin, bitching on about Eduardo and Pieter again, something I was doing a lot lately.

'For God's sake,' he said. 'Why moan? Do something about it.'

'Yes but what,' I said.

As soon as he'd hit on the plan he went about organizing it like some sort of ringmaster.

'We'll need some staff,' he said.

I just laughed when he paraded them in front of me a few days later.

'For Christ's sake Max,' I said. 'Where the fuck did you find this bunch?'

One was tall and gaunt, with acne, another had a shaven head and cauliflower ears. A third with a combat cap pulled low over his face had the wild eyes of a mercenary, while the other two, one black, one white, were all dreadlocks and beads and dark glasses. And in the middle, Mark, with the looks of a leprechaun, curly hair and earrings and that strange sweet smile on his face. I shook my head.

'This is crazy,' I said, reaching for a cigarette. 'This lot will convince nobody.' Max's face though had darkened with fury.

'These are my friends,' he said, the grand Welsh 'r' rolling out and into infinity as it always did when he was angry. 'They are travellers. Journeymen like me. Gentlemen of the road.'

'So what?' I said.

'They are jacks of all trades, survivors in a new and hostile world. They are actors. They have had to be.'

Max's chin jutted up in the air. The slits of his dark eyes were cold.

'They will do their job well,' he said with a toss of his head. And he was right. They did.

They might have been to butler school so tall and still and dignified did they stand in their white ties and rented frock-coats, their heads inclined with such civility towards their trays of champagne.

Eduardo's mouth fell open along with everyone else's.

'My dear,' he hissed, 'they're *delicious*.' He took my elbow, drawing me away from his boyfriend's hearing.

'I insist you tell me,' he said. 'Where *did* you find them?'

'They're performance artists,' I said.

As I moved among them I heard the behind-hand words and half-phrases trailing me like wisps of ether.

'Clearly some mistake' . . . 'Or she's recovered' . . . 'Well, of course I never did believe this whole bankruptcy thing . . .'

'Darling the place looks wonderful,' Eduardo said and so it did, glittering and glowing with the candles and the cutlery, the damask and cut glass. And all making its last public appearance at Stoneham.

He caught me later, Eduardo, in a corner, a man with much on his mind.

'That money thing Joanie . . . When Francis came . . . You know I was *distraught* when I couldn't help . . .'

'Don't think another thing about it Eduardo,' I said.

A short while later Pieter traced out the marquetry on the George II secretaire, not meeting my eye.

'A misunderstanding Joanie . . . you must know that . . . I tried to get you the next day . . .'

He drew a loving hand down the side of the bookcase, looked up finally with a smile.

'One of the best pieces I ever sold you Joanie,' he said as if it pledged something between us. I smiled back.

'And there were so many Pieter,' I said.

Only Paulette was suspicious.

'Not many people here,' she sniffed. 'You couldn't call it a *party*.'

I smiled at her too as her liar's eyes held my own.

'I just wanted something small you see Paulette . . . something intimate . . . for special friends.

'A sort of thank you,' I said.

Francis had gone last to Paulette. She was staring at her sketches, her glasses dangling on her chest.

'What is it Francis?' she said. 'I'm busy.'

Paulette started back in the Quant years like everyone else but somehow never made it. Her business was about to fold when I met her. For a while what with stage stuff and everything I kept her afloat. I introduced her to other clients too, even bankrolled her for a time. But she'd just done a deal with Harvey Nichols and she shook her head haughtily at Francis.

'For God's sake,' she said. 'I must have told her a thousand times she should be more careful with her money.'

She gave a scornful little twist to her nose.

'All those parties . . .' she said. 'Ridiculous.' Which made Francis confused.

'But . . . but . . . but . . .' he said. 'You were at those parties.' He grew bolder. 'You picked up your best clients at those *parties*.' She took her glasses from her chest, peered at him through them.

'Will that be *all* Francis?' she said coldly.

It wasn't. He was angry now. The day had been too much for him.

'She bailed you out when you had problems,' he shouted at her, almost in tears. 'Now you're just like the rest. You won't lay out a penny to help.'

But her voice was bored and cold. She turned away from him, bent back over her drawings.

'Close the door after you Francis,' she said.

She stared at me now, her head thrown back, her eyes narrowed over the high collar.

'It was a joke wasn't it Joanie . . . all that bankruptcy nonsense . . . I knew it was . . . I told them all so . . .' There was a superior smile on her face.

'By the way,' she said, looking around her, 'I don't see Francis.'

'Francis has gone,' I said. She nodded in satisfaction.

'At last,' she said. She took my arm, drew me away, looked back over her shoulder.

'I've been wanting to tell you for a long time. I'm so glad you've finally got rid of him.

'I'll be frank with you Joanie, I never did trust Francis,' she said.

'My dear who will say grace?'

It was the sort of foolish camp remark that Eduardo liked to make. His silly boyfriend looked pleased at it and giggled. But I had heard the joke before and always in the same fashion with Eduardo's plump hands, old fogey style, across his chest.

There had been the faintest intake of breath around the table as the boys appeared in perfect procession with the silver salvers. Now they lay on the table before them.

'I'll say grace,' I said.

Behind me Max, the perfect butler, inclined his head, drew my chair backwards as I stood up.

'Eyes closed everyone,' I said sternly. 'No peeking.'

At the end of the table though Eduardo winked at me through latticed fingers. Doing it he missed his boyfriend doing the same to dreadlocked Benny. Along the table Paulette's date, a punk queen who swung both ways, was making eyes at Max while Paulette and Gudrun, Pieter's wife, stared at each other playing footsie beneath the table. Only Pieter sat head bowed as I recited; an old Dutch Protestant at prayer.

'*Blessed art Thou O Lord our God, King of the Universe, Creator of the fruit of the earth . . .*'

I clicked my fingers and the boys stepped forward, lifting the silver lids as one.

'And for what you are about to receive,' I said, 'may the Lord make you truly thankful.'

They were staring down at the plates in confusion, the first dawning intimations of disgust on their faces when the whip cracked out like a gun.

As their heads shot upwards Max's best Welsh basso profundo rolled out like thunder.

'Eat . . . *dogs* . . .' he said.

For that was what it was. Dog meat.

It lay on the family crested bone china plates that I'd bought from old Sir Thomas, trembling and glittering with the slimy jelly, oozing the dark doggy gravy. As their noses wrinkled with the stink of it which was heavy now and all over the table, I curved myself into Max who was standing beside me. I laid a hand on his shoulder, put my lips to his ear theatrically in a loud whispering taunt.

'They're not *eating*, Max,' I said.

He caught me to him, a last clasp like Valentino plastering a kiss on my mouth and throwing me aside before striding forward.

It became mayhem then, a Bedlam of sounds and smells; the whip cracking as Max the mad ringmaster strode up and down, raising the dust from the stone floor in a cloud which mingled in the nostrils with the stink of the dog meat; the scrapings first of the chairs as they tried to get away from it and then the coughing and the spluttering, the choking and retching when the boys had stepped forward, bent over them, one hand on either side like wicked nannies, grasping the cutlery for them, pushing it into their palms, shovelling the stuff forcibly from the plates to their mouths.

And over it all Max's rolling Shakespearian Welsh ringing round their heads and rising up to the very hammer beams themselves.

> *Most smiling, smooth detested parasites*
> *Courteous destroyers, affable wolves, meek bears,*
> *You fools of fortune, trench-friends, time's flies,*
> *Cap-and-knee slaves, vapours and minute jacks!*

Undoubtedly his finest performance.

They saw them off, in the end, as once Harold had done Molly, only this time it was the boys snapping at their ankles. They ran to their cars, dragging their coats and their bags, screaming and swearing, the brown still running down their shirt fronts and their breasts, still smeared on their faces.

Only Pieter was left behind at the table. He stared down motionless at his plate still thick with the meat and the oily brown gravy.

As I watched he lifted the napkin slowly and wiped away a last tiny splodge of the stuff still trembling from his chin. There was no resentment in his voice as he spoke and he didn't look at me.

'You're mad,' he said. 'Quite mad.'

'I know,' I said.

I was still sitting at the table later when Max came in.

'For the boys,' I said, pushing the pile of notes towards him.

'They will be pleased,' he said.

Later we had a party, turned up the music in the great

300

hall, even switched on the fairy lights. Feet rising and falling. Eating and drinking.

The boys danced easily together like they were having a good time. They didn't dance like they felt something was missing. At one point they jumped up on the refectory table to dance Greek style, arms round each other's shoulders. They kicked their legs up, stamping on the polished wood. Each had a can in his hand. A joint passed along the line between them. Looking up, I thought I saw an ancestor shudder.

'Don't worry,' I said. 'It'll soon be over.'

We partied through till dawn which turned out to be another of those dewy May mornings. I watched from the window as the mist began to roll back across the lawn till it lay on the lake like candy-floss. By then the sun was out and turning the stone a rich yellow and I went outside and I was standing there, the warmth on my face, the lichen and the ivy beneath my fingers, when I felt Max's hands unbuttoning my shirt.

I knew it was Max. I didn't have to look. He went for my breasts like a man claiming his inheritance. He pushed up the black dress, pulled down the knickers with an impersonality that suited the pair of us. My legs were around his waist, my ass cradled in his hands as he undid himself, a satyr, tails of his frock-coat hanging. I yelled out as he pushed himself into me, pinioning me against the wall, not from the passion but from the pain of the stone grazing my skin. I dragged at a strand of ivy in protest and it came away in my hand.

As he came with a grunt, I opened my eyes slowly, looking over his shoulder, and there they were, the sun behind them, making halos around them, Muff and Rizla, Spider and Jazz and Benny.

They stood in a semi-circle, entirely still, like statues.

301

Their faces were flat, like bystanders, free of any sign of salaciousness or prurience. They looked like they were waiting, politely, for us to finish, and so they were I guess, for as Max's shoulders fell and he let out the last grunt of a spent man, Rizla tipped his hat to me respectfully as they raised their hands in farewell as one and turned to walk away, boots crunching across the gravel.

I watched them as they disappeared into the mist, journeymen in their boots and their great-coats and earrings, walking away down the drive as they might have done since the beginning.

The auctioneers came a week or so later, set up the marquee on the lawn, stuck the little tickets on everything. On the day of the sale I stood with Max and Mark looking down from the bedroom window watching the drive fill up with cars.

'Just like the old days,' I said.

Molly was there, her first return visit since I'd thrown her out. I'd seen her scavenging a few days earlier at the viewing, picking at things, turning them over. Now I caught her walking away like something from *Vanity Fair* with a couple of my dresses over her arm.

'They parted my raiment eh Molly,' I said, pulling at a feather hanging off one of Paulette's more exotic creations. But it didn't mean anything to Molly.

I watched the Bechstein sold from the back of the marquee, amazed as the price spiralled upwards on the back of Pieter's obstinate bidding. I was standing over it touching the keys in farewell as he came up behind me.

'A bad deal for you Pieter,' I said without turning. 'You won't make much buying at that price.'

'Only my commission,' he said.

'Ah,' I said scornfully. 'A relic is it? A *souvenir*. Bought by a fan perhaps?'

302

'You could say that,' he said. He came closer.

'My instructions are to leave it here with you,' he said.

I did not answer for a moment, just continued to press the chord, a D minor, melancholy, contrary, disturbing.

'Tell whoever it is thanks a lot,' I said, taking my hand off the keys and reaching for the lid. I could still hear that 'D' in my head as I lowered it slowly. I didn't turn when I spoke.

'Tell whoever it is thanks a lot. But I won't need a piano where I'm going.'

Which is how my Bechstein comes to be standing in Richard's bay window.

Eduardo was there too, refusing to catch my eye and raising his numbered lollipop for the madonna. He didn't get it though.

It went for £82,000 in the end but not to him and Didi was right. It did make less on the open market.

Didi knows a lot about art. She's highly respected now as a collector.

She has a Picasso, did you know that? A Dali too and a Diego Rivera. She has a Cassatt and a Kahlo and I believe a Gustav Klimt.

And of course she also has my madonna.

V

There's the ones who'd like to eat you
Say they're desperate to meet you
Some who must defeat you
To get what they're looking for . . .

Today the Little Match Girl got what she wanted.

There she was, staring up at us from the front page of Donald's *Guardian*. On the mat. Inside the house. Which is where she so desperately wants to be.

She's pictured standing where she always stands, against the railings opposite. Sometimes she stands there for hours at a time, perfectly still, only her eyes moving, swivelling and roving across the front of the house, searching out the window behind which Richard is dying.

'He's all I have . . .' she said, her face contorted in despair as she grabbed at me a second time, the day we came back from Angus's, her fingers caught again in my hair.

Richard danced with her apparently. That's what it says in the paper. Took her up out of the crowd. Danced with her before an audience stretching back and over the horizon. And things were never the same again. Because of the mighty spell of it, the power, the romance, the sweet dream corkscrewing up we call rock and roll.

'It's not about dreams,' I said once to Richard when we were arguing, 'it's not about romance. Rock and roll's about reality . . .' But I couldn't have been more wrong.

There are other fans now keeping vigil but she does not mix with them. She mixes with nobody, keeps herself to herself, apart, solitary, refusing to exchange in the badinage which has grown up between the rest of them and the press.

Even the two policemen on this soft midsummer beat do their best to protect her. They moved on a photographer once who would have obscured her view by parking his car in front of the spot where she lays out her bedroll.

For at night, here's the thing, she is like Donald, lying

307

down, but never sleeping. Instead she lies there, eyes open. Searching. Fixed. Obsessional. She might as well be blind with those eyes.

An 'intense symbiotic relationship'. Dr Lindquist's words. This thing that passes between the worshipper and the worshipped.

'You hate them. Your fans. I think you must hate them.'

'That's strong. Very strong. Hate them?'

'Of course.'

'Why?'

'Because they make you what you are. They hold your fate in their hands. They force you to be something you're not. To wear this mask that they put on you. That turns you into what they want you to be . . .'

He was right. Especially about the mask. Something any real fan knows instinctively. The real fan would run a mile rather than come face to face with the obscure object of desire, knows it could only ever be a disappointment. The real fan knows that for sure we have feet of clay but it doesn't matter, because what counts is what's up there on stage, that other world fixed for ever beneath the lights, the best part of what you are, the mask, that part you make up.

But then there are the others, the ones who spring out from a cupboard in your dressing room, from behind the hotel bathroom door, who sneak in after relics, nicking anything not nailed down, your favourite jacket, a book you happen to be in the middle of, the only hairbrush you've found that's any good with your hair.

A girl once developed a passion for me, wrote letters every day. A young man changed his name by deed poll to mine.

I got used to them hiding in the shrubbery, appearing suddenly in the shadows, frightening the life out of me, outside the French windows. When I saw them I'd yell for Francis or Austin.

308

Sometimes as they were led away they'd turn on me, begin screaming things, that I was a bitch, a whore.

Once I watched shivering as a middle-aged woman was bundled into a police car holding out her arms to me, yelling and weeping that I was her long-lost child.

'You're a repository of hopes, dreams, sadnesses . . .' that's what Dr Lindquist said.

After Mark died they found his room in the squat where he'd been living before he came to Stoneham papered with pictures of me. One of them was three feet high.

'You're all I have Joanie,' he said. 'Take me with you. Take me with you.'

'He was just a boy.' Mark's mother, black hair from a bottle cut very short, large gold earrings. Crying crocodile tears, keening like some extra in an old Greek movie.

'But old enough for you to throw him out on to the streets.'

'It's not true. That's a lie. We were a family.'

'Oh God, this is such bullshit.'

'Joanie . . .' Milton warning, eyes narrowing, hand slightly raised at the desk.

'Well, so it is. What is all this "my son my son" crap? She didn't care that much when she let her latest lover boy kick the shit out of him.'

'It's not true.'

But it was. Mark told me.

'And then he went for me one night.'

'Yeah?'

We were sitting by the lake. His knees were drawn up

and he had his arms around them staring into the water. It was hot in the sun but despite this he wore his old army greatcoat. He shivered all the time, Mark, as though nothing could get to him any more, neither sun nor fire, as if there was nothing left known to mankind which could warm his thin old man's bones.

'He was rat-assed of course. Came storming into my bedroom. Kicked the shit out my stereo. He hated my music. It was what used to fuck him off most about me.'

It's an old story. Nothing different about it. Told a thousand times up and down this green and pleasant land of ours. Only this time it happened to be Mark.

'I gave him as good as I got but he was a big bastard. He got hold of me in the end, chucked me down the stairs, kicked me out the front door and locked it.'

He spent the night with a friend. Went round the next day, picked up his gear and that was that. He was fifteen years old.

'So what have been doing since?'

He just shrugged.

'Movin' around,' he said. 'Just movin' around.'

Once I said, 'Do you ever call her? Your mother? Tell her you're OK?'

He raised eyes that told me I knew nothing. When he smiled, though, it was apologetic as if he was sorry to have to expose my naivety.

'Nah.'

'But she might be sorry now. She might be regretting everything that's happened.'

'She doesn't care.'

'You don't know that.'

He shook his head, his brow wrinkled as he tried to explain.

'See I don't even blame her really. She's a fuck-up herself. She'd rather have him. And if it wasn't him it would just be another one.'

I didn't try to argue. I figured it would insult him to try.

'Nobody cares,' he said. He didn't say it pitifully, more like it was a matter of fact which I guess it was. As he said it he erupted into one of his deep racking coughs, putting a hand quickly over his mouth as if he feared embarrassing me.

'I care Mark,' I said.

But it wasn't long before Mark had begun to get on my nerves. I was running short of stash by then and it was affecting my temper.

When Milton eventually got round to telling me what my weekly allowance was going to be, I exploded at him down the phone.

'For Christ's sake . . . that's a *clerk's* wage . . . how am I supposed to manage on that?'

'The court feels it's enough to live.'

'Yeah but not to keep up a coke habit,' is what we both knew I needed to say.

Stoneham had been sold by now and I was just waiting for the end of the formalities. The sale had stripped the place bare. It was cold and echoing and we were camped out in a couple of bedrooms.

'Why's he always coughing? What's the matter with him anyway?' I said one night in irritation after Mark had left the room hacking.

'Life,' said Max shortly.

If things weren't good between Mark and me, they were even worse between Max and myself. We didn't even like each other any longer. I guess we never did even at the beginning. We were biding our time now and we both knew it. It ran out the way it always does, just when

311

you're least expecting it, which turned out to be around three o'clock that morning.

We were lying on the bed watching a music programme on the box, a cheap airtime-filler full of videos with one of those bright frenetic I'll-do-anything-to-get-on-the-TV-whatever-time-it-is presenters, when suddenly there was Didi dancing, turning and twirling, the black dress straining across the perfect breasts, pouting and lip-synching into the camera.

'Turn it off,' I snapped.

Max, though, didn't move.

'Turn it off,' I said a second time, lunging for the zapper, but he was too quick for me, snatching it and holding it above my head.

'No, leave it on,' he said calmly. 'I like her.'

I began yelling at him then, called him a string of names, but he just settled back smirking on the pillow.

'You stupid bitch,' he said. 'You're just jealous.'

'Jealous. Ha. Don't make me laugh.'

I was up off the bed now, striding up and down, crossing my arms and picking at my fingers. I jabbed one of them into my chest.

'What have I got to be jealous of? I mean Jesus . . . listen to those lyrics . . .'

'Well, she must be doing something right. She sells forty thousand albums an hour or so I read.'

'Shut up. Shut the fuck up.'

The thin attempt at some sort of show of self-possession had shattered like glass. My hands were in my hair in a frenzy. They covered my ears too as if to hide them from the words. From the bed there came the harsh scornful laughter.

'Jesus Christ look at you. The old rock queen. If they could see you now. God you're *pathetic*.'

The word was like a stake through my heart. For a moment I stood there nailed to the ground then I threw myself at him punching and kicking and screaming.

312

'Cunt . . . bastard . . . asshole . . .'

He was strong, though, Max. He held on to my arms, laughing.

'Dear God, you're eaten up with it aren't you? No wonder you're shot most of the time. You're so jealous of your little *sister*.'

'She's not my sister, she's not my sister,' I screamed. 'She's not even fucking related to me if you want to know the truth.'

'Whoever she is, at least she's hung on to her money not snorted it all away.'

'You've done all right from my money. Living here under my roof. You fucking parasite.'

The violent struggling was over now. Instead we stared at each other in hatred, he still lying back, me kneeling before him on the bed.

He snorted with derisive laughter.

'Your money. What a joke. All your money goes up your nose. There wouldn't be anything in the shagging fridge if Mark and I didn't go out busking.'

'Get out.' I was off the bed now. I could see my face white in the one remaining mirror.

'I want you out of here. Now.'

'My pleasure,' he said. 'My fucking pleasure.'

At the door he stopped and turned.

'You're a junkie,' he said. 'The sooner you realize it the better.'

I reached for the nearest thing, a radio on top of a chest of drawers behind me. He got out just in time as I hurled it. It hit the closed door and crashed into a thousand pieces.

'You're a has-been Joanie,' I heard from the other side.

The next morning, coming to in my pit, I found Mark standing with the mug of tea beside the bed.

'Where's Max?' I said groggily.

'Max is gone,' he said.

'Oh yeah,' I said. 'I remember.'

313

He sat on the floor then, not looking at me. His fingers plucked the bedspread as he told the story.

'He was angry. He called me a fool. He said you wouldn't take me with you.' His eyes when he turned were full of yearning. He was up on his knees by then and kneeling beside the bed.

'But it's not true is it? I told him that. I can't bear it if I'm not with you.'

'Oh Christ Mark,' I said, 'it's too early for all of this,' but he wasn't listening.

'You will take me with you won't you Joanie?' he said.

I tried, I really tried.

'I don't even know where I'm going Mark. I don't know what I'm going to do,' and it was true.

'You know you'll have to decide what you're doing,' Milton kept telling me on the phone.

'I will . . . I will soon . . .' I always answered but somehow I just didn't seem able to get round to it. Meanwhile I tried to choose my words carefully with Mark.

'Look . . . maybe it's time . . . what I mean is maybe you should try making it up with your family. Why don't you ring your mother . . . here . . . look . . .' and I tried to hand him the phone.

'No . . . no . . . no . . .'

It was the only time I saw him angry. He'd jumped up stamping his foot.

'You don't understand. You don't understand. Why would I go back there?'

He was back now kneeling before me.

'You need somebody Joanie . . . to look after you. I could do that for you . . . I could be . . . like . . . your assistant . . . your servant Joanie.'

'Don't be ridiculous.'

314

I spoke sharply, the awful adoration of the thing annoying me.

'I don't need looking after Mark and anyway I can't afford a servant.'

'I didn't mean you to *pay* me.' His voice was joyful now, full of what he perceived to be my mistake. His eyes had lit up with hope.

'I don't want to be *paid*. I'll get work myself. Help you with expenses.' He was striding up and down with enthusiasm for the plan.

'I can keep the place clean for you, cook for you . . . look after you while you work.'

'*Work.*'

I said the word bitterly for it had struck me like a dart to the heart, but he never heard it. He was working himself up to something important that he wanted to say.

'The thing is . . . I can do other things as well . . . I mean I can learn . . . you can show me how . . . what I mean is I can score your stuff for you when you need it.'

'That's enough Mark.' The bitterness changed to a guilt-ridden anger. 'I don't need anyone to score for me. I can do that perfectly well for myself.'

I stubbed the cigarette down hard into the ashtray, watched it as it crumbled away.

'What did Max say when he left?'

'I don't know what you mean.'

'Yes you do. Tell me what Max said to you about me.' He wouldn't answer though.

'He said I was a junkie, right. That I was in trouble. That you were a fool to stay. Well, all of those things are true Mark. Look at me Mark.'

When he turned round there was an expression of such unhappiness on his face that I softened. I took his hands.

'I'm done Mark, like Max said. I'm a junkie and I don't know what I'm going to do next or what's going to happen. He was right. I'm a has-been.'

'Don't say that Joanie.' He was up on his feet again

shouting. The expression of pain and distress had deepened. But he was angry too, angry at me for treading on the legend and debasing the myth and it didn't matter that the myth was me.

'Oh Mark,' I said, shaking my head.

But I was brisk after that, as firm as I could be. I tried to make my voice say it was the end of the discussion.

'It can't work Mark,' I said, 'you have to see that. You'll have to go in the end.'

His eyes when they looked at me said they had one last request.

'OK,' he said, 'but please not yet Joanie.'

And so life fell into some sort of a routine in Stoneham, Mark cooking and cleaning as he had promised. As for me, well, I was taken up with the business of the day, phoning around the numbers from my little black book and organizing my delivery.

When Mark appeared periodically with food on a plate, I wasn't even grateful. Sometimes I'd pick at it, mostly I left it untouched, once I even threw it at the wall.

'I don't want your fucking food Mark. I don't know why you're still here. I'm sick of having you around the place. How many times do I have to tell you to go?'

I'd hurl myself raging and crying on the bed and in a moment or so I'd feel the hand on my back which I'd throw off with an angry shake.

'Don't say that Joanie . . . it'll be all right Joanie . . . I didn't mean to upset you Joanie.'

It was after I'd thrown the food on the floor and shouted at him that I gave him the tour jacket, a satin thing with my name on the back.

His eyes glowed. He was speechless with pleasure. He kept sneaking looks at himself each time he passed the mirror.

'It doesn't mean you can stay Mark,' I told him hastily when I saw the hope flicker in his eyes. 'It was just to say sorry.

'You know you have to go Mark,' I said. But still somehow nothing happened.

Milton meanwhile was growing edgy.

'Look,' he said, ringing for the third time that week, 'why don't I get one of my staff to check out some places for you?'

'OK,' I said dully.

'Where would you like to go?'

'I don't care,' I said.

It was true. I'd dropped down into that old Slough of Despond. I didn't care about anything. Which is when with perfect timing Denis appeared on my doorstep.

In my experience most people progress in the business of drugs for what they tell themselves at the time are the best reasons, i.e. they figure there must be neater cheaper ways to do it, and anyway their noses are hurting with all that snorting. And when this happens, when they get to thinking this way, there's always someone like Denis on hand to advise them.

I'd never had a delivery boy quite like Denis. A dork, that's what we'd call him today. College-boy suit and horn-rimmed glasses. First time he presses the door bell I don't even answer. I'm expecting a delivery but it never occurs to me it could be Denis.

Denis, though, turns out to have special talents. Not only is he a first-class chemist, he has a way with him that makes the whole thing seem *innocent*. He unpacks his bottles and bunsen like some schoolboy in a science lesson. He has the look of a train-spotter about him too. Acne with a soft down of beard.

When he offers me the pipe with the crystals, though, all of a sudden the swot of the Fourth falls away.

'Take it easy,' he says and I want to ask him who the hell he thinks he is. I want to tell him, 'Listen kid ... I was doing drugs when you were still in kindergarten,' but by then it's too late because by then I've taken a hit and 'Woooooow' is the limit of my vocabulary.

First of all my heart pounds, then the room spins around and then I think I'm about to throw up on the spot. But then that passes too and all I'm left with is an idiot smile on my face because by then I'm sooooo *happy*.

I haven't felt this thing called happy for a very long time. I welcome it like an old friend whose face I'd forgotten. There's something about the whole thing too that satisfies me in a new and pleasing way. The crystals for instance which look so *pretty*. They look like something the saints might be hiding at the bottom of the Holy Grail. They sparkle in the petri dish. Beautiful. Clean. Utterly incapable of evil.

'Wow,' I say again, handing the pipe back to Denis.

Later when we burn up the residue from the stem of the pipe the crystals turn a rich glowing amber like a rare and precious gem.

The Chinese call it chasing the dragon. A suitable occupation for the Dragon Lady I thought.

Soon Denis is a permanent fixture around the place. He's willing to teach me to cook the stuff up myself but I'm not interested. I was never that good at chemistry and besides that I'd rather watch him at work. It happens to coke-heads in the end. They always retreat into ritual. I can sit for hours silently watching him brew up in the bathroom. I feel aesthetic and holy and cleaned out as I watch him, like the whole thing is a religious experience.

One day as he hands me the pipe, I smile the smile of the truly converted.

'You know I don't even know your second name Denis,' I say.

Denis the dork, the swot, the train-spotter merely smiles.

'That's true,' he says.

But the more Denis visits, the more nervous Mark becomes. He watches the pair of us, an outsider, a shadow, huddled, arms crossed in the corner.

Once he says desperately, hopelessly, like a last test of loyalty, 'Give me a go then. I want to try.'

My reaction is amazing. I shout at him, lecture him with astonishing hypocritical severity.

'If I ever find out . . . if I ever see you . . . if you ever touch any of this stuff Mark I swear to God . . .'

I'm not telling him to go any more, though, but that's because I'm not telling anyone to do anything. My life has disappeared into the bottom of a test-tube where I lie curled up like a foetus, waiting for the pipe or watching the crystals sparkle, watching them turn to that priceless glowing amber.

I've just taken a hit when Milton phones.

'I think we've found somewhere Joanie,' he says.

I pass the pipe back to Denis. It's all I can do to keep from laughing.

'Lovely Milton . . . thanks so much . . . yes I'd *looove* to go down and see it . . .' I'm so absurdly happy he's suspicious.

'Is everything all right Joanie?' he says.

I never do get to check out the cottage. For some reason I can't seem to make it. Milton even sends me a train ticket but I can't get it together sufficiently to get to the station. I think I'll drive and I set out but I don't make it past the end of the road.

In the end I lie to Milton.

'It's perfect,' I say. 'Please do go ahead and rent it.'

Putting down the phone I find Mark staring at me in the one remaining mirror. He has the red tour jacket on and his face is white against it.

'You're not going to take me are you?' he whispers.

319

'We've been through all this Mark,' I say.

'Look,' I say, turning, trying to do the best I can. 'You can come and visit me Mark. It's not like I'm going to the ends of the earth. You can come and stay . . . any time you like . . . Christmas . . . Easter . . . holidays . . .' But it's no good and we both know it. The look of suffering and disappointment on his face turns me defensive.

'You've always known you couldn't come with me. I told you that right at the beginning.' He kicks a foot along the ground, stares down at it.

'You hadn't said anything for a while. I thought maybe you'd changed your mind,' he says.

But I'm getting angry now and quickly. My mood swings up and down like this all the time. Also I'm waiting for Denis to arrive and my last hit of free-base is running out in my soul like sand in a timer.

'I told you I wouldn't change my mind. I made that clear all along.'

'I know you did. I know you did.' He's dropped down miserable on the floor, back to the wall, hands clasped about his knees.

'Don't *do* that Mark.' I'm shouting it.

'I can't help it Joanie. I can't help it.' For now he's weeping, juddering, shuddering sobs. He's coughing too and wiping his eyes and the snot from his nose on the blood-red of the tour jacket.

'Stop it Mark. Just stop it.'

'I can't live without you Joanie.' It's the howl of someone who has no farther down that they can go. 'I can't live without you. I can't lose you. You're all I've got.'

And so there he sits on the floor weeping and I look at him surprised that I don't even feel sorry for him any more, and when I take a quick dip down into my soul to find why it is, I discover the thing empty. Nothing there any more, just that old free-base running out.

No, I'm not feeling anything now. I'm living in a cotton-wool world, nothing to feel and nothing to touch, not even the sides as I go down.

I've got nothing left to say to Mark. I'm dead inside. I'm relieved when the phone rings.

'Joanie,' says a voice I haven't heard in a while. 'It's Kent . . . just checking to see if you're coming to the party tonight.'

The party is for the opening of his new studio, a purpose-built block the other side of the farm-yard. When the invitation arrived I put it for old times' sake on the top of the bureau, an oak thing I bought from Pieter, eighteenth-century and now my only remaining piece of fine furniture.

It's always been in the bedroom, this bureau. It's always been my place for invitations. Once the top of it was crammed with the things, launches of other people's albums, openings of new restaurants and art galleries, galas and premieres, first nights and end-of-tour parties. Now there's just this one square of card, because no one sends me invitations any more. Makes your heart bleed, huh? But still it's true. I've died as far as the world is concerned, or rather disappeared into the ether reserved for the has-beens and the also-rans. Quite fitting really with the smell of the stuff pervading the place from Denis's chemistry set which is a permanent fixture now next door in the bathroom.

I never went to Kent for money you see. You might have thought he'd be first call. But I was too proud for that. I told myself that Kent was always too much given to lectures for me. And it was true. But it was also true that I didn't fancy facing up to him in the state I was in and with my life in such disrepair.

321

I didn't go to Kent so in the end Kent came to me.

He appeared outside the house one day, swinging himself out heavily from the Landrover. In the great hall he stared unhappily out of the window.

'Bit stretched at the moment Joanie . . . with the new studio and everything . . .'

'Don't . . .' I said wearily. 'It's OK Kent.'

'No,' he said, 'listen . . .'

When he told me the amount he figured he could raise, I was overcome. I put my hands over my face. Then I began to shout the staccato phrases fiercely.

'No . . . *No* . . . Shut up . . . go away . . . leave me alone . . . don't offer . . .' His face was creased up in confusion.

'Don't you understand . . . for Christ's sake you can see the situation . . . *I won't pay it back.*'

But he was down on the floor beside me by then, pulling my hands away from my eyes.

'But you *could* pay it back Joanie. That's the point. Don't you see that? It could all be so different. You could start working again.'

'Oh come *on*. I can't even get a deal Kent.' I was scornful, but something else too. Clutching at straws. Because things were too far gone by then. I'd didn't want to be told I could fight back. It was too much trouble, too much effort. I just wanted to be allowed to curl up in the bottom of my test-tube where I told myself I was happy, to be carried out to sea in it, bobbing in it like a bottle.

Kent, though, wasn't giving in so easily.

'So you can't get a deal at the moment? There's session work. You could get that easily enough. It would get you back into the swing of things. You'd get a deal again in the end.'

'It's too late.' The effort of the conversation was beginning to annoy me. I pulled away from him, jumped up, turned away.

322

'It's not too late. Don't say that.' Behind me now he was trying to take that old bull by the horns.

'There's this new place Joanie . . . I know this bass player who went there . . . he swears by it . . .'

'Don't lecture me . . . don't lecture me . . . you're always lecturing me.' My voice was raised now. I did my best to calm it.

'I'm sorry. I didn't mean that. But just leave it Kent. Thanks for the offer. I appreciate it. You're a friend . . .' The last words had a finality about them. They sounded more like a farewell.

Behind me there was silence, then he said in a dull, flat voice, 'So that's it is it? Just like that? All over?'

'Yeah, that's it,' I said, still refusing to look at him.

'I never figured you for this Joanie.'

'For what?'

'I don't know . . . a coward . . . a quitter . . . someone who would just give in.'

'Don't talk about things you don't understand Kent,' I said and there was some truth in that. Perhaps he acknowledged it. There was a sort of hopeless acquiescence in his voice when he spoke.

'If that's what you want . . .'

'It's what I want.'

He had his back to me when I finally turned, a hand on the door-knob. He didn't look at me when he said it.

'If you change your mind . . .'

'I won't,' I said.

He still phoned, though, through everything, once a week or so to see how I was. Sometimes, transparently, obviously, he'd try to interest me in something he was doing.

'I've got this track Joanie . . . I just wondered . . . it could do with some piano on it.'

'Forget it,' I'd say shortly.

Unknown to me he bought Didi's Mini at the Stoneham sale, afterwards calling up in his careful fashion.

323

'The garage is a bit full at the moment . . . I'll tell you when I want it.'

'Thanks,' I said grudgingly, ungratefully.

When he heard from Milton that I was looking for a place to live he rang up with an offer.

'The farm manager's in the cottage at the moment but we've got this other place . . . needs a bit of work but we could get that done . . .' I just laughed sarcastically down the phone.

'Oh just what you need . . . a junkie down on the farm . . .'

Beneath the bravura though I couldn't bear it.

'Thanks but no thanks,' I said.

Eventually when he called I preferred not to come to the phone. I'd get Max to say I was out. Once he dropped over unexpectedly. Looking out of the window I saw them exchanging a few terse sentences on the gravel. There was a thin line of disgust on Kent's face as he clambered back into the Landrover.

Now hearing his voice on the end of the phone, I was sorry that I'd answered. I needed Denis and badly. Meanwhile he was chatting, trying to be kind, trying to pretend he didn't know from the tone of my voice that there was only one thing on my mind.

'Can't wait for you to see the place Joanie . . . I think you'll like it . . . we've matched up the stone you know . . .'

'I suppose Richard will be there,' I say sarcastically for no good reason except the main one that it's the way I always speak his name. His voice has a small chill on it.

'He's away,' he says. 'Visiting some friend in New York.' As he said it I saw Denis's old Beetle chugging up the drive.

'I'll try and make it then,' I say, but only to get rid of him. I know I'll be too busy bobbing away in my little bottle to go to his stupid party.

'I have to go now,' I say and I put the phone down.

Some time later, though, in the way these things happen,

my mood begins to swing. Suddenly I'm restless, feeling caged up. I turn on Mark for want of something better to do, where he sits huddled against the wall hacking.

'For fuck's sake. Can't you do anything about that cough? It's like fucking *Cancer Ward* in here.'

He looks even more shrunken than usual tonight. Against the bright red of the tour jacket his skin appears even more yellow.

'Sorry . . . don't know what's the matter . . . can't seem to stop.'

I hate it when he apologizes humbly like this. It makes me feel even worse. I get defensive when he does it, start shouting at him. And that's exactly what happens now.

'You shouldn't be here Mark . . . it's not good for you . . . the house is cold . . .'

He tries to argue then. 'It's OK . . . I'm all right . . . I like it . . .' which is when it snaps inside me.

'But I don't like it Mark. I'm sick of having you around the place. I've been asking you to go for the last couple of weeks. How many more times do I have to say it?' I put my hand over my eyes, shake my head.

'Christ,' I say, snapping it up. 'I have to get out of this place. I need a change. I'm going over to the party.'

I'm slapping on some make-up and waiting for the taxi to arrive to take me over to Kent's, I'm in no shape to drive, when Mark comes into the bedroom twisting his hands.

'I just wondered Joanie . . . what time you would be getting back?'

I'm still full of self-righteous wrath so I snap back at him, jumping to the the wrong conclusion.

'What the fuck business is it of yours what time I get back? What a nerve.' But already he's raising a hand to ward me off.

'No, no. You don't understand.' His hands are screwed up like the fists of a child, then they fold humbly before him.

'I just thought . . . well . . . I know you want me to go and I thought it would be easier if I did it while you were out that's all.'

The worst thing afterwards is remembering the relief. How it flooded over me. For I didn't say, 'Where will you go Mark?' or 'At this time of night Mark?' or 'It would be more sensible to wait till the morning Mark.' No, I said, 'Maybe you're right Mark' and 'If you think it's best Mark' and 'Why don't you take a lift with Denis, Mark, he's going back up to town.'

At the door with the taxi waiting, I take his hands in my own, give him all the shit about holidays. I say, 'Don't forget to let me know where you're staying,' the craziest thing for someone like Mark.

At the door I betray him finally with a kiss.

'Don't forget you're a *friend* now Mark,' I say.

As it turns out it's not my sort of party, a sedate affair full of talk of patchbay options and bandwidths and pitch shifting. Christ these people really have come to check out the facilities, I think.

In the studio as Kent shows me round they're discussing jack access. A voice is raised, it's true, but only over dynamic voice allocation.

'Excuse me,' I say.

Things are so bad it's actually a relief to find Molly in the toilet.

'Hey good to see you Molly,' I say and she stares in surprise.

Naturally we're both there for the same reason.

'So how's things Joanie?' she says although she doesn't need to ask. She can look down on me now free-basing from the high moral ground of her line of coke.

I guess it's about two in the morning when I suddenly have this crazy idea that I want to play. There's no logic to it. How would there be? Suddenly though I'm blundering my way through what's left of the party. Around me the eyebrows are raising and the glances flying as I grab hold of Kent.

'Come on man,' I say. 'Let's do some of the old stuff . . .'

I'm blown up by the dope then. What I say goes. Which is why I can't understand why he's waiting.

'For Christ's sake,' I say, 'you're the one who's always telling me to play.'

He seems to be leading me away. I tear my elbow from his arm.

'Come on,' I say, pouting, 'or has that old country shit softened you up?

'Come on baby,' I say. 'Let's play some *real* rock and roll.'

Because the truth is that it hit me hard when Kent started playing with Miranda. The first time I caught them on *Whistle Test* and I saw his face lift up the way I had seen it do that first time, the way I knew I only wanted it to do with me, well, it was like someone stuck a knife in my belly.

'So I see you're playing *country* now,' I said, trying to make a thing of it next time he phoned.

'It's good stuff Joanie,' he said.

He sounded irritated and I was glad. I figured I'd hit some sort of Achilles' heel.

'And you an old rock and roller,' I said, determined to press the point. But he just smiled then, peacemaker to the last.

'Well . . .' he said, 'I never did believe much in labels.'

It's not an overstatement of things to say that Miranda rescued Kent. She took him as he blundered about in pain and sorrow following Andrew's death, gave him steadily,

327

slowly, new life and hope. Gently, unobtrusively beneath her hands, the husk which he had become began to fill out again, began to turn back into a human being. But how was I to know all this was beginning to happen, holed up in the bottom of a bong in Stoneham? And who am I to know it, fucking and blinding and being bundled away by Kent?

'But she's a fan of mine,' I say, laughing like a mad woman. 'Has been since schooldays. Hasn't she told you Kent?'

When I turn at the door she's still staring at me from eyes beneath the mass of dark hair. The look of sadness on her face makes me angry.

'End of a legend for you is it Miranda . . .?' I shout. 'End of a dream?'

'Oh just shut up Joanie,' Kent says wearily but I'm not finished.

'Better get used to it baby,' I shout. 'You're going to see a lot of it in this business.'

I won't get in the taxi so in the end he has to drive me home, shoving me into the Landrover swearing.

'For Christ's sake,' I say, lighting up. 'What's all the hassle about? It was just a joke.' But he just stares fixedly out through the windscreen.

'Tell me something, do you have to make a scene wherever you go?' he says coldly.

I begin to rant at him then.

'You make me sick . . . why don't you just drop off your pedestal for once . . . you never know it might do something for you.'

A shaft of light from a street-lamp shows his face tight with dislike.

'Like the something it does for you?' he says.

Still, when he pulls up outside the house I don't want to let him go. I want him to come in and when he won't I refuse to get out of the Landrover. I begin to drag at him, pounding him angrily on the arm.

328

'You're fucking her aren't you?' I say. 'You're fucking Miranda.

'Christ,' I say, 'You're old enough to be her father.'

'Hardly,' he says, jumping out, clashing his door closed and coming round to my side.

'Where's your keys?' he says, pulling me out roughly, beginning to feel for them, but all the time I'm still screaming it at him, 'You're fucking her, you're fucking her,' all the time still laughing like a maniac.

He finds the keys and shoves me forward up the steps, cursing as he tries them in the lock. As the door opens he gives me a shove and I stagger inside. He's getting into the Landrover when I scream it from the steps.

'I don't care that you fucked her, what hurts me is that you played with her.'

Still staggering a little I storm into the great hall and snap on the wall lights. The first thing I see is the red tour jacket. In the half-light I think it's just draped and he left it there. Then I see the feet sticking up over the end of the sofa.

'What the fuck are you still doing here you bastard?' I say, but he doesn't move.

Furious, I storm across to him. There's a peaceful smile on his face. He's not even coughing.

'Why aren't you gone?' I say, kicking his feet viciously.

As if in answer his body slips slowly and heavily to the floor.

Kent was already pulling away when I flung open the front door and screamed his name. I'd been screaming a lot that night but I guess there was something in that scream that showed him this time it was different.

I don't remember a lot about what happened after that. From then on it just seemed like a series of images, the blue lights from the police cars flashing through the leaded

329

windows in the great hall, Mark being carried off peacefully on the stretcher, Kent turning away from me as he spoke to Miranda.

'Something's happened . . . I'll be a while . . . don't worry . . .'

I watched everything from the wall, already disconnected. I sat with my back against it, huddled, my hands round my knees, the way Mark used to sit, like I was taking his place. Before me a policeman was down on his haunches asking me questions. I heard a voice I didn't recognize as my own and watched his pen running across the notebook.

At some point, I'm not sure when, Milton arrived. I just looked up to find him there. And it was because I sat this way hunched up and refusing to move that he and Kent decided to get me into the clinic. It was Kent down in front of me now and speaking to me very slowly.

'We don't think you should stay here tonight Joanie. We're going to take you somewhere. Do you understand me?'

I spent the first two days at the clinic sleeping. I slept straight through. Forty-eight hours. When I woke up there was this figure puffing his pipe beside the bed.

'We don't deal in wires and black boxes here,' he told me. 'Here we believe in getting down to the root of the problem.'

Giving up drugs though was already a formality. Something stopped dead inside me the moment Mark's body rolled on to the floor. A black hole opening up into which I'd now fallen. I knew that no drug on earth could help with the way I was feeling, that it never would again and I figured this was my punishment. To live this way, with this misery, without drugs, for the rest of my life.

'I want to die,' I said flatly to Dr Lindquist the next time I saw him. He nodded in perfect understanding.

'Most people would prefer to die at this stage,' he said.

*

330

'We're not here to try a life-style,' the coroner said sternly to Mark's family's solicitor. But it wasn't true and we all knew it.

The press box was like something from *Alice in Wonderland*. They escaped out of it with their macs and their notebooks. When one got up to leave, the rest collapsed like a pack of cards.

As it turned out, though, the verdict was a disappointment to everyone. The way the pathologist described Mark's heart it sounded bruised, which I guess it was, in more ways than one. A heart diseased. Undetected. Undiagnosed, since childhood.

A small shared sigh of regret wafted along the press box as the coroner hammered the final humdrum nail in Mark's coffin.

'So what we're talking about here then Dr Harvey is a simple heart attack . . .'

'Brought on by neglect, yes. The deceased had obviously been in poor physical shape since childhood.'

It should have been a relief to me. I'd assumed along with everyone else that the drugs, one way or another, were responsible for Mark's death. My worst scenario was that he'd killed himself because he couldn't face leaving, the one only marginally better, that he'd just taken a hit to help with the unhappiness.

I didn't know whether Mark had persuaded Denis to give him a hit, and had passed out, or whether in the end he'd decided not to go with Denis and had helped himself to the free-base when he'd left.

It wasn't possible either to know what part, if any, Denis had played, for instance, if Mark had passed out while he was there and Denis had just left him.

I was the only one who knew about Denis. I didn't tell the police about him. I knew there was no point. The only number I had for him was a call-box in a pub where I knew that if anyone came along asking, no one would have heard of Denis.

Besides that, though, it seemed to me there would be something entirely worthless about me telling them about Denis, and something worse, something demeaning. It would be as if I was trying, in some way, to dissipate the blame.

'So what?' were the first mutinous words that I'd shouted at Milton when he'd told me I would have to give evidence. 'So he died on my sofa. Is that my fault?'

But it was and I knew that now. I knew that blame was a spreading stain, darker in parts and deeper, but still covering everything, and that Mark dying of a heart attack had done nothing more than leave it the merest shade paler.

And so because of all this the pathologist's verdict meant nothing to me. To the family solicitor, though, it was a bitter disappointment.

'But you admit traces of drugs were found in the body?'

'Indeed. Yes. But a trace. Nothing more.'

'Enough to bring on a heart attack, particularly in one not used to the substance?'

'In my opinion no. It was just a trace. In my opinion it had no bearing on the deceased's death.'

He wasn't about to give up, though, and I couldn't blame him. After I'd recited what I had to say in the dull flat voice which had become my way of speaking, he rose to his feet, fiddled in the way solicitors do, with his papers. He was still staring down at them when he said it.

'It would be true to say that you are a habitual drug user . . .'

It was his last question, though, that caused me the pain although not in the way that he thought it. Probably I knew what was coming when he raised his head that way, looked at me with the greedy expression of pleasure. He threw a knowing glance at the press box too as if alerting them.

'And what exactly was your relationship with this *young* man?' he said.

332

The *young* stood out in the air so that Milton jumped to his feet trying to defend me.

'Sir if I may say so I really don't think . . .'

I could see that the coroner who had been kind and considerate to me was about to agree and I didn't want that. I wanted to answer. I wanted to say the words, hear the cock crow, witheringly, one last time, in the air.

'We were friends,' I said.

'But what do they want Milton?' I said wearily when Milton told me Mark's family had asked to meet me. His old lawyer's hands turned upwards at his desk. They said, What does anyone want? The answer had to be money.

I'd seen Mark's brother at the inquest, a string-bean with a bad skin. Twentysomething, going . on fifty. In Milton's office, though, he had spittle on his lips and a salacious look in his eye.

'You're a woman of thirty-five. What was he? A boy of seventeen . . .'

As he spoke Mark's mother kept interrupting, keening, the Greek extra in the corner.

'He could have come home any time . . . I told him . . . I told him . . .'

I shook my head.

'This is all so much shit,' I said in disgust.

That was when Milton jumped in. 'Perhaps,' he said politely to the brother, 'you'd like to tell us why you're here.'

The brother turned pompous then. There was a prim tilt to his mouth but it was spoilt by the greed in his eye.

'We've been offered money . . . from the newspapers . . .' He coughed into his hand as if it somehow excused him.

'Naturally we only what's best . . .'

'What's best for what . . . what's best for who?'

333

'Well. Um . . .'

I'd broken in on him sharply. Now he was disconcerted. He scrabbled around for the words and when he found them finished in triumph.

'For Mark's memory . . . of course.'

'*Oh God.*'

I put my hands over my eyes with the horror of it, with the shame that this was where I'd ended up.

'I'm broke,' I said flatly, looking up. 'Bankrupt. I suggest you say yes to the newspapers.'

They were filing out when I said it to their backs.

'And don't worry, you can buy Mark a nice marble headstone with the money.'

They sold their story along with the rest of them, people from the village, particularly those with unpaid bills, freeloaders from the Stoneham parties, school-friends not even in my form, lovers I'd fucked and forgotten, lovers I'd never fucked at all.

For a week or so, till something else came along, the papers were full of it. Suddenly I was public enemy number one. Suddenly I fucked anything that moved. I was Hecate, I ate young children. Suddenly I had snakes in my hair.

It surprised me, the amount of hate flying around. It seemed to appear out of nowhere. That's when I saw that it must be there all the time, hate, lying in piles just waiting for something to light on.

But I understood this by now. I was into this hating thing too.

'I hate everything and everybody,' I said to Dr Lindquist the last time I saw him. 'And that includes myself.

'But most of all,' I said in a harsh burst of truth, 'I hate Mark for dying.'

*

For their story for which they were paid an undisclosed amount of money, Mark's mother and brother posed by a picture of me in better days still tattered and flapping on Mark's bedroom wall. Robin Phillips used the photo later in the biography.

It was this last scandal in my life apparently which clinched the deal for Robin's book. Which is why he was there scribbling away at the inquest.

Slipping round to the back of the court for an old-fashioned cigarette, I bumped into him skulking beneath the dripping tin roof of a bicycle shed. He was shoving his coke packet back in his pocket.

'Guess this scene will be a bit different in the book Robin,' I said.

He drew out the packet, held it towards me.

'You should cooperate with me Joanie,' he said coldly. 'You might as well. I mean what have you got to lose?'

I reached out, took the coke packet from his fingers. I pulled apart the sealed top, raised it towards my nose. Looking over it towards him, I saw him smile in satisfaction.

I smiled back, upended the packet and enjoyed his curse as the light white cloud floated down to the ground.

'A classic', they called the book when it came out.

'*The* definitive rock biography.'

'A story of our time . . . a book that anyone with an interest in rock music should have . . .'

There was so much coke around at her parties, he wrote, *it was almost impossible to get out of the way of it . . .*

I guess you could say in his defence he never did claim to have managed it.

*

335

Grace rang today, it was cheering and comforting some-how to hear her, even the sound of her cursing, hand over the phone, to Rene in the background.

'Yes I'll do it in a minute Rene . . . I'm talking to Joanie . . . well, just tell them they'll have to wait goddamnit . . .'

It was good too to hear the news from back home.

'Hey,' I said when she told me about Paul. 'Head-hunted yet. An archdeacon . . .' But she only grunted. 'Paul's thinking of turning it down,' she said.

Her voice had all the old affectionate irritation, the tone she takes with him at breakfast for instance, when she berates him across his croissant. Sure enough, in the next instant, I heard the smash of the frying pan hit the stove.

I could see her then, chin tucked into her shoulder, reaching for the butter, the eggs, the herbs for the omelette.

'I told him, "It's what it needs, people like you" but of course he wouldn't listen . . .'

'Listen . . .' I said, laughing, trying to calm her down. 'You think you're mad because he's not going to accept it? Imagine how the Colonel is feeling.'

Things had gone hard, you see, between Paul and the Colonel after the incident of the camel and the needle's eye. And it was only a couple of months after that that the Colonel found himself confronted by Paul making an impassioned speech on behalf of women priests on the six o'clock news on the television.

Now the fact is that the Colonel's grasp of theology isn't all that tight. His objection to women's ordination as it turned out was summed up in that old number about a woman in a cassock being as unnatural to the human eye as a dog walking on its hind legs. His big mistake was mentioning this to Paul.

It's actually quite hard to tell when Paul loses his temper. It's because he does it so quietly. He's like a pot that boils merrily, lifting its lid but never quite managing

336

to shoot it off. Grace puts it down to his Home Counties breeding.

The only way to tell if Paul is angry is to check with his jaw. It goes rigid like someone had clamped it back to his ears. His voice goes stiff too because then he has trouble forcing the words out. And both of these things happened slap bang in the middle of the market-place on the Saturday morning the day after Paul had returned from the General Synod.

At first Paul tried to be polite, as after all befits his calling. But when the Colonel started harrumphing and came out with the dog thing, well, Paul's lid sort of finally phhffffed off.

'Is that how you see it?' he said. 'I mean is that how you actually see the whole thing?'

It was November, well out of season. There were only a few heads in the market-place but let me tell you that Paul's voice was so loud that whatever there were, well, they were turning. I even heard him from the café.

'Hey,' I yelled to Grace, 'get over here.' Because by this time Paul was in full spate.

'You see a woman in a clerical collar and a dog prancing with a ruff around its neck in the same end-of-the-pier tradition. That's appalling. That is absolutely appalling.'

There was genuine pain on his face. The jaw was meeting by this time round the back of his neck. He did the thing he thought best then which was to stump off and leave the Colonel still blustering in the market-place. He got his reward though. He was treated like a returning hero over the croissant and the second cup of coffee which he was comforting himself with, and which, of course, he got free of charge, in the café.

'I can't believe it,' he kept saying. 'That someone would actually say that.'

It had been a dull wet Thursday two days before when he'd made it on to our TV screens and luckily there wasn't much happening in the café. That was just as well

337

because Grace sat all afternoon eyes glued to the television.

'You're such an old hypocrite,' I said. 'You don't even approve of the Church of England.'

'That has *nothing* to do with it,' she said haughtily.

We'd just had a surprise load of tourists in when the result of the voting came through in favour of women priests. She came out from the kitchen punching the air like an old revolutionary.

She bought a bottle with her which she brandished threateningly at the tourists. She said anyone who felt like celebrating like *her* was welcome to a free glass of champagne.

To judge from the response most people seemed heavily in favour of the General Synod decision on the ordination of women.

> *And as I taste this bitter glass*
> *Cast an eye on my past history*
> *And sing the blues for the fool I used to be*
>
> *After last year's jubilee . . .*

For the first year at the cottage I lived the life of a hermit, scarcely communicating with another living soul. It was easy to do, cutting myself off like this, for the cottage stands on its own at the end of a track and the only time I had to face any sort of civilization was when I went into the village for stores. Then I refused the smallest overtures of friendship, grunting at even the mildest 'Good morning'. Since I'd moved in under an assumed name and I always wore wore dark glasses and a head-scarf when I went out, I assumed no one knew who I was.

'Of course we knew,' Grace said airily, years later.

'Come on . . . I mean . . . A *head-scarf* . . . *dark glasses?*'

So much for my view of myself as the mystery woman.

The removal men were just carrying the sofa out on that last day at Stoneham when Kent turned up. He stormed into the great hall, not bothering with the formalities.

'I've been talking to Milton. He won't give me your new address. He says you don't want anyone to know where you're going.'

'That's right,' I said.

It was the first time I'd seen him since I'd gone into the clinic. I'd forbidden him to visit and also to come to the inquest. Now he stood in front of me very angry.

'This is crazy. You're clean now. You could start working again.'

'Don't be ridiculous,' I said curtly.

I turned then. I didn't want to see him any more. Already I didn't want to see anyone. I walked away to the great leaded windows, looked out over the lawns to the lake.

'Even if I wanted to work again, which I don't, I'm a freak-show now. Or haven't you seen the papers?'

There was silence then. Behind us we could hear the shouts of the removal men easing the sofa through the front door. Eventually he said in a cold hard voice, 'So what are you going to do then?'

I traced a finger across the small pane of leaded glass.

'Nothing,' I said.

'And even I don't get to know where you're going?'

'No.'

'Well, that's Joanie . . . never do anything by halves. Always one thing or the other.'

His tone was bitter but I knew that he was also trying to bait me, that it was a last try on his part, all that he could think of now to do. Only I knew how pointless it was and I didn't even bother to answer.

'I see,' he said.

In the end I heard his shoes squeaking as they turned on the polished floorboards, heard them trace their way back across the room to the door. When he spoke his voice sounded like it was trying to be brisk.

'So . . .' he said again. 'Goodbye then Joanie. Good luck.'

'I won't be needing luck,' I said. 'I give mine to you. You deserve it.'

I heard him take the smallest of steps forward. I heard the soft sucking noise he makes when he's deciding if to speak.

'Joanie . . .' he began hesitantly but I cut him short.

'Goodbye Kent,' I said.

I wouldn't have known anything about Marge's death if an empty fridge hadn't driven me out to the village shop that day. I was paying for the groceries, terse and stony-faced as usual at the till, when I saw her picture staring up at me from the pile of papers.

Marge had taken off for LA when she and Leon split up, determined to pursue what she liked to call her 'musical career'. Leon's refusal to help her on this score had been the major running sore of their relationship. For Marge had always fancied herself as a singer. She'd been a regular at the local folk club back home. The night they met, she'd sung all thirty verses of some Border folk ballad. I only know that because it was something Leon liked to throw at her when they were arguing in public about his refusal to plead her case with McGarvey.

In LA, in true Marge style, she took up with a succession of lovers all with dope habits worse than her own and all, to a man, promising to make her a star.

I caught one of Marge's gigs once. It was in some weird artist's hang-out in the Garment District. She sat cross-legged at the front of the stage like some Nico clone, singing a dirge that she'd written herself and dragging the nails of her right hand mournfully across her zither. Behind her an acid-head smashed his hands down on a keyboard with an expression on his face that said it sounded good to him, while a bongo player in much the same state made love to his drums. The only thing truly alive on the stage was Linus.

He could only have been thirteen or so then but he was already a master of that heavy, howling, post-punk guitar. He already had that flat-faced ferocity too that he's become famous for now, only then it was still a front, a cover for his agonizing desire to protect his mother. His look told prospective hecklers, 'Fuck with my mother and you fuck with me.' And there were none. I'll tell you, even at thirteen anyone with any sense believed Linus.

At half-time while Marge went off to jam some more chemicals up her nose, Linus did a number himself. I wouldn't call it a song, more of a primal scream. But it made the hairs stand up on the back of my neck, and at the end of the gig when the whisper kisses were over with Marge and all the phoney formalities, I took him aside.

'I can't pretend to know what you're doing there Linus,' I said, 'but you have one hell of a voice.'

There was a gleam of something that must have been pleasure in his eyes when I said it. As soon as it appeared, though, it was gone, and afterwards I figured that was because in praising him and not his mother (Marge was dreadful, Marge was always dreadful), I'd turned a compliment round into an insult.

When Marge smashed off the freeway with the latest of the coke-heads she was calling her manager she achieved with her death what had eluded her in life. Fame. Or at least that fleeting fifteen minutes of it which is all, really, you can hope for from the front page of a newspaper. What she wouldn't have liked was that it was still, in the end, all down to Leon.

341

For when Leon died she'd written one of those *My Life with Leon* books. At least she actually lived with him which is more than could be said for the rest of the collection of wannabees and one-night stands who did the same thing. They were using some of the stuff from the book in the film about Leon which was just about to go into production. Her manager who lived to toot another day after the car crash claimed she was acting as a consultant.

I found out the stuff about the film from the piece in the paper. It was the first I'd bought since I moved down to the cottage and when I'd read it I picked up the phone and dialled Marge's number.

I still don't know why I figured I ought to speak to Linus. It wasn't, after all, the sort of thing I was doing. Maybe it was the memory of him, shit-filled nappy, wide-eyed and toddling from room to room in search of some human being not half out of their brain (I include myself in this scenario), or that flat-faced ferocity I'd seen in the club. Either way I guess I felt whatever Linus was, there wasn't any of us there at the time who wasn't at least in some small way responsible.

Somehow I hadn't been expecting Linus to answer. When he did it shook me. It might have been his father's voice coming down the line. It had all the old belligerence about it but it sounded hurt too, and when I said I was sorry about Marge he just let out a long empty 'Yeah . . .'

I was about to hang up when he said, 'Maybe I'll come over . . . see you sometime Joanie . . .' and I said, 'Sure . . . do that . . .' the way you do at such a time, and I didn't think any more about it.

It was about two months later, early evening, when there was a knock at the front door. I didn't answer. I never did because I was never expecting anyone and there wasn't anyone I wanted to see. I'd only ever opened up once. It was against my better judgement and naturally it turned out to be the Jehovah's Witnesses.

This time though the banging was so determined that in

342

the end I had to give in. I was pretty mad when I got to the door. It was dark and at first I couldn't see anything. Then the figure stepped forward from the shadows.

It was a young man, lanky and blond, dark glasses despite the dark.

'Joanie . . .' he said with a belligerent growl.

'Good God . . .' I said. 'Linus.'

He stayed for about a month in the end.

He was seventeen by now. Bringing him in, sitting him down at the kitchen table, I saw that his eyes were sparkling but not with the natural exuberance of youth. So I laid it on the line, right at the beginning, as I put his coffee down before him.

'There's only one rule of the house Linus and I'm sure you know what it is.'

'Don't tell me you're going to lecture me Joanie,' he said disdainfully, his lips twisting in a way too old for his years. I shook my head sadly.

'No,' I said. 'Unfortunately Linus I'm not in a position to lecture anyone. But remember, it's not that cute for me to have to tell someone twenty years my junior not to bring stuff into the house because I can't take the risk. Believe me, it doesn't make me feel that good.'

He looked across the table at me, shrewd eyes unwavering.

'The rule stands Linus,' I said. 'Stay as long as you like and welcome. But bring any stuff in and you're out. You don't get a second chance.'

'It's a deal,' he said.

We fell surprisingly quickly into an easy way. It was disconcerting, the thought that it had happened once before, a decade earlier with his father. At first it was strange having someone around. It made me realize how long I'd been holed up in my solitary state, just how used

I'd become to not doing that most basic thing of life, talking.

Because we did talk. We talked a lot. It became part of the routine to cook a meal every night, something else I hadn't done since moving down to the cottage. Afterwards we'd carry the last of the wine into the sitting room. I'd sit on the sofa, he'd lounge the way young men do, peroxide blond on the rug before the fire staring into his glass of wine. We'd talk about everything. Love, God. But always it would get round to his father and in the end I figured that was probably why he'd come.

I told him all I thought he should know. I was honest about some things, lied about others.

'Did you *like* him?'

'Yeah but it's a weird thing you know. Being in a band. It's not like anything else. There's a sort of a bottom line there, a bass line, a sort of given. It's a bit like having a brother or a sister. They just are and you never get around to asking simple questions like whether you like them or not.'

'He didn't care about me,' he said bitterly. 'He never even came to see me when he was in LA.'

You couldn't play games with Linus. You couldn't insult him with banalities so I didn't try.

'Well you know Linus . . . your father wasn't that good at relationships.'

He stared moodily into the fire.

'Did he ever love anyone?' he said.

I looked into the fire, biding my time, debating with myself what I should say. In the end I settled for the simplest answer.

'I don't know, Linus,' I said.

It was the week before Christmas that he left.

We'd already got around to planning the Christmas lunch. We were going to have the works, turkey, crackers.

I'd already started the shopping that day, the first instalment, Christmas puddings, cake, some mince pies. I'd even bought a tree and some lights. I shouted for Linus from the front door to help but there was no answer. Linus wasn't there. Neither was my guitar, and the kitchen window was stoved in to make it look like there'd been a burglary.

The guitar was the only thing of value in the house, a Martin that Kent had given me for my thirtieth birthday. It was the only personal possession of value rescued from the sale. Once I might not even have cared that it was gone. It must have been a sign of life returning that I did.

His eyes were shining when he came through the door a few hours later just like I knew they would be. He was whistling jauntily.

'Been for a walk . . .' he began but I'd already thrown myself on him and was punching him and slapping him.

'You selfish bastard,' I said. 'Don't you know what you almost did to me?'

Because I guess that's what made me maddest of all. That in the hours I waited for his return I'd sat on the sofa not moving, just scrunching and unscrunching my hands, wanting a hit in the way that I'd forgotten. Wanting a hit like I'd thought I'd never want one again.

He slipped his coat off, threw it down on the sofa, playing dumb. 'Don't fuck with me Linus,' I said angrily.

I called him then all the things you call someone at such a time, 'Selfish son of a bitch . . . asshole . . .' and some things which were worse. Then I said coldly, 'You betrayed me Linus,' which was true and which was what hurt most of all.

'You'll end up selling your grandmother for that stuff,' I said, reaching for the worst sort of cliché. I got my reward with the curl of his lip.

'Luckily,' he said, 'I don't have a grandmother to sell. I'd sell my mother but unfortunately she's gone too.'

'And you think that makes it all right don't you?' I said.

345

'You think that puts you in credit. Well, let me tell you Linus, I've done that trip and it's all so much shit.'

He leaned back against the wall, folding his arms.

'Tell me about it,' he said scornfully.

'Why bother?' I said, turning away. 'You know it all Linus. You're seventeen years old and the way the world has been for you, you've seen it all and done it all. But if you're interested I can tell you it doesn't mean shit Linus.'

I wasn't telling him of course. I was telling myself. I got up, walked to a small table, lifted a pack of cigarettes with my back to him, lit it with a shaking hand.

'Life deals you some bad cards,' I said, turning. 'So what? You think the rest of the world gets to live in paradise? It deals you some lousy cards and it deals you some good ones. That's the way life is. And all you have to be sure of is that you don't confuse the two, that you're ready to recognize the good ones when they arrive.'

From the wall there was a movement as he pushed himself off. He walked over to where I was, lifted a cigarette from my pocket. As he struck the match the light flared on the old face. He shook the match out contemptuously in front of me.

'Spare me,' he said.

I slapped his face then, smashed the cigarette from his lips. It fell on the carpet still burning and I ground it in angrily with my foot. His face went white with fury and his eyes glittered.

'And who are you anyway to lecture me?' he said. 'So what? You think your life has been whiter than white? Look at the things you've done. You're no better than the rest of them. You're no better than my father.'

'Oh yes I am,' I hissed. 'I'm a lot better. I'm alive for one thing.'

I snatched his coat from the sofa and threw it at him. It hit him full in the face.

'Now get the fuck out of here,' I said.

346

He stood there for a moment holding his coat. A crooked smile that was too easy and too charming spread over his face.

'You can't throw me out,' he said. 'It's almost Christmas.'

'So what?' I said.

As I heard him throwing things into a bag upstairs, I gave the Christmas tree a vicious kick where it lay the way I'd left it on the floor.

He was determinedly nonchalant when he came down a short while later with his bag in his hand.

'I'm off then,' he said. But I wouldn't look at him.

'Here,' I said, holding out a hand behind me with some notes in it.

'I don't need it,' he said.

'You need it,' I said.

I felt him take the money.

'Take this too,' I said, holding out Dr Lindquist's card the same way. 'You may need it and if you do tell him I sent you.'

He was opening the door when I said the last words.

'Be hard if you like Linus,' I said. 'But remember. It's no big deal. It doesn't mean a thing in the end.' But he didn't answer and a second later I heard the door close behind him.

The week that followed was the worst in my life, so much worse than anything that had gone before. I kept remembering the curl of Linus's lips as he said those words, *Look at the things you've done* . . . and truly they seemed now terrible. Mark's death came back to me in a way it had never done before, not even just after it had happened, laid out before me in rich guilty colours. The blame now seemed inescapable, a stone lying on top of me, a great weight I would never be able to get away from. One night

347

I woke sweating from a dream in which he lay in bed dead next to me. Another time he was there on the sofa at Stoneham while a party went on all around him. The Dentist was there, Molly, Eduardo, Robin Phillips, but no matter how much I shouted at them they wouldn't help me call an ambulance. In a third dream I was driving in the Aston with Max. He turned to me quite conversationally. 'You killed him,' he said.

One night, too frightened to sleep any more, I threw down a handful of sleeping tablets with some wine. As I drifted off I thought probably I should not wake up and I was glad. I wasn't conscious of wanting to kill myself. Only of not wanting to wake up.

I did wake, though, although it was late the following afternoon. Slopping downstairs to make some tea with the light dying through the window, I tripped over the Christmas tree where it still lay on the floor and I realized suddenly that it was Christmas Eve.

I was sitting on the sofa curled up, my hands around my knees, sipping tea, staring into space the way I'd sat for several hours, when I heard the first strains of the carol singers. They were singing 'In the Bleak Midwinter', the only carol I'd ever liked.

When I heard it, I always thought of Mirabel. Each year she and De Vere gave a party on Christmas Eve for the carol singers. It became, by tradition, their last port of call.

Each year I'd have to beg my father to let me go.

'Please . . .' I'd hear them outside Richard's house. They never came to ours.

'Please, oh *please*.'

'Oh very *well*,' he would say tetchily, and I'd jump up and run next door where Richard would be waiting for me already making faces as Mirabel handed out the mince pies and the mulled wine, and tossed her scarf theatrically about her.

Each year, too, she'd say the same thing, laying a hand on her heart when they asked her to sing.

348

'Oh no ... darlings ... I don't think so ... not this year ...'

But then the church organist who also played for the operatic society would take his place at the grand piano in the lounge and Mirabel would walk over, still protesting, tossing her scarf, but taking the hand from her heart to lay it on the top of the piano.

She'd do selections from the shows first, *Lilac Time*, *Merry Widow*, some simple Puccini, 'O mio bambino caro' usually.

She'd pretend to finish then, begin to walk away, but everyone would say, 'Oh *do* Mirabel' and 'You *must* Mirabel' and 'It wouldn't be the same Mirabel', so that in the end she'd go back to the piano to finish with 'In the Bleak Midwinter', her clear soprano soaring up into the air with the rest of the singers around her.

Paul told me later that they'd never come up the track before. He couldn't say why they did it this night. There was no light on at the cottage.

After 'In the Bleak Midwinter' they sang 'Silent Night' which is when I felt the wetness and the stinging in my eyes. Corny of course but I've come to the conclusion that some of the best things in life are corny.

As I listened to them every nerve in my body seemed to be straining. It was as if I was held to the sofa by wires, pulled tight, quivering and threatening to snap with the yearning to throw my feet off and walk to the door and throw it open.

And in the end that's what happened. In the end it was as if the legs did it themselves, so that suddenly there I was flinging open the top of the stable door saying in an odd awkward voice that didn't sound like my own, 'Perhaps it's too late ... I don't know ... but if you'd like to ...'

And as it happens they were glad of the offer for it was a freezing night and they were cold and tired. I opened a couple of bottles of wine that I'd bought for Linus and myself at Christmas.

'I'm sorry,' I said. 'I don't think I've got enough mince pies to go round.'

'Don't worry,' a voice said, 'we'll break them in half, divide them up.' A woman stepped forward.

'I'll help you,' she said.

And that was how I met Grace.

And so here I am, arriving at my new beginning while at the same time Richard reaches his end. For it will not be long now, I know that. Because he can go now. Beriol has been. And because of it at last Donald accepts that Richard is dying.

It's French, *Beriol*. Or maybe Belgian. Gavin isn't sure which. Beriol. Angel of Death in an anorak.

Donald was out of the room. I was beside the bed. I'd had a glass of wine at lunch-time which always makes me drowsy. It was so silent, just the heavy rhythm of Richard's breathing.

I'd only meant to put my head down for a moment but somehow I must have gone right out. One of those amazing deep sleeps you fall into in a second. I was lying there like this, head on my arms on the side of the bed, when his fingers clawed into my hair.

It was like a clasp from the other side of the grave, a hand coming up through the soil. I started up to see Richard's eyes wide open before me. There was no mistiness in them as there had been. No opaqueness. None of that look of the fixed camera staring emptily out at the room. Instead they were fixed and focused, staring at me as clear and alive and as urgent as the claw of his hand which opened and closed on the coverlet. I laid my head on it, feeling its distress beneath my fingers.

'What is it Richard? Tell me,' I said.

I was down on my knees by this time, leaning forward, so his lips were almost at my ear. His breath on my face was old and tired and used up. The dry grey lips formed the syllable painfully.

'Ber . . . Ber . . . Ber . . .' he said.

He swallowed as he said it, expelling it, with enormous effort managing a second syllable.

'Ber . . . eee . . .'

'Help me Richard. Help me,' I said, clutching his fingers as desperately as he clutched my own.

'I'll get Donald,' I said, half rising, but he threw his head to one side in a silent howl on the pillow, a rattle of resistance in his throat.

'You don't want me to. It's OK. It's OK. I won't. I won't,' I said, tears of frustration at his anguish springing to my eyes.

He took a great breath then, preparing himself, his lips drew out for the word.

'Ga . . . Gav . . .' he said.

'Gavin will know. Gavin will know, right?' I said joyfully and I saw all the muscles of his face relax on the pillow and his head dip in the very faintest of nods.

'Gavin will know about . . . *Beree* . . . I'll talk to him . . . don't worry Richard . . . I'll see him straight away . . .' But Richard's eyelids had already misted over again and had begun to droop. In a moment they were closed and the heavy rhythmic breathing had begun again.

Gavin slapped his hand hard on his forehead when I got him aside a short while later, told him what had happened.

'Of course,' he said. 'Beriol. Why didn't I think of it before?' He was moving towards the phone already.

'I'll call him now,' he said. He was dialling the number when he said, 'Don't whatever you do tell Donald.'

Beriol turned up a couple of hours later. He stood on the doorstep, tall, thin, with a ring in his ear, the peak of the anorak standing upwards like the beak of a hawk. Or the wings of an angel. A couple of reporters fluttered about him like sparrows but he looked like he didn't even see them.

351

When I showed him into the bedroom Donald started up beside the bed. He went pale, dropped his eyes dutifully like a child.

'Beriol,' he said dully.

I was surprised at the violence of it. The way it had to be done. But I saw too that it was right, and I stood back amazed at it all, admiring too and respectful, but most of all envying them, this thing that they had, Donald and Gavin and Beriol.

Donald's face was against the panelling of the corridor along from the bedroom. He was crying but Beriol was merciless and would not stop.

'You know the rules Donald,' he said. 'You of all people know the rules.' His English was perfect. There was none of the Clouseau about it. Yet it had this curt French edge to it that added to his air of harsh inflexibility.

'I should not have had to come Donald,' he said.

Then though, he put a hand on Donald's shoulder and with that Donald turned and Beriol clasped him in his long thin arms.

'You've trussed him up Donald,' he said. 'You know that. You're binding him, holding him back, with your own hope.'

He cradled him as Donald's shoulders shook.

'You have to let him go Donald,' he said.

It was later, after Beriol had left, that Donald and I were beside the bed. I saw his chin go up in the air like a man making a decision which I guess he was. He swallowed as he said it, stared straight ahead.

'He wants the ashes scattered in Antigua,' he said.

I squeezed his hand, understanding the nature of what he was saying, how now, at last, he was letting Richard go. He turned with a sad smile, trying to make some gentle conversation from it.

'Why Antigua anyway? He would never tell me,' he said.

I just answered vaguely in the end. Told him about how we'd put down some of the tracks for the second album in the studio there.

'I guess it was a good time for us,' I said. 'We were working well. It was before all the problems started happening.' And all this was true.

We lived in white-washed cabanas with thatched roofs grouped around the pool which was deep blue but still not as blue as the sea behind us which you reached through a sweet-smelling tunnel of rich dark foliage drooping its head with the weight of its flowers, frangipani and hibiscus.

At night the air was full of the scent of them, and with the sound of the cicadas which whirred and clicked like some infinitely soft machinery whose purpose it was to keep this paradise working.

At nights we'd take a break, sit out by the pool. Often we'd run a cassette off of the stuff we'd been working on. We'd stick it on the machine, jam the volume up, sit back and roll a joint as we discussed it.

I can hear it now, see it, feel it, that peculiar combination, rock and roll echoing out over this heavy sweet-scented paradise, drifting up into the velvet star-encrusted sky.

'. . . *a thousand twangling instruments* . . .'

'What . . .?'

It was Donald. Donald the old English teacher with some Shakespeare for every occasion. He fetched his copy of the play, read it out. I write it here to remember it and what happened.

> *Be not afeard; the isle is full of noises,*
> *Sounds, and sweet airs, that give delight, and hurt not.*
> *Sometimes a thousand twangling instruments*
> *Will hum about mine ears; and sometimes voices*
> *That, if I then had wak'd after long sleep,*
> *Will make me sleep again . . .*

I had my eyes closed as he was reading it. As he finished I said, 'Yeah that's how it was,' and as I opened them slowly I saw that Richard's too had fluttered up.

Donald had seen it now as well. The book had slipped to the floor. He held Richard's hand, grasping it with both of his own. There was a mistiness about Richard's eyes but something else, a sort of effort, as if he was trying to focus.

Donald said, 'Joanie's been telling me about Antigua Richard.' He had given in to the inevitable now and he wanted Richard to know.

'I understand now why you loved the place.' The eyes had overflowed and the tears were beginning to edge down his face.

'I know it's time now Richard. I know you want to go. I know it's time. Go when you want to my darling.'

And I can't tell you what happened next. Because I had to get up from beside the bed. I had to let myself out and close the door behind me and lean my face against the corridor wall and let the tears go myself.

And it was as I was there that I felt the arms gently on my shoulders, farmer's boy's hands turning me round and pulling me inwards and against him, and stroking my hair as I wept and wept for the loss of it all, for the waste of the years I might have had with Richard and for other wastes too. I wept and wept for the waste of it all into Kent's chest.

And now it's all over.

It was late, around midnight, after Kent had gone, that I persuaded Donald to lie down on the couch, close his eyes while I watched by the bed.

'I won't sleep mind,' he said.

A short while later though there was a sound I had not heard before, a light snore from the couch. It counterpointed with the empty rattling of Richard's breathing and as I sat scribbling by the bed became a lullaby, the way it had before, in the back of my head.

It must have been an hour or so later when the door opened and Gavin came in to check Richard's pulse and do all the other small things he does about the bed.

I looked up to give him a smile of welcome but when I saw his face I turned to the bed with a start, dropping the book and the pen with a small smothered exclamation.

The clatter of the book falling to the floor though woke Donald who raised his head, putting a vague confused hand to his forehead.

'I've been asleep,' he said reproachfully but then he saw our faces.

'What's happening?' he said, for already Gavin was beside the bed. I stared at him not knowing what to say.

'Why are you looking at me like that . . .?' he said, knowing already, hurling himself from the couch.

Why all this coming and going?

For he knew, just like Rodolfo, and he let out the same cry of despair and threw himself in the same way and with the same racking sobs upon the bed. But it was only for a moment. In a moment he was up and scrabbling with the equipment and swearing at us in a voice no longer his own.

Beside the bed, though, before Richard's body, Gavin had taken a stand like a man defending, arms slightly outstretched on either side. And as Donald tore at the equipment, so I tore at his back, crying, trying to make him stop.

'It's no good Donald . . . let him go Donald . . .'

It was then that I felt myself lifted backwards, not even urgently, just calmly and forcibly.

To this day I do not know and nor have I ever asked how it was that Beriol should be there. But it was him, taking Donald in his arms and holding him, the great sobs shaking him, a frail tree in a violent storm.

355

He howled and tore and beat his fists upon Beriol's chest but Beriol would not let him go, just held on to him, stroking him, this turning and twisting creature.

'But I wasn't there . . . I wasn't *there* . . .' Donald kept howling.

'Of course,' said Beriol calmly. 'But how else would he have been able to go . . .?'

Later Beriol forced Donald to take a sleeping tablet, laid him out on the couch, covering him with a blanket like a child, sat beside him, holding his hand and stroking his head, just the way Donald had done once for Richard.

On the bed Richard lay as if asleep, the more peaceful for the absence of breath no longer troubling him, no longer rattling in and out.

I phoned Kent later from the kitchen.

'You're still up,' I said.

'Haven't been to bed yet,' he said and there was a loud moo from the end of the phone.

'God where are you?' I said.

'In the yard,' he said. 'Mobile phone. Farmer's best friend. Daisy's calving.'

'Daisy . . .?'

'Yeah . . . well . . .' he said, mildly embarrassed. 'No point in pissing about with fancy names. It has to be Daisy or Primrose.'

Later he said, my friend Kent, 'I can jump in the Landrover. Come up.'

'No,' I said. 'No need. Everything's quiet here.'

We talked for a short while then he said, 'The stars are wonderful tonight Joanie.'

'Just a minute,' I said. I pushed open the French windows, walked out on to the square of paving and looked up.

'God they are,' I said, and so they were, a great swathe of them across the heavens. The one they call the Milky Way.

'So long dead,' I said, 'and still shining so brightly.'

'It's a good thought,' said Kent.

'Yeah,' I said. And it was. For tonight. It was a good thought.

I'm tired now. I'm writing this in bed. Outside the window the dawn is breaking and the city is waking up. I can hear the sound of a milk float, the shuttle of a tube.

Somewhere, away from here, a cow is lowing, a calf is born. Somewhere the cicadas are singing. Somewhere, everywhere, the planet is playing its own sweet airs.

And I only hope Richard can hear them.

VI

I pray the endless river will release you
From the journey you have just begun
When you reach that journey's end
I hope you find a friend
Who'll take you by the hand
And say hello the settin' sun . . .

'So why Antigua anyway?' Linus said carelessly. It was the same question Donald had asked although asked this time in a much different manner. I gave him pretty much the same answer though. 'Oh you know . . . it was a good time for us there . . . things were going well for us . . .' But the truth is, that's not the real reason we're flying to Antigua tomorrow.

I couldn't have been more surprised when Linus phoned. It was the day before the funeral and we hadn't spoken for a decade.

'I'm in town,' he said with the old belligerence, despite the years of not bothering with any of the formalities.

'Any chance of getting to see you Joanie?'

He sent a car for me in the end. The press who were still outside watching the comings and goings followed it for lack of anything better to do. When they saw where it pulled up they had no doubts who it was I was going to see.

It takes a crowd outside a hotel to show you how big someone is, and when I saw the size of the one waiting for Linus I had no doubts about what he'd become. They took over most of the pavement opposite. They were curiously quiet, though, more like disciples than fans. And all dressed exactly like Linus.

He was just passing through apparently. He'd stopped off to see Angus who was producing some tracks for him. It was Angus who said he'd seen me, and told him where I was staying.

He didn't look a lot different from the last time I'd seen

361

him, just ten years older that's all. All the fashion accessories were there, the designer stubble, the lank peroxide hair, the disappearing hips, and I told myself that his thinness and the sallowness of his skin could be all part of that, and not to worry, because there wasn't any point anyway in trying to play the fond mama with Linus.

'So ...' I said briskly after I'd forced him into an awkward hug just for the hell of it and sat down on the sofa. 'You're married so I hear. A father Linus.'

'Yeah.'

'Is that good?'

For a few seconds then he dropped the attitude. There was even the beginnings of a kid's crooked grin on his face.

'Yeah. I like it. Maybe it's what I always wanted. A wife. A kid. A family.'

'I'm glad Linus.'

'Yeah ... well ... anyway ... the reason why you're here.'

He'd reached behind the sofa and was pulling something up. It was a guitar case.

'For you. To replace the one that was ... lost.'

The lips twisted over the last word like he was defending himself, getting in ahead of the game lest anyone should try and get there before him. I opened up the case and there was a Martin inside, a twin to the one he had taken.

I held it up by the neck. It was a beauty. I said, 'You didn't have to do this Linus.' He leaned back, attitude restored before me.

'Wouldn't have done it if I'd had to. You know me Joanie.' And it was true. I saw that. I knew Linus. To my soul.

He said, 'I wanted to give it to you a while back.'

'Why didn't you then?' I said as belligerently as him, giving back as much as I was getting.

'You knew where I lived. You were the only one. Why didn't you come to see me?'

362

'Didn't know I'd be welcome.'

'Yeah,' I said. 'And besides that.'

He shrugged. 'Well . . .' he said. 'You know . . .' he said. And I did. And I wished I didn't.

I began to strum the guitar softly. I didn't look at him. I said, 'You've got a kid now Linus.'

He tapped the cigarette in the ashtray, the old bitter twist on his lips.

'Are you lecturing me Joanie?'

'I guess so Linus,' I said.

At the door as I was leaving, I held on to him as I hugged him. I put my forehead against his and when I drew back I held his chin, straining up to him, hard between my fingers.

'Don't let it slip away Linus,' I said. 'For all of our sakes.' He pulled his face away in the end. Afterwards though he laid it on my shoulder, and for a moment that's how we stood there, me held like that feeling the thin lanky frame. Then he pulled away again and when we were apart raised his hand in one of his cool careless waves.

'Take care Joanie,' he said.

'And you Linus,' I said. 'And you.'

I was halfway down the corridor when the door to his room flung open and he yelled it down to me.

'I'm doing Wembley in the autumn.'

I smiled at him.

'See you there,' I said.

'Put a coin in my mouth Joanie,' Richard said cheerfully not long before he died. 'See me over the Styx darling . . .' And I guess you could say I did in the end. That was how it felt anyway watching that strange moment of modern reverence as the coffin disappeared through the curtains. Although I guess the boatman had long since ferried him over.

363

Steve was one of the pall-bearers.

'It's me Joanie . . . Steve . . . don't put the phone down,' he said when he heard my voice. It was a good start I guess. You could say I liked his attitude.

He still had that brushed hush-puppy look about him when we met for a coffee in the park, even more so in the light-weight evangelist's suit with the careful tie and the suspicious-looking badge with the Bible and the flame winking discreetly from the button-hole.

He was over for some evangelical conference. Genuinely wanted to be at the funeral. Still, I wasn't giving in without a fight.

'Just don't try any of that hot gospel stuff Steve,' I said after we'd ordered the coffees.

'I wasn't going to Joanie,' he said looking hurt, and afterwards I saw that he wasn't.

Later we sat on a bench in the sun watching the ducks on the Serpentine.

'So where do you stand on this plague from God business?' I said just to be sure. He looked down at his hands clasped between his knees, a new Steve I didn't know.

'I don't think God *sends* anything,' he said.

As we parted he said, 'Just one thing Joanie . . . I've wanted to say it for a while . . . I'm sorry . . . about the things I said . . . back at the beginning.'

He was staring down, hands in his pockets, moving his feet in embarrassment. Like I say, I liked his attitude.

'It was difficult . . . at first . . . I didn't really know what I was doing.' He looked up then, gave me a grimace.

'Just put it down to the first flush of enthusiasm,' he said.

'Don't do this to me Steve,' I said, refusing the out-stretched hand, laughing, giving him a light kiss in farewell.

'Don't make me start liking you after all these years.'

*

364

It was always a forlorn hope I guess that the funeral could be just family and friends the way Donald wanted it. 'Friend' after all is a generic term in the music business, and there was more of a scattering of the great and good there, including several who wouldn't qualify as either and who Richard would have laughed at if they'd called themselves friends.

As for family, well, Richard has no family left. Just his mother who in truth has long since been carried over by Charon.

The funeral fell on the day that Donald normally goes to see her so he went the day before, hiding his grief.

She didn't notice that he was a day early but she asked him where Richard was as usual. He told her what he always told her, that he was away on tour.

He came back red-eyed and weepy.

'She said, "Tell him I want to see him as soon as he gets back,"' he said.

The fans were out in force of course and I could see there was some logic there. For after all wasn't it *He's a friend of mine* that the Little Match Girl shouted at me that first day I arrived at Richard's as she tried to fight her way in? And isn't that, in some way, at the root of it all?

She was there at the front of the crowd, first in line behind the row of police, clutching her posy.

By some small irony she'd got herself next to the demonstrators. Not that she noticed a thing.

They were mainly there for the press, making a point about what they saw as the media conspiracy, Richard the gay man dying wrapped up in that old flag of convenience that goes by the name of *bisexuality*.

I had sympathy for them. It was a dignified protest, no shouting or anything, taking full account of the occasion. Still though their faces were full of that deadly inflexible zeal that acknowledges ends never means, answers never questions, that flattens the whole, steam-rolling over other considerations.

One of the placards said something about the personal being political, which I've never really understood, at least not when it comes to your sexuality. For your sexuality it seems to me is next to your soul. And if your soul can't be private what can?

And I can see now how they could feel betrayed by Richard, how they could feel he'd sold his sexuality for his success down the river. But then I think of Richard on stage, skin glowing against the white of the singlet, the lights shining on the hair, the sweat running, and I ask myself where is it written that we must retreat into ghettos? Where is it written that because Richard preferred men and was loved by men, he might not also be desired the same way by women?

He said once, calmly, 'You know I'd always marry you if you wanted me to Joanie.'

It was on Antigua. We were lying on the beach, just the two of us. The moon was painting the white sand silver, sending out a silver pathway too across the sea towards us.

'Oh yeah,' I said a little crossly. 'A real showbiz marriage. You go your way. I go mine.'

'Well, why not?' he said looking hurt. 'We've known each other a long time.' He took a long drag of the joint, passed it back over to me. By this time he was laughing himself.

'Well, let's face it,' he said in the old campy tone, 'I'd be a lot better for you than most of the jerks you take up with.'

I laugh when I think about. It was such a *Richard* thing to do. But no, that's not the reason we're going to Antigua.

*

Milton was at the funeral of course and with Lois beside him. When she kissed me her lips were cool beneath the don't-fuck-with-me eyes. Still, I was glad that there was a certain new warmth in the way she said, 'Good to see you Joanie.'

Milton took me aside afterwards at the house.

'I know this isn't really the time or the place for business,' he said, 'but really I don't think Richard would mind.'

'If it was business,' I said, 'he'd be only too delighted. But *business*. With *me* Milton?'

When he told me I said, 'Oh he'd love that. He'd love that. I just wish he was here to share it.'

'You don't mind then?' Milton said. 'I mean it's toothpaste of course.'

I said, 'Yeah, but it's all *money* Milton.'

When McGarvey sold out, you see, he sold to another larger record company which a few years later was hoovered up along with half the rest of the world by a Japanese multinational conglomerate.

> She swallowed the spider to catch the fly
> I don't know why . . .

The company makes just about everything now, toasters, electric fans, kettles, washing machines and, of course, stereos, a nice touch when I think about it. Because stereos in their own way need soap just like washing machines.

They wanted the record companies because they wanted the records to put on the stereos, they wanted the distribution, but they weren't that bothered in the end with some of the publishing deals that went with them. So they broke up the companies to raise some fast cash, offered up the back catalogues as nice little earners to people with investment portfolios.

And it's no shame now in the business to have lost the

367

rights to your songs. Much bigger names than mine have suffered it. And while it must stick in their craw to request permission to sing their own songs, well, for me obviously it hasn't been much of a problem. The worst thing about the whole deal for those of a nervous disposition is that they can find their master-works popping up on the television used to sell anything from toothpaste to tampons. So all in all it could have been worse. And if you haven't guessed it already, it's Didi's portfolio my songs are lying in. I'll have her to thank every time my riff pops up and that's OK by me, believe me. Because I'll just think of the pennies dropping into the pot, and I'll grin right back when those brightly cleaned teeth flash up on my television.

That Japanese company by the way also makes samplers and some of the world's finest pianos. It's like Angus said, if Mozart was here today he'd have one. And it would almost certainly be Japanese.

On the subject of pianos, there's still a problem to solve. Just how we're going to fit the Bechstein into the cottage. *You won't refuse it this time* Richard said, and I won't. Perhaps I'll have to move in the end but I know I must have the Bechstein back. Anyway Milton's already muttering about mortgages, throwing dark hints about bringing in David to help me deal with my new windfall of money.

And speaking of money, it goes without saying that McGarvey wasn't at the funeral. After all, it would take more than someone dying to pull McGarvey away from his money.

Given the chance, Donald would have flown off to Antigua with the ashes the day after the funeral. He has taken Richard's death very hard and scattering the ashes is his last consolation.

But Donald is a very rich man now, and wealth, as we all know, weighs down with responsibility. He's already had to take some major decisions. For instance he's point-blank refused to consider Robin Phillips for a new (author-ized) biography.

For in the way of these things Richard's death has only added to his popularity.

The re-released, tastefully packaged, one new track added, greatest hits which was only waiting for the formal-ity of Richard's death to be born is lodged in at number one, probably in perpetuity. Death and resurrection. A speciality of the music business.

Pressing close upon its heels, naturally, are the plans for the memorial concert. Don't take offence at my tone. He knew it would be so and laughed about it.

'So what will you do then Joanie?' he said one day.

'Richard . . .' I protested embarrassed.

'Oh, come on come on,' he said. 'Don't play the inno-cent with me. My only comfort in dying is that it might kick-start your career.' And we were back on the same old argument.

'But I don't want my career kick-started.'

It was one of the few times he ended up shouting at me.

'Why should I want to get into it again?' I said.

'Because it's what you *do* Joanie,' he said angrily.

> *Would you deny the greatest moment*
> *If the status quo meant*
> *You should turn it down . . .*

I wrote that for Richard and now it comes back to me. Would I? Do I want to put a toe in again? Should I play at the memorial concert?

'If you ask me . . .?'

'Which after all I haven't . . .'

369

'Well, tough because I'm going to tell you anyway . . .'

Grace can grow very cantankerous in her cups, let me tell you.

It was wonderful to see the pair of them again, though, her and Paul, and that was part of the problem. Seeing how easily I slotted back into my life there, how rich it was to me, how sweet and important. Maybe it was a mistake though to mention that thing about the memorial concert, about Kent and Donald both telling me I should do it.

'I've wanted to say this for a long time Joanie . . .'

'It astonishes me that you haven't . . .'

'I think you're entirely *pathetic*. I mean just because you fucked up once doesn't mean you have to do it again.'

'You have a way with words Grace.'

'You have this great talent and Richard was right. It's a waste . . .' She turned on Paul then.

'Tell her Paul,' she commanded.

He cleared his throat, adjusted his glasses, aware he couldn't possibly come up to the moment.

'Well, there is the parable of the talents . . .' he began but he was drowned out by the explosion of disgust.

'*Oh for God's sake,*' she said.

The café was busy when I went in the next day on my way back to town so I stopped off for a couple of hours, helped out with the lunch-time rush.

Rene was floundering with a hangover and suffering from Grace's scathing tongue so it was me who took the tray of soups out to the four in the corner.

The same solarium tans, the same sunglasses, the same shirt-sleeves rolled up.

'Excuse me,' said the girl, holding out the napkin and the pen, 'would you mind . . .'

I just laughed. It felt such a dumb thing, being asked to sign my name. I made them laugh scrawling Didi's.

Which is when, for no good reason, I decided I'd play at the concert.

Kent has the task of organizing the thing. It's one of the reasons he hasn't gone on tour this time with Miranda.

He gave the oration at the funeral, far too pompous a term for the simple speech that he made. I was so proud of him, I couldn't help it, to see him standing there, the farmer's boy trussed up and uncomfortable in his suit.

He was one of the pall-bearers too. He and Steve and Donald down one side. Gavin and Beriol and an actor friend of Richard's down the other.

The actor read the sonnet that Richard had chosen.

> *Let me not to the marriage of true minds*
> *Admit impediments. Love is not love*
> *Which alters when it alteration finds . . .*

I had to brush away a tear, a selfish one, one for myself as much as Richard.

I thought of how Kent said to me once, sadly, when things had got bad, 'Sometimes I don't think I know you any more Joanie.' And it was true but still he didn't stop caring.

He was on his own at the funeral. Miranda had already left for the States. He stood at the door of the house afterwards, staring into the setting sun. He gave the old sucking sound he makes when he's deciding whether to speak. He said, 'You'll come down to the farm soon then Joanie?'

*

371

And so we fly out for Antigua tomorrow. I'm glad we're going at long last. Apart from anything else, Donald needs the holiday. We're staying at a hotel, not of course at the studio. But we'll go to the private beach there, take the ashes.

I'll show the place to Donald, the pool, the cabanas, he'll smell the hibiscus, hear the cicadas and feel the deep night-time velvet of the sky. And all this will help. He will feel close to Richard.

'There's something else isn't there Joanie?' he said to me one night after Richard had died.

'You're not telling me everything that happened in Antigua.'

I tried to fudge it again but he wasn't having any of it.

'Don't you understand?' he said. 'I want to know everything about Richard.' And so I told him.

It was late. We'd worked all night. It was three, maybe four in the morning. I was walking by the pool when I saw the door of Richard's cabana ajar. Thinking he might still be up and around I tapped lightly on the door and receiving no answer pushed it open.

At first I thought there was no one there but then I saw the bedroom door was also open and a soft light escaping out. When I called his name quietly, I heard, 'Here Joanie' and 'Come in' so I did.

Pushing open the bedroom door, I stood there transfixed for a moment by the scene, the flickering candles, dozens of them, throwing the shadows on to the white-washed walls.

It had the feel of a cell about it, or maybe a small chapel. Two thick stumpy candles on either end of a high bureau made it look like an altar. In front of it Richard stood and in front of him again Leon, his eyes vacant and glowing. Around Richard's shoulders there was the weird

372

black cloak with strange signs on it that we'd watched him buy earlier in the day from a peddler. But apart from that both of them were naked.

'You're just in time Joanie,' Richard said.

I slipped down on the bed watching them. As I did Richard raised the cloak on either side of him, carrying Leon's hands with his own, and for a moment they stood there like that, arms stretched out, until Richard's arms dropped again, enfolding Leon.

Suddenly there was a flash of something in Richard's right palm and an arm rose up once more in an arc in the air, freeing the cloak which fell back from his shoulders.

Like a bird then the hand swooped down one last time to his arm, palm flat against Leon's chest. There was a sharp intake of breath from Richard and a crack of red appeared on his own left forearm and began running down on to his elbow. His mouth nuzzled the side of Leon's head. He lifted the bleeding forearm, wiped it across Leon's cheek leaving the smear of blood.

'For love of thee,' he whispered hoarsely, 'I cut my arm.' As he did it Leon feeling the wet against his cheek turned, and like a man I had never seen before began sucking lovingly at the blood.

And I must say that I have thought many times of that scene and, as well, of my own finest moments of passion, and in the end I have concluded that in my life I have seen nothing to compare with what I saw that night between Richard and Leon.

I did not tell Donald this although I told him the rest of the story. When I had finished he did not look sad or angry or bitter. He simply said, his brow wrinkled in confusion, 'But I still don't understand. Did he love Leon then do you think?' and I said, 'I don't know Donald,' shaking my head. Then he said, 'And what about Leon?' 'Who can know?' I said. And it's true. For who can know in the end if, or why, one human being loves another?

Who can know for instance why Kent kept caring

about me through those dark years, a question perhaps you're asking too now that we come to the end of the story.

I was re-reading *Emma* that day that seems so long ago now when Kent came for me in the café. I'd picked up a copy on my last visit to the charity shop. In the introduction it says that when she wrote it Jane Austen wanted to create a heroine that no one would like, and I can't help thinking, looking back through these pages, that if this was a novel I'd have managed the same thing.

And so, defending myself, all I can say is that I have regretted the mistakes that I made, repented of them and bitterly, and I've been punished for them too. I've paid the price, and if you ask what the price is then I'll tell you. It's Kent.

It's true too, although not an excuse, that it's a wicked business I was in, a business of the gods, where suddenly nothing is forbidden, where the hollow basket-work people, which is what I was then, come to grief and only those with a solid core inside them survive.

And yet I did survive. That's all I can say in the end. My last and final defence. I'm still here. And like me or not, so are you.

'So . . .' Linus said as we walked over to the door together that day I went to see him, 'you were all happy in Antigua?' He spoke carelessly in the way he always did when something mattered.

'Yes,' I said.

'And my father,' he said, 'was he happy there?'

I did not fool with him. I never fooled with Linus.

'As *happy*,' I said hesitantly, 'as he was happy anywhere I guess.'

I did not tell Linus, perhaps I should have done, that *happiness* is not a word I care much about any more. After all, *I can be happy here* was what I said the first time I curled up in my private coke world. It's easy to be happy with things like coke, I've found. Which is why *happiness* is not something that greatly interests me any more. Joy interests me. Sorrow. But these are different things altogether, and things not connected to chemicals.

Perhaps that's why I'm not concerned with happy endings any more. Contented ones have become more to my taste. And so I shall be contented to visit my good friend Kent on his farm, to walk his fields with him, those fields that belonged to his father, and his father before that. Perhaps it doesn't seem much to you but as for myself, well, it's like the bard said. 'Tis enough. 'Twill serve.

It will be enough to walk back to the farm arm in arm in that camaraderie of which that other great countryman wrote. And while it is true that if the gods were prepared to descend one last time and offer to rewrite my story then I would choose that I might say of Kent, *Whenever you look up, there I shall be and whenever I look up, there you will be*, still there is a deeper truth than this one.

Once Donald, weeping, said, 'Sometimes I think I love him more than life itself,' and I stroked his arm and let him weep on.

I didn't tell him what I was thinking because I knew he wouldn't want to hear it and anyway he'll know it himself one day.

It will pass, I wanted to say. For all things pass.

And nothing is worth more than life itself.